BLOOD ALONE

Blood Alone is published under Reverie, a sectionalized division under Di Angelo Publications, Inc.

Reverie is an imprint of Di Angelo Publications.
Copyright 2024.
All rights reserved.
Printed in the United States of America.

Di Angelo Publications
Los Angeles, California

Library of Congress
Blood Alone
ISBN: 978-1-962603-07-2
Paperback

Words: Mark Miller
Cover Design: Savina Deianova
Interior Design: Kimberly James
Editors: Cody Wootton, Shelley Romero, Willy Rowberry

Downloadable via www.dapbooks.shop and other e-book retailers

For educational, business, and bulk orders, contact sales@diangelopublications.com.

1. Fiction --- Fantasy --- Action & Adventure
2. Fiction --- Thriller --- Political
3. Fiction --- Fantasy --- Military

BLOOD ALONE

MARK MILLER

Contents

Dream

Pinella

Pinella peered out through the wet window at her husband in the distance. Ron was a big man. She loved watching him stoop down so the tree branches would not hit his head. All but the way he walked reminded her of her father. All at once she felt safe, nervous, and excited. She never missed an opportunity to relish a good man coming home. It may fill the chest of a thousand men to hear of a fallen hero, but nothing set her heart on fire more fiercely than her husband.

He had a bow in one hand while leading a mule with the other. The little valley they had chosen to build their house in stretched out between them. She hurried to stoke the fire and called out to Reff, "You can finish chopping the wood. Your father is back." She could hear him breathe and gather the firewood.

Pinella shut the hearth door with a squeak and brushed off her dress with her hand. She was just starting to brush her hair out when she noticed her trembling hand. That was it. She dropped her brush and ran out the front door.

"Mom? What's wrong?"

She thundered across the wooden porch and out in the tall grass toward Ron. She could feel tears in that place behind her tongue. He had not noticed her yet. He was fussing at the mule that never wanted to cross the little bridge. Her feet thumped on the bridge's wood planks and he looked up at her just a moment before she wrapped her arms around him to squeeze him.

"Pin! You scared me!" Her head found that perfect spot under his chin. Her hands always tried to touch his broad shoulders but never were able to. This was home to her. All they had built together. The house, the valley, their family. It was all good, but this was all she really needed. Her Ron, safe and in her arms. She wanted to cry.

"Pin . . . What is it? Is Reff okay?" Ron was asking her as he looked down at her eyes filling with tears. Why was she crying? Everything was okay, was it not? If it was a normal day, then why was she so emotional?

Then she remembered, and just like that, the dream was over and Pinella was awake.

She tried to fall back asleep, working to remember her husband's face. She could not. She laid in her hot room, wanting to go back just long enough to kiss him or hear another word. She was starting to breathe fast as tears began to flood her eyes and run down her face into her ears. He was gone and her life and home went with him. Her tears gave way to sobs and she whimpered.

"What's going on? Why are you crying?" She'd forgotten about the man lying next to her. She was so disparaged, she didn't say anything — just turned over to face away from him. "You're a lousy whore! I want my money back. You're acting like a child!" The stranger pushed up from the bed, grabbed his clothes, and walked out. But it made no difference. Pinella was always alone nowadays.

Dream

Cicero

It had finally started raining in Hocklee, and Cicero took off his jacket, the only thing he'd ever owned. The people were gathered in the muddy main street, around the soldier who stood over the boy he'd just killed. The soldier began yelling again: "Hocklee has been taken for King Leander of Kalesia, and every Hockleet must submit to the king's law! The punishment for theft is now death. Our laws apply to the young and old!"

Cicero watched as the dead boy's little brother kneeled in the bloody ground at his side. Their parents wept together. People whispered and shook their heads. Cicero approached the brothers, and the living one spoke to him through tears. "They let all of his blood out."

Cicero didn't know what to say. He never did, but he knew it should have been him to die; no one would miss an orphan.

"Here, Gallo, this will keep him dry." Cicero held his jacket out for Gallo to give to his dead brother.

Gallo blinked against the rain and tears. "But this is your only jacket."

Cicero held it out insistently. "You are my only friend."

Cicero woke up with a startled gasp. For now, he was far from Hocklee and, thankfully, further from his past. His eyes swept over the beautiful view of Trofaim's legendary orchard wrapping around him as if he'd fallen into a dream rather than waking up from one. The fruit trees were like none he had ever seen back in Hocklee. The oldest of the great fruit trees of this orchard pushed up as far into the sky as the high pines north of his homeland. He'd heard that one of these great fruit trees could be traded for an entire army.

His hope was that one day, his home would have a great orchard of its own with fruit trees as great as one of these. After all that he'd destroyed in war, a symbol of peace would be a good first step toward redemption. Maybe one day his little hamlet in the South would become like this great city. His eyes drifted toward the modern stately building just outside the orchard. He saw a woman's face in a window and wished he had the fortunate life of a person of Trofaim.

CHAPTER ONE

THE SON

PINELLA

The leaves were changing in the city of Trofaim and the sound of its people herding in the streets crowded Pinella's empty room as they gathered for the harvest festival. She had to stand on the edge of her bed to see out from her high window. Her father and husband loved harvest, always insisting that they observe tradition by hanging a bell wherever fruit was picked. It was widely believed that if a family did not celebrate a city festival in Trofaim, it was bad luck. A harbinger of chaos. Pinella looked around her private room and wondered when last she had any luck of her own. Unless you counted all her bad luck, that is.

Now the city was filled with the sound of bells as people repeated the practice throughout. The sound that meant new fruit and abundance throughout Trofaim hung heavy with lamentation in that little room. Pinella's room had a window at the top of the exterior wall above her bed, which she looked through by climbing on top of it. She didn't look out of her window often, but now she remembered why she so rarely did. In the orchard across the street, she noticed a man on horseback lifting a boy up into the apple tree. It was the one planted by her father, Akten Bennault, after his famous victory at Paveneli. It hurt Pinella to see what always reminded her of her father, now dead. No matter how far away her life had carried her from the tree, she watched it and made sure it was always healthy and fruitful. The sight of it always hurt her in those old, scarred wounds within the heart, but the sight of the man and young boy counting their bells brought back those more pleasant memories of her husband with their son.

As her eyes filled with tears, she looked through her blurred vision at the street her father had triumphantly strode down at the head of Trofaim's noble army, the Songbird Army, so many years ago.

'Akten Bennault saved Trofaim and ended the famine,' the people said, awarding him with the highest honor of the Grass Crown and showering him and the street with paper flowers. The award had seldom been bestowed upon the greatest heroes of Trofaim. It could only be presented by the commoners of the city to their heroes. She could remember her father so clearly, marching at the head of the Songbird Army before burying the seeds of fruit he'd taken from other great cities in the Great Orchard of Trofaim. It was then, after his great victory in the northern city of Paveneli, that her father planted the apple tree that would become his favorite and, after his death, the tallest.

Pinella watered it with her father as a child and continued after he was gone. She often felt his nostalgic essence at the sight of the huge tree. Hundreds of people from all over Trofaim had taken the fruit from the Great Orchard to start smaller orchards, believing the old city's prosperity would follow with it. It was a token of comfort to imagine how many families and villages with their own fruit trees had been blessed by the red apples from her father's tree. She could only hope their luck had been better than hers. She remembered Ron planting a new tree each year in their own little valley orchard when the young trees would bear fruit.

She smiled at the memory of Ron hoisting Reff onto his shoulders to hang bells on the tree as he picked the fruit himself. Ron with the basket of fruit, Pinella with the basket of bells, handing Reff a bell as needed.

Ceremony for the people in the city was now a plague song for her. It was the old familiar music played intentionally amidst the chaos of a sea of bells that made her heart ache. Pinella had lived in the River District in the heart of the Great Orchard long enough to hear the sagely music of the forest bard, Henna. The woman played a tune that hid in the bellsong and somehow wove it all into a great harmony. Every note produced in Trofaim, both great and small, conTributed to the song of the city.

Pinella stepped down from the ladder and sat on one edge of her bed. It didn't feel like a bed. To her, it felt like some work-bench. She heard Gobber, the manager of the brothel, speaking to a client as he showed him to the girl one door down from her. She heard the door shut a moment before he knocked on her door.

"Pinella, sweetheart."

"Yes?" Her skin crawled and she tried not to sound like she had been crying for the last half hour.

"You've got another visitor."

At once she was scrambling to put herself together. She had used her intermission to look out the window instead of getting ready. She was about to lose another thing; without her job how would she eat? How would she send money for Reff's education? She knew she should have hung a stupid bell or two. She felt a fool now. There is always more to lose. Hadn't life taught her that already?

"It's alright. I have been with her before, so I won't need an introduction."

She froze. A mixture of fear and embarrassment squeezed

tears from her eyes when she heard the familiar voice. The door opened and shut. The tears began to really flow now as she stared away, facing the window above her bed. Her hand covered her mouth to muffle the sob. Pinella was so ashamed. She did not know what he would think. It had been years since the last time they'd seen one another. He was so grown. It reminded her further of her husband and father. She was so ashamed that she barely knew what to think of herself.

"Hey, Mom, I brought a bell for you to hang outside."

She was biting her hand now to keep the sobs from bursting out, wondering if her son knew the deeds of his own mother. If he knew what she had done to pay for his schooling, his father's debts . . .

"The people have picked all the low-hanging fruit. The rest will be too high for me to reach, son." She was able to keep the tears out of her voice just long enough to speak for a moment.

"It's okay . . . I can lift you on my shoulders . . . The same way dad did for me."

&

Pinella looked at her son with a heart full of pride. The son of her youth, now a year older than she was when she brought him into this world. Still though, he seemed to be far too young to be in garments of war. On his jacket was the mark of the city, a songbird in flight. The greatest warriors eventually took on the name of the Songbird as their title, Shrike. In some ways, he looked like a stranger now. There was no way of knowing how much death he had seen in the past months. Maybe death had come close to him.

"How was the Western territory?" Pinella set a gentle hand on Reff's shoulder. Her son just looked into the distance for a moment before blinking back what looked like tears forming in his eyes. "It was bad then, wasn't it?" Pinella's hand moved instinctually to wipe a tear, catching it as soon as it rolled from his eye.

"It was . . . I was . . ."

"I know. It was bad, but now you are back and it's over."

He took a breath, collecting himself before his eyes met her with a hint of joy. "You don't have to anymore. You won't have to work now that we're defeating the rebels. They'll be giving us some of the land we liberated as soon as their leader, The Fowler, is brought to justice. They say I will have land in Kornata."

Pinella felt a lump in her throat.

Anyone who followed The Fowler and rebelled against the Republic of Trofaim could be considered treasonous and lose everything to the loyalists who subdued them. The rebel leader was named satirically because he'd sworn to kill all the Shrikes. Pinella's own father had been the commanding Shrike of the of the Songbird Army. She remembered how years after her father died, they split up her own husband's land as incentives for young recruits. The same farm they bought together, and that the greatest of her father's trees.

"We can go together and start over with new land." Reff continued.

"You, son, you have cleared your name. You already have started over, but I can never leave the orchard."

Reff shook his head in frustration, having anticipated this. "You are the mother of a Charger to the Waymar family. Owen Waymar is the Commander of the Songbird—"

"But I was the wife of a rebel."

There was a pregnant silence, and Reff's eyes searched the orchard around him for another truth, finding only the ringing of bells for a response.

"It was Waymar's appointed Tribune who judged our case, and Reff, he was merciful." Pinella set down the small basket of bells.

"How is confinement to the orchard any mercy at all? There is so much more for you!"

"Reff, listen to me." She hardened her voice enough to soften the will of her son long enough to make him understand. "I saw hundreds of women and children imprisoned."

Reff couldn't hold the weight of her gaze. But she continued. "It was only thanks to my father's legacy that we were not dealt with accordingly for the actions of my husband." He needed to learn this in order to be truly free of her. The guilt of condemning her own beloved stabbed her.

"I was lucky to stay here. It was the Tribune Fabrien's mercy alone that allowed me to work to pay for your training. It was not kindness, Reff. They broke laws for us. I will always live here in the River District, and I am thankful to live." Pinella paused, looking deeply into her son's tear-filled eyes and smiling softly. "But you can continue to reclaim honor. You also have a great Tree of the orchard in your possession. You can appeal to the Tribunes and gain prominence with it."

Prominence was nothing like the height of the distinguished nobles, but the Prominents were still nobles, even if lower nobility. She wished she could give her son more, but how many families of the city could say they had a fruit tree of the orchard?

"Oh, son, You have done so much for your city and republic." Her tone softened. "You've grown so quickly and accomplished so much in a little time. I may be confined here but now you can make a way for yourself. It is as you said, I don't have to work anymore. You've set me free!"

Pinella didn't say anything about the fact that her work in the brothel had been entirely for him. Most men just needed to feel like a savior. Pinella stooped to pick up the basket of jingling bells.

"Come on, Reff, let's hang our bells."

≥•

They picked apples from her father's tree in the silence of their disagreement. The bells they hung made the only sound that came from the rest of their time together. The bellsong continued as they left them in the trees to sing for the protection of Trofaim. As they walked, it made her feel liberated to see that her son had finally found his own way. She wouldn't need to work so hard to support him. As a man who had served as a recruit in the Songbird Army, Reff would be independent and receive land of his own for his service. A smile pulled its way across her face at the thought of never returning to that brothel. She may be stuck in the orchard, but she was more free than she had been in years.

Reff broke the silence between them, lifting his voice to compete with the bellsong. "If you have to stay here, you should have a home here. I can buy you a house in the River District."

Pinella let him see her confusion. "Son, a room rented for a year is more expensive here in the Canals than an entire house with land in the Lower City. I cannot sell your grandfather's apple tree."

Reff hesitated. Pinella could see his resolve searching for another way.

"Then I will trade my land claims in Kornata. Some landowners will have property here to sell us."

"Reff, it is too expensive here, and the land will be undervalued until the turmoil of the rebellion comes to an end. You won't get what's fair for it."

Pinella knew land near the river town of Kornata would be worth so much more in a year once the rebels were put down and their leader, The Fowler, was no longer ripping Trofaim's armies and farmland apart.

"You are my mother. For all you've given me, there is no fair return. If you have to stay here, I won't leave you homeless."

Pinella considered all of it. How hard had she worked in the River District serving food, cleaning homes, and pruning trees? Had she spent the last three months working in a brothel for her son to forget about her?

Pinella nodded, moved by the heart of her son. It didn't make all she had done somehow worth it, but it was something.

If he could regain honor for himself, if he could establish a name and live in peace, that would be worth it all for her.

Chapter Two

The Festival

Cicero

Cicero gently spurred his young mare, Doe, through the spectacle that was Trofaim in its harvest. The young portion of this ancient city seemed to be alive with festival everywhere he looked. Bells rang in the trees high and low, their music adding to the harvest song of this legendary city. Cicero usually hated the chaotic press of large cities. Everyone pushing and moving in their separate ways all at once. It always brought him back the emotions of battle.

Trofaim was different though. Music was made by instrumentalists and other harvesters who knew the tune. People clamored across narrow canal bridges under leafy canopies into this otherwise sparsely populated area of the city they called the River District. It was aptly named for its river splitting into a web of canals, feeding the greatest orchard in all of Alssae. The river split after falling from the Upper City cliff and rejoined as it entered the old Lower City. Trofaim's Great Orchard was a source of wealth that sat between the two parts of Trofaim. It was held in high esteem as the burial place of the old dynasty of kings that once held the now broken lands of Alssae together under a peaceful monarchy.

At least, that was the story they told to him and the other orphans growing up in Hocklee. He knew little of the old capital city, but he was amazed at how, unlike most things, Trofaim was greater than the stories they told about it. Each canopy stretched like clouds darkening the ground with shade. Cicero hoisted Swain over his head to reach the lowest branch of their next tree. The boy had been his traveling companion to the great city. Upward, he climbed, high in a tree half-full of red apples, the lower half full of little bells. Some of them were wind chimes both made of wood and metal, ringing as he shook the fruits from the branches. Somehow Swain hummed harmoniously with the tune of the city. How had he learned this song?

"Cicero!" the boy called, full of joy. "Have you ever seen an apple this big before?" Swain tossed an apple the size of a baby's head down to Cicero. Cicero caught the apple and threw a bell up to Swain so he could replace it, then admired the huge fruit himself, shining it on his shirt. He noticed the bottom of the basket of fruit beginning to sag with the plentiful harvest they'd gleaned from Trofaim's Great Orchard. His arm grew tired, so he hung the basket from the side of Doe's saddle horn. The girl never fussed at holding him all day, what was a few more pounds?

"Okay, Swain. Come on down! Your mother asked me to bring her some figs, and we've only a dozen or so bells left." The boy poked his head from a leafy bush in the treetop.

"But my dad loves red apples the most!" Mag, Cicero's dog, barked at Swain as if she would climb up the tree to him if only she had not been leashed up to the horse. Doe stood still, unmoved by Mag as she pulled at the rope linking them together.

"Swain, have you ever had a fig before?" Cicero asked the boy, all the while attempting to calm Mag down.

Swain looked back at Cicero, kind of puzzled. "Is it hairy?"

Cicero just laughed, knowing he meant a peach. "Yeah, that's the one. Now come on down so that we can get some figs for your mother. You and I can share some on the way back."

Cicero, Swain, Mag, and Doe made their way through the Great Orchard City on their way back to Hocklee with a huge basket of fruits in tow. As they passed through the River District, Cicero noticed that the city got more aged the farther away from the Upper City they were. He heard the ringing of bells and chimes making a melodious tune in his ears. It was reminiscent of the time he had spent at war in Hocklee with Swain's father, Lain. He would play his thumb harp, a small rectangular wooden box with a hole cut in the center and wooden tongues that rang when they were plucked. It's a shame Swain never knew what type of man his father had been before the wars, before Gallo Bloodway came back to Hocklee.

The sun was beginning to set on Trofaim and Swain kept telling Cicero how he would grow up to be rich enough to move his family to this orchard. So he could bring his mother figs every day. Cicero didn't bother telling the boy that fruit only came during harvest. He knew that life had a way of making everyone wise, but the dream made the boy happy and no doubt put fire in his belly to live for more than what he had been given.

Cicero just smiled and told Swain to bring him golden pears while he got the figs for Swain's mother. He'd told Swain they were his favorite and they'd used most of their bells for the little pears. Cicero found himself caught in the charm of the beautiful city, hoping his little hamlet in the South might become like this famous City of Bells one day. It all almost made Cicero wonder if anyone in a city like Trofaim ever got worried about the rain or if the clouds would bring enough water for the crops to grow. Probably not like they did in Hocklee. Crops in Hocklee weren't as plentiful as they were in Trofaim. Things and people always died there. It seemed like nothing out there ever got a fighting chance at life. His heart hoped that the little city state that he first called free could truly find the freedom that he wanted for it. Would Cicero's home on the hill ever make something rather than orphans and burned fields?

ଈ

As the festival began to slow, travelers started to go back all over Alssae to their homes. Few people came from the South, and no one else came from Hocklee. Swain had never seen anyone outside of the borderlands of where he'd been raised. Cicero could tell the boy was amazed at all the different people he'd seen over the past week here in Trofaim. They all said Trofaim had the most beautiful women and Cicero had thought it to be an exaggeration until his own first time in the Orchard City. But he was most amazed by the beauty of Trofaim itself. No doubt Swain was too.

Every part of the city was a child's notion of a fairytale. Cicero wondered if he couldn't do any better if asked to imagine a more dream-like place. In the northern part of the city, the Virtuin River flowed in from the Orobos Mountains. The cleanest river in Alssae, named after its first king, by all accounts ran hard and fast in shallow rapids through what they called the Upper City until it slowed at a cliff, spilling down into the orchard. The river slowed in the orchard and splintered all throughout the forested expanse of the central part of the city they called the River District. It was in this quiet, sparsely populated area that Cicero and Swain had spent most of their time, camping under the trees.

Cicero could hear the falls from where they were picking fruit. The waterfall itself wasn't visible for the trees, but Cicero could just see the Upper City perched next to the waterfall. The great stone structures seemed to lean over the orchard beneath. The larger buildings were topped with towers each painted different colors so they brightly stuck out into the purple sunset-stained sky. Cicero could only imagine how hard of a task it must have been to paint the things.

"Cicero, should we spend another week in Trofaim? We could get more fruit!" Swain's face looked hopeful.

"We can't afford any more bells." They had spent all the money they'd brought on bells in the Lower City from the great bell making families who lived there. "If you work hard on your farm with me, maybe we can come next year. We can even plant some of these so we can start an orchard back home in Hocklee. We'll leave tomorrow and be home for the harvest." The boy agreed respectfully, but Cicero could see his disappointment. He didn't want to leave either, but their lives were in Hocklee. His first time in the city, Cicero had come alone and he'd only had enough money to afford a single bell. He ate mostly fallen fruit that year, but he hadn't come for the festival and this year he did. So Cicero looked back indulgently toward the sunset and took a bite out of the pear that had caught his eye.

ॐ

They left after four days spent in Trofaim just before the Harvest Festival ended. It had taken much longer to venture from Hocklee than the time they'd spent in the city, but Swain needed more understanding of all the Free Cities of Alssae so that he could govern their lands one day after Cicero. When Cicero was his age, he heard the stories of the kings and the Alssaen City states, passed down from those who could read or afford to travel. It was a priority to him that Swain see the things that gave Cicero the vision for peace and what it could look like. Since Cicero couldn't read, he chose to travel and show Swain himself. He did not expect famed places to live up to their legend, but Trofaim had done it. If war and evil would be an inevitability in the young man's life, Cicero thought it important for him first to know how good life can be. He had seen young allegiants serving great warriors in Trofaim and adopted the approach with his best friend's son. Rather than teaching Swain how to kill, Cicero had decided to teach him how to farm.

Broad, raft-like riverboats cruised along the river, carrying families and traders. The route down river would take them most of the way home, so Cicero paid for their group to ride on one of the boats. It cost him extra to take Doe, but she was the best horse he had and the journey up to Trofaim would have taken them much longer without her. He owed her for many other things, he thought. He was thankful to pay the larger toll. The river was smooth and some passengers fished off the side of the boat. They ate some of the fruit from the orchard, always keeping seeds for the trees they'd planned to start together on Swain's land in Cicero's region.

They often dreamed together about what the future could look like for the farmland and homesteads they called the South Hamlet. For years it had been one of many scenes of war in the conflict between Kalesia and Galanoa, and again later as Hocklee declared its own independence. It'd been seven years since the Hockleets repelled both armies and made them give up the war-torn land to something like peace.

It was nothing compared to the sustained state of peace in Trofaim. The great city enjoyed superior strength and immense prosperity that far surpassed the Southern city-states. If Trofaim was the most powerful city state in Alssae, Hocklee was the weakest. The land was teaming with killers and war criminals who'd fled from other states. Many locals in the territory, like Cicero, were orphaned as children by the endless turmoil. The land, like its people, was burned and scarred from years of war. The only similarity to this good was the occasional public execution of rebels. Most of whom reminded Cicero of himself. To think he'd fought since he was a boy not much older than Swain made him want a better life for Swain. An orchard in Hocklee was just the thing the region needed. He hoped it would bring a sense of shared pride to the region. If some of the farming families had something to be proud of, they might just defend it. Certainly the trees would have a great caretaker after Cicero. Swain had often spoken of his plans to reserve many of the fig trees, once they were grown, solely for his mother. Perhaps the boy would teach killers how to be farmers.

It made Cicero happy to know Swain had his whole family despite all that Hocklee had been through. Lain, The boy's father, was Cicero's closest all throughout the wars before he got struck in the head and lost most of his reasoning. He was no less kind for it, but he was changed, always mumbling to himself and saying little that made sense. It wasn't fair, but they had their whole family, which was a rarity in the South.

Swain took good care of them, and it pleased Cicero to help him. He'd always wondered what life would've been like had Cicero known his own father or had his mother wanted him. Cicero didn't get to have a regular family, but he reckoned it his chance to taste the feeling on account that Swain always had plenty of memories to share. So Cicero smiled and listened to all the boy's endless stories about his parents and his big sister. The stories made Cicero's heart ache, scratching at those oldest and deepest wounds. It hurt but he figured it hurts worse in the long run if you don't dress your wounds. The wound, small as it may be, can rot a whole arm, or even a leg, eventually rotting a man to death if left to fester. So he let the stories both hurt and heal his wounded heart.

The river seemed to be twice as wide and half as fast as it'd run through Trofaim. Now they drifted past small fishing towns and waved at children running with them along the riverbank. The aroma of food cooking went up from the little town. Cicero watched as the other passengers asked if they could stop in the town, but the Polemen refused to slow down, no doubt needing to meet some deadline for the delivery of their cargo. It would've been nice, Cicero thought, to get some cooked meat out from that village. The Polemen didn't allow any cooking on board for risk of fire. Cicero considered a good meal worth the risk since the raft was little more than hollow wood tied together. They hadn't packed any smoked meats or dried vegetables for the trip, so they only had silver coins and fruit from Trofaim. They were saving the fruit for when they got home, and silver isn't worth much if you try to eat it. Fortunately, some other rafts came along and Cicero was able to toss some coins across for which they tossed some bread back in return.

They passed wheat fields that seemed to extend for miles over the state territory of Trofaim. As they went, the Polemen announced that they'd be leaving Trofaim and entering that portion of the river that served as the border between Carnae in the north and Storins in the south. The cultures of both the city-states were similar but divided by the large span of river between them. The Sister States, as they were often referred to, helped each other against one another's rebellions. Swain's own father had come as a Storinian mercenary before becoming Cicero's closest, a friendship many traditionalist Galanoans despised him for. Cicero had fought men from both states who'd been paid to aid Kalesia against Galanoa. Cicero had grown up with and fought beside Storinians who had settled in his homeland. Many had come as mercenaries in aid of the Kingdom of Kalesia in its occupation. Cicero didn't doubt the fact that he may have enemies somewhere in these countries. Come to think of it, how many enemies did he have? Could they be reckoned as an army if they were all together in one place?

"Have you ever met anyone from Carnae, Cicero?" Swain asked, seeming to know Cicero's thoughts.

"A few men in the past." The only Carnaens Cicero had met were men he'd killed.

"What were they like?" Swain was expecting to hear about brave, good men rather than the killers he'd fought in the wars.

Not knowing what to tell the boy, Cicero settled with, "They were like me." Even though Swain beamed at Cicero's response, it stabbed him with guilt. Being good to a few doesn't make a man good. He had heard it said that even an evil man is good to someone. From what Cicero could tell, Swain admired him, but that still didn't change who Cicero was or how he'd once lived. Partly it felt like a second chance, to have so much admiration, but mostly it felt like a lie that could not hold up forever.

CHAPTER THREE

THE WAYMARS

PINELLA

Pinella walked through the streets of the Upper City for the first time in a decade. She almost didn't recognize the buildings with all their new facades and colors. Buildings that had once been faced with brightly painted wood or shingles now were adorned with cut stone or cooked clay held together with miles of mortar. The street, similarly, had evolved from packed gravel and earth to grand avenues of granite and cobblestone. The only detail congruent with her memory was the constant rush of the river. The River of Alssae was louder here, running quick and shallow between rocks and rocky banks.

Her eyes drifted up to the towers of apartment buildings that served as townhomes for the noble families who only came to the Upper City on business or service obligations. The Upper City didn't smell like a city, she noticed. It smelled only of food. Pinella remembered how the use of horses and livestock were pushed further and further from the city so that the river would remain clean for those who lived along the outskirts. She'd come up the ascending river steps from the River District for the first time in eleven years. Eleven years earlier, it was still congenial and warm with heritage. Now the upper part of Trofaim felt busy and embellished. She understood that most every noble family had sold their land in the lower, older part of the city for great expanses in the territory and ornate apartments in the newer Upper City.

Pinella's feet were sore from the long walk that she was so unaccustomed to. Her heavy breathing added to her heart's heavy beating with nerves. Today she would again face the Tribunes, one of whom decided that she would never again be given the freedom of leaving the River District. For every season since, Pinella obediently stayed among the rural middle city orchard, caring for her family's trees and what remained of its legacy. Perhaps the old Tribune would demand her execution. Maybe her leaving the orchard would bring disgrace upon her son, Reff.

She waited in the place her son had told her to meet him the day before. The King's Forum had been the place where both hearings of subjects and executions of criminals were done for the people by the kings. The tradition was carried out in the Lower City's Great Arcade now. The Forum was covered in uniform freestanding marble pillars. Each pillar stood as tall as three men. Each of the marble columns stood twenty paces from the last. A harold down the street shouting news about The Fowler and how many Shrikes had been killed at a battle a week earlier. He said something about a Shrike betraying Trofaim to join The Fowler in rebellion.

"Twenty-five affiliates have been sentenced to death for conspiring with the traitor Elmo Deep. The Tribunal has doubled the reward for uncovering a criminal." The harold continued to publicly disclose the latest insights of the rebel army. It was troubling, but Pinella had enough to worry about with her meeting to come. She directed her focus to the columns of the square around her, finding a lighthearted distraction from her inner tension. Pinella overheard a tutor with his young student as she waited expectantly.

"On that platform, two nations have been born. Over three centuries before I was even born, King Barrence stood on that platform and raised his own flag over Trofaim. Almost two-hundred years after that, his ninth-generation grandson was beheaded by the descendants that cheered for the first king." Pinella found herself cringing at the brutally honest rendition of Trofaim's history. Sure, it was true, but it was oddly sharp to hear so much of the detail left out. The tutor continued, "The nobles didn't just stop with the king. They executed the entire royal family and buried them in the place where the orchard is now."

"They planted the trees because they were sorry for what they did to the royals?" The young student asserted his question.

"No, it was the lady of the orchard, Henna, who planted the trees. The people helped care for the trees out of respect for their kings." Pinella's attention was caught by the rare historical opinion.

"My mother says Henna is a mythical figure, that she was never real." The tutor smiled and took a moment before responding.

"Mom!" Pinella's head turned instinctually at the sound of her son's voice. He was smiling wide as he came running toward her.

"Reff!" she responded with surprise. "Is it time?"

"Soon the nobles I told you about will be arriving. We should have several moments for making acquaintances, then we will go before a delegation of Tribunes in court." Pinella felt nervous. She already felt so out of place here. Now she was about to formally appeal to a powerful family for a pardon. She had no idea what to say to them. Pinella had nothing to offer in return. It all just added to the weight of worry she felt in her stomach. So much was on the line.

They waited for the nobles to arrive. Reff's gaze searched for them, his head swiveling constantly. Pinella didn't know the appearance of the people she looked for, so she just waited, watching her son arrayed in leather stained a rusty red.

"The Shrikes of the Songbird Army rule Trofaim for now." Pinella was caught again by the teaching of the old man. "The noblemen who own trees in the orchard claim ties to the life of the royal family. The nobles hoard the prestigious positions within the army to themselves so that they control the power of the army."

"The Shrikes claim to be descendants of the royal family?" Pinella agreed. That's how the old man made it sound.

The old teacher took on a spiteful tone in his voice, "I already told you, they killed the royal family. No, they don't claim royal heritage, but a kind of bond through the orchard." The boy tried to hide his confusion. But it was plain even for Pinella to see.

"I'll make it simple," the tutor began again with a sigh. "The bodies are proven to give nutrients to the soil, which the trees rely on. I'm sure your parents taught you that when you eat the orchard fruit, you honor the people who built Trofaim." The old man awaited, but the boy's blushing face was a sign of his youthful ignorance. The old man sighed again. "The rich of this city have gotten too busy to raise their own children."

"If we all eat the fruit, then what makes the owner of the trees so special? Shouldn't we all be allowed to claim to be the next nobles?" This time the old man looked puzzled as he considered the boy's question. Pinella hadn't considered that. It was a good question, and she looked forward to the old man's answer.

It was at that moment that Reff touched her shoulder, saying, "They're over there, coming from the Garden District." Pinella laid eyes on the people her son had spoken of. An unmistakable Shrike, a celebrated one. He was crowded by an entourage of beautiful young woman each beautifully dressed. Their attire had been made to reflect his armor. Both the woman's dress and the soldier's city armor dripped with ceremony. The breastplate of the armor and the bust and corset of the dress were burnt red. The shoulders and arms of the dress were blue like the sky. Pinella knew the other armored Shrikes must have been his Chargers, his most trusted aids and advisors given charge of his estate. Reff began to lead her to them.

"They look so . . ." Pinella hadn't expected so much open display of distinguishment just to hear her appeal.

"Distinguished? They are!" Pinella was going to say pomp. Reff's thrill was palpable as he led her in their direction.

As they neared, a Charger stepped between him and the small crowd of rich nobles. Reff began to customarily disarm himself when a man spoke out an interruption, "That's entirely unnecessary!" His words rang like a warm greeting. The man spoke to his guard, but his words were directed at Reff. "Bennault is my friend. If I am in danger here, better to be close to him." The man's smile was his most pronounced adornment. Every word was edged with laughter. His armor, though indicative of a noble soldier, was humble. If he had any awards or ribbons of honor, he didn't wear them. Pinella wondered how many people would think him a hanger-on rather than the Sire of his house.

Her son pushed his sword back down into its sheath and bowed his head. Pinella followed suit. "My lord victorious, thank you for meeting me to hear my request today."

The nobleman waved off Reff's address. "Not victorious yet! Not until I impale this *Fowler* in the way he did those men in Kornata. Until then, a title unearned is just weight." Pinella noticed a certain joy in the man's expression at seeing Reff. It was good to see her son making such an impression.

"Well said, my Lord!" Pinella noticed Reff beaming in the nobleman's presence like a lily in the sun.

"This must be your mother then?" Reff turned his head to her with an odd look mixed with embarrassment. It was contagious.

"Yes, lord, this is Pinella Bennault, my mother." Reff said it like he was asking a store owner to excuse him for bringing a dog inside rather than introducing his mother. He had a flush of red to match. The nobleman looked at her appraisingly.

"How pleasant it is to meet a woman of Trofaim," he said, sweeping one arm over the well-dressed collective around him. "My name is Owen Waymar. And this is my household."

She had to force out a response, "Well met. This is to us a very high honor!" The herd of overdressed nobles just looked at her, smiling expectantly. She had to force her head to stop nodding. Pinella felt like an actor on a stage who had forgotten her lines. "Thank you for meeting us. We're indebted to you!" Waymar shook his head in protest, giving a thoughtful look at Reff.

"Your son saved my life at Kornata, you know." Reff turned his head, smiling, to see his mother's reaction. "Because of his turning the tide of battle, my cousins were able to pursue him with their army. Unfortunately for them though, they did not have this young man at their side."

"You . . ." Pinella felt a smile tug its way across her face along with her pride as a mother. "Reff, you turned a battle?"

"It was greatly done! Your son is a hero!" Lord Waymar set a hand on Reff's shoulder, glowing with a fatherly expression.

"Bennault found my bodyguard surrounding me in a terribly vulnerable position!" Lord Waymar began proclaiming his story like an actor setting a play. "Many of my men were wounded and faltering. Many of the hired soldiers had fallen away. I wasn't sure if we were what remained of the army of Trofaim. My only thought was that we should under no circumstance surrender!" At the word surrender, he smashed his fist into an open palm. "Soon

I was forced to draw steel and deal as much justice as I could." A sly smile sparked in the nobleman's eyes as he stole a glance back at Reff, who just smiled on, blushing. "That's when Reff Bennault here broke through at the head of two hundred hired swords!"

Pinella joined the Waymar family, who he still had not introduced, in light applause. Reff hadn't told her any of this. And she couldn't believe it. Owen Waymar's eyes settled again on her. "Two hundred thralls of the territory looked like the sun rising for me and my guards. Like melted snow, the rebels surrounding our position were set to flight . . ." His voice quieted and the nobleman spoke directly to Pinella. "I tell you all this so you will see that this affair of yours, whatever your problem, it is my problem as well. But first you should meet the Waymar family — my family."

Lord Waymar turned on his heel like a door on a hinge, his arm outstretched to reveal his family beyond him. He was considerably less audacious in his dressings than they. He began by introducing his three wives, the two younger of them with two or three young children of their own. "This is my wife Livra." The first of Lord Owen's wives may have once been a beautiful woman, but hadn't aged well. Her gray-black hair and facial features made her look far older than her husband. She spoke warmly through tired eyes. His other two wives were much more beautiful and excited to make Pinella's acquaintance.

Kessa and Karianna Waymar looked like they were relatives. The only difference was that Kessa, while just as pretty, was clearly older than Karianna. Lord Owen introduced his sixteen-year-old son Otrin, whose mother was Kessa. After Otrin, Lord Waymar introduced his younger two children by Kessa. A twelve-year-old girl named Omera and a nine-year-old boy named Ogwin. Pinella was already forgetting their names, and she had so many more family members to meet.

Lord Waymar introduced his youngest daughters next, who he'd had with his youngest wife, Karianna. The young girls were named Owella and Olanna. Olanna had was still too young to walk. "I regret that my sister Octavia is not here to meet you. She attends to our business in the Lower City. She is eager to meet you, though"

Lord Waymar went on to introduce a small troops of Chargers, veterans, and a litany of respected servants and aids. Pinella just gave up trying to remember all their names. She knew there was some deeper reason for all these members of their family to come to the Kings Forum than to meet her. He ended the introduction by surprising Pinella. "And this is Reff Bennault, my twelfth and newest of my Chargers!"

Her head swiveled on its own to see her son's gaping smile. "Oh, Reff, congratulations!"

Lord Waymar beamed with the announcement. "Just as his title implies, he will be given charge over a number of my soldiers in times of war and charge over parcels of my land in times of peace."

"You do my son a great honor in recruiting him. I'm beyond words with gratitude."

Lord Waymar just waved off her thanks again, reserving the right to gratitude for Reff saving his life before dismissing his wives and other Chargers to enjoy the Kings Forum and the nearby fruit sellers and traders among the booths between the Forum's pillars. Owen Waymar shifted into thoughtful discomfort before exposing his thoughts.

"Now, to the issue of your own social standing, lady Bennault . . ."

Pinella shook her head in protest, feeling awkward by the honorable address. "Please, Lord, you do your servant too much honor. My name is Pinella." She let her head bow forward slightly in reverence. The nobleman acquiesced to Pinella's insistent humility. She then held out the record book her father had given her, containing the story and deeds of the Bennault family. Pinella watched the Waymar family enjoy the Forum as she waited for their sire to read the account of her mostly common family.

"Akten Bennault! A classic hero of mine," he said, before continuing to read silently. He scanned the writings with his little finger pointing to the place he read on the page. Every time she looked at her son, he seemed nervous, hanging on every facial expression on Lord Waymar's face. She knew that his angst came from the shame he carried for what his father had done. Reff had not known his father. Not really. The sad part to Pinella was that he was not interested in who his father had been or what kind of man he was. He only cared about detaching his own reputation from the criminal that ruined his family name. She could never tell Reff how much he reminded her of his father. He had already made up his mind to resent him. Father and son were alike in that one couldn't change their mind when it was made up.

"I see here that it was the Tribune Sullemn Fabrien who proposed the ruling of your case." Waymar took in and let out a chestfull of breath, appraising. "He writes: *Life in the orchard to care for what remains of your family's legacy.*" He looked up from reading the record book to Pinella. "You have spent all this time taking care of the apple tree your father planted after his famous victory."

"And working to pay the recurring criminal debt payments I owe the Republic." She added. It was embarrassing, but it was better if she got it all out there now before the Waymar family extended her their help.

"Tribune Fabrien is not known to recall any of his legal decisions. But I will speak to him before we make our appeal in the

Court of Tribunes. If he was the primary influence on the first ruling, he will be necessary in our appeal for a more favorable ruling."

Pinella felt a touch of worry in her stomach. *His first ruling was more favorable than most of the other wives of rebels received.* Pinella felt an unfamiliar feeling that brought a twinge of nausea with it. Hope.

Chapter Four

The Broken Borderland
Cicero

Alssae was broken. Their trip through the free cities of Storins and Brevalti was a reminder of how shattered it truly was. Cicero remembered nights around campfires when the other civil warriors would tell stories of how the city-states of Alssae were once a united nation under a single king, fighting against the mighty Aravacans who enslaved monsters called shrouds to fight their wars. *Fairytales,* he thought, *that a nation so divided and broken may have ever been whole.* The notion was made even more ludicrous to Cicero as he occasionally saw familiar pillars of smoke in the distance. He could tell the difference between a brushfire and a burning house. They had been too frequent to be anything but conflict fires. None of that stopped him from telling what he remembered of the old stories to Swain when he didn't know how to answer his many questions about the war-torn lands. Cicero loved the fabled stories of the armies of singing men fighting an impossible battle against the monsters from the South. Somehow their songs helped, but Cicero couldn't remember how. He loved the old tales and Swain did too.

"What was the king like?" the boy asked, wanting to be impressed.

"He was . . . amazing!" Cicero used his hands to help him explain. "He wore purple robes that dragged four strides behind him."

"Did his robe get dirty?" Swain asked confusedly.

"He could always buy more!" Cicero had no idea why any idiot would let his clothes drag on the ground behind him. It sounded better when the old soldiers told the story.

"The king was evil!" a man said from nearby, sitting with his family. "The king declared it unlawful to wear purple if you weren't of royal blood. Started killing the poor folks that did all throughout Alssae. Especially in Trofaim." Both Swain and Cicero were listening to the interrupting man. Cicero wanted to tell the man it was just a story, but clearly it was more to him.

"Had it not been for the Shrikes killing the purple fools, we'd still be killed and persecuted in his royal purges." Cicero was thinking the man must've been from Storins by his accent. "Rumeneddan kings have been cut from the same canvas, far as I'm concerned." The old eastern coastal kingdom of Rumenedda was more ancient than the Alssaen Kingdom by all accounts, and a powerful army lived there. "Storins is free . . . for now. These rebel insurrections conspire to reinstate the Rumeneddan Monarchy over the city." Cicero found himself just listening to the man fervently talk about his offenses held with the political enemies.

"We're from Hocklee!" said Swain abruptly. The man looked puzzled from Cicero, to Swain, and back.

"You know hard times then." Swain looked up at Cicero for his response.

Cicero took his moment before responding, "The nation is long broken. I doubt that any of us are strangers to the hard times."

The rest of the boat ride was somber as the other families and groups began trading stories of family members lost. Some killed in war, others starved or fell victim to plague. Seemed to Cicero, the old monarchy would have been a thing worth having, even with an evil king. He may have killed a few hundred people, but what was that against the wars that left countless dead. One evil man should have been an easier compromise than a nation teeming with evil men.

≈

The old roads of South Hocklee were rocky and winding as it twisted through the pine covered hills of the region. Swain's company had grown gloomy as he evidently grew more homesick on the roughest part of the journey. As they neared though, Swain became excited to be reunited with his family, again humming the tune they'd heard in Trofaim. Cicero couldn't help a stab of sadness at the thought of an empty house after a long absence.

Soon enough, the road came to that familiar fork toward Swain's own yielding patch. He felt for a strange moment that he was a child wanting to ask Swain to stay with him or to let him go with the boy to see his old war companion. Cicero just turned to Swain, suppressing the lonely orphan within. "Well. I'm sure your family misses you!" Cicero looked off toward the home of Swain's family. He squinted against the bright sky, noticing a great deal of smoke in the direction of Swain's home. Strange smoke.

"Looks like my mom's burning off some brush. I'd better go help her!" said Swain, just before sliding down off of Doe where he rode in the saddle behind Cicero. He kissed Mag, scratched her ear, and strolled toward his home. "I'll come tomorrow to help you with the reaping," the boy called back. Cicero watched the dark smoke and then smelled it. It was more than brush. It reminded him of *that* smell. But Cicero thought the boy's mother was probably just burning some dead animals. It's good when you can afford to burn something you would have killed for in wartime. He was thankful that his miserable life of fighting had brought some peace. He also had Swain's father to thank for it. He took a deep breath and reminded himself that fires didn't always mean fights now. He looked down, finding Mag's empathetic gaze. Cicero leaned down to give Doe a scratch right above her saddle, how she always liked.

"Let's go, girls." And they went in the homeward.

❧

Cicero stood in disbelief, watching the soot and scant smoke lift slowly off the scorched turf. There were roughly twenty-five good acres of farmland just days from harvest. What had been a great body of golden wheat that seemed to flow in the breeze had now been burned black as midnight. He watched the breeze push and pull the smoke across the plain. He wanted to cry. Cicero turned back to his horse to leave. "All our work burned while we were gone." He looked at Doe. She barely even seemed to care that all her work pulling the plow was wasted. He could tell the saddle had been on her back too long, so he unstrapped it and lifted it off her back and let it fall to the dirt.

"Mag, what do you think?" The dog responded with an empathetic mix between a growl and a hum. She was looking out across the fiery wheat fields with even more concern than him. "What do you make of this, gal?" But she just licked her lips. It was clear he'd lost a season's work as well as a season's pay. It was a serious loss to be sure, but he could not help but to think of all the farms he had burned in his day. He was coming out of this one in the best condition by far. He still had his girls, Doe and Mag. Cicero had decided to sit on an old log on the treeline and wait for

Swain. He pulled out some moldy bread and stale water from his satchel and began to eat. He was sitting, staring at that last piece of blueish green bread. In his head, he weighed out which was worse, his hunger or the sour taste of the loaf. Every time he took a bite, it made him want to cough. He was still just hungry enough to think it might be worth it, so he took another bite and tried not to breathe. It had that effect where you smell it more than you taste it, and it smelled like the handkerchief it had been wrapped in was wrapped around his foot rather than his food. It should have been bread from freshly ground wheat flour. So much work was lost.

His mouth was still full of nasty bread when he heard his own name.

"Cicero? Are you there?"

Cicero patted his dog as soon as she began to growl. "It's okay, Mag. That you, Swain?"

"Yessir!" the boy came out of the treeline fifty strides away. The youngster looked around, evidently seeing nobody.

"I'm down here, Swain." Cicero pushed up from the log and spat as much of the moldy bread out as he could. He could tell the boy was worried. Cicero smiled. "Looks like I haven't got any work for you after all." Cicero gestured toward the burned field, trying not to show the pain of his loss. Swain didn't say anything. He didn't even look at the field. Just kept walking, looking concerned, looking right at Cicero. "What is it, Swain?" Cicero was starting to get nervous seeing him look so worried and saying nothing.

"They're burned . . ."

Cicero's neck and face started to feel hot. His stomach tightened as he made sense of Swain's demeanor.

"All of them?" Cicero felt himself shaking with worry.

"I couldn't find my sister." That was all it took. Cicero could barely think.

"Whi . . . Which way did they go?" Swain just shook his head, looking flush. Cicero looked around, waiting for some obvious answer to pop up. None did. "We'll speak to the other families in the region."

꒰꒱

They had not said anything to each other. Aside from Cicero's words to Mag and his horse, it had been silent. He could only imagine what Swain was going through. The village they looked for came into view. But soon they could tell it had been burned out and abandoned as well. Cicero was starting to worry more than ever. There were hundreds of tough hardened veterans who lived in the region. So far, all of them had left their farms and towns. He desperately needed to know what had happened in the region, but it was abandoned. The strangest part of it all was that there were no bodies. Those old Storinians like Swain's father would've fought like animals. But he saw no bodies. Cicero wanted to keep going west in search of survivors, but his warlike instincts were beginning to set back in from years of being dormant. Cicero looked at the north sky. A storm would be coming and the opportunity to track whoever had done this would be lost. Anger enveloped Cicero and he again turned homeward.

꒰꒱

Cicero led the horse on foot for the long stretch back to his farm in their valley while Mag and Swain followed close behind. "Keep an eye out. If you see anyone, call out." Cicero went off alone to the ashy pile of sticks that remained of his shack farmhouse. Cicero only ever felt disdain for the place, but now that it was picked over and burned, it might as well have been his life's pride and joy they'd burned. Cicero went to the back under the stall where he kept Doe tied up at night and started digging. Gradually as he dug, he felt the canvas bag underneath the collapsed roof and charred turf. He pulled it out of the earth, not stopping to even brush off the dirt from the bag. He walked back to Swain, who was holding Doe's reins in one hand and petting Mag with the other. Swain was looking out across the field, looking with tears in his eyes. Cicero's heart was angered.

"Swain, we're going after them. We can't mourn yet. First, we need to get some work done. Then you can go home, and I'll help you bury your family. I don't think I can do this without you." Cicero stopped and realized he'd spoken more just now than he had all day to Swain. His voice was grim and foreign "Are you coming?"

Swain nodded his head, and they were off. Cicero was careful to leave one thing behind. Hope.

Chapter Five

Before the Court of Tribunes

Pinella

Pinella followed Lord Waymar and her son down the long corridor to the large familiar door to the Tribunal Court. Nearly as tall as three men, the double doors were cased in ornate basketwork of polished brass. She could see her own distorted appearance in the reflection. A guard, standing with the appearance of one possessing no greater capacity to guard than a sick house cat, stood as doorman. Together they awaited their appointment within the chamber before the Tribunes. Pinella remembered waiting here before the same door so many years ago, her wrists chained and Reff at her side. Lord Waymar quietly advised them on how to approach and address the Tribunes.

"Remember, these are almost all delegates. They have no real authority of their own, so a little flattery is in high demand. Any chance to stroke their ego should be taken." Lord Waymar described a very different experience than what Pinella remembered years before.

Soon the doors were opened to them, and they entered the most greatly feared room in Trofaim. How many powerful and great men had been reduced to criminals in the court of the Tribunes? Pinella followed Lord Waymar alongside her son into a much more different court than the one she remembered. A somber room filled with somber Tribunes had evolved into a bright courtroom filled with conversation and even laughter. Pinella tried not to look at any of the officials for fear she may be recognized, so she looked straight ahead to the pleading floor. Oddly enough, she saw no desperate person begging for a favorable sentence. Instead, she saw what looked like props and a backdrop for a show of entertainment. "What's all this?" Pinella whispered, leaning to Waymar.

"That is Kasriotti! The great actor from Rumenedda!" Waymar seemed a little disappointed to have missed the performance. "A variety of entertaining performances are held regularly in the High Court." Somehow that seemed a little inappropriate to Pinella. The Tribunes soon were hushed by a master of ceremony with the strike of a gavel, though most of them just continued their conversation quietly to each other.

"Our next point of order will be hearing an appeal from the Bennault family and their debts of guilt to the city." With that, the men flipped a sand clock, nodded, and Owen Waymar led Reff and Pinella to the center of the fifty or so elevated platforms of desks and cushioned chairs. To Pinella, it seemed the Tribunes of the High Court should have at least been sober. Her eyes drifted up through the dozens of seated officials. They all spoke idly among themselves, all of them laughing and chumming with one another like a theatre audience may in recess. Would they even consider her pleadings?

Her son stirred nervously, pulling and adjusting his ceremonial soldier's garb as though it were made for someone else. She let out a breath she didn't know she was holding. Lord Waymar stood in a wide stance, his whole appearance pensive and intense. Time stretched. Officially they were taking these moments to gather notes and any records of their own concerning Pinella's case. But she kept hearing the light remarks and shared commentary of the actor's performance that had just ended.

When the last of the sand fell to the bottom, the administrator again called the court to order. "May the account be read aloud." One of the scribes who sat in the front of many shelved archives of scrolls stood and thoroughly cleared his throat. The moment he opened his mouth to speak, an interruption came from a Tribune seated high up and to the left. Pinella strained a moment before the cold realization of who it was who'd spoken out. Tribune Sullemn Fabrien's hair gained some gray. His face was familiar though.

"The scroll is over three spans in length. For the sake of the court's time, I would give an abridged account." The administrator nodded respectfully to the esteemed Tribune with a visible look of reverence.

"If the rest of the court endorses, we may—"

"I endorse!" one Tribune with far too much makeup shouted. Delegates stuck their thumbs up, signaling their endorsement. The announcer didn't bother counting the obvious majority endorsement. Likely it was as Waymar had said, Sullemn may have been the only ranking Tribune in a court of representing delegates. His influence was already apparent. Pinella prayed Waymar had enough history with the man to gain his favor. She certainly had enough of her own history. All of which was likely to make Fabrien unfavorable. She took Reff by the hand and squeezed against his own nervous grip. The respected Tribune looked familiarly to Lord Waymar, who Pinella noticed giving the slightest nod in return.

"Have you reviewed the account, good sir?" asked the announcer.

"I wrote the account," he responded levelly.

"Ahh . . . excuse my ignorance! May the court pay its attention to the esteemed Tribune, Sullemn Fabrien, trustee of some two and two-dozen estates." The announcer finished Fabrien's introduction with a hammer strike, silencing the court. The senior Tribune pushed up from his desk about two stories higher than the pleading floor where Reff and Pinella stood behind Lord Waymar.

"Please . . ." whispered Reff.

"Good men and women of the court. The name Bennault is that of our city's late hero, Akten Bennault. The same Akten Bennault who defeated the Mottravan Army at Pavenelli and broke the famine. To our long dead hero, we owe much. This woman is the daughter of Akten Bennault." Many among the delegation gained some observable interest at the understanding of her heritage. "She is a criminal though, for her association to the Highwater Rebellion that so greatly threatened the Republic." Pinella felt the blood rush around her eyes in embarrassment. *What will they do to me, the wife of a rebel?* she thought. "She was sentenced to confinement within the River District to spend her years keeping the orchard and paying the debts of Trofaim. In the interest of brevity, as we are in a state of civil conflict with this new rebel, The Fowler, I propose we lift Pinella's confinement as her involvement to the rebellion was not of any real consequence. A relative of her and her son's may have sowed discord among the republic, but not as much as Akten Bennault sowed to our unity and stability.

"She's been quiet and without disobedience in her sentence. Her son here wears a soldier's garb. He fought at Kornata where he was recognized for exceptional accomplishments."

The Tribune left the host of delegates and scribes in a state of suspense as he took a drink from the cup on his desk in front of him. Pinella hadn't anticipated Fabrien gaining so much favor as a senior Tribune. It was either Sullemn's mercy or Lord Waymar's influence or both that he referred to her husband as a 'relative' of theirs.

"Good people of the delegation, I suggest we deal favorably toward this family." Fabrien turned his attention to Lord Waymar. "Now, Lord Owen Waymar of House Waymar, you may present your plea." Lord Waymar nodded to the announcer before addressing the judicial delegation.

"I ask that the only daughter of Lord Akten Bennault would be entirely pardoned and that the remainder of her debts be forgiven." That must have been a tall order. Pinella watched their faces show concern and hesitation. After some whispers and looks were exchanged among the desks. A Tribune on the bottom level on the far right side stood with a hand raised. The announcer called out in response.

"Tribune Kellen! You may endorse or protest." Kellen waited, staring at the announcer with an impatient look. *Has he improperly addressed a Tribune?* she thought. After a moment of pregnant silence, the announcer remembered to ratify his own announcement with a belated hammer strike on the gavel. Kellen blinked his eyes in a rapid succession to show his annoyance.

"Lord Waymar, while you are a distinguished man of this republic, it isn't simple to pardon the offense of treason. The Highwater Rebellion may have been over a decade ago, but many families still suffer the loss of it. We face a new uprising, and soon we will be called upon to judge associates and rebels for their disloyalty. To simply excuse the past is to forget our duty. Ultimately this would be short-sighted. A parole or even some sort of criminal sub-citizenship would be a lenient ruling in a time where the rule of law must be upheld." The Tribune finished with a spiteful look over his shoulder up at Fabrien. Lord Waymar raised one of his muscular arms, to which the announcer introduced him and struck the gavel.

"It is not just for freedom that I propose we set her free. My brother-in-law was struck down by The Fowler's men at Shephard's Pass. This uprising must be put to an end. The Waymar family and its subordinating families are finished hiring mercenaries to fight our war. I, Owen Waymar of the distinguished Waymar family, officially declare war against The Fowler and his rebellion! All vassal of houses and allied families will be called upon."

Without missing a beat, Tribune Fabrien stood to his feet and loudly endorsed Lord Waymar. Before speaking to the tables of notaries, scrawling the record down as fast as they could.

"Lord Waymar has made his first declaration of war here in court. Let the record show that Tribune Sullemn Fabrien is first to endorse the war against the enemies of our republic!" Nearly the entire delegation stood to their feet, shouting their endorsements mixed with applause for Lord Waymar. They didn't want to miss such an opportunity to be in the pages of the Trofaim's history. Pinella didn't know much about the court, the Tribunal delegates, or why this Tribune Kellen opposed her pardon, but she could tell Lord Waymar had stolen the upper hand decisively. She watched Kellen endorse acquiescently. Lord Waymar raised his hand again to speak, but it took a moment for the applause to die.

"My family will need hands and minds, as many as possible together to best serve Trofaim." Turning to Reff, Lord Waymar put his unraised hand on his shoulder. "Young Bennault has agreed to join me once again in arms. But I won't let him bless that republic which retains offense against him. His family must be pardoned and their honor restored so that he should fight for the state that has fought for him."

The court ruptured with applause. Sullemn Fabrien, who Pinella now held eye contact with, gave her a sad smile. She felt his pain, the pain she'd caused him years before.

Chapter Six

The Sister

Cicero

The two of them had been tracking the raiders since midday. The sun was setting fast and the clouds squeezed the light out of the sky in their boast of a storm. It was nearly dusk when they found a wooded grove that smelled of sap.

Cicero stared up at the sky. It was a beautifully peaceful display of gray storm clouds rolling in on a gradient sky. Cicero took a moment, if nothing else, to admire the scene before stepping into the moments to come. "We haven't got much daylight, and the clouds are shrouding over the little light we do have. Better if we just plan to fight in the rainy dark. It's going to be a very dark night judging by the clouds, and by the smell of the air, it'll probably rain on us soon."

Swain looked at Cicero with a confused look on his face. "Fight?" The boy was starting to look more worried. Cicero just laid the canvas bag on the ground and started to break the stitching. He opened a hole on one end and slid out a long, smooth piece of wood as well as another similar one that was curved just as smooth but not quite as long.

"Hand me that log, Swain." He took the piece of firewood they carried from the camp and stomped it with one boot. There was a hollow crack as the wood broke under his foot. Cicero thought he had hidden more arrows in the wood, but the seventeen he counted seemed to be in good enough condition. He took the long, straight piece of wood and strung the bowstring through the two notches on both ends. The bow was tight and resisted the bend like a brand new bow. That was good, maybe even a little lucky. The second bow was easier to string. Its curved ends flexed against the pull of a cord. His two bows, unlike him, had not aged a day. They were smooth and glassy as if they had just been polished. "We will wait until the rain starts to fall before we get near them, but working in the rain means getting close."

The rain came on hard. Cicero taught Swain how to shoot an arrow but even an expert bowman prayed for accuracy in rain. Swain was a good boy, always caught on quick. Now Cicero needed him to learn how to end a life. Or was he learning how to save one? Cicero tried to clear his head and set his mind to the plan. They had counted eleven men down in the camp, a maddening number to think about. He had to simplify it in his head. Just another quota. That made him think of all the times he had painted three blue rings on his arrows so he could recognize and retrieve them. That made him notice a faded blue ring on the shaft in his hand. He heard someone and remembered where he was. His head jerked upright. He saw the men scrambling, one with an arrow through his neck just above the collarbone. Cicero wiped raindrops out of his eyes. He nocked an arrow, picked one man out, and loosed. The arrow caught the man in the ribs, causing him to stumble and fall. Another one of Swain's arrows stuck in the mud. Cicero loosed another arrow and caught a man through the face just below the eye. Men began to yell as they hid behind trees and the logs where they had been sitting. While the men were still scrambling to find cover, Cicero took this moment to run left and let an arrow fly. The men in the camp were starting to think they were surrounded. Cicero hit another man in the chest before running back the other way. Everything was going as well as Cicero could have hoped for in the camp. They were all peering out into the rain, looking for a target. That's when things took a sour turn.

Another one of Swain's arrows took a man in the shoulder. Cicero aimed at another man. Pointing the arrow at the man's chest, he let the bowstring rip it out of his grip through the rain, lodging in the man's thigh as he made an effort to stand.

"Five and two!" Cicero called out loudly to Swain, reminding him to make a swift exit on Doe. The men were well hidden now.

"The fire!" A man down in the camp crawled over to the flickering fire and began to choke out the flame with loose dirt and rocks. Cicero shot but he was low to the ground on the opposite side of the camp. Seeing that he had no shot, he ran again. Rounding the camp while looking for an open shot. This time he was focused on the man putting out the fire. The man was down low between a log and a saddle, stretching out his hand toward the hole that the flames were coming from. An arrow stuck out from behind the man's cover and Cicero could tell it had taken the man in the back. One of Swain's.

"Good boy," Cicero whispered in disbelief. The flame was small now and the other men were hidden in the night.

"That way!" Cicero could make out a man running in Swain's direction. He pulled an arrow back and waited for another man to pass through the low light in the center of the camp. He shot as a man crossed the fire and heard him yelp. He fell, bringing the fire canopy down with him to the ground. With nothing left to cover the fire, it wasn't long until the rain soaked out what remained of the embers. That left Cicero in the dark and rain with no sight.

He ran in Swain's direction. He wasn't sure where the boy was, but he followed the voices of the men through the trees. His feet found puddles, and his head ducked under branches. He was beginning to lose his focus. These men could kill Swain, and no doubt would if given the chance. He could hear Mag barking. He started running faster. Not caring about his footing, looking straight ahead. His breath started coming fast. He should have stayed focused but he was afraid. His foot caught a tree root and all at once he was in the air. Cicero threw both of his hands out to catch himself, but his hands were still wrapped tight around the bow and remaining arrow shafts. He heard wood cracking as he hit the ground. One of them stabbed through his calf muscle of his left leg.

Cicero let out a loud groan as he realized the new wound. One of his broken arrows. He brought himself up to one knee. Cicero grabbed the bow, looking for breaks and cracks. It was lucky to still be in the shape it was in. As he checked the arrows, he could tell they were all broken but one. That was not lucky. He picked himself up onto his feet again and continued toward Swain. His leg screamed with pain where his arrow stabbed him. He had to help Swain.

As he hurried through the dark woods with the rain adding to the confusing darkness, he caught some movement on his left. He instinctively put his hand up to shield his face and caught something against his forearm just before a blade cut into the side of his face. He flinched away from the movement, stumbling, barely staying on his feet, slowing his pace from a run. He darted behind a large tree and waited, not knowing if he was hidden or not. He loosened a strap on that perfect knife in his chest belt and peeked around one side of the tree. He made eye contact with a man holding an axe only feet from where he was. There was no hiding now. The man swung the axe across the air too far for Cicero to even need to dodge. Cicero was starting to understand now. The man couldn't see very well. That explained the poor swing at his head. That was lucky. Cicero slid the knife out and lifted it over his head. The man tried to swipe again and missed. He croaked as Cicero's knife flew through the air and into his chest at the base of his neck. Best place to throw a knife. You could always tell if it was fatal when the victim made that wheeze. The man was heaving and clawing at his throat with one hand. His mouth made him look like he was screaming but a whisper was the only noise the man made.

Cicero backed away from the man, still coming on through the plight, wildly swinging his axe in one hand. He couldn't breathe yet seemed capable of a fight. There was no sense in killing a man twice. He didn't have time to wait for this man to die before he helped Swain. He would come back for the knife. So Cicero grabbed his bow and left back in the direction of Swain. The wind changed directions and rain increased. Cicero gripped his bow tight and kept searching. Now he had not heard anything for some time. He wondered if he should turn back. He was starting to feel desperate.

"Mag!" he called out, hearing a bark. He couldn't hear or see much beside the rain and darkness. He hoped Swain had gotten somewhere safe out there in the wet forest. Or that Doe had taken him back to camp where they started. He just stood there looking all around, not knowing if another killer was moments away from him, or if they were killing Swain, or if they were killing Mag. But worrying had only ever got him wounded and his friends killed, so he let himself calm down and tried to analyze the situation.

Doe was a good horse and she knew how to get Swain out of trouble. Those men were probably looking for someone on foot but would be trying to stay hidden from whoever it was that shot up half their crew without warning. That explained the half blind man staying back. He was just hiding from the chaos of the camp. So Cicero crouched and circled back around towards their camp.

He was limping badly. He couldn't tell how much blood he was losing with all the rain soaking in his clothes. The mud was starting to make everything hard to do. He had rain in his eyes, making him blink at the wet blur constantly. Any light that made it through the clouds was blotted out by the trees. His lungs were burning from running and falling. His head ached from the blow of the axe. He couldn't tell where the camp was anymore. He was just walking around in the dark. Was he lost?

He started to feel dizzy. He must have slipped on a tree root because he was starting to fall forward. The balance was drawing out of his legs and he couldn't find his footing. He was on his face in the mud, trying to push himself up again, but his body was made of wet blankets. He could only roll over to breathe slowly. His breath grew slower. Cicero just laid there listening. Hoping nobody found him.

❧

Cicero woke up on his back. Some orange sunlight was poking at his eyes. That brought the urgency back fast. He tried to sit up, but something was heavy on him. A large tree stump was laid over his body. He tried to push it off of his chest, but he was tethered to it somehow. A rope around his torso fastened him tight to the wood. Another one around his legs just below his knees.

"He's awake." Cicero heard someone say in a strange accent.

"Good. Let's ask him some questions." Cicero could tell they weren't from anywhere in Alssae by their accent, which was starting to sound more like Aravacan. Cicero could pick out bits and pieces of the conversation since he'd spent some time with Arava-can mercenaries in the wars against Galanoa and Kalesia.

A man came into view. He stood over Cicero and kicked the spot in his leg where the arrow caught him. This made it feel like the arrow was there again, and Cicero yelped from the pain of it. He could hear someone groaning somewhere nearby but he could only see the one man. Cicero recognized the man by the scarf he was wearing. He remembered seeing the man in the camp by the fire.

"You're alive and awake too, I see."

The voice that had been moaning came next with some effort: "He ain't gonna go to sleep again till he dies slow."

Cicero was trying to blink the mud out of his eyes when Blue Scarf kicked more right into his face, making it even worse. He felt the man roll him over with the log so the log's weight was on the ground. He could see the camp now. There were three men, counting Blue Scarf. The other two were sitting around the re-ignited fire. Each one wounded, one from Cicero's arrow to the thigh, the other with Swain's arrow to his shoulder. Another man called out from a ways off by the sound of it.

"Don't kill him till I get my share."

Blue Scarf yelled back, "Don't worry. He's got a while before then."

Cicero was trying to work out some way free of the situation, but he was held so tightly to the log that the rope dug into his back with every move. He was horrified that he saw no sign of Swain or his sister anywhere. Cicero's heart felt like it was in his stomach. Blue Scarf took an iron from the fire and brought it close to Cice-ro's face. It was so close he could feel the heat of it.

"In case you think lying might be a good idea, this is what you got coming." Blue Scarf turned to Shoulder Wound. "Alright, who's first?"

The two men looked at each other before Thigh Wound spoke, "I'll go . . ."

Cicero couldn't make out what else was said for the man's accent. So Blue Scarf handed the iron to Shoulder Wound and held Thigh Wound's arms so he couldn't move. After chanting together, the two men pulled out the arrow and seared the wound shut with the iron. Gray smoke spilt out from between the orange metal and the man's flesh, filling the morning air between the three men. Cicero heard the man's flesh sizzle before screaming from the pain so loud, it seemed out of place in the early morning. Cicero wanted to look for some means of escape from the log, from the camp, and from these men, but he was petrified by what he was watching which no doubt would happen to him shortly. They poured water on the red flesh and bandaged it. They all repositioned, this time to close the other man's shoulder. The same thing. They chanted, which Cicero figured was them counting down in some number in their Aravacan tongue. Then ripped out the arrow and *tssss*, the iron, and the pained shouting. Dark gray smoke billowed up into the air just before the man screamed like a bull being castrated.

This time, he saw someone sit up over by the bodies opposite the camp. At first it didn't make sense that a girl would be sitting hogtied with the bodies, but Cicero remembered it to be Swain's sister. She had something tied around her face so she couldn't speak. That made things even worse. All that risk taken, nothing gained, everything lost. The problem they set out to fix was probably made worse by their failed attempt.

As the men finished their crude medicinal practice, cursing at one another in Aravacan, Cicero flinched at the feeling of a blade cutting just above his elbow.

"I didn't have any more arrows." It was Swain cutting the rope that was holding Cicero to the log. A rush of emotions made the ache come back to Cicero's head.

"Good boy, Swain," Cicero said.

"What the . . ." Shoulder Wound was looking at Cicero and Swain.

"Hurry!" the words came from deep inside Cicero. "Swain, Hurry!"

He could see the men scrambling for weapons. The world shrunk down to a knife in a shaking hand and a rope. The rope severed and it went slack around him. Cicero ripped the knife from Swain's hand and flung it right through the blue scarf and into the man's throat, just a few strides away. The other two cripples were just finding their weapons.

"Swain, get her and run."

Blue Scarf was on one knee, holding his neck when he caught Swain's foot, sending him falling to the ground. He was close enough that Cicero reached for the knife and ripped it out, opening the man's neck wide. The blue scarf quickly turned red. Cicero brought the bloody knife down to cut the rope at his legs. Distracted by the men coming at Swain and himself, Cicero cut himself along with the rope, just by where the arrow caught him.

"I'll get the boy," Leg Wound said as Shoulder Wound lifted an axe over his head.

Cicero, still half covered by the log, pushed with his hurt leg against the dirt and rolled the piece of wood over him, half a breath before the axe blade chopped hard against the log with a hollow *clonk*. Cicero shoved out from under it and rolled over. He struggled to his feet. The man was struggling with only one good arm to free the axe. Cicero pounced, just missing the man's neck with the knife. The man shuffled back, leaving the axe, and

Cicero followed. He faked with his knife and brought his other fist hard across the man's face. Now, bringing the knife hard across his outstretched hand, Cicero side-stepped and kicked out one of his knees and held the knife tight to the man's throat.

"Stop!" Cicero called out loudly to the other man. Leg Wound had Swain on the ground in front of him with a sword in one hand. Noticing his companion with a knife to his throat seemed to make Leg Wound forget about the boy. As Leg Wound turned toward Cicero, he slit Shoulder Wound's throat and threw the knife at Leg Wound. The throw went high, clattering with the man's forehead. "Agh!" The man yelped as the knife's pommel connected with his head.

Cicero reckoned he understood Leg Wound's language now. He picked up the hot iron at the edge of the fire on his left and held it out in time to block a slash of the man's sword. Cicero dodged the neck slash. The man was clumsy. The wound in his thigh stole his balance. Cicero ducked below another swing, caught Leg Wound's hand, and gripped it long enough to press the hot iron to his neck. Leg Wound — or rather, Neck Wound — screamed and Cicero was able to pull the sword from his weakened grip.

Cicero brought the sword low and up into Neck Wound's groin. He squealed as Cicero pulled it out. There was an expectant pause, and an apologetic wince from Cicero as they looked at each other for a moment. Neck Wound stood there, his eyes wide open, looking back and forth between Cicero and his own bloody sword in Cicero's right hand. He held one hand on his bloody groin and the other in front of him as though he could catch a sword with it. No doubt wondering how everything had gotten so far away from him. Cicero clubbed Neck Wound's hand away with the hot iron in his left hand and drove the sword right through Neck Wound's torso. Cicero stepped back and let the man fall.

"Swain, are you okay?" Swain looked up at Cicero, watching him in silence. "Go find your sister, I'll take care of these guys."

With that, Cicero handed the knife to the boy and watched as he ran over to his sister. For the first time in two days, Cicero watched the boy let himself be a boy. Swain was batting tears out of his eyes and sniffing back a whimper as he freed his big sister. "Good boy, Swain." Cicero thought to himself as he stood there watching. He was covered in blood. He looked around the camp as ten men laid out dead on their faces in the mud. Red Scarf was still wiggling his feet, gasping for air. The bandit's horses were tied to a fallen tree at the edge of the camp. Ten riders and two pack horses. Out to his left, he saw a man riding hard away from the camp. Cicero looked back at Swain and his sister and watched them embracing each other while rocking to and fro, crying.

Cicero gathered the valuables while Swain went to go get Mag and Doe. He made sure Swain's sister ate and drank. When Swain got back, he gave the longbow back to Cicero. Cicero let Swain's sister ride Doe while he and Swain rode the bandits' horses. It was midmorning when they left the camp, and Cicero hoped it was the last time Swain would have to partake in this work. Cicero wondered if he could ever be free of it himself. He did not feel some heroic glow, only the gloom of leaving ten men unburied on the turf behind them.

CHAPTER SEVEN

ENDLESS CELEBRATION

PINELLA

In the following weeks, Lord Waymar gave both Reff and Pinella a place to stay in their opulent estate. Pinella spent her mornings on the western balcony, watching Reff and Lord Waymar sharpen their abilities over dozens of hours of duels and training. Her nights were spent at elegant galas where Waymar's little sister hosted the many allied and vassal family heads. It amazed her to think each house governed and administered justice to dozens of families under them. So much authority, all disTributed to these stewards by Lord Owen Waymar. Pinella's father was an extraordinarily famous Shrike in his time. But his land holdings were less than a tenth of that of the Waymar family and of far less value than some of the Waymar Lands. As one of Trofaims oldest and greatest houses, they were known for their wealth.

Lady Tavia Waymar was an astute hostess. She shined in her ability to entertain the many stewards and allied distinguished families night after night with excellence. Pinella enjoyed them at first but, after the first week, she found it strenuous to remember all the names and titles of Lady Waymar's guests. It all became so monotonous. It was a new dress every night with just as many tight straps and buttons. Pinella often envied the servants with their fake soldier costumes and unsocial tasks. Lord Owen had said Reff was the future of their family but Pinella was its legacy and both of them had their part to play in the Waymar's war effort.

While Reff prepared himself to fight and lead soldiers, Pinella learned names and stories of dozens of families so that she could gain enough favor to ask them to pledge some of their young men to join the Waymars. It was all more than enough without the pressure to drink at the same rate as the guests. Pinella had no preference for wine no matter how great the vintage. Lady Waymar's was famed for the spiced red wine and Brandywine. No two dinners were the same in their sequence or phases except for Octavia Waymar's ritualistic pouring of the spirits at the third and seventh phases of the party. Every night, she would announce the vintage and producer before uncorking a jar nearly thrice the size of her torso.

"Rumenedda produces the finest wine and Brandywine with its renowned vineyards! And Trofaim produces the only people fine enough to drink it!" she would say, just before toasting her older brother, Owen Waymar, and his efforts of war. At the sound of metallic cups colliding, a banner depicting the leafy branch of a thornapple tree was lifted. Lord Waymar's personal bottle standard. It was to her guests a constant reminder of the central focus of why they had been invited. To Pinella, it made her shudder at the notion of another morning spent hungover to come.

One night in particular Pinella had spent most the evening entertaining some member of a prestigious family. His name was Vestin Almott and he spoke to Pinella with far too much familiarity, so that his intentions with her were clear. She was happy to be distracted by the arrival of a new guest of wide prestige. Tribune Sullemn Fabrien made his entry into the party. Unlike the other families who demonstrated their strength and size by showing their many family members with half as many Chargers and vassal families among their entourage, the legendary politician arrived alone, save for his low-born bodyguard confidant named Rulver. Fabrien was the only guest to somehow draw more attention with less followers. The noble Almott family didn't even bother to excuse themselves when they realized Tribune Fabrien had arrived. Pinella was left to watch him make his entry.

Sullemn Fabrien had aged well, she noticed. His light brown hair was shocked with white but still as curly as ever. He seemed to be as prestigious as Lord Owen Waymar himself. Fabrien's renowned political aptitude and economic insight gave him popularity, whereas Owen Waymar's celebrity was mostly inherited. Pinella guessed that besides all of the Waymar family's wealth that wasn't compacted and passed through their generations, was because of Fabrien's stewardship. Families all over Trofaim sought out the man to invest, consult, and manage their estates. Just like his father, Sullemn Fabrien was among the greatest Tribunes in the republic. Unlike Pinella, he had kept his father's legacy.

As families rich enough to afford top academy graduates as proteges clamored to greet the Tribune, hoping for an audience with the man, he focused on the hostess of the party, Lady Waymar. Though she sat higher in the social order as a distinguished noblewoman and sister of a Captain of Shrikes, Tavia Waymar was passed in popularity by Sullemn Fabrien. He was the man responsible for so many families' rise in riches and political standing. Although the party guests flocked to him, he was not stopped by any of them until making his formal greetings to the Ladies of Waymar. Some of the single woman of higher standing didn't even hide their infatuation as they lavished him with adulation. A prominent woman could elevate her family to distinguishment by marrying him.

Fabrien made his way straight to Octavia Waymar so that he could pay his respects and compliments to her elegant hosting. The other guests become a peripheral of agreement and endorsement for every perfectly articulated sentence he made. Fabrien was a remarkable orator. Whether he argued the legitimacy of proposed laws in court or simply told a story of his life as a Tribune, Fabrien shined every time he spoke. Pinella took advantage of the moment by pouring her cup full of priceless Brandywine into a nearby houseplant while the guests were focused on Fabrien now extending his compliments to two of Owen's wives; lady Livra and lady Kessa Waymar.

While greeting Kessa, Fabrien asked, "Where is Lady Karianna? She has claim to my respects as well." It was gracious of him to pay respect to all the Waymars rather than just Octavia as most of the guests had done. Kessa spoke before Octavia and with half as much grace.

"She keeps with the children. We will relay your gratitude to her." Kessa spoke dismissively of her own sister wife. Pinella had to keep her face from sneering as she watched Kessa disregard Karianna. The two sister wives should have been the closest of the Waymar women, seeing as they were cousin from house Mance. But Pinella always observed a certain coldness between the two very different women. Ladies Livra and Octavia just listened to Kessa with noticeable embarrassment.

Pinella was thankful that Fabrien came to the party. She'd worried that he may eventually make an appearance at one of Octavia Waymar's parties. *Maybe he will confront me about my sin.* Funny enough, the Tribune was too preoccupied by his own fame to create an awkward moment of confrontation with her. Thankfully, between the celebrity of the Ladies Waymar and Sullemn Fabrien, Pinella spent the party mostly alone and almost sober. She only had to execute the toast to Lord Waymar and his Chargers at the uncorking of the second vintage after the poultry was served on burnished platters to a hundred inebriated party guests. She'd found it hard to mess up an announcement of more alcohol to a crowd of drunks.

Pinella was able to spend at least an hour and a half sitting near a window looking into the torchlit city of Trofaim. The Waymars had a spectacular view near the falls and from it the Great Orchard looked like a black abyss between the Waymar estate in the Upper City and the Lower City — beyond a half league of fruit trees.

From where she sat, Pinella could see so many torches and candles that lit the old city streets and rooftops. Some of them she knew were smaller parties hosted by some of the vassal families who championed the Waymar family war effort. Recruitment of men and support was a citywide endeavor. The thousands of little yellow firelights were beneath a clear, dark sky so filled with white stars, they all looked like sand on a beach.

She heard someone approach her from behind, reminding her where she was and that she was obliged to give a toast soon.

"Is it time for second toast already?" she asked before looking to see that it wasn't a servant come to fetch her, but Sullemn Fabrien with his hand on her shoulder.

"Do you think our fathers met at parties like this?" He asked the question as though some deep part of him had always wondered it.

"Mine never told me." The comment was the only thing she could think of in the moment. She faced him and leaned back to create more distance between them. Somehow she felt more comfortable with added distance. His eyes peered out the window in search of what she'd seen through it.

"I guess we will never know then. But I've wondered how it began. Nearly two decades after their deaths, their deeds together continue to ramify as though they are still doing them." Fabrien's searchful gaze settled on Pinella. His eyes seemed to find what they couldn't find outside the window. "I am still sought out as much as any high born noble of Trofaim's republic. I'm not sought out for who I am or my dreams of what their republic can become. I'm sought out by nobles who only want a bigger piece of it for themselves." Sullemn's eyes looked back out the window. "They want what their parents already gave them. They want distinguishment." Pinella tried not to let her own discomfort be known. She tried to break the tension under which she was struggling to breathe normally.

"I should thank you!" She forced a smile onto her face. "You helped Lord Waymar in his appeal for my pardon in court. Thanks to you, I'm loosed from a sentence that was merciful to begin with. On both accounts, you have so much of my gratitude." Hoping she had changed the subject to a less personal nature, she raised her glass in such a way as to drink in his honor, but her glass was empty. She'd poured it out.

The Tribune just nodded dismissively and sighed quietly. Subtle disappointment mixed with his expression before acquiescing to her distraction.

"Well," he started, suppressing whatever deep feelings and reflections he tried to engage her with, "you weren't the rebel who put his own countrymen to the sword's edge, were you?" Fabrien painfully referred to her husband.

"I . . ."

"No. A murderous traitor must himself be murdered. His wife, though, should be afforded a chance to make amends. Shouldn't she?" The Tribune awaited a response from her with cold expectancy. His change of tone shifted to an air of accusation. "Even if she did leave her city and obligations to be with him."

"Of course . . . my fair Tribune." It became harder than ever to meet his gaze.

"Pinella." The disruption cut through the tension. It was Octavia's handwoman Hess come at the height of Pinella's stress. She felt her shoulders loosen.

"Yes?"

"I'm sorry to interrupt the both of you, but it's time for second toast." The servant woman had no idea how she was rescuing Pinella. With equal parts grace and haste, she excused herself and followed the heavy woman toward the elevated platform in the center of the dining tables. Pinella set her mind to making her toast. "I need a fresh glass," confessed Pinella, holding up the empty wine cup. Hess looked at it with an eyebrow cocked up in judgment.

"I hope you're not too drunk to make the toast." Pinella realized how it must have looked to be at the end of her second helping of a particularly intoxicating wine. The servant woman enjoyed a tone above her station.

"I'm fine. I do this every night."

Hess studied Pinella's face probably still red with embarrassment from her conversation with Fabrien.

"I hope you're *fine* enough to make the grand toast," said the handwoman, gesturing for her servants to bring out the second jar of Brandywine spirit. Pinella wondered how this woman had become accustomed to speaking this way to elevated persons. She adjusted a few of Pinella's hairs and inspected her appearance. "You look beautiful, Pinella. It's time for you to introduce the heroes. Don't ruin this party."

Pinella nodded and went up onto the small platform from

which the monologues were made.

Pinella carried out a careful articulation of the grand speech while the Waymar family servants pried open the large wooden shipping box. Pinella did not look at him, but she could feel Fabrien's gaze on her. She spoke as some attendants pulled out the glossy black jar painted with ivory-colored depictions of the coastal city of vineyards from which this highly demanded wine had come. It always took two strong servants to tip and pour the expensive liquor from the huge pottery art piece into smaller vessels which the other servants used to disTribute the brandy to the esteemed guests of the Waymar family. The servants were all dressed in prop-armor and costumes that looked like the battle garments of a Waymar soldier. Pinella paced her speech so as to end it soon after every guest held a cup in their hand.

"With you, great matriarchs and patriarchs of families who, like me, matriarch of the Bennault family, pledge your allegiance to Lord and Lady Waymar, I now raise my cup of finest Brandywine along with my support to the Waymar family!" A cheer roared out from the body of the gathered guests. Pinella had to catch her breath after the long-winded conclusion of her toast. It was her first time saying it all in one breath. She tried not to shudder in disgust for the stinging bitter liquid. *Just don't puke!* she thought, trying not to cough or gag.

When the applause reached its apex, the procession of war captains began from behind Pinella. She endeavored to keep the substance in her stomach as dashing captains entered the host of clapping guests. After the captains came, Lord Waymar's dashing young officers were led by her son, Reff, and ended by Bermellin, Lord Waymar's most trusted and capable Charger.

Guests held ceramic prop swords over their heads as other guests had done each night before them. Pinella felt safe and unnoticed as the crowd clapped for and greeted the honored soldiers. Once she no longer felt a threat of nausea, she clinked her bronze cup against a pewter plate laden with fruit. Soon she again held the collective attention of the room. Her head was already swirling slightly from the strong alcohol of the second toast.

"I ask now that you award your highest applause to the high captain of six hundred Shrikes and head of the war effort against the rebel known as The Fowler: Lord Owen Waymar!" The room began to vibrate with a roar. Pinella tried to focus on standing straight.

Only three more parties . . .

❧

"We received one hundred and twelve more pledges last night. Couriers from the vassal houses will be arriving at noon." Lady Waymar's voice was painfully cheery against Pinella's routine morning headache. *How does she drink so much without a hangover?* "Thirteen of which are young noblemen!" Octavia Waymar spoke over the loud wooded clacking sounds of practice blades colliding in the courtyard below.

"How many does that give us?!" asked the oldest of Lord Waymar's wives, Livra Waymar. Lord Owen's sister, Octavia, took a moment to tally up totals, before smiling up at her sister-in-law suspensefully.

"One thousand one hundred and forty-four."

The balcony overlooking the practice yard below was occupied with the Waymar house women. There were some woman present who Pinella didn't know or take the time to meet on account of the cheap conversation sanctioned by Kessa Waymar. Octavia tolerated them from her place in the front row of seats with Pinella and her handmaid, the Kalesian woman in her sixties named Hess. The older woman lived more well off than the other servants. Hess was shrewd in her dealing with most of the workers. Pinella witnessed one woman who she treated with a particular sharpness. A young woman named Riva. Two of Lord Owen's wives were present along with some of the other Chargers' wives or betrothed, most of which spent their time discussing city gossip or anything aside from the war effort that was supposedly the central focus.

Pinella heard Octavia say her name and she gave her attention back to the discussion at hand.

"I'm sorry. Come again, My Lady?"

"I asked what your thoughts were on my brother with nearly ten maniples!"

"He will be a Company Commander, my husband!" The younger of Lord Waymar's wives answered as though her name was Pinella as well. Kessa Waymar had the least social grace of his wives. Pinella figured Lord Waymar must have married Kessa and Karianna for their youthful beauty with ignorance of their lack of likeability.

"A cohort is what you mean, dear sister. He will be a Cohort Captain." Lady Octavia Waymar waited for the epiphany to be visible on Kessa Waymar's face. The younger woman remained a picture of confusion now that she was expected to know anything besides the business of other affluent families.

"You mean he won't be a commander?" The rest of the women sat in the awkward moment. The woman had spent months lobbying and recruiting for her husband's war effort without understanding it's most basic workings. Her sister wife Livra shook her head in condescension. The other women had silenced from their otherwise endless gossiping. No doubt, taking careful note of the moment in order to gossip about Lady Kessa at the first opportunity.

"A commander leads a company of men composed of multiple cohorts . . ."

Kessa Waymar, clearly not understanding, began to laugh to herself as her face flushed with blood, trying to conceal her own ignorance. "Of course! What did I say?"

No one else laughed along with her. Pinella felt the rest of the women on the balcony judging Lord Waymar's second wife. Tavia just sighed, turning her attention back down to the yard below.

Dozens of men sharpened their technique for battle. Lord Waymar fought two of his Chargers at once with confident proficiency. Reff fought a man twice his age and thrice his skill. Pinella watched the next sire-to-be of the Golan Family. Pinella felt guilty; she'd been the one to convince Golan's reluctant old father to join the Waymars at the second War Gala a week before. Now his son was making hers look and feel inexperienced.

"This is good for him, Pinella!" Lady Octavia reassured with a pat on the hand. "My father says a little shame and exhaustion now may result in glory and prestige in the end. The result is worth the process." Pinella smiled and nodded in agreement.

"Of course, Lady Way—"

"Eh!" Octavia interrupted her abruptly with a fresh wash of annoyance. "You must begin calling me Octavia, or else I'd rather you didn't at all." Octavia had corrected Pinella a number of times but never so pointedly as this. It stunned her slightly, to hear Octavia speak to her in such a way. There was so much custom to this new way of life she was living. A month ago, she'd been prostituting herself to pay her own criminal debts. Now she was running into situations where she had little idea of how to act. She just agreed and returned to watching the men train quietly.

Reff was forced to train the most rigorously with the other Chargers. Lord Waymar and the other veteran Shrikes seemed to be at a social gathering. They often joked with one another and took breaks to eat or rest. Bermellin pushed the Chargers and the other recruits so that they were sluggish and sweaty with exhaustion. This humiliating form of training was designed to strengthen the younger men's will for war. Her son was strong and a veteran, but he was the least trained of these men. The next week was all he had to prepare for war, so Bermellin pushed him hard.

Pinella watched as Lord Waymar repeatedly outdid the other Shrikes in single duels. They were more sport than the intense training her son endured. He would best his opponent, men would cheer, and he would look up at his wives in the balcony to see if any of them noticed his skill. Each of the sister wives preoccupied themselves though. Livra, his first love and wife of his youth, always busied herself with ordering the servants and attending to her stepchildren. His second wife Kessa laughed with her friends over drinks of tea steeped in diluted wine. The servants made it so that the women would not get completely drunk before the parties. She drank a lot though. The thirty-five-year-old constantly neglected her husband and her children to the care of her sister wives. The third wife of Lord Owen, Karianna, could rarely be seen engaging in any other pursuit except caring for her two young children and Kessa's three adolescents. Of all Lord Waymar's children, Pinella could only remember the name of Kessa's oldest son, Otrin. Otrin was polite and spoke like his father, but his blue eyes reminded Pinella of Kessa's grandfather Lord Tribune Kellin Mance.

After four hours of watching the men train with one another over two meals on the balcony, the women finally went inside to prepare for another banquet. Lord Waymar's wives had been the last to join and the first to leave. They had that attitude that nobles get after achieving what they wanted: forget their social obligations and the people who cared about them. When the servants and lower family women left with their children, Pinella took the moment to speak to Lady Waymar.

"Why only me?"

Octavia looked at Pinella inquisitively, waiting for her to continue.

"Why do you insist on me using your first name? I'm in your debt to even be here."

The younger woman looked back out at the training ground as she formed her response.

"I am not to you what I am the rest of these women." Pinella took her own turn to understand. "They are women beneath my station. To them, I am their matriarch. My brother's plan is that you would be my sister — not my servant — and that they see that." Pinella felt her eyebrows pinch together. "I know you have probably noticed all the men who find you suited to them as a wife or their son's wives. If . . . If you ever choose to remarry, it's not in your best interest to be steward woman to one of our vassal families. Now that you're pardoned and your son and father are successful soldiers, you'll be sought out by many noblemen."

As Pinella considered that, Octavia stood to her feet. "You're a valuable ally because of so many things. Your father and son. You are single and beautiful." Lady Waymar's eyes narrowed. "You've brokered more unaffiliated families into agreement with us than Kessa or Livra." She laughed to herself, "Karianna, too, but that goes without saying." They shared a laugh.

"Pinella, you're my friend. I feel like I can trust you, and I do. So distinguish yourself from the other women. They respect you." With that, Octavia left Pinella alone on the balcony.

Chapter Eight

The Road

Cicero

They had been riding continuously for three days. They were able to move quickly because there was always a fresh horse when one got tired. Cicero had always been impressed with Swain's courage, but now he got to watch Swain's big sister, Noon. Swain kept reminding him of her name even though Cicero hadn't forgotten. Swain had become familiar quickly. Every time they made camp, Noon and Swain cooked good meals. Better even than anything sold in Begatto. Cicero supposed that to be a weak standard of good food, but it was a stride better than what he was used to having. And this, more than a stride better than that even. It made Cicero keep having to remind himself that they were children.

"Cicero?" Noon asked. His eyes met hers. "Where is your family?"

He actually had to think for a second before he remembered, "They're right here." Cicero pointed at Mag and then up at Doe. Thinking about the two gave him a smooth feeling. "If I asked for more family besides them, folk would reckon me greedy." He smiled and gave Mag a pat on the rump. That seemed to be enough for the children judging by how they smiled up at Doe and asked Mag to speak just to hear her bark. It's a rare thing to find a dog and horse as well trained as Mag and Doe.

"Where did you get 'em?" Swain asked.

Cicero said while smiling at each one, "I found Mag's mother in the old borderlands between Hocklee and Kalesia, where I fought against—"

"Hocklee City?" Swain interrupted. Noon bumped her brother. "Don't interrupt, Swain."

Cicero just smiled and continued, "Yes, near the big city. She came up to me, looking to share some of my food. I kept with a Galanoan Army back then. I saw her for the first time while she was looking for food. She would sit near some of the men's cook-circles and beg for food. Trouble was, she had been burned in the fires and she was scarred up real good and missing most of her fur. She looked bad and the soldiers treated her worse. She looked pitiful, so by the time she got to my lonely little fire, I gave her something to eat. After that she just stayed with me.

"Then one night, about four years ago, she ran off to Begatto. I got pretty worried she'd run off chasin' wolves and got hurt. But she came back two months later, and she had a litter. I didn't even know she had been pregnant till I heard Mag whimpering under the shed on my plot. She had a small litter. Only four. Mag lived and the others were stillborn. It was wintertime and she got lean from feeding Mag. She got sick and wouldn't let me feed her, so I had to choose between Mag and her because I knew she couldn't make it through the winter in her condition. Especially with Mag pulling any energy she had left every time she nursed.

"I was almost sure I would choose her mother, but remembered feeding her the last of what I had from the cookpot. I remembered thinking, if it's not me, then nobody would feed her. Me and Mag's mom were both alone, so I thought it would be better to raise Mag and she wouldn't have to learn what it was like to be alone."

Mag was asleep now, curled up warm next to Cicero. He looked back at the two kids and smiled. They were leaning back against Doe with the fire at their feet. "That same winter," Cicero continued, realizing how much more he had said in the last five minutes than the last five days, "Mag's mom died and somebody stole the pack mule I had just bought with most of my meager harvest money. I remember telling everyone how out of luck I was, but in honesty, I couldn't help but laugh. The man who sold the mule to me lied. That animal had never worked a day in its life, and back then I couldn't tell the difference between mules and squirrels!" That made Cicero laugh again. "So I went to the horse ranch, and the owner must have felt bad for me after hearing my story and seeing Mag as a little puppy. So the rancher sold Doe to me for everything I had left if I agreed to feed her mother while she nursed. So I used her mother to plow my plot early before sowing season. While I plowed the field, Mag and Doe would play and sleep together, and I was able to give Mag some of the milk that Doe drank."

Both the children looked like they tasted something sour. "You milked a horse?!" Noon asked as Swain laughed.

"Yeah!" Cicero said with a bright smile on his face. "I sure did, and Mag loved it! So I was the only one going hungry that year. I reckoned that was a bargain. Mag and Doe grew up thinking they were sisters, and we've been living like a little family ever since." The kids both smiled and laughed. Apparently the story worked on them because they didn't look sorry for him at all. He supposed that it worked for him too. Swain was starting to struggle to keep his eyes open and eventually gave in and started to snore a little bit.

"You should sleep too, Noon. Me and Mag will keep watch."

Noon sat there watching the fire flicker. "It's hard to forget about those men that took me. I keep thinking about what they were saying they would do to me. I keep remembering how happy I was when you and Swain killed them." A tear was glowing in the firelight and it ran down her cheek. Her lip started to quiver as she spoke, "I wish they didn't have to die because of me. And I don't want to be happy that they died."

Cicero sat there at a loss for words. He knew all too well how words were a pointless gesture at times. Cicero whispered to Mag and she stood up, stretched, and slowly rounded the fire to Noon. The girl had begun to cry with her face in her palms. Cicero couldn't help smiling watching Mag work her magic on someone other than himself for once. Mag pushed her nose up under Noon's arm until the girl unintentionally had one arm around Mag. She stopped crying just long enough to see that it was Mag. About that time, she whimpered and licked at the tears on Noon's face. Noon began to laugh a little as her face was being assaulted by Mag's tongue.

"Mag never lets me cry alone." Cicero laughed with the girl as she calmed down. He was starting to notice how much he made himself laugh.

Chapter Nine

Flight of Shrikes

Pinella

Pinella and the other women of the Waymar family left the Waymar estate two hours after sunrise to the Lower City. Descending on the lift powered by the falls, they went through the orchard on the wide road past the River District on to the Lower City. The traditional city of Trofaim was either called the Lower City by the nobles who considered themselves 'higher' than the people who lived there, or it was called Old Trofaim by just about everyone else. It was home to scores of thousands of people who seemed to always bustle with activity and goings on of every nature. Today though, the city was as vibrant as an ant colony after a rainstorm. The people of Trofaim gathered to see the army off to war against the rebels.

Pinella noticed people dining on the rooftops lining the crowded main street that the troops would march through. They arrived at the Great Arcade in the heart of the city just as the morning air began to heat up. The City Center had often seemed full but not enough to keep countless other people from cramming in to see off their army. Luckily, Octavia had arranged for one of the steward families in her service to host them on their balcony overlooking the square. When they got there, Pinella recognized a few of

Lady Waymar's servants. She must have been sent ahead of them to host them during their visit to the Lower City. Tavia was always making sure the rest of her household were well taken care of. Hess, Tavia's handwoman, was already there to greet them. Lady Tavia gave the women an hour to eat from the extravagant brunch spread with fruit and cheese.

Soon they were all on the balcony high above the street, vibrating with excitement from the people below excited people. Pinella could see a fight breaking out between several men at least four stories below where she sat. It was a hot, clear day today. A few servants had been posted along the edges of the balcony seating with fans to cool Lady Tavia and her companions. For once, all of Lord Waymar's wives were present in the same place. They were here, even if they were sitting as far from each other as they could.

"Do you think they'll be okay?" Pinella asked. Tavia's head turned to show a face full of concern to Pinella.

"Of course I think that, Pinella. Your son and my brother are going to be back in a couple months, and we'll shower them with paper flowers from this same balcony." Pinella said nothing but nodded her head and directed her gaze back out to the cluster of brawling citizens. Tavia again attempted to ease Pinella. "They're armed and prepared for the task at hand. Your son is a Shrike of Trofaim, Pinella. For your own sake, you must believe in him."

Pinella didn't feel better or pretend to. Reff was again putting himself in war for his mother. She was sick with guilt. *Come home, Reff. Until you do, farewell.*

CHAPTER TEN

RESPONSIBILITIES

PINELLA

Pinella's delegated responsibility was to meet with family stewards who each oversaw landholding owned by the Waymars. Two thousand apartment buildings, 122 storefronts, 7,000 hired employees, and four orphanages. Each of these were overseen by a collection of stewards who had proven themselves to the Waymars. The Waymar estate was so vast, the only thing they could count on was theft and corruption. Octavia had shown Pinella the current records of income and what they should have been, and Pinella realized why Reff had made such a powerful impression on Lord Waymar. The Patriarch had said the thing he needed most was trustworthy people around him. You would never tell just by talking to them, but many of the trusted stewards of the vassal families were masters at concealing their embezzlements and bribery.

It was roughly noontime when Pinella entered the old town center called the Great Arcade. Aside from the usual business and trade being conducted, the main display was an official reading the verdicts of several convicted rebels. It did not keep the venders from raising their voices for public attention. Pinella walked with a young woman named Riva, whom she had rewuested to accompany her. They said little of note to each other on their descent from the Upper City.

"Are you from the city?" Pinella began her erosion of the unfamiliarity between the women.

"Not this one, ma'am." That surprised Pinella.

"No?"

"No, ma'am. My parents were from Galanoa, but I wasn't born until her captors sold my mother in Brevalti." So much tragedy in such few words left Pinella without any of her own. Rather than some worthless words of sympathy, Pinella tried to listen.

"That's why my name is of Trofaim; I was named in Bravalti. How about you? Were you born here?" Pinella had to think of a response, bothered by Riva's personal history.

"I was born he—" Pinella had to raise her voice over an executioner shouting the crimes of a rebel supporter. "I was born here. My father was a Shrike." Riva nodded in mild interest before giving her attention to the executions.

The Waymar house in the Lower City was a stark contrast to its counterpart in the Upper City. Pinella was used to an opulent home made up of large open rooms each with high ceilings hung with candle chandeliers. The home here in the Lower City was utilitarian in nature. Money wasn't spent on decor here but on parchment and ink for so many records stored on shelves so high a ladder was necessary to reach the top. The furniture was desks and conference tables. Even the beds were half the size of her bed she'd slept in over the last month. A distant relative of Lord Waymar's second wife lived at the house and greeted Pinella and Riva upon their arrival.

"Welcome, Lady Bennault! My assistant will show you your rooms. We received the baggage you sent and unpacked your things."

Riva spoke out of her confusion. "I'm not a woman of station.

There's a mistake. I am a—"

"Handwoman."

Riva's confused face turned to Pinella.

"You are my hand. I sent my request with our bags that you're my consultant. A full guest room next to mine. Did you think you were going to clean up after me?"

By Riva's expression, she must have thought so..

"It's all been arranged. The servants will show you so that you can get settled in." Pinella nodded to the man and Riva followed the servant to their rooms on the second story. Before Pinella went into her room, she spoke to Riva, who looked into her own cluttered study room with an expression she might have used if seeing a sunset for the first time.

"The Waymar's have plenty of house servants that I could have brought. So don't worry about my comfort or anything else that the servants here can manage. I need someone to keep records and appointments for me. There are hundreds of individuals to interview and hundreds of numbers and details with each one. I'll need you to assist me in earnest. I don't expect you to do it on your own, either. You'll need to go to the Arcade and hire a notary and an accountant."

"The Waymar's have accountants though," Riva informed.

"I'm starting over. I have to trust every record keeper. I know you don't have much experience with numbers, but you'll warm to the task and I'll tire of it." Pinella gave her the most approving smile. "So use the room to get some rest until the first reports of stewards this evening. I'll need your help with each one."

"But Lady Bennault . . . You couldn't trust any of the bookkeepers, so why me?"

"You can read and write . . . and you looked like needed a break from Hess." Riva smiles with realization. "Consider it a vacation."

Pinella left the dark-haired woman in the hall for a nap in her own room.

Chapter Eleven

The Lone

Cicero

The wound in Cicero's leg was starting to send pain through his upper leg so bad it was all that he could do not to pass out from pain and exhaustion. They spent so much time on the road that he never had time to check on it. All he had time to do was make sure all the horses had food and keep watch every time they set up camp. Once he ate with the children, he had to walk around the camp to keep watch since Mag was starting to sleep with the kids at night. The only sleep he got was on the road while Doe pulled all the horses. Cicero strode off away from the camp for a minute and took stock of his new injuries while he finally had time, and he realized it was the first time his boot had been off since he found his plot burned out. That arrow had made the skin on most of his shin a puffy blue color. He had been foolish to neglect his injury. He wanted to cut the limb off now, but he had to wait. If they could just make it to Hocklee in time—

"Cicero!" It was Swain coming from their freshly made camp.

"What is it, Swain?" Cicero asked, trying to keep the intensity of the situation out of his voice.

"There were some men with weapons on the road," Swain said, out of breath. "Mag found 'em. They found the camp and asked if I knew murdering horse thieves with a bow. They didn't know I was keeping the horses. They were looking through the camp when I walked up on 'em."

"Are they still there? Where's your sister?"

"Dunno. Said she was gonna go down to the stream to wash up." Swain said. He held his hands behind his head with his fingers locked, taking a moment to catch his breath. Cicero shoved his burning leg back into his boot. It started to lance with pain just before going numb. He fought the urge to limp as he ran to Swain.

"Get your sister and meet me by the horses." At that, Swain gave Cicero a dutiful nod. It was the same kind of nod his father would have given to Cicero so many years ago. Then, without hesitation, Swain scampered off into the woods toward the stream nearby.

Cicero was in utter disbelief. They had tracked him from the borderlands, nearly fifty miles now. The man that survived must have been among the trackers. The sky was almost dark and the horses were fussing to be on the move again already. It was no simple thing to get all the horses moving fast and in one direction. Soon enough, Swain returned with Noon in tow. Cicero assumed they must have been running since both were panting and took a moment to catch their breath before speaking.

"Mr. Cicero, who were they?" Noon asked, fully aware of the situation.

Cicero wasn't sure who they could be. Then Swain spoke out, "One of them said you broke the law, kidnapped a girl, and stole horses from an Aravacan envoy and his guards. I didn't tell him that I knew you. But they counted all the horses and studied their saddles."

Cicero looked back out at the road and tried to think of what that could mean. He was so tired from the hard ride. He was still sore from the fight. His wounded leg was spitting pain again. His fever was making him cold but sweaty at the same time. He was strung out and, for all he knew, eleven more men could be very close to killing him.

"Mr. Cicero, are you sick?" Noon was studying Cicero's face.

Swain's voice came before Cicero could respond, brimful with fear: "That's them." The boy was looking over his shoulder. Cicero looked behind and peered out into what little daylight was left. Four lit torches, all coming down the far slope after them. Cicero could just make out a horse under one of the torches.

"They must be coming from the camp." Cicero pulled on the reins. "We'll never outrun them. Swain, take your sister and the horses into the trees. I'll need Mag and Doe." He took all the baggage off Doe except for the holster for his long bow. It had three good arrows and a cracked one. Long odds that he was getting out of this one without a close fight, so he took the sheathed short sword too. "Just keep going, Swain. And don't stop."

"What about you? I can help again."

"No, help your sister. I'll handle this and when we're done, Mag will come and get you and bring you back." Swain looked out at those torches, then back at Cicero. He had that look on him. That kind of look that made Cicero want to reassure him that everything will be okay. A fight is never an easy thing to go back to. "Go on, Swain. And stop when you hear Mag." There was a slight pause as Swain looked at Cicero with fear smothering his face.

"Go!"

Noon gave her horse her heels and gave Swain's a slap on the rump. And with that, they galloped into the woods with eight horses behind them. It was just the three of them now. Mag was growling low while Doe nickered along with her. He led Doe off into the brush opposite the way that Swain had gone. He loosely tied Doe facing away from the road. "Stay with Doe, Mag." With that, he left the pair and stood in the middle of the road. Watching. Waiting. Trying to find the violence in him.

વ

"Four men, four horses, four torches." Cicero tried not to look at one thing for too long or he would feel dizzy. He was taking deep breaths like he had been running. It was the fever for sure. It was made worse by the lack of sleep. Now it was getting dark though. The four men couldn't see him. That was good. They wouldn't be able to see the longbow leaning against his back. That was good. They couldn't see Doe or Mag in the brush. All good. But no matter how you look at it, each of the four men looking for the man who killed ten had to be dangerous. Cicero couldn't comprehend another fight. He had to try talking. Talking was always the thing more dangerous than fighting. So Cicero bit the inside of his cheek and made himself violent — or, rather, he made himself into violence.

The four men rode up, not far from where he stood. They stayed spread out on their horses. The one on the far right spoke first. "Any particular reason you're standing in the middle of the road?"

Cicero couldn't think why he would be in the middle of the road. Well, since he could think of nothing good to say, he whipped the bow out with his left hand, nocking the arrow with his right, then, needing more time than usual, he shot the best arrow he had right at the man who had asked. The arrow whistled, thudding gently into the man's face. The torch dropped from the man's hand, scaring his horse.

"Three." He pulled the second arrow out of the ground behind him.

"Shields! He's the man we're looking for!"

Cicero leveled the arrow at the next man in line, but he couldn't get a shot for the man's circular shield and darkness. The other two spurred their horses and rode right at Cicero, shields raised, while the last man slid down from his horse. These three had a devil of a plan, and a hell of a knack for making his bow worthless. Cicero threw his bow to the right and dove to the left, feeling a spear shaft slide against his skull. He hit the ground and ran back the opposite direction towards Doe, but the one man was already down from his horse, lifting a hatchet for a swing. Cicero went low just as the man pulled the axe through space, only just missing his head. Cicero felt the blade hit his hair dragging behind his head. Cicero was slow.

The man flinched as Cicero knocked hard against the man's shield. Grabbing it with one hand, Cicero pulled his knife and stabbed it twice around the shield. The dagger stuck on the second drive, so he pulled it and ran. Giving the man a parting shove as he darted away. Cicero's back prickled with the anticipation of an axe blade burying itself in him, but it didn't come. The horsemen were circling around to finish him up. He scooped his bow up and ripped the arrow out of his jerkin and nocked it.

He was trying to make the blurring dark shapes into a target when he heard one say, "Let's get him by daylight. We've pushed it too far." The wounded man was groaning as he mounted his horse. They all three put their shields on their backs and rode away faster than they had come. That felt like the luckiest thing that had ever happened to Cicero.

❧

It was still dark when Cicero caught up with Swain and Noon. It didn't take long riding with Doe while Mag tracked their route. The kids were tired. Cicero judged them to have been riding as hard as they could since dusk. Even though there was a chance the riders would be following them, Cicero was confident they wouldn't fight until morning. Cicero had made a mess of his chance at peaceful resolve, but now they'd be careful in their approach. When they woke up, Cicero felt worse. The rest sharpened his mind but the fever was worsening, prodding at his focus. They started moving again, slowly veering back to the road.

They were riding hard but not fast due to their high number of horses in a heavily wooded terrain. As they crossed a clearing in a meadow, they picked up speed again.

"Cicero! Is that you?" Cicero's back went cold. He had been so relieved to pick up the pace, he hadn't looked to make sure the meadow was clear. The voice had come from a dismounted man standing in plain sight, just outside a treeline on the edge of the meadow.

"Swain, Noon, both of you get between the horses." He didn't wait for the children to dismount before he rode out between them and the man.

"Don't pull that bow," the man held up his hands as he walked closer. "I'm here alone." Cicero kept his arrow trained on him and drew the string back. "It's Tork! I came to talk. It's you, isn't it, Cicero?"

Cicero slowly eased on the string as he lowered the bow, keeping the arrow nocked. "How'd you find me?"

"I'm the peace authority out here now. When I saw which way you went off the road, it was a safe bet which way you would come." Cicero thought on that for a moment.

"I need your help, Tork." The two men had fought together

for Hocklee for three years. Before that, they had been enemies, fighting each other for four years. Tork for Kalesia and Cicero for Galanoa. It was after Cicero turned on his own people in Galanoa for Hocklee's independence, that Tork betrayed his own people in Kalesia to join the fight for independence.

The old warrior started again, "I know you do. That's why I've come!" Cicero knew he could trust Tork's word when he gave it. So he rode to speak to Tork.

"I'm being followed by bandits." He said, feeling the relief of a friend. "They've tracked me from my plot in the borderlands. Every Storinian settlement in Hocklee was attacked by bandits. It wasn't just Storinian people though. My land was burned completely. When I caught up with some of the raiders, about a dozen men who had burned and raided farmland, they made a captive out of my neighbors. It was Lain's daughter. They must have sent some of their own to catch me before I could notify other Hockleet for help. Last night four men attacked me on horseb—"

"Slow down, Cicero. It's not bandits who are hunting you," Tork sighed, shaking his head at the ground like he didn't know how to say something. Then he blurted it out: "It's a mix of Galanoan andH ockleet men. They've been following you throughout the region. They have an order to catch you for killing an Aravacan unit of men at arms. They came to speak to us about raids along their northern border. Those were my men on horseback who met you. I know it was you who attacked them unprovoked."

Cicero was filled with surprise. They had been Kalesian men . . . that explained their lack of skill on horseback. Tork had sent men against his own ally? "No—"

"Yes," Tork interrupted. "They have witnesses on you. They said it was an archer with long bow. They showed me the blue rings on the shaft of the arrow you used to shoot my man in the face with . . . But I already knew it was you, Cicero. No other man in Hocklee could sow ten bodies with a bow by himself."

"The Hockleets are looking for me?" Cicero began to feel fresh hope. All the information was confusing.

"Four hundred fighting men led by Gallo Bloodway. They're looking to turn you over to the Aravacans. They agree you led the raids."

Cicero was almost sick to think of his old enemy, Bloodway. No two men fought for the same cause as long as they did and still hated each other all the way through it. Gallo got his name for putting all the Kalesians in Hocklee to death after taking the city back for Galanoa. He filled the city's main street with corpses. When it rained, the people always called it the Mudway. It was raining when Gallo stacked the bodies of all the Kalesian immigrants, sparking his soldiers to call it the Bloodway as long as they held the city. When Tork took the city back, he referred to him as Gallo Bloodway, and the name stuck ever since.

"You're working with him? I thought you were the only one who hated him more than me!"

"Cicero, it's about avoiding a war with Aravaca. They've demanded the captive be returned along with you and whoever it was who helped you murder those men. Cicero, I think I can stage your death, and your companions to Aravaca, and save this place from another war. I'll tell them you fought hard and that I had to kill you."

"Tork, that captive was Lain's daughter! His son helped me save his own sister. What else should I have done? They were burning farms — my farm too.. Those men burned out three separate Storinian villages." Tork took a second to think on what Cicero was saying. "Tork, you've got to help me save those children."

Tork took in a deep breath and slowly exhaled. "This is war,

Cicero. The Storinians attacked first. The Aravacan envoy told
us that some of their own lands were raided months ago. They
responded by recovering their own losses and retaliating. They
could have just invaded the rest of Hocklee, but they chose to
peacefully send demand that we give you and their captive over
to them . . . I know it's not easy, but they might let the child live in
Aravaca. How many more children will die if they bring war back
to our land? You know good as anyone what war brings. You saved
a lot of lives in Hocklee. We both did . . . We have to make some
hard choices again to prevent war."

"It's been a while since the sieges, Tork. I think we remember
things differently. I don't remember our reasons, but I can't forget
our doings. We always had a new cause worthy of bringing hell
along with us everywhere we went."

"Cicero, you're bringing war back now! Everyone else is trying
to keep peace. It doesn't matter if you hate Bloodway, or Kalesia,
or me, or all of Aravaca! The Storinians provoked war. They retaliated and took prisoners of their own. We can negotiate with
them for her acquittal. But we have to return her first. This must
be done, and I've still got some loyalty to you because I have seen
you do the right thing. So do the right thing now!"

Cicero knew there would be no agreement between them. His
heart wanted to argue and persuade the man, but Tork wasn't one
to be persuaded. Cicero looked at the kids and back to Tork. "I
was glad the day I came to Hocklee. The day we agreed and traded knives was better than a hundred days as your enemy. I knew
making you my friend was worth all the enemies it brought me.
But I won't be an enemy to myself by betraying children to murderous slavers, Tork. Even if that makes you my enemy too."

Cicero pulled a sharp blackened steel blade from his chest belt
and came close to Tork. The old fighter didn't flinch, just pulled

out an old crude-looking dagger of his own. There was a pause. The two men close enough now, they could almost headbutt one another. Cicero pressed the dagger flat against Tork's chest, then snatched his own out of Tork's hand.

"This is a dagger I never wanted back in all my life. I knew a good man had it."

Cicero's response came harsh and low, "I wish I could say the same for the man that held mine."

CHAPTER TWELVE

Old City Stewards

Pinella

Three weeks after the departure of the army and nearly two months since she'd been pardoned from her criminal sentence, Pinella spent her third day interviewing stewards. She was almost finished. Riva sat next to her, scrawling furiously at a book of notes. She'd employed two other servants to aid her and Pinella couldn't have been more pleased with the woman. She'd turned days of steward's reports into miles of written notes before consolidating it into another report for Pinella. All Pinella was left to do was conduct interviews and implement solutions to any problems that the stewards couldn't solve. Even then, the woman was a shrewd consultant. Pinella couldn't have found a better fit for the role. The secretary entered the double doors of the house's primary study. Pinella had been using the room to conduct interviews.

"Lady Bennault, your last steward interview of the day."

Pinella rubbed her sore eyes. "Riva?"

"I'm almost finished. Just another moment." After exactly one moment, Riva was finished scrawling down her notes and Pinella motioned for the final stewards to enter the office.

Pinella repeated her greeting, "Welcome! I am Pinella Bennault, ally of the Waymar family. Lady Octavia Waymar has asked me to conduct her interviews and act as consultant while her brother is away with many of the couriers and consultants that are needed in the field." The steward was a woman younger than Lady Octavia. She had reddish-blonde hair with bright green eyes. She generously gave her bright white smile before addressing Pinella.

"Tro-Bennault." Her tone was corrective. Pinella didn't understand.

"Come again?"

"Pinella 'Tro-'Bennault. The Aspins, my family, are careful to properly address the members of our republic. Your father was awarded the Grass Crown after his heroics in Paveneli. My father was a common man in those days but still brags about being the one who wove your father's Grass Crown together. He says he used leopard lily stalks every time he tells the story, sometimes with tears in his eyes. Me and my brothers threw paper flowers from the roof after he returned from his second campaign." Pinella at a loss. "Few citizens are worthy of merging the name of the city with their own. And who more worthy than he of the Grass Crown?"

Pinella accepted the payment of respect for her father.

"What's your name?"

"Greyah Aspin."

"Greyah, you would have been a young child when my father turned back the Mottravan invasion."

"I was. I was six years old, and I can still remember how the bread tasted after your father's men passed out the grain. My father was a humble baker in those days. He became rich after that. Your father appointed mine as steward over famine relief."

Pinella shared an impressed look with Riva as she sat forward in her chair. She was not used to being recognized.

"I'm honored by your account of my father."

"It's the account of how my family changed forever." The young Aspin woman was a touch intense with her gratitude but none the worse for it. Pinella went on to conduct a very typical interview of the woman who stood as steward over several bakeries and food stands throughout the city. She and her family also managed several farms within the Fork Region. Every word was backed with specifics and citations of extensive records she had sent a day prior to Pinella's arrival in the Lower City. As representative of her family, Greyah Aspin dripped with professionalism.

When the young steward woman finished her report, she thanked Pinella, saying, "When I heard who it was that would hear our report of stewardship, I told my father, who told me to tell you that our family is your family." Pinella smiled thankfully.

"How is it that your family came to serve the Waymars?" asked Pinella.

"The Waymars have allied closely to Tribune Sullemn Fabrien. His father, Caulen Fabrien, was our overseer before Sullemn. After your father was . . . had died, Caulen Fabrien set us under the lordship of the Owen Waymar's father, Otrin Waymar, before he died in the Highwater Rebellion."

"I don't remember any Aspins among the pledges for Lord Waymar's army. Didn't you say you had brothers, Greyah?"

"Yes, my Lady, but it is the reaping season and Lord Waymar raised his army so quickly. We must be wheat farmers before we can be bread makers, and my brothers are still at work in harvest. That's also why I'm here alone." It was easy to like this woman and her stories of her father.

"Fair enough. When can we expect your harvest tax?"

"My brothers will bring five percent of their yield in wagons along with seven percent of what they sell at the markets in Elos."

Pinella wasn't used to stewards paying too much Tribute.

"Seven? The rate is only five percent." Pinella double checked with Riva to make sure she had it right.

"Two percent honorarium for you, Lady Tro-Bennault."

Pinella didn't understand and neither did Riva, by her expression.

"My father wants to keep his word of pledge to your father by extending his allegiance to you. Two percent is, to us, a small gratuity in expression of our loyalty." Pinella wondered what Octavia would have said. She wondered what Sullemn Fabrien might have thought.

"Both virtues will be remembered, Aspen. Tell your father that mine would be very grateful." Soon, Greyah finished her report and Pinella was almost as happy as Riva to be done hearing reports from the stewardship.

After bathing and taking a nap, Pinella and Riva sat together to look over the condensed report Riva had made. They compared the abridged document with hundreds of notes taken by Riva and her hired assistants. Pinella was impressed by how Riva had done it all. It had given Pinella confidence with the stewards and made her feel confident to give a report of her own to Octavia.

"Why did you bring me? You couldn't have known we would work this well together." Pinella was happy to see Riva speaking to her comfortably.

"Honestly, I hate how that woman treats you." Pinella closed the large binder full of all the records they'd made. She was satisfied knowing that her first task had been done well.

"What woman?" asked Riva.

"I forget her name. The Kalesian handwoman. What's her name?"

"Hess?"

"Yes! Hess! That's it! I got sick of watching her criticize you. She does often seem critical, but I couldn't help but notice that with you, it is cruel."

Riva considered that, looking at the floor with a thoughtful expression.

"I don't know if she's like that to the others, but I noticed with you. I thought you'd like a break and a chance to prove your hand at something besides serving food with a revealing dress for the enjoyment of Lady Waymar's guests."

Riva's thoughtful gaze was directed at Pinella now, still saying nothing.

"I can tell you've liked it, which makes me happy. But . . . It's late. I want to say again, thank you for all your help." Pinella set a hand on Riva's forearm. "I wouldn't be halfway done interviewing stewards if I hadn't brought you." Pinella patted Riva's arm and stood. "Now, enjoy your last night in your own bedroom." With that, Pinella left Riva in the office, went to her dark bedroom upstairs, laid in bed, and closed her heavy eyes.

&.

Pinella stole another day to enjoy the Old City. She thought about leaving as soon as possible to get back to Lady Waymar, but they were a half week ahead of schedule and Riva seemed a different woman entirely. So she thought it'd be good to take a day to see the city, how it'd changed, and how it'd stayed the same. Pinella always loved to go with her father to the seller's Great Arcade to hear the heralds and their news of the Alssaen heartlands. Since Pinella hadn't been since leaving the city with Reff's father, she decided to pay good money to listen up close.

For a distinguished family in Trofaim, all news was carried

quickly by couriers. For the undistinguished commoners though, heralds would shout out the current events from boxes or balconies at odd hours of the day. Some would climb atop the arches that encircled the Great Arcade. Only a few famous heralds were known to be accurate. Most heralds were more entertaining for the masses. They told summaries and abbreviated pieces of the stories they'd allegedly witnessed. They usually sold tickets to the rest of their news announcements in rented venues where the held performances like storytellings of Alssae.

Pinella and Riva went together to listen to a particularly celebrated herald named Gannon. Unlike many other heralds who shouted into oceans of mostly uninterested crowds, Gannon had at least a thousand people quietly gathered in the seller's corner of the Arcade before he'd even begun speaking. Most heralds dripped with celebrity and pomp so as to better appeal to their urban audiences. Gannon, though, wore a simple cloth shirt and trousers. It was obvious his hair had been dark before turning mostly white, hanging past his shoulders and tied behind his head.

He began his story by telling of all he'd seen in the state of Trofaim.

"The heartlands surrounding the Fork Region are sharply divided." Gannon let his pauses stretch until the silence was pregnant with suspense. "This rebel they call The Fowler has routed the third army to be fielded by the City and Republic of Trofaim."

Pinella looked around at the sober expressions of people around her.

"This third army was unlike the two before, though. The Fowler's first two victories were unthinkable in their own respect. The third is already coming to be known as the Battle of Shepherd's pass. Named after the mountain route between the mountain lakes of the North, this victory has given the army access uninhibited to the lands west of Kornata. In the low valleys of the territory, the rebels have had time to collect resources, indoctrinate, and recruit more followers, gaining strength to grow . . . Until now!" At that one statement of hope, the crowd immediately went into an uproar of applause so great, Pinella thought the ground might be shaking beneath her. Thousands of proud citizens cheered for their latest army sent out a month earlier.

Gannon's face remained unmoved, like he'd already lived this moment. After the audible part of the crowd died a slow death, the herald began his speech where he left off. "Lord Waymar marches at the head of nearly four cohorts of men. He is accompanied by one hundred Shrikes, Alssae's greatest soldiers. He is projected to gain at least a thousand more men-of-war between Kornata and the rebels. Lord Waymar is himself a Shrike and a renowned man of war in a long line of veteran soldiers. When he is victorious and the criminals are judged in the court of Tribunes, Trofaim's people will still be divided. They may be pacified in time, but their heart is against us who live here in the Orchard City. To them, you are the reason their taxes are so high. It is their opinion that your lives are easy at their expense." Gannon had to yield to the crowd's *boo*s of disapproval. It took a long moment of the herald's hands gesturing for silence before the crowd acquiesced.

Riva looked at Pinella to see if she could gain some insight as to what her political opinion might be. "Is that true? Is Trofaim divided?"

Pinella wasn't sure how to answer. This was her first trip to the Old City in over a decade of working in the orchard. She'd only been allowed to leave the River District for a few months.

"I'm not sure. Lady Waymar handles the greater politics. You know that. She's asked me to manage the stewards."

Soon, Gannon began again, "I don't share their sentiment. I share it yours, the free people of Trofaim. Soon we will again be free of The Fowler and the criminals who sow dissension among our brothers and sisters in the outer regions of the territory. And when we are, we must host all of our brothers who travel her from the far country for the Orphan Holiday." That brought the applause back. All the people of Trofaim loved the Orphan Holiday.

Pinella and Riva left before the legendary herald finished his news. Pinella could tell Riva wanted to stay longer, but it all just reminded Pinella of her husband and the pursuits that led him to his death. For the whole walk home, her heart was sick with questions. *Were the heralds this biased against you?* Maybe if Pinella hadn't once been married to such a rebel herself, she would've been caught up, intoxicated by the crowd's collective opinion. *But I was married to one. I did live as a rural citizen. Did he lie about her?*

CHAPTER THIRTEEN

THE WOUND

CICERO

"I'll be back soon. Stay in the cave and wait for me," Cicero told the two children. They were making their camps in pits and caves now to avoid attention. His leg was dead and dying, filling his body with fever and feverish heat. It had been three days since they had a fire and Cicero could tell that it was damaging morale.

Tonight Cicero hid the children before sundown and took nine of the horses to a small village nearby. It was named Gladney after a Brevaltine Tradesmen. He came south to Hocklee during its wars to bring supportive trade to the infant state, making a fortune. He passed three trading villages to his children who named each operation Gladney. The family made a fortune on importing weapons and armor. Cicero could remember buying Kalesian swords from the Gladney traders just before fighting with nine hundred Kalesians that wore Galanoan leather armor. After the battle was won, they were ready to buy all the extra supplies and other spoils from Cicero and the other Galanoans at a lower price. Soldiers remarked at how the Gladneys always made it so you were trading with your own enemies. When the Galanoans set siege to the city of Hocklee, Gladney supplied them. They sold supplies to the Kalesians when they returned a year later in their attempt to retake Hocklee from the Galanoans. They made even more money when Cicero united several groups of the local soldiers from each side, kicking out the Kalesians and starting a revolution against both nations. Gladney employed mercenaries from all over Alssae to fight in the revolution and against it. Now Gladney controlled most of the territory in Hocklee, making the family from Brevalti the richest in Hocklee, which was not necessarily hard to achieve, since Hocklee was not much more than a coalition of farmers, warmen, and farmers who were warmen in the winter.

Cicero rode a black stallion he used to pull the horses into the fenced village. He rode up to the first stable he saw.

"Those are some good horses, friend! Have you brought them to sell or store them?" The old man sitting at the front of the stable yard had asked Cicero without even looking at the horses. He only looked at Cicero. The man had sun-tanned leathery skin with wrinkles around his eyes so pronounced that Cicero debated whether or not the man could defend himself if he was robbed. Cicero was done fighting though and, with his leg in this condition, decided that it was best not to test it.

"I need to sell."

"Ten silver Brevalts for the lot," he said, smiling warmly up at Cicero. The man had to be joking with him. He hadn't even looked at the horses before making the low offer.

"Twenty each. And four for each of the saddles." Cicero remembered buying Doe for thirty before she was even weaned. The man studied the horses for the first time.

"The best I can do is forty for the horses and their leather. It'd be the most I've paid for horses." The man was lying and it was clear he didn't care if Cicero knew he was just from his expression.

"Do you cheat everyone who sells here?"

The man's smile widened. "No, but I am willing to buy stolen horses." Cicero's stomach tightened like a fist. This man knew more about Cicero than he thought. Cicero stayed silent.

The man spoke again, "The bounty is for a man with ten horses, and you only have seven, but, judging by those saddles and the shape you're in, you're no horse breeder." He looked at Cicero and shook his head "Forty-five silver Brevalts is the most I would pay for a stolen horse without telling the militia." The more Cicero thought on that, the more he considered how badly he needed the money and how much the horses slowed him. It seemed as though the man could read his thoughts.

"Fifty silvers and a bone saw."

The man's grin turned into a frown of confusion. Slowly his expression became a sympathetic appraisal of Cicero. "I'll make that deal." Cicero took the money as quickly as he could, anxious to leave town. "Here's your money. For what it's worth, there's a man who can replace body parts in Hocklee." Cicero just took the money and limped back to the black stallion he had chosen to be his new rider.

Cicero got out of Gladney as quick as he could. He rode out of the village through its weak fence, noticing a band of fighting men were entering the town. Cicero could tell they weren't hunters by how they were armed. They definitely weren't soldiers, but they were a notch up from the thugs who captured Noon. The detail that scared him most was that he didn't recognize any of them. He began to wonder if the horse breeder would tell the men as soon as they passed the stable.

Cicero kicked, bringing the horse to a faster trot away from town. He left Gladney and rode back to where he hid Swain and Noon. Cicero's fever was starting to really pull him down. He had been paring the numb, rotting flesh away for over a week now and he was only slowing the infection. He was sweating and freezing all at once. On the way, he could see the sun sinking into the trees on the horizon and was thankful for what might be his last sunset.

≈

"First, I have to off your leg. If I don't see blood, then I have to cut more off until I do. Then wash your wound and put a bandage over it. I'm supposed to put on a new bandage at night if you don't wake up, and I'm not supposed to take off your gag until you wake up." Swain repeated the steps as Cicero said.

"And if I don't wake up?"

Swain's lip quivered. "If you don't wake up . . . If you don't wake up, then I have to drag your body to the road and take my sister to Hocklee."

Cicero snapped a finger, making Swain flinch. "Take her to Storins. We're in Hocklee. Noon, you have to make sure that Swain does everything right. Remember, if I'm hard to pull, tie my legs to Doe and have her drag me." The kids were both silent at that. Cicero took a thin leather strap and made a tourniquet around the middle of his thigh. He sat against a tree and let the children tie him fast to its base. He drank three bottles of whiskey to numb the pain. Then they stuffed his mouth with a cloth and gagged him with a leather strap all the way around the tree. Now Cicero could only breathe through his nose. Noon held his hand and told Cicero he'd be okay. That came as little comfort to him as she had never done this before and had no idea if he would be okay or not. He just nodded along to make her feel better. With that, she strapped his leg tightly to a root coming from the bottom of the tree. The area still had feeling, but there was no better way to make sure to cut away all the rot. The boy began to cut. It was agonizing. Then it was dark.

&

Cicero woke up with his head spinning and sick from the alcohol. He was still tied to the tree but really had to relieve himself. Just as he began to struggle, Noon was standing over him, holding a finger over her lips, telling him to stay quiet. He realized her other hand was over his mouth. Cicero noticed his bloody stump where his left leg had been. Now that he was looking at it, it felt like his leg was still attached and dipped in a fire. Only his leg was gone, and they hadn't had a fire in days. He felt weak and drawn down like his fever mixed with lack of rest were finally coming to a violent point.

"Mag is with Swain," Noon said in a sharp whisper. "Some of the men are nearby. They're with that big man you talked to a couple days ago." Cicero wanted to worry and run and fight but there was nothing left in him. Not to mention the fact that he was extremely drunk and really had to puke. He could only sit still and hope they were not found. Tork was a good man, but when he said he would do something, he always saw it through. That's what made him such a powerful enemy years ago. Cicero remembered being tired of fighting Tork and the relief that came with making him an ally. Cicero again found himself fighting a man that always inspired the men around him. Even Cicero had followed him back in the days when they were both sided against Gallo.

Tork always led dangerous men. That's how he led the revolution with nothing but a few hundred tired men and some Brevaltine silver. Tork repelled the numerous Kalesians and their mercenaries in three pitched battles. He even won a battle against the Galanoans led by Gallo Bloodway. Now he was tired of war himself and compromised that dream to appease some foreign nation. The thought of Tork working with Gallo Bloodway to kill Cicero made him more worried than losing a leg or fighting ten men. Those two men cooperating meant something bad. Cicero didn't know any Aravacans, but they must have really threatened Hocklee. Cicero had never heard anything about any raids into the south. They must have thought Cicero was the raider. Now he was thought to be the cause of a new war where he had given everything to make peace.

Cicero sat there tied to that tree trunk. Hoping that, for all the war he would cause, these two children might go somewhere and make crops grow where war had burned them out. "Noon, help me up."

She looked at him for a moment. She looked as if she was trying desperately not to lose hope. "Yes, sir."

CHAPTER FOURTEEN

THE CITY ON STILTS

CICERO

"Cicero?" Noon was sitting over him when he opened his eyes. "We don't know where we are."

Cicero took a moment to look around. It was only three days since he had lost the leg, but it hurt like it hadn't even been an hour. The only thing that aided Cicero's rest the night of the amputation was the liquor and the fact that they had their first fire in a week.

He took a moment longer to judge their situation. They were surrounded by tall pine trees and the sunrise poked from between the branches. Cicero deduced that they were south of the city by about a few hours worth of riding. If they were quick enough, they could make it there before the sun set.

"Where's your brother?" Cicero cleared his throat and rubbed the sleep from his eyes.

"He's getting the horses ready. He's been keeping an eye out just like you did before you got sick." That reminded Cicero, his fever had broken. His leg still burned like crackling firewood but his thoughts were clear. "It should be fine from here. I changed your bandages while you slept. You didn't sleep long enough but at least I didn't wake you." Cicero remembered the agony of her clumsy hands touching his wounds. Anytime he fell asleep, it wasn't long before pain woke him up. He didn't dare mention that to her though.

"I . . . I'm sorry I caused all of this." Noon was looking Cicero in the eye. "It's my fault this happened. I know I didn't choose this, but I also know it's because of me." She started to cry. "I'm sorry you lost your leg and got sick because of me."

Cicero watched for a moment, Mag under Noon's arm. He knew he had to say something even though he hated this much talking. Cicero took his moment, trying to let the words come. He tossed another log on the flame, throwing sparks into the air like fearful fireflies. "Don't apologize or you'll just blame yourself. Better to be thankful for what I've done than sorry that I had to do it. Value this so that you can live up to it. I trust that you'll help someone when they need you. Don't be sorry for what's happened, Noon. Just be thankful." Cicero realized he hadn't smiled at that point since he had started talking. So Cicero wore his biggest grin he had. The smile made him a touch sad, seeing how rarely he smiled these days. "You won't leave the helpless people you meet to help themselves. You'll just help them. By helping you, I'm helping them as well."

Noon finally began to smile as she considered that. Her face was still full of tears but now mixed with hope.

Cicero smiled warmly at her. "Go get your brother."

She wiped her tears, collected herself, and slowly got up and told Mag to show the way to Swain. Mag always knew the way.

He started to notice how the kids were bonding with the animals. For so long he hadn't spent a long period of time with anyone besides Doe and Mag. Now that Mag and Doe trusted the children, Cicero noticed himself growing fonder of them as well. He knew that even if something were to happen to him, his dog and horse would be taken care of. However, he also knew that if anything were to happen to him now, the kids would still be hunted. Cicero could not die yet. He had to keep working to find some scenario that didn't end with Swain and Noon dying.

Cicero sat there, thinking of what his next move would be when the kids got back. He took a moment to admire the woods around him. Everything around him was peaceful. The pain in his leg was awful. It seemed like it wasn't getting any worse, but it certainly still had the potential to kill him.

Cicero thought about his situation. The best bet he had of surviving this was to go see this body trader in Hocklee, who the horse trader had spoken of. Gallo Bloodway had been accused of dealing with a body trader in his siege against Hocklee with the help of his monstrosities that were made from severed limbs of dead soldiers. Cicero reflected on what he had heard about the monsters made from the corpses of his fallen allies and was snapped back to reality when he heard Mag's quickened breathing coming up from behind.

"Cicero, are you feeling better?" Swain called out from the road. The boy was sitting tall on Doe's back with Mag and Noon walking at his side. It was then that Cicero saw Swain as more than just a boy. He was quickly becoming a man. Even while Cicero felt pride swell in his chest, he couldn't help a twinge of regret for teaching the boy the ways of killing. He knew all too well how difficult it is to leave that life behind.

"Yes! Much better," Cicero replied. He lied. His leg — or rather, stump — was a source of furious agony that made everything else hurt. "We're going to start moving again today. It's starting to get cold out."

A couple hours down the road, Cicero began to recognize the countryside near Hocklee. The old memories were coming back to him. He asked that old bittersweet question he could not help but ask himself every time he'd come back here, *Till I leave Hocklee alive?* This was Cicero's fourth time entering the city, his second time on the run, and his first time on one leg.

The old fort, now called the Hilltop, sat where it always did at the top of the Green Hill overlooking the River Darm. The rest of the city had grown from the west around to the southeastern base of the hill. The main thoroughfare was a canyon cut from the water that flowed from hilltop. The mud and water running down made it near impossible for invaders to climb during the rainy season. Which, in Hocklee, referred to most of the year. They named the street the Mudway because anyone who climbed it was muddy to the waist if he was lucky enough not to have slid back down to the base at least once.

The Green Hill would have been reckoned to be a mountain in some regions of Alssae due to how tall it was. The old town made it look even taller with its high walls that began at the summit. The unique city never built a gate because the Mudway was too wide to stretch a gate across. The Mudway connected the old fort on top of the hill to the village at the bottom which became more visible as they drew nearer to the city.

Cicero had always thought it an exaggeration calling the collection of lean-to shacks and hovels a city, but now it was fitting. Nearly the whole western base of the hill had become occupied with houses and storefronts built up off the muddy ground on stilts. Some of the buildings were as high as a tree. The whole place was fit with walls and defenses more than a sight better than what he had in the Upper City years before. Of all the things that surprised him about Hocklee, nothing shocked him as much as the amount of people that had come here. As they rode into the village, he stared at the busy, crowded walkways under the city that hovered on stilts. There must have been hundreds of people.

Cicero had once defended this place with less than a quarter of the people that congregated under the now floating city. It made Cicero happy that at least some of his efforts had made his hometown better.

Each tower had at least five floating bridges connecting to other buildings at different levels. Almost as many people passed across the bridges above as did beneath the wooden towers. Cicero noticed the muddy bottom of the city to be the poorest part of Hocklee. Travelers tied up canvas sheets between the stilts like tents. Many of the inhabitants also set up booths and tables as makeshift storefronts. Prostitutes could be seen around a huddle of small tents. Amateur musicians were playing loudly to mask the sound of the make-shift brothels conducting their business inside the tents. People called to him trying to sell him their meager effects for too much or to buy his for too little. You might have thought his clothes weren't blood-stained and dusty from travel with how they called out to him. But he was in fact covered in brown, blood-stained clothes with one leg.

"Eight Brevalts for the Black stallion." Cicero completely ignored the low offer.

"My friend, I'll pay a silver for him!" Now Cicero was curious at who would make such a stupid offer. He turned to see a man tied to a post the way you might tie up a slave or prisoner. Cicero recognized the man to be one of the men who'd fought with him years ago against Gallo Bloodway. His name was Vanno, but everyone started calling him Redeye after being stabbed in the eye while guarding a stretch of wall. He never patched it, so as to scare his enemies and some of his friends. He always had a tear of blood running from it, so the others knew him for it.

"Remember me?"

"Of course I remember you." He still hadn't patched it, *but he should,* Cicero thought as he looked at the dry wrinkly skin sunken deep into the man's eye socket.

"What brings the Hood back home, eh?" Cicero reminisced at the mention of the old name that Tork gave him at Brierly Hill.

"The same thing that's always brought me."

Redeye smiled like he knew exactly what Cicero meant, "War follows you like death follows the plague. Yellow-tooth used to say, 'Every time there is killin' being done in Hocklee, it's because Cicero brought it with him.' I wonder though, is it old man Tork or Bloodway coming after you?"

Cicero pulled his horse around so Redeye could see his missing leg, "Both I hear. Maybe some Aravacans." Redeye had to think on that a moment.

"What does Aravaca have have against you?"

Cicero ignored the question, pitching his own, "Why are you in Hocklee?"

Redeye looked at his chains as if remembering where he was. "I was with Yellowtooth. Not too long ago he went back to raiding."

Cicero couldn't believe the old raider had gone back to his old ways. "How does a man turn to back to violence after he's won a lifetime of battles?"

Redeye smiled, "It's peacetime that makes the warrior restless. Yellowtooth took over the whole outfit a year or two after you left. Though, we probably should've called him Blacktooth. Would fit better." Redeye kicked at a greedy blackbird trying to steal some of the food he'd been given. "We went southeast hitting the borderland south of Hocklee. We took anything good for the take and you wouldn't believe it, but Aravaca came looking for us with an army the size of one of those old stories Tork used to tell. It was too big an army to just be looking for us though. We thought they must be doing something big . . . Big enough for us to flee back up North."

Cicero began to understand. His old companions had been the ones to spark war between Hocklee and Aravaca. Cicero wanted with everything he had for that to be false, but he knew it was true. The problem was that too many men like Gallo Bloodway wanted to believe it was Cicero. It gave them a reason to get even on several old accounts.

"I hear there's a man in town who can replace a limb. If I pay your guild, will you take me to him?" Cicero asked, causing Redeye to smile again, knowing full well that he was back in trouble.

The body trader's face was pale and hairless. The man of middle age had a deceptively boyish face with an oblivious smile. "You're the body trader?" Cicero ventured.

The man nodded with a smile like he was about to laugh at some joke. Cicero just nodded.

"My leg, can you do anything for me?"

CHAPTER FIFTEEN

GOOD NEWS

PINELLA

Pinella was reading bi-weekly reports sent from the stewards in the Lower City. She had practically split the paperwork with Riva. It would be impossible to proofread all of her servants' work, but every formal request needed a proper response and each failure of payment demanded a formal notice. So she trusted the young woman. She had become invaluable to Pinella over the past weeks.

Riva's discernment and likeability had made her a reliable companion. Because of Lady Octavia's head house servant, Pinella employed her as an assistant and a courier to the Lower City in order to avoid the servant woman's cruel and spiteful treatment. It made Pinella smile to think of the woman raised a slave, with little autonomy, now a scribe. Pinella owed much of her own productivity to Riva's shrewd advice and ability with records and numbers. No wonder she frustrated Hess as a housemaid. Riva was above the repetitive monotony of housework. Anyone with a mild education would feel stifled by it. The memory of brothel work came to mind. Pinella was also better suited to the work than her previous alternative.

Pinella was still smiling down at a report from Greyah Aspen when Lady Octavia walked into the quiet study. Though they lived together, they had not seen one another in days. Octavia spent time in politics among the nobles and Tribunes in the Upper City while Pinella spent her days in Old Trofaim managing stewards and vassal families of the so-called lower nobility. Pinella had not realized how she'd missed her friend until seeing her now. A smile was spread wide across her face because of a note she held out in one hand.

"You're not going to believe it!"

Pinella shot up to her feet to respectfully greet the woman. Pinella hadn't spoken to Lady Waymar in three days. "Octavia! Welcome home. How long have you been back from the Tribunal?"

"Less than an hour." Lady Waymar held that single piece of parchment next to her face, smiling at Pinella. "This is a message. I'll give you one guess who it's from." Pinella felt her eyes widen as excitement filled her chest.

"The men?"

Octavia Waymar's grin spread all the way into a laughing smile. "They've won a battle! My brother says it was decisive! The rebels are in retreat!" Octavia's voice gained excitement with each announcement. "They're heroes, Pinella! Our houses and every vassal house beneath us will grow because of this. We can expect more families to send support, as this will greater establish our purpose!" Lady Waymar laughed as Pinella stared out the window, considering the celebration of the of the moment. The nagging sense of worry melted off of her.

"Were they injured? Did your brother say how many of the rebels were left?" Octavia closed smiling eyes and breathed.

"They're fine. We are finished with these worry-filled nights. We're okay. We can be okay now. They are safe." She began to tremble as here face twisted and began to cry. "I'm so relieved Pinella." Lady Waymar wrapped her arms around Pinella. "My brother is the only family I've left. I'm so glad he was victorious." Tavia let go of Pinella and wiped her tearing eyes, regaining her composure.

The good washed over Pinella's worried heart like a warm sunrise. She breathed air deep in her chest and hoped along with the relieving news.

"Did they say how much longer it would take?"

Octavia gestured back at the letter. "My brother estimates a few months before they're caught, a few weeks to reestablish stable rule before, then they can come home."

A few more months, Reff.

"That's not all though," said Octavia with a sniffle and smile. "Owen writes of your son's heroics. He has given the rank of Shrike when he returns. He's already become a senior among my brother's leading men."

"Shrike?" At first she felt disbelief. Then remembered his words in the orchard.

"I'm good at this," he'd said of war.

"The army has made him a suit of armor from the weapons of defeated foes. They even put the honor symbol on his breastplate." Pinella remembered a picture of a skewered rat on a thorn branch next to the bird who'd skewered it there, a Shrike. Pinella let it all sink in. Everything had already changed so much since her son returned from battle a hero. Now he was twice a hero and everything was soon to change even more, all for the better. Octavia continued to speak and dream, but Pinella only pretended to listen. All she could think about was how her only son had followed his grandfather's legacy and redeemed himself of his father's shame. Like his grandfather, he had attained the standing of Shrike. She had dreamt and hoped for so long that he would just be able to outlive the shame. Now here he was, achieving glory for himself. So much pride filled her heart for her son.

You have done it, son.

At that moment, the door opened abruptly as Riva entered the study, interrupting Tavia's speech.

"I'm back my La—" Riva was caught off guard to see both Lady Waymar and Lady Bennault, crying together. Her eyes went back and forth in confusion.

"Riva!" said Pinella. "It's good news! You're not going to believe it."

CHAPTER SIXTEEN

THE MATH

FINNION

Finnion ducked under the low branches of many sweet-smelling cedar trees, stepping out into the clearing. A field yawned in front of him, revealing a wide landscape that was perfect for battle. The wet air was chilled for the first time that season. Smelling crisp, it subtly threatened of winter. His eyes scanned the details of the terrain. Finnion resisted the urge to envision it's potential as a farm with fruit trees strategically planted for beauty and good luck. Tragically, Finnion had to make it into a mass grave for the tyrannical Army of Trofaim. A gradual slope with tall grass that hid rocky treachery. The lowest point leveled off well where the loose soil washed down to the base of the hill. The night had brought rain with it and with the rain came the cold. The base of the slope would be filled deep with wet soil, creating a mire hidden in the tall grass.

The top of the slope was the smoothest part of the field with few trees or rocks. He was sure it would deceive the Army of Trofaim into attacking down the rocky slope as it seemed to afford them a perfect opportunity to annihilate the rebels. The uneven downward terrain would break up their lines enough for Finnion's troops to have an unexpected advantage. The bottom of the hill would be soaked from the heavy rain they had seen the night before. With a broken line of over-armored men stuck in the mire, Finnnion would pull his ranks back and target his arrows at the Shrikes. The rebels, still outnumbered, could then fight in the mud at the bottom of a hill. The field Finnion had chosen would be doing most the fighting. His rebels would be up against sixteen hundred of the finest warriors in all of Alssae. Everyone had always said that a Songbird Army couldn't be defeated. They had said the same thing about the other army he defeated three weeks ago. They were betrayed by one of their own Shrikes, Elmo Deep. Deep and his Shrikes now fought for the Fowler's rebellion, rejecting their old Title of Shrike and dubbing themselves Kites. Elmo Deep and the other renowned soldiers of Trofaim took the moniker, saying Kites are known to be fowling birds and that they're known to kill Shrikes. Finnion wasn't sure about any of that. To him it just seemed they were taking the whole bird analogy a bit too far. Finnion didn't care though. The man betrayed the Army of Trofaim after fighting and leading among the Shrikes for over two decades. He could call himself a turkey if he wanted. That made Finnion laugh before directing his mind back to business.

Today, Finnion and his 2,253 men would die as treacherous rebels or win as victorious revolutionaries and bring a new way of life to the city-state of Trofaim, perhaps even the rest of Alssae. As the old saying goes, "The one who rules Trofaim rules Alssae." Could be that the people would remember his name. Maybe even use it as a byword for freedom or justice. But then he thought he'd probably just die in some mansion in Trofaim, listening to bells a decade before some hypocrite would rise up and knock down all that he'd built.

That made Finnion laugh to himself again. Revolution and Alssae paired better together than singing and dancing. It wouldn't be long until someone else thought of a more just system to live by and rise to power long enough to see it go to someone else. The vicious cycle had been the theme of Alssae for over a hundred years. The city-states inherited hatred and warfare as the norm. All of them except Trofaim. The armies of Trofaim, that once held the monarchy in place for a century, tore it down taking power for themselves as an elite class of soldier citizen. The Shrikes now practiced their own form of tyranny from their perch in Trofaim while the rest of Alssae was left to swallow itself in rebellion. They needed a leader.

"Sir, the Songbird Army has been seen. The captains are ready for orders." Finnion remembered where he was, looking at a muddy field in the cold.

"Blakes?" Finnion asked.

"Yes, sir?" The young man sounded nervous. No doubt thinking of his first battle to come.

"Can there be any true lasting peace without it eventually leading to tyranny?" Young Blakes was silenced by the question. "Can tyranny last without giving way to rebellion? What if peace will always come at the cost of tyranny and justice can only come at the cost of rebellion?"

"Sir," Blakes said as if to dodge answering, "the captains have asked me to find you." Finnion turned to look at the twenty-five-year-old with a physique belonging to anyone but a soldier. How could this be his bodyguard?

"Tell them to gather at my tent. I will give them battle plans there."

"Yessir!" the unathletic boy said, hurrying back into the treeline.

Finnion took one last look at the battlefield to be. "Where was I? Oh, yes . . . fighting uphill, outnumbered, in the mud."

꙳

It wasn't long before Finnion had made his way back to the circle of tents where they had made camp. There's only so much planning that can happen before you start second guessing. He entered his tent where his closest allies stood in a circle. These were the nine men that led his rebellion and would lead Trofaim one day. It was Jonas Blakes, Timothy Blakes' older brother, that spoke first as he reached out to shake Finn's hand. Their hands gripped with that familiar firmness they had felt before a dozen battles. Jonas was stronger and more broad-shouldered than his little brother, but they still shared a powerful resemblance.

"You ready for the big fight?" Jonas' words came smooth and level on his smoking breath. Finn nodded and looked around the circle of men one set of eyes at a time. Gilmor wore a proud expression as well as Jonas. Dan Tro-Gabion, whose father added "Tro-" to their family name after repelling the Bletharine invasion from Trofaim, stood at attention with his eyes locked on Finnion. Jentree, Berricks, and Childress, Finnion's greatest scouts, all gave Finnion a dutiful nod and waited for Finnion's response. Felix, Elmo Tro-Deep, who got his name from the Highwater Rebellion after he had been labeled a traitor for chasing the rebels into the bogs and cutting every one of them down, and the Yilian all looked at each other and back to Finnion, expecting him to continue.

"We're ready for your orders, my king!" Gilmor said.

Finnion didn't understand why Gilmor had called him king, so he grunted at the sarcasm but as he peered around the ring, Greenan, Jentree, and Felix began to bow. They were all bowing now, even Jonas.

"What is this? I don't understand," Finnion said. Timothy was the only one standing now, looking just as confused as Finnion.

"Whether we win today or are vanquished, you are our king!" said Childress, the captain of the scouts. The man was older and no doubt the one who would've been hardest to convince out of the old traditions.

"My Lord," Berricks said, looking up from bowing his head, "Trofaim needs a king again."

Elmo spoke next, across the circle from Finn, "All of Alssae needs a king. Lord Finnion, you are our bid for the throne." Elmo Deep had been a Shrike once and put down two rebellions during his tenure. Finnion was in disbelief that these old conservatives of Trofaim were choosing a king from a rebellion they themselves headed. Men like Jentree, Gilmor, and Childress all made sense. They didn't have the understanding of history or government to oppose monarchy. They would follow Dan Gabion, and Felix was loyal to Elmo.

Three men would've been necessary to make a decision like this: Jonas Blakes, Dan Tro-Gabion, and Elmo Tro-Deep. Gabion was awarded the "Tro-" on his name for his participation in repelling the Motravan invasion at the city of Pavanelli. Finnion knew Elmo had gained an honor prefix to his own name for destroying the preceding rebellion to this one. *He broke the Highwater rebellion led by the mysterious Fowler, and now he follows me as I use the same handle . . . How ironic.*

"How did you all come to this decision?" Finnion has to give voice to his confusion. "You haven't even asked me."

Jonas stood and faced him. "We need an absolute power. We will restore the monarchy and set Alssae on a new path toward security. If the throne is re-established, peace can be restored." The rest of the men voiced their agreement. Finn could tell this was Jonas' idea. *The nobles of Trofaim will painfully regret having a hand*

*in the death of his two young brothers when Jonas Blakes marches at
the head of my army through the Kings Forum in Trofaim. Who will
be able to stand his fury then, I wonder?* Finnion had heard Jonas
tell him how a man named Kellen in particular had to face justice.

"Alright," Finnion was amazed at his friend. "For now." Jonas
smiled and nodded.

One man Finnion couldn't understand, though, was Berrick,
the one they called the Yilian. He just stood looking at Finn. He
knew Berrick to be the most dangerous man in the rebellion.
Most of the men had taken up calling him Champion on account
of his heroics. He didn't seem heroic now though. He just seemed
mournful or regretful even. "If I am to be king, it is only because
of my men, my captains who have raised me up on their own
shoulders, that this nation might once again know peace." Finnion felt silly talking like that. He waited for them all to bust out
laughing in ridicule. But they all agreed with grunts and nods. He
gave them the credit as he always had for his victories. Deep in his
heart, he knew he could have done it without them.

"Your orders, my King!" Gabion requested. The men all began
to stir.

"We've come to name our king here in the presence of a few,"
said Jentree. "Now we need orders for our men." Finn smiled. *Of
course they did*, he thought. It was his tactful planning that won
them three decisive victories against mercenary armies and one
against the Army of Trofaim led by a Shrike. Had it not been for
Finnion, this rebellion wouldn't be a threat to Trofaim and these
men would be forgotten by now. He cleared his throat and explained his battle strategy in detail.

No aspect of it was left out. Each one of the three captains would
hide their forces in the woods at the base of the hill surrounding
Elmo Deep and his Kites with the auxiliaries. His standards and

those stolen from Owen Waymar's cousins would be positioned at the center in plain view from the top of the hill. The Songbirds would see the auxiliary forces with their tents and cookfires from atop the hill. If their luck was good, the Shrikes underestimation would mix with their hunger for revenge against Elmo and come pouring down the slope in numbers, intent on ending the rebellion with one downhill charge. If they took the bait, they would be stuck in the bog and surrounded on three sides by the captains of the rebellion. So many birds in a fowler's trap. They would no doubt be heavily armored, which would make them even less mobile in the mud. Elmo and his men would be wearing the armor of typical regulars while the surrounding three units of regulars would be lightly dressed like unto auxiliary.

"They'll be light and fast enough to crush the enemy encumbered by their own armor. The charge will happen after Childress and Gilmor swing around their backside and give them arrows." Finnion let his eyes round to Elmo Deep. "Elmo, you get to prove your loyalty by baiting them in." Elmo Deep may have betrayed his own men among the Songbird Army a few weeks earlier, but something about him still seemed unreliable to Finnion. After all, the man was famed as a patriot for killing the notorious Fowler before putting down his rebellion. Trust for this turncoat would be slow in the coming. "Once we have the wing mired and pricked with arrows, we will surround and squeeze the life out of them. It will all end today."

"Hahaha!" Felix laughed in amazement. "You're always amazing me with your mastery of tactics!"

Gabion was smiling at Elmo, eyebrows raised. "Seems like it'll work to me," he said.

Jonas turned to address Timothy, "Get the men ready. The time is coming." But Timothy stood still. "Go, Timothy. The men need to be assembled!"

"They will be. Without you!" Childress sneered, bringing a knife up through Jonas' throat.

No sooner than the knife could go through his neck, Jonas ripped it from his own throat with his right hand, cupping Childress by the nape with his left, and put the same blade through the great scout's right eye.

Finnion almost screamed for the invaluable loss of the scout.

Childress dropped like a bag of rocks, leaving Jonas Blakes holding his bloody throat and gasping with the knife ready in hand. With a shiver, Finnion realized what was happening. He'd been a fool for ever letting a man of Trofaim into his circle. He and his closest friend were the only ones lost in that circle of traitors. Even as he died, Jonas Blakes beckoned the others on for a fight. Even with more than a pint of blood running down one arm and a dull cook's knife, he still intimidated all challengers.

Spinning madly, Jonas warded off the veteran soldiers as if they were nervous coyotes. Even now he would have killed any man who tried him. Maybe one of them should have tried their luck to find it lacking up against the feared Jonas Blakes. But it was Berrick who came to meet him. The two men were the tallest in the midst. They squared up to fight one another, never losing each other's gaze.

Finnion realized he was frozen watching. He gripped the hilt of his sword to help Jonas, but a hand held it still. Elmo was looking at him grimly just before headbutting Finnion so hard in the face he heard his own nose crunch against the man's forehead. He felt himself hit the ground. His head was thick and fuzzy. Dizzy, he looked back to his lifelong friend bleeding and struggling to balance. It didn't take Berrick long to move past Jonas' blade and put his own through Jonas' chest. That's what made Berrick, the

Yilian, the deadliest man of the rebellion. Finnion rolled over to one side, trying to stand. He could see Gabion and the rest conversing,

"You heard him. We'll follow his plan to the letter." The men started to walk back towards the camp. Elmo turned back to Berrick, who was cleaning the blood from his sword. "Kill the king and take his body somewhere it won't be found." Elmo looked back down at Finnion, clicking his tongue. "You might've done it," he said before walking away toward the camp.

Finn looked back to the Yilian. He tasted the blood running down his throat from his broken nose.

"You were the better man," Berrick said. "Elmo's just got more in his pocket." And with that, he lurched forward and kicked Finnion in the head, and all was dark.

Chapter Seventeen

The Body Trader

Cicero

It was a creaking mass of towers and stilts above the mud. Cicero had always thought no structure could last at the bottom of the Mudway after it rained. That's what made it so hard to put siege to by invaders. But there were people, all who had come to trade and settle who had done what an army could not. They funneled the spring water into channels that rolled down between the gatherings of tents and pop-up shops like a network of vines on a wall. Everything down here on the bottom was temporary. Even the bridges between them looked like they could be folded up and taken away. The homes were all tents and carts that could be taken up the towers when the rains flooded the Mudway.

Cicero purchased the rest of Redeye's bond who in turn brought him to an associate of man Cicero was looking for. Both he and Redeye followed the healer, if you could call him that, into a smokey tent filled with different kinds of people, most of whom weren't Alssaen. They looked like Aravacans. The foreigners were each distorted, their limbs disproportionate to their bodies and other limbs. One man looked like his arms may drag the ground if he let them. A woman with one leg had arms that should've belonged to a child. Cicero judged the body trader himself to be from Aravaca.

"You're from Aravaca then?" Cicero asked, stretching out the hand that wasn't keeping his balance to shake Karrick's. Cicero had only met a few people from the South and yet fewer who dared to bring the forbidden switch practice to Alssae.

"Born, raised, and orphaned all in the 'land of monsters,' as the people here call it. But I've come to the North to conduct my master's business. The same business you've come to partake of, I suspect." The man was very polite, using manners like a language so foreign to Cicero, he felt like an alien in his own land. He always found the people of Aravaca to be very odd when it came to social interaction.

"I need a new leg." Cicero said matter-of-factly.

"I see that," said Karrick, as lightly as he would if he were a shoemaker rather than a switch. "Your name, sir?" He had that wide smile that Cicero had seen on a wolf in a cage. He had seen body trading switches use the same smile on so many desperate men.

"Cicero . . . of Hocklee," he replied, half scared and a little anxious.

"And have you any idea of the quality of leg you'd like to purchase, my good Cicero of Hocklee?" He did not. Cicero sat in the chair across from Karrick and let his assistant tether his arms and good leg into the restraints. Seemed more like he was about to be tortured rather than healed. Was he? Cicero noticed Redeye bristling like a guard dog. The man was always anxious to fight. "The leg will not be exactly suited to you. Our inventory is scarce due to the recent . . ."

"Peace?" Cicero suggested. The switch let a yielding smile spread over his face and nodded respectfully. Cicero knew all too well how peace could afflict a switch's business.

"Peace isn't good for those necessary men who fight to bring it." Something in the way he said that made Cicero wonder if the man knew him. His tone felt like accusation.

⁊

Cicero watched as Karrick cleaned utensils that seemed more suited to a scribe or artist than a switch. Cicero had expected a torturer's box, filled with blades and needles. Instead it was all brushes, quills, and ink wells, each neatly in its own place. Karrick began to hum gently an eerie, foreign tune as he popped the cork from a bottle he'd been mixing chemicals in. As elegant as a tenured physician, he removed the bandages and emptied the small jar over the scabbed, bloody stump where Cicero's knee had been. Cicero's jaw clenched shut as a cold feeling washed over his leg.

"First, we let the primer set a moment." Karrick nodded to some silent man looming huge in the corner. The giant left the inner tent with less emotion than a corpse. Cicero hadn't noticed the motionless being until Karrick's silent command. The switch uncorked another smaller bottle on beat with the tune he was humming. He gently stirred its contents before mixing another mystery ingredient in. He dipped a feather quill into the mixture, without moving off tempo with his own humming. He began to write or draw symbols on the wound.

After being gone a moment, the big man returned with another box that Cicero found impossible to look away from. The big man stood there patiently and working his jaw muscles constantly. In accord with one of Karrick's music, he opened the box lid. The rusty hinge squealed and he pulled out what Cicero reckoned must be his new leg. The lump of flesh was wrapped tightly in dark linens before the switch undressed it and began drawing similar markings on it as he had put on Cicero. Karrick finished

134

the inkwork and his tune at the same time. He felt sick in anticipation.

"I'll meet you outside, Cicero." Redeye said with a look of disgust on his face before exiting the tent. Cicero couldn't blame him. He didn't really want to watch this happen either.

Karrick took the top half of Cicero's leg in his left hand and the bottom half of someone else's in his right. He cocked his neck to one side as a sort of warning and, at his nod, the man who worked for the trader of bodies pushed the two legs together so that the markings met like thread and needle stitching two cloths into one.

To Cicero, it was like fire, then like balm to a burn. He couldn't feel the pain of the wound that had plagued him constantly. His racing heart slowed as agony subsided. His eyes closed. Breath came smooth and fresh. The strange tune became like a breeze in the summer sun. Cicero's entire being became a sigh of relief.

Cicero was already wiggling the toes of the borrowed leg by the time Karrick was putting his instruments away.

"The limb may feel numb for a few hours, but soon it will be subject to you."

Cicero thought his choice of words were odd but he had no choice but to put it out of his mind. "Do I . . . Does it need anything?" Cicero felt the exchange was far more simple than it should have been.

"Do not immerse it in water," Karrick said simply, but Cicero didn't miss the warning tone in his voice.

"Is that all?" Cicero asked.

The switch snapped his box shut and said, "That is all," all while holding his hand toward the door, smiling as if to say, *Get on, I've work to do.* Cicero got on. The first steps were unbalanced, and the foot was very numb, but he could use it. That was good.

He would need it.

❧

"You're back and you have a new leg!" mused Redeye as he looked Cicero up and down. "So, have you some bloody business in mind? I'm sure you wouldn't have gone through all of that if you didn't need it."

Cicero ignored him, thinking of any way Swain and Noon might make it out of Hocklee alive.

Chapter Eighteen

Bloody Business

Cicero

The red morning sun broke across the pale sky the way blood stains a sheet. Cicero was first awake that morning. He hadn't really slept that night, but for the first time in weeks, his energy seemed to be heightened with the new leg. It had been three days since they'd left Hocklee. They'd made it as far as the North-western Region about ten miles from the border of Hocklee and Brevalti and things were seeming to calm down among their group. So much so that one couldn't tell that there wasn't an incredibly deadly group of men looking to kill them because their own lives depended on it.

"How's the watch?" Redeye's voice came breathy and relaxed. It took Cicero back to times passed when he and Redeye hid, waiting for the same man they waited for now. Perhaps some of the men who fought with them back then were now searching to fight against them both. That was a frightening thought, as all those men were so skilled at one thing above all others, and they may be coming after him. They were men who now followed the lead of Tork and Gallo, with orders to kill Cicero. Tork of Kalesia was one of those men that made his friends feel brave and his enemies fearful.

"Do you remember fighting alongside Tork?" Cicero asked

over one shoulder.

"I remember. I remember fighting against him too. Thinking I was unbeatable until we met him at River Beach." How many times had Cicero relived that nightmare? "Made me wonder why I ever took up a blade in the first place." Cicero remembered that same hopeless feeling after the battle. Tork and his men fought outnumbered against a Hockleet ambush with as much confidence as a man who'd picked the field to fight on.

After that battle, Cicero told himself he would never pick up a weapon again. "They were made of stone," Cicero said.

"And we had the ground." Redeye added, rendering both men quiet. There was no doubt that both of them wondered how they were once again on the opposite side of the worst enemies a man could have. Only this time without the allies that once stood with them.

"You know he's working with Bloodway?" Cicero asked rhetorically.

Redeye looked up in disbelief at that. "They're together?!" So now, not only were they on the opposite side of the worst enemy a man could have, they seemed to also be on the opposite side of history as well. Cicero noticed something in Redeye's expression. It looked to be childlike fear but quickly it changed to irrational confidence.

"I like our odds." He said, hacking out a cold laugh. Cicero could tell a decade of killing and banditry with Yellowtooth had taken its toll on the once softhearted orphan. He wished he had more time with Redeye back when Cicero led the Hockleet Army against Gallo. He should have spent more time with him when Redeye was young after losing his mother and his eye. Maybe if he did, he could undo some of the evil Yellowtooth had put in him. There was nothing he could do now. All he could do is make sure he didn't make the same mistakes with Swain and Noon.

Cicero walked back to the camp where the fire had conceded all but a few glowing embers. His back was starting to feel misaligned. The new leg must've been too long or too short. He reckoned it to be a good trade though, to have a misshapen leg rather than no leg at all.

"We've got to move," he said, waking the children. Noon woke slowly and peacefully. Swain woke with a troubling start, the way a warrior does when he's afraid that the fight's come to him in his sleep. The way Cicero had awoken from so many nightmares. He wanted to give the boy some soothing words, to give him peace, but he wondered if there were any words to help. Instead, Cicero just offered one hand to help the boy stand. Thankfully Swain was settled as fast as the fit had come. At first Noon tried to comfort him, but Swain didn't show a sign of softening.

Catching a sight of Doe, Swain made his way toward her. Cicero watched as Swain patted his mare the way you might calm a horse after bucking wild. Cicero felt a smile spread across his face. He found Noon was watching her brother with a look of relief as she ran her hands through Mag's shaggy coat. It seemed like the kids gained comfort from his horse and dog again the same way he had so many times. He couldn't count how many nights those two animals had been his only companions.

They rode out northwest from Hocklee, toward Galanoa, hoping Tork might head northeast, toward Kalesia, searching for them. Cicero told Redeye to scout ahead of the group so as to catch any enemies before they stumbled upon them. He guessed Bloodway would be in the borderlands near his home country in Galanoa. If he could get them as far as Brevalti, he could get lost in the land he knew to be foreign to both Tork and Bloodway. Once he got there, he could sell the horses, save for Doe, and take the children to the sea where he could go to Lithura in the east or west to Yilia — or anywhere they could live peacefully. Anywhere they could live at all.

Cicero gave his heels to the gray-spotted Gelding, and he heard the leg speak. His new leg seemed to whisper about memories he didn't have. He was reminded of spurring a horse he'd never ridden, reminded of some enemy at his back. But when he jerked his head to look behind him, the enemy was gone and he only saw Noon looking worriedly back at him. When he looked at the horse, the spotted Gelding was gone and he was on top of the stallion he picked from the lot. "Are they behind us?"

Noon looked back, trying to see what he had seen.

"No," she said. "We just have to keep riding."

As they rode, Cicero could barely see Redeye riding full gallop towards them. Redeye coming back like this meant he'd seen something — seen someone.

"Cicero!" he called, riding higher in the saddle as he came close. "It's Tork's men, Kalesians. I saw four, but there should be more." Cicero didn't want to believe there could be more, but Redeye had fought against Kalesia as long as Cicero had in the wars; he knew his business as good as Cicero or any other Hockleet.

A plan came to Cicero as Redeye rode toward him. "Take the kids to the treeline." Cicero began to examine the ground. It was lightly wooded, rocky with tall grass. "Swain, remember how I showed you?" he asked as he tossed his long bow to the boy. Swain nodded and caught the bow. Cicero dismounted and tied the black stallion to a nearby tree. "Swain, you'll go on my mark. Redeye, go on Swain's mark."

Cicero laid in the tall grass watching three men come over the hill on horseback at a wary trot. The fourth was nowhere to be seen. They must have seen Redeye then. The other rider could be getting more help, setting a trap of his own, or flanking them. Cicero didn't have time to worry about him though. He could only set to work on the men he had.

He watched the riders come closer. He looked up at the position he'd told Swain to take. Cicero couldn't see Redeye. That was deadly company he was keeping. Redeye was a demon in the grass, waiting to kill an innocent man just obeying his chief. No doubt they only wanted to keep their own families safe. No doubt, though, he had to protect his as well.

Cicero threw the knife from the grass at a rider who'd come close. His old knife was heavy and his hand wasn't used to the old crude blade. He knew it wouldn't land the moment it left his hand. The poorly thrown dagger slapped against the horse's rump harmlessly, but Cicero was already on his feet. The new leg was strong and he was fast coming at the rider now trying to control his horse. Cicero was on him, ripping him from the horse to the ground. He wrestled against Cicero, trying to reach for something, but Cicero's second knife was buried in his neck. The man held the knife there with one hand trying to hold Cicero down, but Cicero bit the man's hand, left him with a knife in his neck, and stood to face the other two horsemen riding at him. Cicero yelled out to Swain but no arrow. Swain must have been in trouble. One bowman and one rider missing. The closer man dismounted far enough away to draw a sword. Cicero could hear the first man choking on his knife in the grass behind him. The killing in him was starting to rise. The second horseman rode around behind Cicero and dismounted.

One man behind him, one man in front. Each several strides from him. Cicero sprung forward at the man in front of him, letting a growl mount until it was a shout. The man was armed well. He pulled his shield up, looking over the rim and hiding his sword. Cicero pondered on the man behind him but he was already committed, charging, and shouting. He was only a moment away from contact when Redeye took the man's sword arm at the elbow and stabbed his own knife somewhere in the man's back. Cicero pulled the man's shield to one side and his short sword from the soldier. Cicero drew it and ran it through the man's chest at the same moment Redeye was pulling the knife and moving past them to the man behind. Cicero took the man's shield and joined Redeye.

The first man must have sliced Redeye's scalp, because he had blood all down his face. The two men were getting one another's measure, circling. Cicero charged at his enemy, throwing the shield to Redeye. The stolen short sword thumped against the wood of the man's shield, then clanged against his sword. Cicero backed off and drove his foot into the shield like he was trying to kick a door down. The man pushed against the kick, but Cicero was off running towards the trees, leaving the man behind to Redeye.

"Swain!" Cicero called out for the second time, not seeing either of the children, Mag, or Doe. The more he ran, the more thick the surroundings became. Batting shrubs and tree branches out of his war, he noticed rapid movement off to his left. There was Swain and the other rider sprawling on the ground. Cicero moved and he was on his back. Suddenly he was tied hand and foot looking at . . . a campfire? He tried to speak but he was gagged. He didn't know where he was or what had happened. He'd been dreaming? He heard some familiar tune somewhere in the darkness. He could see a large man carrying a box. He recognized them from somewhere, the box and the man. Had he been dreaming about them? No. He'd dreamt about a boy and a girl. That humming was still audible out there somewhere in the dark.

Where was he?

"Mr. Cicero!" Cicero saw Noon's face looking right at him worriedly. Mag leaning against him, front paws against his ribs. And just like that, he was back. He looked up and saw that Swain was struggling against the Kalesian by himself. At the same time, his heart was both relieved and worried.

Cicero mounted Doe. It was as familiar as sitting in an old chair. The horse he'd been riding was like a stranger to him, but Doe was like an extension of himself, reacting to all of his movements exactly the way he needed her to. His horse. He only had to lean forward and suggest his heels and they were moving fast. Swain dodged as the man swung a longsword at him. Cicero called out to the boy, "Swain!" and Swain rolled out of the way as Cicero dove off his horse, thrusting his dagger. It hit nothing as Cicero's body collided against the man, then against the ground, leaving both men rolling. The man's forearm must have snapped against Cicero's torso because his breath was driven out of him. When the rolling stopped, they were already struggling with one another.

Cicero was dizzy, gasping for air but not breathing in any. The other man's arm was definitely broken but his right arm was hitting Cicero again and again. He tried to block, tried to breathe, tried to find that dagger he'd brought with him. But he was stuck under the weight of the man. The Kalesian pulled his fist high to punch Cicero as hard as he could when an arrow lodged itself inside the man's head right behind his ear. The fist still came, but slowly and weakly as it hit Cicero's chest.

He looked over, and Swain was holding the bow out, one eye still closed.

"Good boy, Swain," he murmured as the man fell limp onto Cicero.

Chapter Nineteen

The Aftermath

Finnion

Finnion woke slowly. He had that tight comfortable feeling like waking up in a pile of pillows. He took in that big breath he always took with a stretch in the morning. That's when the smell hit him. His eyes came open as he remembered the battle.

His body flinched as he tried to get up, but he was hemmed in tight on every side. He squirmed for freedom but was held suffocatingly tight from all around. He was trapped in some sort of stinking heap of flesh. He pushed, pulled, and clawed at limbs and body parts. Corpses? Was he in a pile of corpses? Was he a corpse? If he was, how was he moving? But then he couldn't move, so was this death?

Finn started fighting, pushing against the crush. He gave out a breath and heaved in the stench. Everything was vile and dead. But he had to live. The people had to know the generals had turned on him. He used his legs, but his right knee felt tight for a second and then there was only white hot pain. The pain took his breath away. He gasped in the rotten air between the dead, and he could smell and taste that stuffy reek of rotten decay. He could barely move his right foot, so he pushed with his left as he climbed with his hands and fought his way between the bodies, pushing past each one. Pushing past the urge to puke. His progress seemed to take years.

The urge to vomit got the better of him. Bile burned at his throat and behind his nose. He kept pushing onward, gradually and painfully making it half way. He felt the wind on his shoulder and the left side of his face, but the stench on top was little better. Now that he could see what had happened, he was horrified. There were too many dead. Finnion wondered again if he was really alive, but the great pain in his knee would have to be none at all for that to be true. Regretfully, he was very much alive and alone by the look of it. He guessed he was thought to be dead and they had thrown him into a pit with the corpses.

He peered out into the dark, wondering if anyone was left from the battle. This was no time to find an enemy. He would have been little more than an inconvenience to kill, given his current state. His body was weak, full of pain, and half held by the grave. He may have been alive, but his chances at staying that way were less than slim. He took the moment to find himself. The field was covered up with death. There were other piles of corpses just like the one he was in, some about a dozen bodies while others consisted of hundreds of corpses. Though he saw dozens of piles, that wasn't the extent of the carnage. What had been a scenic green slope at the mouth of the valley was now barely green anywhere. Muddy and bloody, it showed no sign of life. How it must have manifested hell the day before.

The only sign of life, aside from the flies swarming around him, were the hosts of birds picking through the horror, scavenging for their meal. That reminded him of the smell, which in turn, reminded him of the inevitability of plague. Finn knew he probably would not last long with his wounded body, but he refused to die like this with plague. So, sticking his head out of the heap of death like a mushroom out of a turd, he pulled the vile air into his lungs, tightened his body, and tugged on his lower half. Slowly and painfully, he worked himself out of the tangle of limbs. Finnion tried to balance on his numb legs, but his right leg didn't want to move.

He fell into the mud, scattering a few greedy birds. The mess he had risen from was about three men tall and as wide as a house. Half of the great pile was charred black with ash. They had tried to burn the pile he was in, but it must have gone out. Tears and whimpering came out of a deep place within him as he lay there, soaked in blood and cooled by the night breeze. The relief to still be alive was too much to bear for a moment.

As he laid there crying, he became aware of himself. His relief to be alive turned into guilt for authoring the carnage around him. This had all come from him starting this war. Why should he get to live? Maybe he still had to suffer the way he had made so many others suffer. He had orchestrated so many massacres in the past and ordered the piling and burning of the bodies. He remembered telling a reluctant soldier to be thorough. One could never be sure an enemy was dead until he'd been burned or beheaded, and since the fires are less trouble, they became common after a battle. He'd always expected to die because of his orders not being followed. Now, here he was, clinging to life because some man had half-heartedly followed orders. He quietly thanked that man.

Sitting up, Finnion tried to get his leg to work but it had been constricted and without flow of blood for many hours. The limb felt lifeless. Now that he was looking at it, the skin of his leg was pale as a corpse. His head rolled back. He would take care of that later. For now, he had to get away from this graveyard. Gradually, he stood up on his left leg and limped away. He came to the scrap pile, a heap of shattered and broken armaments amounting to little more than firewood. He found a broken piece of a cartwheel he thought would serve as a crutch. He leaned on it and looked for something to use as a weapon. All of it was trash. Broken shields, fragments of broken wood and iron, and no weapons. Then he found a sword blade broken at its hilt. It probably wouldn't make a difference in a fight, but he had to make do somehow. He picked it up, the blade gouged and notched from use in the battle.

Finn dragged himself from the wreck, hobbling on one leg and a piece of a cartwheel. He found that he was smiling and talking to himself. He had been stacked with the dead and forgotten. He had been knocked out and his knee dislocated while he was out. He reckoned the trouble breathing was from being trampled in battle. That made him think on how hard his head must've been hit. And that made him wonder how long he'd been unconscious, which brought hunger into his guts. He'd been lucky to live, but now thinking about it, living hungry was a sorry way of living, and he hadn't eaten before the fight. He rarely ate before battles. Made him slow and heavy. Now he felt slower and heavier than ever, thinking it a stupid notion to skip a meal. Finnion was hurt, hungry, and exhausted. But for the first time in a long time, he was free.

"Free." His own voice was so cracked and raspy, he laughed. Laughing tickled his wounded lungs and made him cough, which only made him laugh and cough more. He was free! Free of marching, free of leading men, free of responsibility, free of fighting for other men's freedom. He wondered what he would do with his life and savored his ability to do anything he wanted. He might not live long but what little life he had left was free.

He hobbled through carnage unimaginable. The birds and bugs would have swarmed him had it not been for the bounty of dead flesh around him. Many of the mounds of bodies still burned brightly, blinding bright in the night. The fires blinded his eyes from seeing anything but the fires themselves. So many shadows shifted and flickered hiding from the light. Finnion heard noise that made his body still as ice and chilled him with fear. His eyes widened to find what his ears had heard. Voices. Low tones were distinct amongst the sound of roaring and crackling flames. Were they Shrikes? Men of Trofaim? Or were they rebels?

Who won the battle? he wondered. He tried to study the dead but even if he were able to recognize their faces in the firelight, they were all maimed and naked, stripped of their armor and markings. His heart was pounding and his breaths were coming faster, painfully. He decided against making himself known to the strangers. They may have been thieves or scavengers, violent men come to take anything of value. Finnion went as quietly as he could in the opposite direction. He didn't know where he was going, but he was heading away from all of this.

As he went, his good leg sank to the knee into thick mud. The wet ground sucked and held his foot like the earth was trying to swallow him. This is where the Army of Trofaim would have been surrounded. His leg was held tightly. He thought about the men picking through the remains and finding him stuck. An image of a songbird caught in a fowler's trap came to mind. With a great effort, he pulled against the mud. With a grunt from his chest and a sucking sound from the mud, he was loosed.

"Hello?"

Finnion's head shot up, his eyes wide. Someone had heard him. The realization washed over him in horror.

"Is someone there?" The voice was labored and rugged. Finnion didn't move. He peered all around, his eyes straining to see in the darkness. Seeing nothing, he proceeded to continue away from the field, this time more quietly than before.

"Please!"

Finnion nearly fell back with a startle at the voice near his legs. He gasped, holding one hand out between him and the voice. But nothing happened to him. Finnion took a moment to look and found a man in a pile of bodies a stride from where he stood.

"Can you please help me? Please . . ." The man was begging now. Finnion took a moment to kneel and squint against the darkness. It was a young man, staked to a small corpse stack with a standard pole. A humiliating mockery of the birds from which these men took their title. Just as a Shrike may impale a mouse on a thorn, here was a Shrike impaled by his own standard. But that's why Finnion was called the Fowler. This was his own creativity. This was the first survivor he'd seen in the darkness and the first to still be clothed with his armor. The armor of a Shrike. He seemed young. He was broken. Bloody and trembling, he begged Finnion for something to drink, but Finnion shook his head.

"I don't have any water . . . I'm sorry."

"Can you please help me? I can't get up." The kid Shrike said everything with snorts and sobs. His face contorted and twitched with suffering. This was too young.

"I'm sorry. They left you beyond my ability to help." The boy tried begging more, but Finnion just turned around. It hurt, but this was a Shrike. This was exactly the type of man he'd come to kill.

"If you can't help me, please, can you kill me?"

It wasn't what the soldier said but how he said it that made Finnion's heart ache with guilt.

CHAPTER TWENTY

REMAINS

FINNION

Finnion fought for every step. He was wounded and tired. He could barely breathe through his broken nose but for a little wind that tickled, with a whistling noise every time he breathed through it. He often forgot his nose was broken, rubbing at the itch it made. It made his eyes water from the pain. He had a deep splitting headache from the Yilian's boot kick to his head. His ribs were sore with every inhale, probably from being crushed by so many bodies. His leg at least had begun working again. When Finnion fell from the pile of bodies, he'd thought he must have survived in order to suffer for what he had caused. He wondered now if he had survived in order to pay some of his debt.

The young Shrike lay pale and crusted with dried blood and dirt as Finnion dragged him on a cot behind him. He made the cot from part of a hay wagon he'd found in the wreckage of the battle. All that was left was a two wheeled axle attached to a bed to make a type of trailer. The young man had said something about how it was lucky they found the scrap wagon. Finnion thought it would've been lucky if it still had all four wheels so he didn't have to lift the front end.

Finnion walked gingerly over the ground, his bare feet raw from miles of walking over pine needles and occasional stones so small and sharp they brought tears to his eyes. Thankfully he still had his pants on and he used the Shrike banner flag to cover his own bruised body. It took Finnion what felt like the whole night, looking for the right kind of forested area with a creek or small pond where they could hide and rest. Realistically, it couldn't have been more than a mile or two from where they'd left the field of battle, but it felt like Finnion had never walked so much in his life. His pain and exhaustion gave him excruciating attention to every detail.

Finnion finally found a good enough hiding place. He thought it must have been a black willow tree, but he hadn't been able to tell in the low light of early morning.

He was right. Willows are always near water. As he got closer, he could hear it flowing along with the cooing of a pair of mourning doves. That was good. Flowing water is the best kind. He thought the young Shrike in his care was unconscious, but as he approached the stream, the young man began to moan for a drink. Finnion took the scarf still wrapped around the boy's neck and rinsed out the blood and grime from it. Having cleaned it, he let the cloth saturate with the cold creek water and wrung it out into the thirsty kid's mouth.

Finnion thought he should've been sick of nurturing a pathetic nursling. He was not sick, though, and he did not feel enmity for the youth; Finnion only felt a primal sense of compassion.

When he had had his fill, Finnion drank in the same way, unsure if the dirty taste was from the creek or the rag. Regardless, he was thankful to have it. When he finished drinking, he used the same rag to clean his wounds and wash his body. Much of the dark colors did not wash off; he was stained all over with bluish brown bruising.

When Finnion was clean, he did the same for the young man.

His armor took an effort to strip off. It was bound to him with belts and straps of leather. You might have thought Finnion was torturing him with how he croaked and whined. His body was bad. Joints pulled out of sockets made his flesh look lumpy and unnatural. They'd done this to him so that he would be unable to move from the pile of bodies they staked him to. The wound the stake had left in his gut was the worst by far. It would have drained all his blood if not for the way they packed it so that it wouldn't kill him for days. This was the height of cruelty, cold and beyond ruthless.

Finnion sat against a fallen tree trunk across from the youth he'd saved. After a few moments of shut eye in what remained of the morning darkness, Finnion opened his eyes to the deep red beginnings of sunrise. He desperately wanted to sit by this quiet little stream for days. Maybe if he wasn't helping an enemy of the Rebellion, he would be taken for a harmless vagabond or rebel survivor. If they found him taking care of this young man, they'd kill him with all the righteous anger they had for Trofaim's Nobility. For a long moment, he watched the boy from Trofaim laying on the makeshift bodycart, breathing heavily with his eyes closed.

"Thank you for . . . ugh . . . nd for cleaning my wound." He sounded delirious from all his pain. Finnion wished the pain was over for him.

"Look at me." The boy's good eye opened to look at Finnion. "Do you see this?" Finnion pointed to his nose with a finger. The boy was silent, looking at Finnion's nose. "My nose is broken, so I have to force it back into the right place." Just hearing himself say those words brought shivers to his spine. He tried to convince himself with the truth. "If I don't, I won't be able to breathe through it anymore. You understand?"

Finnion took a deep breath, stilled himself, and in one motion with a horrible cracking sound, set his own nose straight. He should have grabbed something to bite down into. Immense pain surged from behind his eyeballs and in his cheeks. His teeth clenched so hard one of his molders cracked. A deep moan came up involuntarily. Tears and bloody snot poured out of his face. He was dizzy. His face felt like caving in any moment.

Finnion splashed a little of the cool water against his face. It only frustrated him how it didn't help at all. No escape. He wanted it to subside but it did not . . . until slowly, he could think again.

He looked again to the young man, who was still watching Finnion. "My name is Finnion. What's your name, boy?" For a moment, Finnion thought he may be unconscious before he responded.

"Reff . . . is my name. Are you one of the reb—"

"Reff, your arms are out of place. Your knee is also. It's like my nose, Reff; if they're not put right, they aren't going to work right ever again. Do you understand, Reff? I need to do this, and it's going to hurt."

Reff was crying now. His tears were rolling down his swollen cheeks. "They're going to heal. My wounds . . . ugh."

Finnion knew what he had to do. He closed his eyes for a moment and ignored the young man's dreadful whimpering. He breathed slowly. His nose throbbed. Blood dripped down his face and chest. Those mourning doves were still cooing gently. Finnion wished he were patching things up with Jonas Blakes the way they always had after a battle. Taking a day alone together, they wouldn't speak or cry or sing or drink like the rest of their army. They would just cook, eat, and spend time staring at the sky or a campfire after bandaging themselves up.

Eventually Jonas would say, "We should be getting back." With that, Finnion would agree and both men would rejoin the army and all the worry and duty that came with it.

The young man's lip quivered as he begged Finnion not to work his body. Finnion knew what was best though. He took the man's right arm, the one with both shoulder and elbow out of place. Every little movement made the boy flinch and grunt in pain. Finnion, standing next to the boy, placed his foot in Reff's armpit.

"No, please! No. No . . . AGHH! . . . Hmhmhm . . ." Finnion felt the boy's shoulder come back into place. His face twisted terribly with pain. And again as Finnion did his elbow and opposite shoulder. Just as Finnion lifted Reff's leg, making it go straight and pushing it so that it clicked back, he heard something distant that made his body move before his mind told it to. Men's voices. Someone was coming. Reff had been making a lot of noise. Still was. Had it been foolish to do all this so close to where he knew deadly men would be nearby? He pulled Reff's body off the cart and drug him close to the base of the thickly leaved willow tree.

"Please be quiet. I think men are coming." But The boy was out of his mind with pain. Finnion cupped his hand over his mouth and held it shut, muffling his whines. The voices came near. Finnion held his breath. His heart beat so loudly in his chest he thought they might hear it. But they didn't. Slowly, the voices got quieter and whoever they were, they kept on moving. Finnion rolled off of Reff to the ground next to him, letting out the breath of air he'd been holding painfully long.

"We've got to move soon." But Finnion noticed Reff was unconscious now, breathing softly.

Somehow, Finnion felt like it was an act of defiance to help this boy. There was no way of knowing if the republic or Trofaim would reason with the rebels or continue efforts to defeat them. Maybe the rebellion would thrive now that they'd destroyed the bulk of the army and taken its resources. There were so many results that could come of things now. If this kid was to survive, he, like Finnion, would stop at nothing to bring down the men who led The Fowler's rebellion. Finnion's rebellion.

As time went and their wounds healed slowly, they were able to rest more and hide less, enjoying fires at night and some sparse conversation. One morning the sun rose on the two men and the smoking pile of embers that had been their fire the night before. Finn watched Reff struggling as he slept. Nightmares probably. They needed to start moving, so Finnion thought he should wake him up. But then he remembered his own first battle and thought better of it. If he was anything like Finnion, the night was long and peaceful sleep was still hard to find. It takes time to make the death of battle scale to a normality.

How long did it take for me to sleep at night? he thought. *How long until my heart healed? I didn't heal, did I?* As he watched the young man sleep with his body tightly wrapped against the cool air, Finnion noticed a cart stacked high with wheat crossing the distant plane.

It made him smile to think some folk could keep going. Some people could still live through it all. His wife had told him, "Heroes have their place in stories and in books, but the world needs its men." She'd been the best thing he ever had. Shame, he thought, to miss most the things he enjoyed the least.

The little farm was hard work, but it was all that work that made him hungry enough for her bad cooking. And he had that small broken bed to thank for always pushing him closer to her each night. The only comfortable thing in the old farmhouse had been her warm company. The memory of her shone bright against his hard youth. He knew if he still had her there with him, he wouldn't have spent thousands of lives to kill thousands more for justice to be done. If they wouldn't have killed her, perhaps it would have always been someone else's war. She could make Finnion happy in injustice like a pig in the mud. She was his happiness. With her, he had been a different man. He would've been just another unhappy farmer, mad at the clouds for not giving him his fair share of rain. He laughed as he realized he'd never met a happy farmer.

"What's funny?" croaked Reff, now awake and peering through one black sleepy eye. Finnion noticed himself still smiling off distantly at the cart of wheat.

"Can you ever truly appreciate a thing while you have it? Must one lose it?"

Reff looked to the cart of wheat and back to Finnion.

"What are you talking about? The sun's not even all the way up yet."

That made Finn laugh again. "It's too early for philosophizing, isn't it?" The young man's only response was a judgmental look of puzzlement. It seemed to Finn he did love her more now that she was gone. *That settles it then,* he thought, *I have not healed.*

They were far west of Trofaim near the eastern boundary of Agrephens, not far from where the battle had been. They spoke little to one another, likely because the young man was fighting that inner battle every warrior fights. Finnion wondered how long Reff would need to discover the battle with oneself is a battle with no victors.

CHAPTER TWENTY-ONE

THE ORPHAN'S HERO

CICERO

They were riding hard. They had been for a day and a half. The horses were all tired. Redeye still had dried blood on the side of his head, lank hair curling around his bony face. "How long do you see this going, Cis?"

Cicero ignored the question then spoke, "We've only got eight miles until the border of Galanoa. I know the land there." Cicero looked at Redeye for his opinion on the plan, but his look was grim.

"You know who will be guarding the Galanoan borderlands . . ."

"Bloodway should be following us. There is no way he could have gotten around." Cicero again was looking at Redeye's face for an expression of agreement but again, he only grimaced.

"I spoke with a farmer and some search bands looking for you," Redeye said reluctantly. "They all said they aim to find you first and bring you back to him alive. just east of Galanoa. He wants to unite the Southern States with the Aravacans against the North. This could do it."

"Tork told me they didn't offer Hocklee a chance to pledge," Cicero argued, but Redeye wasn't surprised.

"That was before Gallo spoke to the foreigners. Now he is say-ing this is how he will save Hocklee. Seeing as how the people don't want war so badly, they've even got the immigrants looking for you."

If what Redeye was saying was true, Tork was on his right to the west and Bloodway on his left to the east. There were no worse enemies in Hocklee, or all of Alssae to Cicero's mind. Here he was, smashed between them. Herded by one toward the other.

"Brevalti then?" Cicero asked.

Redeye shrugged. "Only place we haven't each left a trail of blood through . . . Tork's men will meet us on the way doubtless." Cicero was trying to avoid the decision. "It's a choice between Tork and Bloodway. You chose to fight against Bloodway in the wars—"

"Yes, but that was *with* Tork." Cicero was in disbelief at the situation. It was more real than ever now. But it had never really been a hard choice. He knew what had to be done.

"Swain, Noon." The children rode near to him, not a worry on their tired faces. "Tie all the horses to Doe. Redeye, take up the watch." Redeye, understanding what was happening, nodded and rode up a hill. "Swain, we've been riding northwest toward my home in Galanoa, but I need you to move due north." Cicero pointed out the way. "Brevalti is to the north. You won't be wanted there, but you'll have to keep moving. I'm afraid you may always be moving from now on. That's no life at all, and I'm sorry that's the best I could do." He looked at the children, thinking he may cry in front of them for the first time, but he kept speaking through his cracking voice and wet nose. "Keep moving north until you get to Brevalti. You should get a fair price for the horses there. Keep moving, across the sea if you have to. The money should last, but if it doesn't, sell Doe and Mag if you have to. Just keep going. Just be okay. You're both strong. You'll be fine if you have one another—"

"But Cicero! It's because of you we have each other!" With that, Swain wrapped his arms about Cicero.

"And because of you, we're well!" And Noon came on hugging him too. They stayed there one more moment. They were a family one more moment.

&

Cicero took his stallion and tied it to Doe in the long line with the rest.

"What will you ride?" Noon asked.

"You both need the money. I won't be needing it." Cicero bagged them all up and noticed Swain trying to hand him his bow. "No, Swain. Why do you think I taught you to use it? Take them both and keep your sister safe with them." He knelt, getting his small bag together. Two short swords, a longsword, and . . . he couldn't find his old dagger from Tork. "Agh . . ." He couldn't see for the tears that kept suddenly filling his vision. He wiped his eyes and found it wrapped in his old green hood. Cicero sheathed the knife and held the hood up to Swain. "You'll need this now, Green Hood."

The boy began to cry. Cicero had to crouch down, looking back into his pack, pointlessly trying to hide the tears from the kids. It was then when he felt Mag licking his face while she whimpered and Doe nickered softly. "Farewell, girls. I know you will keep them safe."

He drove the horses north, then turned west for Tork.

CHAPTER TWENTY-TWO

THE ORPHANED HERO

CICERO

"Best thing you could've done for 'em," Redeye remarked as he watched the children ride away, patting his horse as Cicero ran up the hill. He spat out the brown liquid contents of his mouth, still watching the children ride. "Everyone in Hocklee, they all know what you look like. Some of them might even be some of your boys."

Redeye began checking the equipment he'd been collecting. He looked down the edges of blades and felt their sharpness. "We've been in worse shape before. We can really make a go of it if we get some of the old boys. Leito and the cousins will be out there. They'd join us." Redeye was starting to sound excited, tightening the strap of a leather chest piece.

"We aren't dividing Hocklee. I won't be needing you to come with me. Just go to Gallo and tell him you found me."

Redeye looked confused, pushing the sweaty hair out of his one eye. "Where do you want me to take them?"

"To me," Cicero said. "Bring them after me. And tell the truth so they won't have a reason to suspect you as helping me. That should clear your name with the Galanoans and the Hockleets. You'll be a free man." Cicero wondered if it was a good or bad thing letting an evil sort like Redeye free. No doubt he was tied up justly in Hocklee. Probably hurt someone or stole something. He knew Redeye since he was a boy crying in the Bloodway. He was like Cicero; he needed a second chance and needed someone to show him how to use it. Redeye might've been guilty, but Cicero knew good as any. Sometimes an orphan just needed a fighting chance.

"I'll stand with you, Cicero. We can outrun 'em or kill as many as we can on our way down." Redeye may have been a killer, but he was a loyal one for sure.

"You are talking like death is your only option."

"It's either die or get chased until they—"

"Those are my options. We're splitting up. It's better this way. They'll believe you and you'll pull 'em off the kids' trail. They know you've fought with me and won't doubt you. So just take them in the direction I'm going, and with any luck, I'll get to see if your sword arm is worth the guild I paid for it."

Redeye looked troubled, studying Cicero, thinking.

"You sure about this?"

"I want you to find the boys and take care of them. I miss them. Gallo will round them up and try to turn you all against each other." Cicero thought back on the nights he'd dreamed of more for the orphans of this little land. Many of them were orphans because of Gallo Bloodway. And now he would be leading them.

"Make sure the youngest stays away from Yellowtooth and his men. Hezro is a good boy. If Lairo is there, he will have Drux with him. They will look out for you. You'll have a little crew."

Redeye looked like he had a question but was too afraid to ask. Knowing Redeye's thoughts, Cicero gave him the hard truth. "I don't think Rector could have made it out of Begatto. It was burned real bad. They killed a whole lot of Stornians." Redeye nodded to himself, and in that moment, Cicero saw the expression of the innocent boy named Vanno, before killers named him Redeye. "But if he is with the rest of them, he'll be looking for you."

Cicero thought about what else to say. He wanted to share so many things in his heart for Redeye to do. But that wasn't why Cicero freed him. It wasn't so that he would make Cicero's dreams come true. Cicero had helped him for the same reason he helped Swain. So that an orphan could live to have his own life and dreams

"Go on. Tell 'em I'll be moving hard and fast towards the river cliffs."

Redeye looked like he might cry if he tried to say anything, so he just nodded, clearing his throat. And with that, he left Cicero alone on the hill.

&

Cicero squatted under branches and ran through vines, bushes, and all manner of undergrowth. He was constantly moving, always feeling his pursuers were close. He'd seen several parties of horsemen searching the country. So he'd chosen forested woody terrain where it would be harder to find him. He was always worrying about Swain and Noon, wondering if they'd already been caught. If Redeye brought Gallo and Tork was in the west, he should attract enough attention to make a hole for Swain to get through. It was all subject to chance though. Any farmer with a horse and weapon could catch them, and there would be many searching all over the countryside for them.

He found a clearing and began to move faster until he was sprinting. His right foot hit the ground and at once, he was awake again at the campfire with the strange tune being hummed. It sounded closer than before. He'd kept falling asleep into the same dream.

The large man was horrifyingly close. "Why are you doing this?! What do you want from me?!" But the monster was silent, and the humming could not be interrupted. He wriggled at the ropes that held him, and something must have come loose because the rope went slack.

He scrambled to his feet somehow with his hands still tied behind his back. He could feel the abomination chasing him. Its footsteps were loud on the ground just behind. Scared, horrified, Cicero's heart was beating loudly, painfully. *Cicero? Who's that?* He thought. He could hear a river running. He ran toward it. He looked over his shoulder, not hearing the footsteps. The giant freak had fallen behind. He didn't slow though. He ran hard, and with everything he had, he leaped high off a bank and into the water below, cold, fast, and flowing as it took him in.

Cicero pulled air in with a loud gasp.

"What was that?" He heard someone say. Cicero was laying on his back in the thicket, looking up at the treetop canopy above him, gently swaying in the cold autumn wind blowing in. They'd been looking for him. Why was he laying on his back? He'd dreamt about something but he couldn't remember what. Cicero heard a man coming close, his steps crunching in dead leaves maybe four steps from where he lay. His hand gripped the handle of one of the short swords in the pack. He slid it out slowly and silently, not moving the bush at all. The man walked up and turned, facing Cicero's left. He was looking right past Cicero. The man choked on the blade as he sat up fast, thrusting it through the man's neck. His head jolted to the left with the movement of the sword as Cicero chopped it forward, slicing the man's neck open so wide that it sprayed Cicero with hot blood.

The man went down to his knees, half falling on Cicero. He

shoved the coughing bloody man over and stood facing the others. There were two men looking, not making sense of how fast their man had been killed. Cicero beckoned to them. He knew he had them. One came on with a wood axe in two hands raised high. *A fool,* he thought, *to come so confidently at death.*

Yes . . . here was the violence coming in nice and steady. Cicero would usually have thrown a knife, but this clumsy man could have his sword if he, like the other man, came running to join his friends. One dying. One about to die. The axe came high and Cicero went slow to let the wood of it hit the short sword's blade, taking the head of the axe right off. The axe head whizzed by his head, shaft hitting hard against his collarbone. Cicero, absorbing the blow and bringing in the sword, swung out wide in a backhanded motion, into the man's side. It went deep and he pushed off from the man, leaving the sword buried in his guts.

He fixed on the next man, pulling the longsword, holding it in one hand. The man slowed, his eyes darting between his dying companions and Cicero. They'd each been killed in a few quick motions from Cicero. He noticed the man hesitantly working on the situation. Cicero felt the man's confidence leaking out the way his friends leaked blood.

Something grabbed Cicero's sword hand as the man lurched forward with a sword of his own. Not good. He pulled out his dagger in his hip belt to block the sword coming down at his face. The metallic sound of steel against steel was muffled as the dagger's blade lodged into his forearm from the sword hack. Cicero kicked the man with the sword in his gut and reached behind to grab his short sword, still deep in the other man's torso. His hand found it somewhere on the blade and pulled up the steel like a lever, ripping his other arm from the man's grip, now weakened. In one motion, the longswords clanged together.

He swiped and the man leaped back in a dodge, giving Cicero enough room to turn and free his short sword from where it was sunk in the other man's chest. He threw it straight at the man, thinking it would distract him, but luckily the blade sliced his face, making him stumble. He weakly blocked Cicero's cut but was victim to another kick. Cicero swiped hard, and the man's resistance was weak enough for Cicero's blade to connect with the man's head. His eyes looked up and to the left where the blade stuck in his skull the way an axe sticks in the side of a tree. The longsword came loose with effort, and pain shot through his left forearm where his dagger had cut him.

Cicero looked about, frantically looking for another opponent. Three lives ended in the span of roughly seven or eight breaths. He searched for danger but there was only choking gasps aside from his own loud breathing. He looked to the dying man he'd stabbed in the torso and the man met his eyes. "If they ask, I'm headed that way." Then Cicero ran northwest as he had indicated.

Cicero could remember the dream he'd had when he fell in the brush, but just barely. It made him wonder for a second if the giant was chasing him still. He had to tell himself to focus on the business with Tork and Bloodway. He kept remembering the feelings of the dreams and forgetting his task at hand.

Cicero heard something behind him and turned around quickly to see what it was. The odd-looking monster from the dream was now deadly familiar in front of him. Cicero gripped the long iron in his hand, but the beast was gone, replaced with a normal man slowly approaching with a sword and shield at the ready. Cicero had to blink, not knowing what he was really looking at.

The man came fast, and Cicero drew steel. His sword missed Cicero's face as close as a bug buzzing around his ear. His own sword hacked a splinter out of the wooden shield, sending the man back a step but not off balance. Cicero's head leaned back, letting a swipe breeze by before he feinted with a high overhead swing and followed with a kick that landed hard against the shield. Cicero swung his sword around fast at the man's side, letting his grip go slack as his other hand drew his dagger. The man was backing up and blocking the longsword when Cicero sprang into the man's shield, letting go of the longsword to grab the shield with his newly free hand.

The man was off balance now, so when Cicero pulled on his shield, Cicero was close enough to breathe on his face. He brought the knife around into the man's body somewhere behind the shield. Again, Cicero stabbed him, this time getting a quarter turn from twisting the knife. The man groaned, trying to get at Cicero, but his balance was stolen by Cicero and his sword was too long, clumsy for a fight this close. He almost got the point of the big blade pointed toward Cicero, but he pushed free in time to evade the stab.

The man let the space between them widen. He was breathing hard, looking down where Cicero had knifed him. His eyes bulged as the knife thudded into that perfect spot. He made that familiar gasp, then slumped back. Cicero couldn't wait for this man to die. Pity for the man stung at him as he picked up his longsword. He was holding his bloody throat with one hand, trying to cover with the shield, but Cicero pinned the shield aside with one foot and thrust the blade through his heart. He growled to get past the guilt, then retrieved his gear and ran farther west.

ে

As he ran, his lungs hurt from the dry, cold wind at his face. The rest of his body was worn out from exhaustion and raked bloody from all the brush. He stayed in the thick so that he could stay hidden, but it slowed him. Everything scratched at his body, tearing his skin repeatedly. It was especially painful when the brush drug across the open wound on his left forearm.

Cicero kept thinking on the children. Had they already escaped? Or had Tork's men caught up to them? Had they been waiting just past the horizon to catch the kids? The thought of Swain's face showing fear surrounded by armed soldiers invaded Cicero's mind. It all pulled at his heart. Cicero could hear dogs barking in the distance behind him and he pushed through the world clawing at him.

This was not his first time to run from his enemies. He'd had Gallo chasing him before. The barking brought it all back. Cicero wondered if those were the same hounds that chased him seven years before. *Let them come*, he thought. *Let them all come. Let that dog, Gallo, come with all his men and monsters and hounds and devils.* Cicero remembered this moment like he'd never been a farmer, maybe he'd only ever been a killer. He and Gallo had fought like animals, one against the other for their farms and families longer than he could remember. Why try to forget this part of life? Twice they'd try to be allies, but the man was a hellion. Only in death could he be forgotten, and dead Cicero would make him.

The men's voices were now far off but audible. The beast of mix-matched men screaming like animals accompanied the barking. Redeye was right, Cicero was the one who brought death with him. He'd spent years unable to sleep for the memories of moments like these. But now that he was here again, the nightmares gave him comfort. He knew what to expect. Cicero probably knew Gallo Bloodway better than he knew anyone else. So he let go of the worries. The worries about the children and Doe and Mag. All of them weren't his responsibility now. Cicero's only responsibility was to kill these men and as many as he could.

On through the thick he pushed.

❧

The forest was growing thin and Cicero ran faster with stamina he didn't know he had, or had he forgotten it was there all along? He looked over his shoulder at the thick brush behind him and turned north towards the open landscapes. They'd be expecting him to continue in the thick, so he risked the far more dangerous purple woodlands. Cicero knew the dogs would lead Gallo to him, but he'd send a few to continue north. That would give him more time to cut each man down until he got a chance at Bloodway. Cicero wondered if any of the old warriors were with Gallo. Yellowtooth no doubt. Probably all the old Galanoan faces he'd fought with and fought against for so long. He wondered which wretch he would give to the ground first.

The voices had faded and Cicero could barely hear the dogs barking now. The further he brought them, the better. So he ran.

❧

He stopped, his feet sliding.

Cicero's heart leaped, and his rasping breath couldn't keep up with his thumping heart, horrified. First, Swain's face. Then Noon came into focus. Tork himself led Doe with the reigns in one hand, all the horses tied to her and the children on top. *How had he caught them? How did he know where they'd come?*

Cicero looked behind again. There was no time. Gallo behind him, Tork before him. Cicero's feet kicked before he knew it. Leather hissed as he drew the longsword and charged at Tork.

CHAPTER TWENTY-THREE

MONSTERS

CICERO

The older man must've heard Cicero, because he turned to face him while Cicero was still a ways off. He dropped the reins and drew his blade and shield. Cicero stopped before he got too close.

Tork got his reputation for ending fights as soon as they'd begun. Cicero had to wait for a moment, a chance, anything. Tork was quiet as the grave and poised to send Cicero there. Both of them knew the situation. Tork wasn't going to charge like those thralls in the woods. The grizzled old soldier just needed to wait for help, help from Bloodway. Cicero looked sideways at the children; both had their hands tied behind their backs, watching Cicero. Noon had that same fearful look with tears in her eyes as when those bandits captured her.

"You've got to come on, Cicero. We both know I've got men coming. Bloodway won't be far either. We predicted the way you'd come. Give battle or give up."

Cicero waited. Every second was an eternity. Compassion for these two kids bubbled up from his heart and manifested hatred for his old ally.

"Chief!" a voice came from behind Cicero. "You found him?" Two men who came from Kalesia with Tork to Hocklee. One man was named Golf. Cicero forgot the other's name.

"Time's up!" barked Tork. "It's over, Cicero. Don't try bringing any more men to the ground with you!" The men were close to Cicero now, easing their way towards him, trying to do it fast and smooth as possible. That was Tork's way.

Tork's voice came cautiously, "Please, Cicero . . . no more death."

Cicero stood as still against all his anger. Despite the almighty urge to rage against these men, he waited . . . He waited until his heart thumped. His breath came faster. They waited for Cicero to say something. People always wanted to talk more than they wanted to fight. But not Cicero. The Kalesians had unknowingly come too close. The moment was coming. Not an event or some opportunity arising. The moment was coming from within him.

When it did, Tork tried to warn the men behind, but it was too late.

Mag was on one, and Cicero spun with the sword out. It hit Golf's shield first, but that was the problem with Kalesians: they trusted their shields too much. The sword thudded hard against the shield, but the man's skull is what stopped the momentum. The man sprawled back like he'd been slapped and lost his balance. Cicero pulled his old familiar dagger, and it made no sound going between Golf's ribs. By the time he gave a gasp, Cicero was past him, twisting the knife as he went. The other just looked confused, his eyes only inches from Cicero's. He'd only begun to address Mag when he'd gotten a knife in his throat.

Golf was on all fours, trying to hold his wound. The other man just tottered around, trying to breathe with a knife in his throat and Mag ravaging his leg. *Tag? Was that his name? No, Tag would've been older by now.*

Tork didn't charge, but came slow, shield raised. His eyes

were looking over the shield rim between Cicero and whatever his name was, choking on Cicero's knife. Golf croaked over to the left, one hand trying to plug the hole in his chest. The other man, down on one knee now, tried to hold his bleeding neck but couldn't reach it for the shield in his hand. Mag bit and tugged on his sword arm relentlessly.

The horses were already stirring when Cicero threw one of the short swords at Tork. It wasn't much, but it was enough for Cicero to slip past. But not without a slash to his back as he went. Cicero could feel Tork behind him, not sparing a half second to look back. Cicero cut through one, two, three of the straps tethering the horses to each other, slapping the horses as he passed with his free hand. There was chaos as horses bucked. One reared up, nearly knocking Cicero with one hoof as it came back down.

He knew the blade would cut Swain's hand, but he had to cut the ropes around his hand quickly. The hands spread apart and Cicero slapped a hand against Doe's leg so hard it burned. "Yah!" he yelled, and Doe was off pulling at the horse Swain was on. Cicero turned, expecting Tork to be on him but pleasantly finding him occupied with the mean red stallion. Tork raised his shield just in time to catch one hoof against the wood. Tork fell back though, and for a short moment, Cicero hoped he was okay before remembering: they were trying to kill each other.

Cicero whistled and Mag ran after Doe, leaving Golf in a bloody mess, kicking and gasping for air. Cicero could hear the dogs barking again in the direction he'd come. Tork spit red from his bloody mouth. Cicero could see the stallion had broken his nose. The horse was bucking at Mag as she ran by, but she was too quick and the hoof went high.

Cicero passed the short sword from his right hand to his left and let Mag's fur slide under one hand as she passed. One last pet as he remembered the puppy born in winter. He remembered her hungry mother burned from war, and with that she was gone. *Farewell, Mag.*

The stallion was trotting toward him now, Tork waiting just behind. Cicero lurched back only just dodging the front hooves as it stood on its hind legs. At the moment the stallion stomped down, Cicero scrambled back up. Cicero was doing everything he could to keep from getting his head kicked in while Tork stood behind the stallion, goading him with his sword toward Cicero. He was yelling and waving, trying to herd the animal forward to attack for him. That barking was getting closer now with every moment. The stallion bucked high. Cicero braced, but the stallion bucked its hind legs this time just before trotting away to his left.

Cicero originally thought Tork dropped to dodge the bucking horse, but as he noticed, the old man's leg was broken backwards at the shin, making the leg bend unnaturally. Cicero looked at the horse coming back at him again. The dogs were close now and apparently the horse could see one because it ran toward the sound, leaving Tork and Cicero alone. He heard the sound of fighting. Maybe there were several dogs. Cicero's eyes swept over to Tork, spitting out more blood and trying and failing to stand on his broken leg.

"You should have left me to go, Tork. I didn't have to be your enemy again. I didn't want this."

Tork just sighed, and with a wince, pushed himself standing on one leg, sword in the ground like a cane. "I didn't want this either. I didn't want war." Cicero was approaching him as he leaned against a tree, watching. "That's what this business is . . . It's war, Cicero. And now it's come back to Hocklee. For the guilty and the innocent."

Cicero remembered what Redeye had said: 'Death follows the

hood like death follows the plague."

"You know what Bloodway told me when I tried convincing him to let you go? He said you only want war. He said you can't live without the battle." Tork balanced on that one last leg as Cicero came close. "I loved you like a brother, but I see that I only knew you at war. You were living well while the rest of us were fighting to survive. I see it now . . ." He looked across the body of the man Cicero still couldn't remember the name of and Golf, who was now twitching a little. "You thrive in the chaos of all this. But at least Bloodway'll have you . . . Him and those . . . things. They'll be just out in the woods there." Tork nodded out toward the barking and noises out in the distant forest. "He'll catch you and those children and give you all the slow death I wanted to save you from. But at least Hocklee will be safe, and all my dead friends won't be wasted. So go on, Hood. At least I know you'll be right behind me." Tork pulled out his knife and threw it down at Cicero's feet. "I'll take your knife back now."

Cicero killed him there with the first crude knife he ever had. He felt like a monster in the windy darkness between the trees, still living among the dead and dying. Cicero moved for the familiar knife he loved. He picked up Tork's knife, leaving his own blade buried in his old friend, running in the opposite direction of Swain. His leg still burned but less so now. The stranger's limb was numbing, but Cicero trusted it. He had to trust it. The leg was the only thing he had at this point. His friends, his animals, even his bow with its arrows were all gone. So he ran with another man's leg, another man's sword, even Tork's well-fashioned knife. It felt like his, but he knew it wasn't. He had never had much of anyone or anything of his own that lasted. Now he ran, limping on someone else's leg away from Hocklee. Away from his home he was being chased out of.

Cicero ran with the monstrous growls in the forest behind him and trusted everything he had to getting Swain and Noon to safety. It wasn't fair that they'd been orphaned. Cicero felt that pang of injustice, familiar to his own childhood, pronounced when Swain came to him for help. It was as if he'd been given a chance to do things differently. The boy may have not known it, but those stories of his family had been the closest thing this orphan ever had to family. Cicero wondered if this was what it was to have the love of a family. The willingness to lay one's own life down for another.

Giant footsteps were close now. Cicero could feel the ground vibrating from the monster's weight. Which way was the river again? "Go help more orphans, Swain," he whispered through his winded rasp. "The way we helped each other."

The monster was on him now, huge and strong in the darkness. Cicero felt flesh tear painfully against jagged claws raking him. A second slash gripped him with overwhelming strength, shattering Cicero's weak balance. He fell, his face dragging in the dirt and grass. A huge leg rammed his ribs as the huge man tripped over Cicero's body, having fallen in front.

First, the great weight of borrowed bones and stolen limbs collided against Cicero, then rolled with its momentum beyond him. Vomit pressed its way up from his stomach through his nose and mouth. Luckily his enemy, whatever it was, was clumsy with all of its estranged limbs. Cicero rose painfully to his feet, puke running warm down his chest. He sank Tork's knife into its torso and it felt like stabbing into a tree trunk. The dagger was set fast so Cicero left it and ran. He couldn't fight this thing. It would outrun him and chase him down again. This monster was coming to kill him. Cicero was thankful though still not to be fighting with Gallo Bloodway or with the stakes so high as a child's life.

Cicero unstrapped the sword, letting it fall behind him. His pack, he left in the darkness. Cicero ran and struggled to breathe, grunting and growling, covered in mud and his own vomit. The guttural noises were made more pronounced by the lurching steps of his — or rather someone else's leg. As the beast rose up and began to near again, Cicero realized how similar their snarlings had become. Was he a monster now? Maybe the monster was once an orphan too. Maybe evil men had only offered war to a boy that didn't understand peace. Cicero recognized the place that marked the northern boundary of Hocklee. Cicero peered into the dark, then he turned to face the coming beast. He waited until it came right toward him to say, pointlessly, "May Swain learn peace." He was wondering if any voice came out of his mouth at all when a huge shoulder beat intensely into him as the two monsters plunged off the cliff, down into the churning river below.

"Don't submerge it in water," the body trader had said. He smiled as the water rushed up at him. Swain's chances were not as bad now that he thought about it. Maybe luck just isn't for everyone, no matter how many bells you hang.

And the cold wet darkness swallowed him whole.

PART II

"Even if I knew that the world would end tomorrow,
I would still plant my apple tree."
—*Martin Luther*

CHAPTER TWENTY-FOUR

THE LOSS

PINELLA

The leaves were falling in Trofaim and the people began to gather in the streets for the funeral commemorations. The fallen Shrikes shared a single funeral observance. Dead warriors were buried below the base of trees that the great heroes of their families had planted after great victories of the past. Next to long lost uncles and fathers who had also fallen in battle, they too would have the honor of closest burial to the trees of their family.

They had not found Reff's body, so Pinella buried the beanie that she made him when he was little.

Pinella picked a spot near the base of the huge red apple tree her father planted after his victory at Paveneli. It was fitting to bury her son by the tree her father planted, the same tree she watered as a little girl before its roots tapped into the river. Every year, Reff filled it with so many bells. For a second, she thought she heard her little son laughing in the treetop, but her son wasn't little or laughing any longer, and all the fruit had been picked.

He was gone, along with her husband and her father.

Pinella pushed the loose dirt over the child's hat, her tears dropping on the turf. Both her husband and father's bodies had not been found, and her son's body may not receive the honor of burial either. She had that familiar desire to wait, telling her if she was patient, he may come home again. But all that waiting had taught her not to hope for heroes to come home. This time she would learn.

CHAPTER TWENTY-FIVE

THE GOOD MAN

REDEYE

Redeye looked down at the corpse, hardly believing his eyes. "Tricky man, your partner Cicero." The stuck-up accent of Aravacan nobility would've caused annoyance, but Redeye was thankful that Karrick interrupted his own endless humming with his words.

"We weren't partners. He paid my guild, so I worked for him just as the law demands . . . and I still betrayed him, didn't I? You wouldn't have come close without me! It's not my fault your monster couldn't get him." Redeye had to calm himself, reassured by the fact that no one could have known he had helped Cicero. The switch only smiled reservedly.

"Don't worry, good Redeye," he purred, smiling. "I don't serve Bloodway either, and it's nice to know who else serves only his own interests." That smile got wider as Karrick winked like he knew every secret Redeye had ever heard. "He was smart to draw Maldor to water like this, but if he is alive, he shouldn't live much longer. The leg will deteriorate much faster now, poisoning the rest of him as a result."

The switch crouched down beside the giant beast he'd called Maldor. Every limb was disgustingly pieced to the others like each one belonged to a different person. Redeye knew this kind of monster, even though this was the biggest he'd seen. They were called shrouds. "The leavings of a ghost," they used to say back in the wars.

Bloodway used shrouds in his fights against the chief of Western Galanoa, then against Tork and Cicero later. Cicero always said it'd been the use of shrouds made by switching limbs that had been the greatest disagreement between the two men. Cicero had to make peace with Gallo, tolerating the evil practice in order to make peace in Hocklee.

"A detestable practice," Cicero had called it, saying it was irreverent to the dead. Redeye found himself in agreement as he looked at the compiled mutilation of at least a half dozen bodies stitched into one.

"It's sick how you do this to good men," Redeye said, feeling his stomach turn. The switch didn't even look up from his work severing limbs.

"Good men like you? You'd be surprised how many of them beg for taller men's legs, or a stronger man's arms."

Redeye was disarmed by that. His mother had always told him to find the good and be a part of it. He always tried to do good, but every time he did it, it cost him. Cost him an eye fighting for the muddy city and its people. In the end, Gallo still tricked them into chasing his men before taking Hocklee and filling the whole Mudway with corpses. All Redeye got out of it was another whisper in a windstorm of evil deeds on his conscience. Now good deeds for those children got Cicero thrown off a cliff into a river. Redeye watched the water run softly onward to the gulfs. Was his old friend floating with all the good he'd done for the two orphans? Redeye decided now wasn't the time to hope for good.

He focused on finding his old friends, the Hockleets.

Redeye looked over as some of the other men made their way

down to the river's edge. Some were the old bandits of Hocklee that went with Yellowtooth. Others were Tork's men who'd come with him from Kalesia. Most, he could tell, hadn't fought in the wars of Hocklee. They all looked fresh and eager to get their weapons wet the way young men do.

"The men of Kalesia will have to choose a new leader. We found him dead on top of that cliff about a mile back."

Redeye felt a stab of sadness at that. Had he hoped deep down to see that old warlord again?

"It was Tork's body up there in the woods. Hoodless killed a hero for his own crimes." The stranger from Kalesia spoke with deep regret.

"Cicero . . . The orphan killed Tork?" Redeye fought back the urge to smile that came with the pride of knowing his old boss brought down the strongest fighter from the old wars. Cicero had never enjoyed the reputations that his deeds gave him. All those fights and sieges, and Cicero had always chosen to be alone when he could after Lain lost his mind. Until he friended Tork, his only companion most nights was that burned up dog he kept with him.

Redeye remembered Tork breaking down Cicero's walls slowly, eventually drawing closer to Cicero than anyone thought possible. After Tork, it'd been all the Kalesians and their honor for one another. The Galanoans lost most of their trust with him, saying he'd become a Kalesian man, saying he'd forgotten who his own were. Redeye didn't blame him though. The Kalesians, for all their fancy traditions, stuck to their ways and their word. Seemed to him that Galanoan men always found reasons to make their allies into enemies. Until Cicero led his warband, the word was you couldn't trust a Galanoan man except in battle against him. That was maybe their only creed, and a poor one in Redeye's opinion. Maybe he didn't care for Tork, but Cicero did, and Cicero was a rare, good man born in so much evil and war. "Those children better be worth it," Redeye grumbled.

They came from a man named Kerbaro. He'd always gone with Yellowtooth in his robbing and fighting. Yellowtooth was notorious for making war in peacetime, a true Galanoan man and Redeye's mentor for years. Even when Kalesians started coming over to the Hockleets, he couldn't get used to them. Maybe Yellowtooth, like Redeye, just needed someone else to fight, so as not to be at war with himself. Truthfully, they all shared a good portion of the blame. Those wars held happenings for which all those men were responsible, even Tork, who everyone called honorable.

And here they were now, having stood over Tork's dead body, all because he wanted to track down children to be tried as murderers. All because Cicero was the one who pledged to protect those children.

Chapter Twenty-Six

The Good Samaritan

Finnion

What had the territory become? Finnion looked at the remains of a supply shipment. Several soldiers in the armor of Trofaim, along with a few dozen noncombatants, all executed and looted along with the contents of their wagons. Finnion wished that the looters could have had the decency to leave a horse for him. He was exhausted from pulling the little makeshift body he'd made for the young Shrike. Finnion was able to find a few scraps of food and a small waterskin before continuing on. Now that he had found a road to travel on, it made everything easier. He wanted to give some of these innocents a decent burial, but there were just too many and Finnion had already chosen more than his own fair share of charity.

As Finnion came back to the little cart, Reff awoke with a groan.

"Uh . . . Hello? Finnion?" Finnion hated how the young man pronounced his name like onion.

"Don't worry. I'm here. We just stopped to see what we could find in the wreck. We are going now." Reff's youthful face became visible as Finnion approached the cart. "Here, take a drink." Finnion held the waterskin in front of the boy's bruised and swollen eyes before putting the tap to his broken lips. "We've got us a decent waterskin! No more sucking creek water from a rag," Finnion laughed.

Reff took a few pained swallows before coughing most of what he'd drank, spitting it onto Finnion.

"My chest . . ." the boy moaned in harmony with Finnion's irritated sigh. He dropped the salvaged items next to Reff and continued his duty as carthorse. Finnion was looking for a town. He knew if he just kept following the road he would find one, but rebels were one of many threats in a land without policing authority. Eventually he found a small community that he could tell the rebels had not yet captured. He made his way toward it in what remained of the daylight, his body aching from travel.

The village and its people were hospitable. Finnion had nothing to trade nor sell, but some of the people were willing to give him a livestock cover to sleep under and some of their communal soup from their common house. Finnion focused on not breathing so as to avoid its terrible flavor. All of these little villages kept a shared cauldron of soup or porridge called a common pot for all their residents. Every little town had their own and was usually comprised of what was left over from a proper meal or whatever was about to spoil if left uncooked. The bowl they served him was poor in taste but rich in warm nourishment that satisfied his burning hunger. After he finished eating, Finnion helped Reff slurp down half a bowl of his own.

"He needs fresh bandages," said one of the old locals as they came with another steaming helping of gross soup. Finnion could not dissagree. Reff's huge wound was still open.

"I can't pay," Finnion admitted.

"I know. Were you both in that battle up in the hills?" The old villager wasn't really asking, but Finnion still confessed. He tried to think of a lie to tell to keep the two of them safe. This village might hang Reff and Finnion if they thought the two of them to be part of Trofaim's army. Maybe worse if they found out Reff was a Shrike.

"We'd really appreciate any help." Finnion tried not to beg, hoping the gray-haired man didn't ask any more questions. After a thoughtful moment, the man agreed to help, leaving and returning with a jar of water and clean strips of cloth for bandaging. Reff winced as the man stitched what Finnion guessed to be miles of scarred flesh. He tied a stint to straighten one of Reff's crooked fingers. Finnion was impressed as he sat comfortably on a stack of hay cuttings, trying to stay awake. He was thankful right then for decent people.

"Maybe when the two of you get where you're going, you can do us a kindness back here in our little town."

Finnion was too lazy to reply to the man making conversation with himself as he worked on Reff, but Reff didn't think similarly.

"The Tribunal will reward you for offering clemency to a Shrike."

Finnion couldn't believe his ears. The stupid kid. Finnion opened his eyes to see the old man's eyes staring wide at Reff, who was barely conscious. The man turned his attention to Finnion. He felt his heart speeding up.

"Did he just say Shrike?" asked Finnion in deceptive amazement. "I was just helping a helpless youth."

"You can help him by leaving at first light!" The man's words stabbed with accusation. "The Fowler's men are everywhere! If they discover a Shrike in our care, they'll deal cruelly with us. If you are here in the morning, we will hang you by your necks to show ourselves not to be hosts of loyalists to the republic." With that, the man stormed out, leaving Finnion and Reff under the livestock shelter.

Finnion fumed with anger at the young Shrike, while Reff laid peacefully, snoring now that he had a cushion under his head.

CHAPTER TWENTY-SEVEN

No Time To Mourn

Pinella

The Waymar manner was quiet. Since Pinella had been affiliated with the family of celebrities, she had never known their favorite home to be so still and without color. A month earlier, a musician would have been stationed on each level in the common space in order to fill the house with a unique ambiance suited to the weather, the time of day, recent family celebrations or an accomplishment. Dozens of leaders of vassal family members could visit in a single day to gain permissions or pay Tributes to the great house. It's lower two levels had been used to conduct Waymar family business and civil administration throughout the city and territory of Trofaim. The courtyard outside the house would have been filled with common families with their children come to enjoy the ornate gardens and fountains. By this time in the day, several small trade stands would have come to sell food and drinks to the vacationers and visiting affiliates of the Waymars.

All the life and clamor that made it feel like a small city was overcome with melancholy.

The Waymars could have all of their sorrows, but someone had to keep the Waymar affairs going. Lord Owen had once said that "Waymar business never stops." He went on to explain how his younger sister Octavia was the only person who seems to keep a continued tab on everything that happened.

Now, one of the greatest minds in Trofaim was halted by tragedy. Pinella gritted her teeth thinking of how they had not only killed one of Trofaim's greatest leaders, but also crippled his delegates with sorrow for the loss.

From the time she began descending the river steps until she crossed the north bridge into the Lower City, she had not stopped thinking of how hard it must be for the vassal families without any leadership or communication from the Waymars. How had they been expected to carry out legal business without any support? She did not take her customary detour through the Arcade against her own desire. There was scarcely ever a time when she would miss an opportunity to go through, but affairs were overdue.

"Lady Bennault!"

Pinella turned her head to see who the gravelly voice belonged to. An old familiar man whose name eluded her. She first remembered only that he was from the large and largely unimpressive Alcott Family to whom Vestin the flirt belonged.

"Ahh, Lord Alcott! A pleasure to see you."

The Old man was followed by a body servant nearly as old as he was and another a quarter his age. He didn't bother introducing either of them. "It is my great sorrow that your noble name has undergone such weight of loss."

Pinella began to realize where the old man was taking this conversation. "I thank you for your concern Lord Alcott but—"

"Please, call me Levin" The old man bowed his head enough for Pinella to see his shimmering bald patch. "I would ask to accompany you to your destination, as you are alone."

"Very well," Pinella reluctantly agreed, fighting the urge to sigh in annoyance.

They began walking together and the old man spared no time before returning to his objective. The Alcott family was large and influential, but Levin and Vestin belonged to the outer branches of the family tree. This man would have inherited far less than his younger cousin, the dame of her family. Her birthright as heir of the middle branch of a noble distinguished family would have been comparable to a moderately sized city in the Fork Region. This old man and his nephew were more so inheritors of duty to support the house than wealth and influence to rule over it. These lower members of large families were constantly vying for relationships and connections that gave them the influence and authority to increase their own respective branches of the house. The large Alcott family was filled with smaller family units like this.

Pinella assumed that Vestin would like to have the prestige of her family name and the resources of his own family to build a family of his own. 'Vestin Bennault.' Pinella tried not to laugh aloud at the thought of it.

"You know, I've heard a great deal about you from my son Vestin. He spoke of your eloquence of speech and way at the Waymar galas. He says you spoke as equal to Octavia herself."

She pretended to be flattered. She knew her own skill of speech fell far short of many distinguished men and women. Even Grayah Aspin, who was only a second generation lower nobility, was often much more articulate than Pinella was.

"The Waymars need good help around. I taught Karianna's father structure and engineering before her grandfather gave her hand to Otrin's son. Oh, what was his name?" The old man was talking about the former sire of house Waymar, as if he and his son weren't both dead.

"Owen."

"Yes, Owen! His father Otrin Waymar was a great man in his time. The time of your great father was not an easy time to be considered great, my dear."

"You remember him?"

"Who? Your father? Of course I do! He's in the histories." His eyes sparked with realization. "I'll wager that you consider him all but forgotten."

Pinella didn't deny. Instead she waited for him to propose a different idea.

"To understand your father, you must first understand Trofaim and our fear of Mottrava. The sense of peerlessness we enjoy over the other states was only ever assumed before your father bested their generals around Pavenali. You see, Trofaim has only fought a single war that wasn't a minor dispute against Mottrava. Until your father defeated them, no one ever knew for sure if our republic and its army could withstand war with Mottrava. It was your father who assured our hegemony in Alssae."

"I haven't ever considered that before."

"Trofaim has been able to remain fairly peaceful, even though the other states struggle constantly. Since the fall of the monarchy, Trofaim has never fought a fully-fledged war against a another state. We have only aided other states in their conflicts. Mottrava is very different. Their armies are continually hardened by war with the peoples of the far north, as well as other Alssaen wars in which they have conquered territory from Agrephens and Rumenedda. It was a dreadful thing to hear that the Mottravan Army was led by a commander of no small repute toward the Fork Region." Pinella loved to see how Levin's voice was impassioned by her father's legacy. She loved hearing her father cast in such a light.

"People were afraid?"

"They were mortified," he corrected. "The people were so ter-rified of the invaders that they abandoned their farms and ranch-es all around the Fork Region, seeking refuge in and around the city. That's how we found ourselves famished and defenseless in the face of war. I can still remember the consensus of the Tribu-nal to bide for time and sue for peace. When your father strode into court with the support of twenty Shrikes, insisting that he march immediately, it shocked all of us. But not so shocked as when we heard news of his victories. And complete victories they were. I won't bore you with all of his tactics, but I do find them terribly fascinating."

Pinella laughed without denying. She was more interested in his rally of the political finesse and capacity for influence than anything. "You were a man of court in those days?"

The old man smiled, having impressed Pinella. "More of a courtier. I was delegate for my cousin Verron at the time. I was one of the fools to doubt your father."

Pinella found herself trying to settle on a single question to ask the man, more interested than ever.

"It looks like we're here at the lower Waymar house. Forgive me! I could talk about your father continually if allowed." The old man chuckled.

"And I'd listen." Said Pinella before thinking. She had not real-ized their arrival.

The old man nodded understandably. "Well, come dine with me tomorrow evening, and I will take even more of your time." They shared a chuckle. "I'll send for you."

"I'll bring my servant woman with me."

"We'll be going now. Please get yourself someone capable to accompany you on your walks. The city can be dangerous."

"I will," said Pinella, knowing she would not. The peace of the River District and Lower City streets were matchless. The old man waved over his shoulder as he went down the street. Pinella turned to face the entrance of the Waymar House. She hurried inside to find work for herself, always endeavoring to outpace the sorrow that awaited her in an idle moment.

She threw herself into the work. Painfully focused, documents and reports that would have taken her days to write up only took her hours to finish. Riva's work was done well. The woman had learned quickly for someone who had never overseen anything of note, but this was by far her best work. Pinella checked through every document, ratifying most of it without the need for revision. These records of Tributes paid, neglected, or appealed for exemption usually required tedious work. Many of the stewards hired accountants to skillfully write lengthy appeals for exemption of Tributes, stating they had afforded the commoners under their jurisdiction the same exemptions. It was the least favorable work because to deny the steward's formal request was to reject their justifications as well. In almost every response, Riva had cited some evidence or reason for the denial or exemptions granted. The Waymar's vassals were mostly faithful in service, but Octavia had warned how they would endeavor to exploit her brother's absence. The Waymars were a patriarchy and had been for generations. Pinella knew that if there was ever a time to test the resolution of their authority, it was now while they were without a family head to fill Owen Waymar's place as Sire.

So she poured herself over the Tributes first. Reading each line in detail, she refused to allow herself to be distracted until Riva arrived in the evening. When she did, she arrived with even more reports from the stewards and their houses. There was so much work to get caught up on. Work that if left alone, Riva would have been expected to fulfill on her own. She was excited at first to see Pinella had come to the Lower City. But then she showed her concern.

"My Lady, you shouldn't be here. The city is still in mourning, and you can't worry on civil affairs during a time like this."

Pinella was touched by Riva's concern but also frustrated because she brought Pinella's own hurt back into focus for a moment. "It's okay. I find this to be—"

"My Lady, this is not where you should be right now."

Pinella took a moment for Riva to calm down before starting again.

"Riva, I want you to call me Pinella. You can save all that formality for the Waymars." She had to raise her hand so that Riva wouldn't interrupt again. "I lived in confinement in the River District a few short months ago, whoring myself out for enough to pay my debts to this court. Debts that I didn't even acquire. My only living hope, my will to survive, was my son. My desire was that my family would live without that debt . . . that shame. Now, my son is gone. I do not need a servant . . ." Pinella stopped speaking even though she felt her heart screaming the rest: *I need a friend.*

She couldn't speak that, because that was where all the pain and tears were. So, Pinella stood there looking at Riva, letting her lip quiver, hoping that Riva could hear what her own heart was screaming. She waited not for the obedience of a servant, but the willingness of a friend. Riva was slow in responding. That was okay, because Pinella was feeling relieved to have confessed some of what had plagued her.

"I don't know what to say . . . except that I was relieved to see you here. I thought all the Waymar affairs were left for me to manage."

"Let's start with the Aspins." Pinella's suggestion made Riva smirk.

"That woman has kept things in line for me out here."

Pinella wondered which one of the Waymars had come to govern without her noticing.

"Which woman?"

"The Aspin woman."

"Greyah Aspin?"

Riva pointed to the stack of letters that Pinella had been swimming in all evening. "Greyah informed me of many of the other stewards' dealings. She has much insight in the Lower City. She serves as steward to the Waymars, but she is not a vassal like most of the stewards. The Aspins don't accept any aid from the Waymars, but they always pay their Tributes without fail." Pinella was unconvinced. That was hard to believe.

"What do you mean 'any aid'?"

Riva responded wordlessly and Pinella questioned further, "How can they go without any aid? How do they protect their holdings outside the city?"

"I don't know, but they've managed. They've managed better in the last several years than any of the families their size — and some larger. I found a correspondence between Lady Waymar and Grayah's father about a formal rise in social standing."

"Seems fitting. Why weren't they elevated?"

"Grayah's father fell ill around the time that Lord Waymar's cousins were defeated by the rebels. Most civil matters were slowed at that point. The Waymars concentrated everything into the war effort."

Pinella thought the family was sure to be hiding something.

"Riva, do you remember what Greyah told us when we met her? I asked her about the men in her family, and she told us why the men hadn't consigned to the war effort."

Riva showed her lack of memory then spoke after a facial spark of realization. "She said they had to bring in the harvest . . . Their primary income are their bakeries throughout the upper and lower cities." Even as Riva spoke, she herself didn't sound convinced. "Do you think they're hiding something?"

"If they are, we will keep it hidden until we decide it doesn't benefit us as much in the dark." Pinella hadn't conceived the words that she spoke. They simply came together. She hadn't ever considered herself separate from the Waymars in any way. Now she was keeping their business to herself. It helped that Riva agreed so heartily.

The woman immediately went to her own workspace and resumed her response letters, leaving Pinella to wonder to herself if the Aspins were criminals. Were they? why didn't she rush off to tell the Waymars? If she was going to tell them, it could wait a few days until she went back to the Upper City. The ladies Waymar were too steeped in tragedy to deal with something like this anyway. She wasn't bothered, though. Why wasn't she offended, hurt by their betrayal of the city? She had time to think about how she felt. What did all of this mean for Pinella?

Pinella had been slightly disobeying Octvia's poorer judgments and often acted independently. Often it had to be done. Octavia had not visited the Lower City in months and was clearly misinformed, so Pinella had at times kept things from Octavia, but this seemed different. It was different. What if the Aspins were what they seemed to be?

.

CHAPTER TWENTY-EIGHT

THE WALK BY THE STREAM

FINNION

The house was small and plain, everything fitting to poverty.

"Is this the safehouse?" The old men looked confused at the three strangers who'd been following Finnion and Reff a moment before. The strangers shrugged, looking to one another for the meaning of Reff's question and not seeing it.

"It's my house, but you're never safe from some poor cooking and poorer company in here!" The other men laughed, a bald man drawing a ladle full of hot soup for his bowl.

Finnion and Reff took their turn to look at one another in confusion.

"I'm the loan man here in town. My friend gave you the job offer in Aldersyde . . . You did meet my friend in Aldersyde, yes?" asked the old man.

The tallest man turned to another, saying, "Strange looking bounty collectors to my mind." The man next to him, who happened to be the shortest one in the room, nodded, equally confused.

Reff and Finnion exchanged another glance, this time with more understanding.

"You work for Cuften Bander then?" asked Finnion.

"Who doesn't work for Bander around here? He eats a portion of everyone's meals from Bilton all the way to Vandt, I'm convinced. But I've heard his control of the South is growing all the time. Have soup. You both look awful." The old man extended two steaming bowls. They took the bowls, still trying to fill in the grand stretch of confusion. Finnion realized his heart was still thumping from the anticipation of a fight moments before. They took the bowls from the man.

"I'm Benneck. These are my associates," he said, pointing to the three men. "Tall man's Elton, short one's Wynter, and the bald one had his ears and scalp taken by a man in the South. He's a Galanoan. We call him Quiet, because he is." The men nodded at the mention of their own names. Finn and Reff just stared at all of them, filling their mouths with soup.

"I'm Finnion, and this is Reff," he said, nodding in return.

"Well, when I heard you both were coming, I prepared a place for each of you to sleep." Benneck stood and opened the door to a room adjacent. "Thank you, boys. I'll see each of you at sunrise," he said, dismissing the three men with a tossed silver coin to dismiss each man. After they left, Benneck shut and locked the door. "I'm sorry for all that confusion. None of them know about my work for the Lark. Actually, only two people in Harmony-Ford know. Both of them also work for the Lark. Those three are all good hands, though. They collect debt that goes unpaid for too long." The old man blew out most of the oil lamps, leaving the one near Reff and another near where Benneck sat down. He sighed, then spoke, "So, how was the way coming?"

They hesitated, then Finnion gestured to his wounded leg, "It would've been much easier had my leg been well."

"Hmm . . . A walking journey with a wounded leg. I commend you and sympathize. I know that had to have been an effort." Benneck lit a tobacco pipe and vented huge puffs of gray smoke. "So I hear you are Shrikes. This is true, yes?" Reff nodded honestly and

Finnion lied his agreement. "Well that's not much, but it is a start."
He took another smoke. "So much has changed in the South since
the rebellion began. I'm sure both of you know that here in the
Southern Territory of Trofaim is where the whole thing started.
Actually, the Highwater Rebellion had its roots here as well."

"Really?" asked Reff, astounded.

"Yes! But not in Harmony-Ford. Both rebellions can be traced
back to Bilton, south of here." Finnion knew all of this, of course,
having built the second rebellion out of the remains of the first
one. He still pretended to be interested to learn new things right
along with Reff. "The Lark was a name for a man who worked for
Akten Tro-Bennault before he was assassinated in the East. After
that, the same people who killed Bennault set a trap for the Lark,
but he eluded capture and remained anonymous." Reff's chest began to move more rapidly with his breathing at the mention of his
grandfather.

That was good, Finn thought. The young man kept that knowledge to himself. His father no doubt would've said knowledge is
power.

"Later, when the Highwater Rebellion began to heat up, the
Lark made it possible for Cazprien, the rebel chief, to remain
anonymous as well. Trofaim has had dozens of small rebellions,
but both the Highwater Rebellion and Cazprien's Rebellion were
made possible by the Lark." Finnion noticed Reff calm down. No
doubt Reff would've been very shocked to know his own father
had led the Highwater Rebellion, and that he, Reff's companion,
was the rebel Cazprien. Both born of a rebel and accompanied by
one, all unbeknownst to the staunch patriot of Trofaim.

"Who led the Highwater Rebellion?" asked Reff, leaning forward in his creaking chair.

"Many say Cazprien led both. This may be fact, since their

organization is the same. The way the fighting improved against the Wing suggests that he learned from his mistakes." Benneck sipped on a silver flask before sucking his pipe again. "But what was most interesting is how well Cazprien used the Lark against Trofaim. He did it so well, it was as if he knew who the Lark was. Since the Battle of Brierly, all the Larks are much less trusting of each other, each one suspicious of the next. With a single battle, Cazprien leveled the strongest army in Trofaim and turned all the leaks against each other, compromising the trust we had gained in Trofaim. It's as if Cazprien knows Trofaim better than the Shrikes did."

Finnion smiled on the inside at his own accomplishments. His only error was trusting the greedy men around at the time. Looking back now, it wasn't pride that brought him down in the end. Though he had been prideful, it wasn't greed or impatience. It was his loneliness that made him include the wrong people in his doings. They may have been evil company, but Finnion could remember that painful loneliness in the wake of his wife's death. It forced a young widower to reach out for companions.

"It's not an unreasonable thought. Many of the men from the Highwater Rebellion also helped lead Cazprien's. Elmo Deep is famous for betraying the Songbird Army in the middle of battle. He was he first traitor to the Shrikes."

"Who is Cazprien?" Reff asked. Finnion closed his eyes as they rolled back in his head.

"If we knew who he was, there would be no rebellion," chuckled Benneck.

"What is the state of the rebellion now?" asked Finnion.

Benneck shrugged and smoked. "Many of us have cut off our communication with that informant for fear that he's a traitor."

"Do you know who the Lark's informant was within the rebels?"

Benneck shook his head again. "I know of a few members of our guild. The man in the rebels is exceedingly dangerous to talk to. All evidence points to the fact that he was speaking to Cazprien."

That disappointed Finnion. He wanted so very badly to know who among his men was speaking to his enemies. It would almost be worth it, he thought, to only ever get vengeance against that one traitor.

"So much has changed. As soon as the Wing was broken, the rebels set their eyes on the Fork Region of the river surrounding the city. With the Wing destroyed and the rebels tightening their grip on the city, bandits blow through, stealing and killing whatever they like. These bandits caused the region to hire Cuften Bander to impose mercenary law."

Finnion knew the reference but saw that Reff was confused at the term. "What is mercenary law?" he asked so that the young man could keep his pride.

"Usually a last resort, mercenary law is when a nation must hire a foreign army to instill order in absence of the army or other keepers of justice. Rumeneddan cities used mercenary law when the capital city was besieged by the old monarchy."

"And how has it been under mercenary law?" asked Reff.

"For towns like Harmony-Ford, it's hard. Taxes are unreasonable, food is scarce, and anyone with Cuften's mark can take whatever they like. So people often hide what they have with little motivation to sell goods due to the threat of having their goods claimed by Bander's men. I haven't been to any other city in years, so I can't speak on that. As for the smaller towns and villages, you saw Aldersyde . . ." Benneck sighed and shook his head. He had a distant, troubled look on his face. "You must revive the Songbird

Army if we are to be free of this cloud of war."

"That is my only goal!" Reff spoke from his chest. "To rebuild what the rebels can never destroy!" Finnion was stirred by Reff's emotions. No doubt he was righteously passionate, but the nobles of Trofaim had not been. Finnion didn't leave a single brick atop the other when he was their adversary. Now this old man was putting too much faith in Reff, who put too much faith in this old spy. Both of them were short on allies and wanted by their numerous enemies. They were now overjoyed to make an ally, even though it was exceedingly more dangerous.

As Finnion thought more and more, he realized, of all the men in Trofaim, Finn himself was the kid's greatest and most dangerous ally. If any of the rebel generals knew about Reff, they would send force certainly, but if they knew Finnion was down here helping the Shrike, they wouldn't rest until they knew he was dead. They would probably even send the Yilian. The thought of Berrick killing his oldest friend flashed back into his head. His jaw clenched tight as barrel bands. His hands clutched with white knuckles. They all had mocked him, using Finnion's pride to make him weak. But Jonas had meant it. It was the first time Finnion considered the reality that Jonas really saw him as a king. He could feel tears stinging his throat and eyes.

Finn wasn't listening to Benneck and Reff anymore. He had a truly great ally in Blakes. Felix, Elmo Dccp, and Dan Gabion must've orchestrated the betrayal. What hurt Finnion more than anything was knowing that Jonas Blakes' greatest weakness was the admiration he had for Finnion. That was the weakness that got him in the end. Finnion's head filled his heart with silent promises to kill those seven treacherous men.

Both Benneck and Reff ended their conversation and succumbed to the exhaustion of the day before. Finnion stayed up though, forcing himself to remember each traitor. He pictured their faces in the low embers of the fire. Elmo Deep and Berrick sparred together. He hoped they were practicing their sword work. Soon enough they'd need every moment of that practice. He saw the Greenan, who led Childress and Gilmor laugh in those last moments. Felix's face popped up, always studying, always prepared. He remembered Jentree spitting on Jonas' body after Berrick killed him. He cycled again and again through the faces of his enemies. The pain of Finnion's leg was lost in the great pain of his heart that night.

CHAPTER TWENTY-NINE

THE HOCKLEETS

REDEYE

Karrick kept smiling at Redeye knowingly. Redeye hated it. The man was the source of a great deal of discomfort as they met with the rest of Gallo's militia. It was strange, meeting with this many old warmen from his past. Men he thought he'd killed with men he knew he killed. Redeye had always looked for the fight, but here, he wondered how so many men could align after they'd all fought each other in the past.

He saw men who'd come fresh from Kalesia to aid Tork. They were wrapped in their fancy armor, all clean and shiny like they were off to some parade in the North. They all were uneasy seeing men of Galanoa armed with ferocity and hard, eager looks rather than heavy weapons and arms.

One man, whom Redeye thought might've been called "Big Crooked," only carried a long, rough halberd that was more of a war axe on a shaft that stood as tall as he was. He eyed some dandy he'd picked for a rival among the Kalesians. If the Kalesian had ever been in a battle, he didn't show it. His armor didn't have a single scratch on it. His face was crammed with daring snarls and hatred. Redeye didn't know this Kalesian, but any man would be wise to avoid scrapping with Big Crooked. If he would've had armor, it would have been scratched and scraped to no end. But

Crooked didn't have armor and his face had scars from a dozen evil strifes. The man's reputation was widely known too.

Redeye wondered if anyone knew his name or stories. Likely most of them just knew him as "Man Without an Eye." Most of the warriors who would've known him weren't in this group, but he felt more comfortable among the angry crowd of warriors.

As they gathered around the place that had been the scene of Tork's death, where Cicero had killed him and his men, Yellowtooth stood there with his killers, all of which were named for their violence or other actions. Like Redeye, they let their names be forgotten so their reputation might be known. For some men, their reputation did the threatening for them. Those men like Crooked and Yellowtooth had the personal history that deterred young warriors from trying something stupid against them. Others like Tork and Cicero were so known for their actions that it took an army or a man made of cold steel to take a chance at one of them. But of that class of killer, only Gallo Bloodway remained whom many would say was the most feared.

Redeye looked down at Tork, the legendary soldier from Kalesia who was the last great ally to join Cicero and the Hockleets in freedom. Everyone who knew the two men spoke of the great irony of it. "The women will sing about this one in their dances for fifty years," said a Galanoan, his men agreeing with him. Nobody had to take command or give orders before men began to gather around their old chief. Men who weren't in the wars gathered with men who followed Tork, adopting the chief as their own. Redeye was happy to be free from all the food chain squabbles and fighting for a leader's approval. He'd followed Cicero because he'd been given no choice. Having to work for the man who paid his guild was law in Hocklee, and he improved because of it. Redeye would miss following a truly good man, but at least he was independent.

"Where's the Hood boy?" came a gruff old voice replete with phlegm. Redeye turned to see Yellowtooth's gaping smile. He was no longer worthy of the name Yellowtooth — now his teeth were brown and broken. Yellowtooth was famous for leading a large portion of Cicero's Hockleets.

"He jumped over a cliff into the river. Must've been his end."

Yellowtooth let the smile slide off his head, somehow becoming less ugly. He looked around the varied company a moment before leaning in to whisper, "Did us all a favor before he went though, huh? Tork would've slowed everything down with his preaching of fairness and traditions. Better to follow Gallo and get it over with." Yellowtooth looked around at the crowding Kalesians and added, "Might let us get some fancy armor too." He winked after that, bringing that big ugly mouthful of teeth into that infamous smile.

Redeye was made uneasy at that. Was he somehow eager to fight Kalesia? That had been little better than going to war with the monarchist in Redeye's mind.

"Glad to have you though, Redeye," Yellowtooth put a skinny arm around Redeye's shoulder, his hand with dirty fingernails inches from Redeye's face. "Bloodway's gathering my friends, few as they are, together with all my enemies, who are as numerous as the trees in Hocklee." Redeye followed Yellowtooth's deadly stare across the clearing where Crooked stood, his men gathering around him. Crooked stared back at his old enemy. The two men had been personal enemies as long as Redeye had been alive.

Redeye felt a shiver creep down his back as Crooked and his men took note of Redeye standing with Yellowtooth and, all at once, he knew what made Cicero a loner.

"I trust you'll follow as loyally as always, Red!"

Redeye felt his stomach drop as one of Crooked's men with a wolf pelt over one shoulder smiled at him and Yellowtooth patted his back. In those few moments with so few words spoken, he was back among the conflicts.

Chapter Thirty

Welcome Distractions

Pinella

The walk to the Upper City was getting colder and Pinella saw fewer people making the trek through the orchard and up the steps. She couldn't help but that she had to make them more often. With the Waymar women forced to take on all the responsibilities of Owen and each of his Chargers, Pinella was forced to keep the communication strong between the vassal families of the Lower City and the Waymars in the upper.

She was happy to at least have Riva with her. Every time Pinella went alone, she was always stuck in her own painful feelings. The younger woman always reminded her to stop in the River District to check on her father's apple tree and to stop for food. Riva was always interested in the porches and the people there. Always finding People she knew, she would take time to speak and listen to their families. The poor families that she befriended always had small personal gifts of food or blankets to give her. The porches were fuller now than they had been in years. Like the rest of Trofaim, refugees had come here out of fear of the rebellion and it's growing strength. These were the families who couldn't afford to rent in the city.

Pinella was watching the river slowly roll under the canopy of fruit trees from her seat on the tavern veranda. She had never been able to afford a drink from this tavern until she knew the owners. She sat with a steaming cup of tea under a blanket, watching the refugees conduct their affairs. This late in winter, the bells were beginning to fall and the impoverished paced underneath the huge trees, looking for any fallen bell they could find. In the short time that she sat outside the tavern, Pinella had counted eight individuals coming to present a bell in exchange for some grain or oil. Pinella made sure the owner gave what was fair for their harvests. It took everyone's participation in hard times like these if they were going to survive as a city.

Riva returned with a basket of gifts veiled under a rag. "How's the tea today?"

Pinella looked down at the cup of honeyed pine needle tea that somehow helped stave off heartache and shame. "It's warm. Should we be going back up?" Pinella stood up, leaving the fur blanket she'd hid under for the past hour.

"Yes. I think we should. I have kept you long enough, and Lady Waymar will be expecting you."

When they neared their arrival, Pinella felt all the emotions threatening her. The Waymar house was the saddest place in Trofaim with its lack of decor and color. It blended into the dead winter landscape around. She almost wanted to turn around.

"I'll go in and report to Hess. Show Octavia the Lellin family appeals first. I changed her letters so that the vassal families wouldn't know we acted independently of Octavia. Their disputes with the other stewards have grown considerably and our latest dealings have helped ease tension. She'll want to see that and should be pleased. I have my journals so will be working on the Tribute payment reports for you."

Pinella just shook her head. The woman was better than if Pinella could multiply herself.

"You are not working for Hess any longer. Instead, tell Hess that I want another desk in my room. I want the servant's bed replaced with a normal one. That's where you'll stay from now on. No more wasting time cleaning while you're here."

"But shouldn't you ask Octavia?" Riva looked confused.

"No, I need someone who knows how I like my tea." Pinella didn't smile back at Riva. "Let's finish those minor crimes reports this evening." Pinella made her way in. She always expected the home and family to begin its course back toward normalcy, but every time she came back from the Lower City it was quiet and still. The huge dining rooms and spacious living areas were always vacant and clean, like nobody had occupied them in months. Riva remarked about how the house felt abandoned. Pinella knew it wasn't abandoned, but that the occupants had become hermits. The loud laughing personality of Owen Waymar was gone, along with Reff and all his youth. Strange how great a hole one person can leave in their absence.

The first people she wanted to check in with were the wives and children. In their normal place above the dining room, Pinella could hear the children playing as she made her ascent toward the family room. When she opened the door, she saw the typical scene.

The youngest were with Livra, who loved the young babies. Having never mothered one of her own, she always looked closely after Karriana's two daughters, two-year-old Owella and Olanna who was not yet weened. She also rocked Kessa's youngest son Ogwin, who Pinella had heard was beginning to walk. While Livra watched those children, Karianna gave music lessons to her nephew Otrin. Pinella noticed Kessa's second oldest, Omera, sitting alone with a book. It didn't seem right to see the girl sitting alone. She would be thirteen years old soon and she was not get-

211

ting the attention a young woman needs. Her mother should have been her, or she should be with her mother, but Pinella knew Kessa Waymar would've been out with her gossiping friends already, drinking early in the day. The woman left her children to be raised by their aunts. Young Omera was a few years younger than Pinella was when she lost her father, and her mother was out playing.

"Hello, Pinella," said Livra, waking the child in her arms.

"Hello, ladies. Hello, children. How are all of you?"

Karianna stopped playing strings a moment to greet Pinella. "We manage . . . It's cold out but we make the most of the indoors with lessons and learning for the children."

Livra agreed. The baby she held began to cry.

"Is Lady Kessa home today?" Pinella knew she started something immediately. Kessa's sister wives began to voice a million frustrations before Livra paused so that Karianna could speak.

"She is never home! Her children have lost their father, and it's bad enough without their mother leaving them for social pursuits with young gossips. You came up with most of her friends. My mother never would've let me socialize with them. They're all treacherous and scornful women."

Pinella felt she'd made it worse by asking about the situation. The women had no inhibition against speaking poorly about Kessa in front of her adolescent children. Otrin, having been tutored in music by Karianna, had hard what was said of his own mother. Luckily Omera sat apart, her attention removed from the room.

"Perhaps she is with Octavia working in government among the Tribunal. Or with the allied families discussing policy." Pinella knew she was wasting breath trying to defend Kessa to the other two.

"She came in drunk last night. None of the women she befriends are married. They're all half her age!" Before Karianna could say more, Livra was handing her the crying child.

"Your daughter must be hungry."

Karianna handed the stringed instrument to her nephew Otrin so that she could nurse. When she prepared to nurse, though, Pinella couldn't help but notice that Karianna made no attempt to conceal herself. She noticed that Otrin failed to conceal his wandering eye as well, watching Karianna with an expression Pinall questioned. As this happened, Livra had the opportunity to speak her piece about Kessa.

"She's left the raising of her own children to us." Livra was clearly embittered by the pain of her own barrenness. Kessa's poor mothering clearly dug at her more because of it. A woman uncapable of baring her own children will despise the mother who fails to raise her own. Both of them were angry though. Pinella didn't feel their pain though. Her heart hurt for the children who were forced to listen to dissention of their aunts in the midst of tragedy. Owen had been a better father than husband, and the children lived in that reality more vividly than ever.

Of all the Waymar women, Octavia seemed to be the only one to truly mourn the loss of her brother. Owen's widows seemed to become unrestrained in their words now without him. Pinella knew that the family had to reunite. These women were raising the future of the family and Octavia and Kessa were managing its presence in Trotaim.

Pinella sought out Octavia. Her friend always knew what the family needed, and it needed leadership now more than ever.

The conference room was filled with scribes and counselors sitting around the long table, at the head of which Octavia sat rubbing her eyes with one hand. She should've been surrounded by family chargers and highly trusted stewards. Most of them had been killed in battle or were at home scrambling to keep their own affairs together. Every family close to the Waymars had lost several young men to the war, so scribes were promoted to counselors. Couriers were elevated to representatives. Competent leadership was scarce, and corruption was rising. Trust was spread thin and Octavia showed it in her exasperated expression. Relief softened her tired eyes when she noticed Pinella standing in the door.

"Pinella! I'm so glad your back! Please have a seat." Octavia gestured to a chair occupied by a twenty-something-year-old dark-haired counselor who barely made it as a courier. The young man reluctantly stood up and stood aside, looking betrayed. Pinella took the chair and sat down. Octavia ordered Hess, who stood nearby, to pour Pinella glass of the wine she hated passionately.

"Lady Octavia, I have a few things to request."

Octavia politely, but impatiently nodded for Pinella to voice her requests.

"Riva, the slave woman you've delegated under me, has been very useful to me in every way. If possible, I would like to ask for her as . . ." Pinella hesitated, feeling the collective attention focused on her. Maybe she should have brought this up at a different time. ". . . I was thinking she would help in many ways if she wasn't a slave."

"Would you like that I sell her to you? Because I would give you the woman." Octavia interrupted. Pinella hadn't thought it would come so easily, and relief washed over her. "I could free her, if you like." Pinella saw Hess turn her head in surprise. That had to hurt. To see a lowly slave girl freed while Hess had been an honorable servant to Octavia for so long must have stabbed. Pinella wasn't expecting this much favor with Octavia.

"Well . . ."

"No. I'll give her to you, then you can free her! She will love you forever. How does that sound?" Octavia smiled wide, having guessed Pinella's heart.

"Thank you, Lady W—" Octavia caught Pinella with a stirn lifted brow. "Thank you, Octavia." Her expression softened in response.

"Of course. You said there were more requests?"

Pinella had to strive to remember what other requests she had. "Yes. I wanted to ask for the right to entrust Riva with more responsibilities. She is very loyal and—"

"Done!" Octavia waved a hand to motion Pinella toward the next topic.

"I have been struggling between the upper and Lower City. With my attention split between our center and the stewards, I keep falling behind."

Octavia uncharacteristically stuck a hand up to silence Pinella. "How about this. You can send your woman as a trusted courier as well as an additional courier sent to you twice as often. As for you, Lady Pinella, you should be given the title of Ward, so that you will have charge over all the stewards. You have proved yourself, and more autonomy will alleviate your need to constantly go up and down." The position was a huge honor that usually belonged to a family member within the house. Owen's senior charger had always held the position. It was the third highest position in most families after the office of Tribune. But Octavia was Tribune, and soon she would be appointed Dame over the entire family, so it was unlikely for anyone to dispute her decision.

Octavia asked anyway. Looking around the table, she consulted them on her decision. "Pinella, you have been the best of my trustees, and in of the districts in your care, we have had best cooperation and least trouble. I'd love to be free of all the difficulties that come from managing the other stewards. Do any of you object to Pinella's being promoted?"

The other officials just looked on, maybe a little jealous. Pinella noticed now for the first time that everyone under Octavia feared her. It was hard to watch her lead like this. She had always been beloved and honored for her wisdom and care for each subordinate. Now, after Owen's passing, she dealt coldly with them. Authoritative was her demeanor, and Pinella felt the effects. Even Hess looked worried and unsure of herself.

Pinella thanked Octavia and the counsel.

"Of course. Now we really need to move onto the topic at hand."

"Of course." Pinella was settling in, having been shook up by so much promotion.

"The greatest issue we face right now is disloyalty to the republic. The Alcott family have put together a rear-guard action to slow the advance of the rebels while locals flee their looting. They have reported Morgimin Alcott is leading their Shrikes and household troops. He reported to the Tribunes that the Fowler's men somehow know all of his movements before he makes them, and that casualties are much higher than they should be. He suggests that the Fowler must have spies informing him on their movements. He reported that the rebels are too small and weak a force to defeat the Waymar army as completely as they did. He urges that our family and holding be investigated by the Tribunal for treasonous individuals."

Pinella nodded and waited for Octavia to proceed. She knew this had to be worse than it sounded so far.

"If we are investigated by the Tribunal, our holdings may fall under temporary governance of another family until we are vindicated. We simply cannot afford to forego payments of Tribute for what could take months. If they find anyone colluding with the rebellion inside our house, we may lose much of our ownership. Our name and standing would be greatly tarnished for at least a generation."

Pinella began to feel alone in the room. "They suspect me of collusion . . . don't they?"

"It's that Tribune Kellen Adhemar who suggested you be investigated. As soon as Alcott brought the issue before the Tribunes, he made a case against you."

"What did Fabrien say?" Pinella regretted asking as soon as she did.

Octavia looked slightly puzzled. "He wasn't in attendance. I'm not sure who his delegate was, but no one outside the Waymars and our allies objected."

"I see."

After the meeting was over, Pinella requested a private conversation with Octavia. She seemed more depressed and exhausted in her demeanor. The weight of responsibility and loss was setting in on her. Pinella felt for her friend. She had been able to occupy herself with work and Waymar affairs, but for Octavia, Waymar affairs must have been a constant reminder of what she lost.

She pinched the bridge of her nose, closed her eyes, and breathed. "Pinella, I feel like I'm fighting the inevitable. It's like I'm arguing with sun about its setting. I now suspect that other families are attacking us politically while we're weak."

"What families? I don't understand how any distinguished family could accuse yours after all you've sacrificed for the city. But you can investigate me, Octavia . . . It makes sense that they would suspect me."

"Pinella . . ."

"No. My husband was a rebel. It's best if you hire someone from a neutral family so that the Tribunes don't question their findings . . . They won't find anything."

"Of course they won't. Your son is a patriot. He died fighting to stop the Fowler. It's foolishness. It's evil that they would accuse you colluding with the ones who he fought." Octavia was working her own frustration into resentment. "Plenty of families would like to force us to sell our holdings and increase their own control over more of the city. Our allies have begun distancing themselves. Soon they will open talks with other upper nobles." Octavia lost control of her quivering lip. When she spoke again, her voice broke. "I wish Owen were here."

Pinella didn't hesitate to embrace Octavia to provide what comfort she could. Pinella wanted to talk about her son and how much she missed him too. She wanted to share the pain with Octavia, but she couldn't. She had to avoid it all.

"It's going to be okay. I welcome the investigation, and I will keep the stewards in order while you sort affairs. Octavia, your family needs your attention." Pinella avoided the urge to accuse Kessa of her shortcomings as a mother.

Octavia sighed. "What do I do? All three of my sisters-in-law argue so much, I sometimes wonder if they'd care if their children's name and inheritance was forfeit as long as they could win their arguments."

"That's exactly why they need you! Losses of wealth and honor are nothing compared to the loss of your family. The Waymars can always regain strength, but your family must remain united."

Octavia acknowledged Pinella's point. "It's Kessa, isn't it? Is she drunk?"

"I don't think she's home. Ogwin is three years old. He needs his mother."

"All three of them do. She was a much better mother when Otrin and Omera were young. I'm not sure when she left their raising to Karianna."

"Karianna is more attentive to Otrin's needs. Livra takes care of Karianna's two. Omera is being left out."

Octavia searched the room for an idea. "Should I bring her with me? I could teach her Tribunal politics."

Pinella disagreed. "Let her come with me and Riva. I think she likes numbers. She can meet the stewards, and I'll have Riva teach her to be a courier. It will be good for her to come away."

"Okay . . . Take care of her, and hire a guard."

Chapter Thirty-One

The Debt Collector

Finnion

The next morning, Benneck was up early. The old man's cooking and talking to himself is what woke Finnion. Reff awoke a moment later. The warm smell was good in the cold morning air of the house. Finnion's leg throbbed with pain and his throat was raw from breathing in the cold. "That soup smells nice!" his voice called out, hoarse and quiet.

"Good!" said Benneck, realizing his guests were awake. "It usually smells better than it tastes!" He chuckled to himself as if he made his soup to taste bad on purpose. "Young Lord, would you get the door please?"

Reff looked confused, getting to his feet. A moment before he reached the door, a knock came at the other side. "CLOCKWORK!" Benneck exclaimed. Reff opened the door to reveal the bald man who they said had no tongue. He nodded to Reff and came in.

"Here's your soup, Quiet!" Benneck handed the bald man a steaming bowl with a sheaf of papers, "These are the people who have requested a loan." Quiet took the two papers with a nod of his earless head. After a moment to get a spoon for his soup, Quiet left as abruptly as he'd come. "Always on time, that man." Benneck served both Reff and Finnion each a piping hot bowl of their own.

"This soup is really good!" said Reff.

"Yes, it is," Finn agreed.

"Why do you say it's so bad?" Benneck rolled his eyes and picked his pipe out of a coat pocket. "Anything is good to the hungry stomach," he said, lighting the pipe's contents with the flame under the soup cauldron. "It's a fact that you can't have many possessions in a little house, but you can warm up a little house with a small fire!"

Finnion noticed the cabin was much warmer since the old man started the cookfire.

Another knock came at the door, this time to Benneck's surprise. "Who could that be?" He walked over and looked through a window to see who it was. "Ah. Elton is even earlier than usual." The door opened to reveal the tall, long-haired man they'd seen the night before. Elton also took a bowl of soup, but rather than taking it with him, he sat carefully at Benneck's small table.

"You're extra early this morning, Elton," said Benneck, "I know it's not the soup that brought you."

"No! Absolutely not for the soup!" Elton turned to Finnion. "Can I interest you in a story?"

Finnion thought about that for a second. "Well, why not?" he said, shrugging.

"No, no. You're not that early!" said Benneck before Elton could speak. "If you wanted to tell us one of your stories, you should've started last night!"

Elton laughed, set his spoon down, and held the bowl up to his mouth to drink the soup. Finnion watched as he downed it like a glass of cool water.

"A story later then!" He smiled at both Reff and Finnion and left, shutting the door behind him.

"That soup must've burned," said Reff.

"Yes, but bitters are best swallowed whole, I find." Benneck replied.

"You know, your soup really is very good," said Reff, presenting his bowl for a second helping.

"You can skip the formalities; it doesn't matter to me as long as my guests don't go hungry." Benneck pulled the ladle out to test the soup's flavor. His face wrinkled as if he smelled a rotten wound. "You two must be starving!" The old man shook his head in disbelief as they ate the soup. "At any rate, this business of giving out and collecting loans is the way I've paid for so many of the Lark's efforts here and in the surrounding areas."

Oh, what Finnion would've given to torture this man a few months ago. Now he was a good a shot as Finnion seeing the same kind of revenge against his traitors.

Benneck went on to talk about how the Highwater Rebellion raised many more soldiers but didn't have the leadership of the current rebellion. "Cazprien was an influencer of crowds. Somehow he motivated thousands to fight without giving a speech or showing his face." The old man pulled out a stash of dry meat and took a bite. "By the time he started this current effort, his infrastructure was impenetrable. Not a single member of his elite staff ever gave him up."

Finnion was careful to select men who already had riches and power. Those men, he theorized, wouldn't be satisfied with anything but leadership of Trofaim. He turned out to be very right. So right, in fact, that they took his own position from him.

"He picked loyal men, huh?" asked Finnion as he tried to get every last drop of soup.

"Oh yes!" said Benneck. "In fact, they were so loyal that—" Just then, a knock at the door interrupted Benneck. "That must be Wynter," he sighed in disappointment. "Behind schedule as usual." Benneck opened the door for the third time that morning. "You're late," he said to Wynter, who still had sleep lines on his face, his hair standing off the side of his head at a weird angle from where he'd laid on the pillow.

"Yes, but earlier than usual!" said Wynter, grinning.

"Come on in. Get some soup and take it to work." Benneck ladled up another portion of soup.

"Thanks, boss. Where am I headed today?" asked Wynter.

"Over to the Eastern piece. Make sure the Velby family doesn't try to leave town without telling Quiet."

"Of course. Is that all?" Wynter asked as Benneck handed him the bowl of soup.

"Watch the gambling rooms for our clients. I've heard a rumor some of them have been breaking the rules."

"Pay it back as soon as possible and use it only for what it's requested for," said Wynter, blowing a spoonful of hot soup. He began to sit down when Benneck slapped his ladle on the table.

"You're already late, Wynter. Get on!" And Wynter stood up, took his bowl, and made for the door. "You better be on time tomorrow!"

"Oh, don't worry. I'll be early!"

"And bring my bowl back!" called Benneck after him. He shut the door and returned to the table. "Lazy sloth never brings my bowls back." He came back and sat in his place across the table from Reff and Finnion. "You both see how I run our little front? This is how I've served my state so many years, and they don't even know my name. Heh heh heh!" Benneck loved his own obscure humor. "This is how I've never been caught. I made my place in the town as an old miser. Anything patriotic or generous I do, I've kept in secret."

Finnion cleared his throat of its dry morning feel. "You've never been suspected?" he asked.

"I've been suspected of being a rebel supporter, but never a loyalist of the state."

That must have surprised Reff because he sat forward and asked, "No one has ever opened a letter of yours or gone through your possessions?"

"Absolutely!" Benneck smiled. "But I never use written letters. My possessions do not accurately reflect my alignment. The most dangerous thing I have is my relationships. This is why we all lost decades of trust when the Wing fell. Someone, or several some-ones, helped the rebels." Benneck let out a long sigh. "Make no mistake," he said soberly, "if I weren't so desperate in these dark times, I wouldn't have so readily trusted you." He took another bite of jerky.

"What is your plan to move forward?" asked Reff. "How can we help your efforts to reunite the Larks?"

"I've been thinking on that ever since I sent for you two." He lowered his voice. "I think it's best if you both work for me for a time. It's best, I think, if we clear your name and stage your deaths. The Shrikes weren't popular in the South to begin with." Finnion gave that look to say *I told you so*. Reff just glared with some malice and tried to ignore the affront to his pride.

"But these people surely will welcome one who brings things back to normal," Reff submitted halfway, trying to convince himself.

"There is a reason rebellions are born here in the South, Young Lord. The *Shrikes*," he said with a sarcastic flourish, "used the land and extorted the people for their political gain in Trofaim." Benneck shook his head. "The rebels have brought hardships in abundance, but they do it with the promise that they'll bring a greater future at the end of it all."

Finnion remembered spreading the word throughout the countryside, saying, "These are the labor pains necessary to bring a rebirth." He first stamped out small tyrannies in throughout the South for the purpose of raising funds to hire mercenaries to secure the South while he focused on the Wing. "A shift of loyalty must first take root and be given time to weaken the common opinion of the rebel Cazprien."

"We don't have time!" Reff exclaimed abruptly. "We cannot waste moments that the rebel army uses to prepare to take the city. It may already be too late!"

"My boy. My boy," Benneck said with a soothing tone. "It won't be done in a week. This uprising is generational." Reff's face softened at that. "The only thing you can do in a rush is get yourself killed."

"There must be something we can do to keep out the rebels now." Reff was almost asking the question rather than convincing himself.

"There is," said Finnion, his voice still hoarse in the morning. Both Benneck and Reff looked at him expectantly. "Defeat them in battle," he said solemnly. The look on Benneck's face showed his agreement. Reff did not understand. "Reff, they plunged confidently down the hill at Brierly. The commander didn't send scouts or make any attempt to surround them."

"The commander did what he thought was right!" Reff was becoming defensive of the man responsible for his near-death experience. "He saw what seemed like a rare opportunity and took a risk."

"And why can't you learn from his failure?!" All at once, Finnion let all of the anger out that had been building up over the days he spent with the ignorant noble. Reff just stared, shocked at Finnion's frustration. "You want so badly to make the same noble,

foolish error to end the war with a single battle! War is many battles won. The man who stakes an entire war on one battle is easily
beaten. It is him that lacks the greatest weapon. King Barrence II
said, 'War is waiting and patience is the almighty tool of it.' Rush-
ing to fight your enemy without learning from your loss is fatal. A
single loss contains the insights for a hundred victories." Finnion
looked to Benneck's surprised and thoughtful face, then back to
Reff's own wounded expression. "Forgive my emotion. Instead
of being lured into attacking them without strength, you may be
able to draw them to attack you. They may think you weak and
weaken themselves unknowingly."

Benneck slowly nodded in agreement, taking a slow drag from
his pipe. "You make an interesting point, eh . . . What was your
name?" he asked through a long, smoky exhale.

"It's Finnion," he said, still feeling the pride of being right. No
doubt it was that same pride his generals used against him. No
man stays with someone who turns everything into a contest.

"I knew you would be a powerful ally," said Reff.

"A what?" Finnion was suddenly confused.

"You've shown yourself astute. Your brain is sharp. All of this
was invisible for my pride." Reff took a deep breath. "I aim to re-
deem the Shrikes, not repeat their tactics."

Finnion noticed Benneck taking care to study him. Benneck
looked at Finnion, trying to see deeper into him as Benneck
puffed hot, dry smoke into the air between them. Reff seemed to
be reaching an unprecedented depth of thought. No doubt he was
thinking of a way to kill the Fowler — to kill Finnion.

"First though," said Benneck with a new train of thought, "before we lay the groundwork for your plan, I have work for you
both."

Finnion remembered what the men had said about them yesterday. "Debt collectors?" he asked, fanning down some of the stagnant smoke hanging unwelcome in the air over the table.

"Yes, but only in name. The men who you'll be collecting from aren't really in debt to me. They're members of the Lark." This man was full of surprises. "What you will collect is for you two."

Finnion and Reff looked at each other. "For . . . us?" asked Reff.

"Yes. I arranged for some funds to be raised for both of you. I assume you may have use for it." They both looked back at each other then back to Benneck, still at a loss. "Unless you haven't the need for it. In which case, I do, because getting any worthwhile amount from anyone right now is like trying to draw blood from a stone."

"No. Of course we need it," Reff said hastily. "You have our gratitude."

"And you'll have mine if you save us from the rebels. For the Larks, this is about survival." Benneck pulled up a local map. "Here is where you will meet the Larks, and I'm going to teach you how to confront them."

Chapter Thirty-Two

The Bloodway

Redeye

Cicero's dog was barking as she led the Hockleets toward their enemy. They squelched and slogged through soggy mud as they neared Hocklee. They could see smoke lifting from inside the walls on top of the green hill. Men who'd run for hours breathed harder, running faster, nobody running as fast as Cicero out in front.

"If . . . they got my daughter . . ." one Hockleet was saying to his partner. "I mean to say, if Gallo's there . . . then I want to be thorough." The two men switched knives as was their custom, nodding knowingly to each other. Vanno didn't want to think about what that could mean, or what it would mean for his mother if Gallo had already gotten into the city.

It was slow going and muddy, but Vanno had never seen anyone climb the Mudway as fast as they did that night. As they got higher up the hill, he started to notice the mud was mixed with blood. Some men's limbs turned red with gore as they climbed, their faces being painted with a familiar shade of brownish red. Vanno looked up from his muddy plight, seeing Cicero at the hilltop standing, watching. What was he looking at? What happened to Hocklee? Vanno fought his way up and tried to suck in enough air to soothe his burning lungs. It took a moment before it all made sense.

"Gallo drew us out," said Cicero, staring at the gore. "He knew I'd risk everything to end the conflict. But I would have never guessed he'd climb the hill so fast this time of year." Men were yelling all around as they crested the hill and invaded their own town, searching the small fortress for survivors. Searching for their families. A man next to Vanno vomited seeing so many dead, broken, and scattered bodies across the muddy street. Vanno took no time to process anything until he reached his home. He found his mother laying down, still breathing softly on the floor in their room.

"Mom?" He rushed to her side and put his hand behind her neck. "Can you hear me?" He looked down, noticing the blood on her in the darkness. He held his mother. He never had siblings or a father, but he had his mother who always told him she was proud of him. That was until he felt his mother breathe out her last breath. His tears began to roll down his face and onto hers.

Hocklee was quiet as men of different families gathered what they could and who they could. The only noise that came was from Cicero's dog as her continued barking echoed through the city. Cicero stood in that same spot now, but instead of facing toward the wrecked city, he was facing outward into the darkness down the hill. Vanmo walked up behind Cicero, covered in blood from the climb. Torches and firelight illuminated the bottom of the Mudway. Gallo's army, composed of thousands of Hockleets and their Galanoan allies, swarmed around the city at the bottom of the hill. "What do we do, Chief?" Vanno asked, tears still clouding both eyes.

Cicero spoke quietly, as if to himself, "He's got us . . ."

Gallo Bloodway walked through the assortment of soldiers in the clearing. Men stepped out of his path as he went. Men honored Tork for his honesty and tactics, but Gallo Bloodway was feared above man and monster alike. Redeye always thought it was because Gallo had no morality. He saw what Gallo fought against and what he used in fights, and it chilled him to the bone just thinking about it.

The man of Galanoa walked on, not challenging anyone. He didn't stare down his enemies like Yellowtooth and Big Crooked. Gallo just looked at the ground in front of him as he walked. The men from far away or those too young seemed confused as to who this was and why, out of all these hard men, he had to be the one to lead. Bloodway paid no attention to them or their murmuring.

Redeye recognized the only man to walk in step with Gallo. The switch known as his body trader. Jaco was the most famous switch in the South, and all the other switches worked for him. Both men wore black, but Jaco's garb was suited to a man of business and Bloodway had the clothing of a Galanoan rider.

"My ally, Callen Tork, is dead," said Bloodway, looking around at the gathered host for the first time. "For nine years he was my ally. He followed my command in this affair of the criminal, Cicero, who they call Hoodless. I will assume sole command of the militia, which will soon become a warband." Scores of men questioned each other at that. "I will not force any of you men of Kalesia to follow, but the Southern Nations of Alssae must be united in this."

Yellowtooth concealed a laugh. Redeye found Big Crooked and one of his old warriors to be smiling as well. They seemed to understand something Bloodway wasn't saying.

"Men of Hocklee, I understand many of you follow Bermand

Broadback. He plans to never allow Galanoa to have peace with Kalesia. As some of you may know, Aravaca will respond to these crimes of Cicero. Initially, they wouldn't hear Tork's requests for responsibility placed upon Cicero, so they demanded Tork bring the criminals to them for justice. They thought us to be divided and quarrelsome. They thought we wouldn't unite without being conquered."

"Kalesia won't be conquered! The South is King Leander's inheritance!" The man, whom he guessed to be a warchief of Kalesia, stepped out from among his armored men, many of them murmuring their agreements.

"But some of you would say the South is not a King's inheritance," Gallo shouted above the Kalesian warchief, "but that it is *our* inheritance. You of Galanoa follow the wardens who your fathers followed before you, as I was once a warden of these lands when it belonged to Galanoa. I wouldn't ask you to follow me because you owe me anything. I only invite the strong to follow. It shall be us, the strong, who unite the Southern States of Alssae." Of all the emotions in the crowd, confusion prevailed. Hundreds of men asked each other about his meaning. Gallo just looked at his hand for a moment as if he noticed an ingrown hair for the first time.

"Ready, boy?" came Yellowtooth's voice in his left ear.

"Ready for what?" asked Redeye, trying to read the old man's smile. Yellowtooth looked back out across the crowd. Redeye followed his gaze to Big Crooked, who looked back, nodding his head to Yellowtooth. Crooked's men were peering around just like Yellowtooth's were.

Bloodway spoke again, "I will follow Astro of Aravaca for the chance he gives to make Southern Alssae a sovereign nation if we fight to give him the North. You Galanoans of Bermand Broadback who would see the South united, who would have peace with Kalesia rather than continued war, show your weapons to me." All throughout the Galanoans, axes, maces, and crude spears went up overhead. Some men pushed at one another as they disagreed.

"Men of Kalesia! Servants of King Leander! If you would leave that stagnant service of a king who taxes your hard-earned money to put a sword in your hand and risk your life for his kingdom, lift that sword so that I may see it!" A little over half of the polished swords rose over the Kalesians. Again, discord rose up in the men at the shifting loyalty.

"To those who have not risen their weapon, I have told you I wouldn't force you to follow. But that does make you my enemy." At some unseen cue, Big Crooked, Yellowtooth, and all their men began lashing out at foreigners nearby.

Blood spattered into Redeye's face as a nearby man cut a nearby Kalesian across the throat. Soon, a Kalesian squared up to fight Redeye. The man came on with his sword, wielding it well. Redeye only had a crude short sword and not a scrap of leather to protect him. Yellowtooth and his men were lost in the murder, so he knew help wouldn't come from them. Unlike the others, he wasn't prepared for a battle. He kept dodging, giving ground, waiting for some impossible opening when he tripped over a body. He looked up, terrified. He held up the bad blade, feeling the need to do something as the Kalesian brought his sword high to chop down into him.

Before he could split Redeye's skull in two, someone grabbed the Kalesian's sword hand, holding it there. The Kalesian's eyes shut tight with pain as a dagger blade stuck out in front of his breastplate. Another Kalesian had killed him before he could kill Redeye. The man went on to kill others.

Redeye laid there a few moments as the killing went on. He

noticed Crooked and his men killing Galanoans all around them. As the killing slowed and men began to beg for another chance to follow, Bloodway called out, "I said I wouldn't make anyone follow. I'm not a king. So if you've had a change of heart, you may follow, but you shall follow the command of those who first raised their weapons. And all of you follow the command of the men of Hocklee." And at once, Yellowtooth's men and Crooked's men were yelling like they were in a battle charge. "Summon all those like-minded to our cause. All of you have allies and brothers and sons. Bring them up. In one week, we go to King Leander."

Everywhere, men began taking armor and weapons from the late joiners.

Redeye turned to see Yellowtooth's brown smile with a voice that was just as dingy. "Hear that, Red?" he rasped. "We're in charge."

Chapter Thirty-Three

The Lead

Redeye

He was starting to feel alone with these men. Redeye had never been in charge before. Not really. He had a few men that minded his say back in the wars, even a few followed for a time, but nothing like this. Redeye looked back over his group of men and tried to keep that knot out of his stomach. He let his eyes wander over what Yellowtooth had said was ten-dozen men. In Alssae, men called that a warscore. Some of them were as old as Tork and older, a few as young as Hezro, the youngest Hockleet. Yellowtooth had given him twenty-six Hockleets to help him lead, seventeen of which followed Cicero back in the wars, eighteen if you count Hezro, who carried messages for Cicero as a boy. Rector, who Redeye trusted most of all, always stayed quiet nearby. Rector and Redeye had once been close, and he found himself building trust with the man again, almost overnight amidst all the foreign killers.

"Redeye. Yellowtooth says he wants your men to go first." He knew the man who had approached him as Igoss, one of Yellowtooth's voicemen. "Bloodway sent his man, Gorring, who will go second with a warscore of line breakers, and then the boss himself goes last with the most men where he's expected least." Igoss's face had no emotion to it at all.

"Fine with me." Redeye looked back to all men starting to look curious, ready to get orders after waiting and polishing the same weapons all morning. Igoss's presence was unmoved. He stood there scratching his nearly bald, stubbly scalp for loose skin and checking his fingernails for findings.

"Is that all?" Redeye had let pointless anger cook up all morning and found the voiceman's blankness unsettling.

Igoss leaned in close so only Redeye would hear. "Yellowtooth wants me to kill Zifix."

Redeye jerked back, looking at the man accusingly, but Igoss still gave no emotion. "No Galanoan kills his ally in battle. Who does he take me for?"

"We haven't been Galanoans since we joined forces to kill the Hood. Now we're all just men of the South. Galanoans and Kalesians can die with their old ways. Bloodway's bringing in a new way."

"Yellow always has someone he can't trust, but what'd Zifix do?" Redeye knew the company of Hockleets to be dangerous, but Gallo was making everyone into a murderer in his bloody sweep through Kalesia. Redeye understood them though. Yellowtooth was always about his old squabbles, bringing everyone around him into them. Here he had only a couple dozen veteran Hockleets who expected him to keep them alive, and here he was given fresh orders to kill one of them. Seemed just like Yellowtooth.

They'd been camped around a large, fortified city named Krahl. It had a large wall around a set of central towers that operated as shelters for locals and battle stations for soldiers in events like these. Most Kalesian settlements were designed with these garrisons so that a small force could repel a large army or sustain sieges until the royal army arrived. It should've made Bloodway's efforts take months while fighting reinforced armies, but unlike other invaders, the Hockleets were siege masters. Each of them had many lifetimes of siege experiences against the hardest fort in the South to take by siege.

For the last month, Gallo had raided the country and pushed deep into central Kalesia. There were five great cities to take, one of which being Kalesia, the capital city itself. First though, was Krahl, the most central city in the state of Kalesia. Bloodway often took forts as soon as he came to them. This quick paced warfare caused the Kalesian Army to move fast from one fortress to another, trying to come to battle with Bloodway's army. They were always moving too fast for him to fully take a small fortress. The Kalesian Army was somewhat small but among the highest quality in Alssae, second only to the Songbird Army. If they could bring the Southern Army to battle, with its divided ranks of Galanoan, Kalesian, and Hockleet forces, they would crush Bloodway's army. So Gallo outpaced them with less armor and better horses. But as fall gave way to winter, the army needed to find a defensive position before inevitably being caught by the Kalesians. Taking the city of Krahl was Yellowtooth's task he was given from Bloodway, so taking the wall and gaining access to the city was the task Redeye was given from Yellowtooth.

Igoss stepped back, watching Redeye. "I'll go with you, and you can help me get it done."

Redeye nodded, acting like he didn't care at all. Even though he did. Redeye didn't want to kill a Hockleet in this host of strangers, especially one so close to him after so many years fighting together. He couldn't help but think Yellowtooth sent Igoss to make sure Redeye got the job done.

How did he get back to being one of these treacherous men again so quickly? Hadn't he been riding against all these evil men to help Cicero save some children? Now he was back to stabbing his fellow men in the back for Yellowtooth. Redeye let out a disappointed sigh. This is what he was and all he could do is accept it. *No point in doing any more good,* he thought. Cicero had bought the guild on him and Redeye was indebted to him for it. Now he was riding for Yellowtooth again and that's where he belonged.

"Okay, it's time we took this place!" Men were grunting their agreements all around at the call. It startled Redeye to see his words spread through the crowd but he managed to keep the look of surprise off his face. Redeye turned to Rector. That man's look really was solid, which lended some mettle to Redeye's weak nerves. He needed it.

"Bring up Zifix."

Rector nodded, turning to get the man. Redeye cleared his throat and stepped up onto his horse, the same one Cicero had given him. All of a sudden, he realized he hadn't been given a horse before. The only horse he'd owned was the one he'd been arrested for stealing in Hocklee.

Most Hockleets were old Galanoans, which made them particularly good on horseback, but Redeye's mother was a Hockleet of Kalesian descent, so he was an average rider. Cicero had given him a horse despite the fact. He tried to tell himself he'd never wanted the horse, but he only told himself that because he never thought he'd have one of his own.

He remembered where he was, looking up from the white mare with black speckles to the soldiers returning his gaze. He weakly cleared his throat. Was he seriously about to cry at the memory of a dead man? No, Redeye's tears are of blood, not sorrow!

"Men of the South!" His throat burned as his voice felt like it might crack. "Some of you are from this town!" A dozen or so Kalesian men clapped their swords against their shields. "That means you know this place and you know a way in. What's more, you know how they may fight and what their strategies might be. All of you should know that if we do not take the fortress, then the Kalesian Army will fall on us with all its strength, our army crushed between them and those walls." Redeye swung his arm to point at the huge walls of the city. "We would be scattered and Aravaca would conquer this place, putting our towns to the sword and fire. Every last one. But if we unite the South in time to help them take the North, we will have forged a nation together!"

The words weren't magic. In fact, all he did was restate the plan Bloodway told them a couple weeks before, but the men roared like they'd never heard a plan like it. One might've thought Bloodway himself had made the call.

"Men who live here, your homes will be protected here. All else that doesn't join the South shall be taken by it!" Another cheer came from the gathered men, and they began to move. It was then he noticed Rector coming up with Zifix and Zeux. Redeye had never betrayed a man in battle. Somehow this is how he would play a part in uniting the Southern States. "Kalesians get in through these channels for water and the secret horse gates you've told me about." Redeye split the one-hundred-four Kalesian men into four groups of twenty-six, one for each secret passage into the city. "Hockleets! We will climb the walls!" The smallest group of men gave the morning's fiercest howls.

"But sir!" One Kalesian man local to the city raised his hand, looking confused. "The walls are ten strides tall; they've never been breached in our lifetime." The other Kalesians looked equally confused. Some of the Galanoans considered that as well.

"Do you hear that, Breachers of Hocklee? The men we're going to fight have never fought a wall breach in their lifetimes!" The wild Hockleets began to laugh. Igoss cracked a smile, trying to fit in but having no idea of the plan and experience Redeye was talking about. "You're about to learn of our skills in city-taking, friend! You just focus on getting them surrounded. I don't want to lose any good Hockleets because a Galanoan forgot how to swim!" A laugh rose up from the Hockleets at that.

"But," the man of Kalesia was stepping forward, his hand going up again. "You have no ladders or hooks, only some rope," he said, looking for some hidden secret.

Redeye was getting tired of being questioned.

"What's your name, Kalesian?" Redeye asked.

"Boban, sir," he said.

"You come with us, Boban, and we'll teach you what we've learned in our lifetimes."

Hockleets were cheering in agreement at that, clapping Boban on the shoulder.

"Call him chief, not . . . sir," said Heelix, the shortest of the Hockleets. Boban looked pale at the notion of being included in their impossible attempt, but Redeye looked at the walls around Krahl in the distance. Hockleet's walls were taller by half and on top of the green hill. Every one of these Hockleets had taken Hockleet before, some with Cicero's arrows snapping down at them.

"Whoever gets in first gets first take at whatever Governor Balt has stored away. Let's go!"

With that, men began to disperse and go to the places they'd chosen to get in through. Redeye found Igoss standing next to Zifix. Zifix didn't know what to expect. Men all around were suiting up to take a city with ease. Redeye pushed down the desire to be out riding with Cicero again.

They snuck through the town buildings surrounding the fort that allowed them to get close to the city without being noticed by the soldiers garrisoned on the walls of Krahl. The Kalesians had said the men in the fort numbered roughly three hundred. All Redeye had to do was get in the city quick enough to get Gorring's men in the fort, then Yellowtooth's after him.

Redeye walked in a house, making sure it was clear. A charge can be made useless if some enemy comes up behind you. Better to leave no worries behind, so he checked the scattered houses that dotted the terrain outside the fort. Igoss's stagnant voice rumbled grumpily behind him in the abandoned house: "I could do it here. No one would think to look down here for him."

"No! We need him on the walls. You'll do him after that, once we're in the city."

Igoss squinted thoughtfully at that. "You don't plan to let him live, do you? I could let Yellowtooth know you chose to let him live." Igoss had that look like he had Redeye figured out.

Redeye felt his face go flush.

"Bring Zifix here, we kill him, and I tell Yellowtooth it's done. Better to seal the wound before it rots."

Rector poked his head in the doorway. "Zifix and I haven't seen anyone, Red. Want us to keep looking?"

Igoss turned to Rector as he spoke. "No, tell Zifix to come speak with us," the ugly man said, raising his eyebrows to Redeye.

"No, we have nothing to talk about. Both of you get the men ready for the walls."

Rector nodded to Redeye's order and left into the quiet town.

"If you plan to cower out of Yellowtooth's orders, then—"

"Why are you so keen to get it over with, Igoss?" Redeye interrupted. "Are you afraid of the walls? You would rather kill one man and come in at the end of the battle?"

Igoss looked only for an instant out a window toward the fort, and Redeye knew he'd guessed right. "Well I'm sorry, Igoss, but

I'd have you work as long as you're here." Redeye strode out of the building, showing his back to the man.

He joined the twenty-seven of them behind a house about twenty strides from the wall. They split up into four groups, one of six and three of seven. Each man looked as calm as if they were going to repair the wall rather than breach it. All except Boban, who looked like he was to be drowned for a war crime.

"You okay, Boban?" Redeye asked. Only a nervous nod came from the man. "You'll go with me, Rector, Zifix, Zeux, and Igoss. We're the smallest group."

Boban's worried eyes looked over the men, then over to Igoss.

"You won't be able to get up there with all that metal," said Rector, eyeing all the Kalesian belts and plates. "A dagger or a hatchet, something you can hold in your teeth." Boban had never looked certain, but the blood drained out of his face at that. Rector dropped his shield and two swords to the ground along with everyone else doing the same. "I'm taking this." Rector held up his old hammer pick, rusted like he'd dug it out of some ancient ruin. Redeye had seen that pick kill many men over the years.

"You get to go third, Boban, best job of the lot and you didn't have to throw dice to get it!" The other men laughed at Redeye's joke. "I'll go up first, I've never been lucky anyway. The rest of you have a minute to decide your fighting orders."

"I'll go second!" said Rector, nodding to Redeye.

"Good, I'll go first, then Rector. Boban, you come next and help up the man behind you." and Zifix's hand went up, then Igoss.

"Guess I'm last?" asked Zeux, feinting a fearful look.

"You're last, but don't worry, Zeux, you're still the ugliest man I know," mused Rector. All the men laughed except Igoss and Boban.

"Okay, boys," said Redeye to all five men around, huddling

together and planning their way up the wall. "Remember what Cicero used to say: the only way this works is with a whole lot of luck, so only take the good sort with you!"

"Who's Cicero?" asked Boban. Redeye just clapped his hands, ignoring the Kalesian. At that, Zeux and Igoss took off toward the walls.

"Wait, I thought they were last!" Boban yelled, more worried than ever.

"Shut up and do what I do after I do it!" said Rector, tired of the man's constant worrying.

Zifix left a moment later and Redeye nodded again to Rector before darting around the corner of the house toward the wall. He watched as three other groups of seven Hockleets were sprinting towards the wall as fast as him, three men each leading their own scaling parties. A man on the wall shouted as he noticed them coming. Zeux and Igoss both crouched their backs, leaning against the wall. Zifix arrived next, stepping on top of their hands so that both Igoss and Zeux were low to the ground, each holding one of Zifix's feet in interlocked fingers. Zifix put his hand out and took Redeye's hand. Redeye used his momentum to jump as high as he could in unison. The men all stood up straight to make a tower the height of three men. Redeye slung one arm over and felt the men below drop down again to make the springlike tower once more. Redeye hung there a moment, taking breath into his lungs but not enough to catch his breath. Then he roared it out, pulling himself over the parapet.

Redeye realized in that split moment he'd never been first over the wall in a breach before. Plenty of times he'd hoisted Cicero and Yellowtooth over the walls of Hocklee and Begatto. He'd even hefted Tork's larger-than-life body up once, but this was Red's first time over. As he settled his footing on the walk, he made eye contact with a lone soldier not ten strides from him. The guard looked in toward the inner city. Redeye followed his gaze to houses and town buildings where men poured into the streets like angry bees from their hive. He heard grunting behind him. Redeye looked back, seeing the Storinian Hockleet named Culver from the middle group struggling with a guard. He realized what little time they had.

His body snapped into motion, running to help the Hockleet. Redeye pulled a knife from his belt and jabbed the blade into the man's neck just under the bear symbol of Kalesia on the back of his helmet. He ripped it out and turned, taking no time to acknowledge if Culver was okay. If he wasn't, Redeye couldn't tend to him now.

He saw a hand coming up where he'd come up the wall seconds before. Redeye took advantage of the moment to pull Rector up over the edge. As he pulled on his ally, he realized the guard also took advantage of the moment. He could hear footsteps coming on. He looked to see the guard pull his spear back for a drive. Redeye curled up, getting ready for a spear in the guts as the Kalesian charged.

It came through the air between them, but Redeye didn't feel it stab him. His mind caught up to what his eyes saw. Rector had knocked it down with his hammer just before lodging the pick end of the weapon in the man's temple with an evil backswing. The Kalesian's eyes went cross and his teeth chattered incessantly. Rector had put it straight through his helmet. He and the guard clattered down to the walk at the top of the wall as Redeye dragged him over the parapet. The sound of emergency bells rang throughout the air behind the voices of men yelling as they ran toward walls to repel the invaders. As Rector and Redeye regained their footing, they heard a problem on the other side.

"Check on that," Rector said, standing to greet whatever defenders were about to come out of the gatehouse. Redeye looked over the wall to see something had gone wrong, to put Zifix and Boban with their backs on the ground, scrambling to get to their feet. They must've fallen. Igoss still waited in the squatted position for the others to get everything together and try again. Further down the wall, the other Hockleets were doing well. One group was setting the rope already, his men easily putting down a guard that was trying to kill them.

"New plan! Get up the rope!" he called down to his squad at the wall's base.

"They fell?" asked Rector.

"Yeah, so we've got to split up," Redeye answered. "Get the Kalesian man up here!" he called over the wall then turned to the man he'd just saved. "Culver, with us!"

Culver left from pulling up the other Hockleets. They ran along the wall, Rector and Culver following Redeye. They got away from the spot where the Kalesians would swarm soon if people began to coordinate. Redeye knew they would if they could. He knew that because Cicero had beaten the otherwise unbeaten Tork by sowing enough chaos to keep the enemy constantly confused. So they ran away, splitting off from their own, which the mighty Tork would've said is as good as dropping one's own weapons.

They sprinted along the wall and found more guards with whom they started a new fight. The Kalesian wall guards yelled as they fought, always giving ground and retreating. They did all they could to buy time for more reinforcements to arrive. That was okay with Redeye as long as they weren't drawn to the rest of the Hockleets breaching the wall. So they yelled along with them, hoping to draw the men of the city toward their harmless three-man invasion. They all stood there a moment in a stalemate, both groups waiting for their allies to arrive when Redeye had a fresh idea.

"We have to run! Come on. Run!" Redeye turned, running back toward the Hockleets, but stopped to tell Rector and Culver to jump. The fall wasn't high enough to hurt a Hockleet. The Kalesians followed but took caution to wait for more arrivals.

"Get Gorring!" Redeye knew Culver to be a fast and long-winded runner usually working as a voiceman. Both men jumped, leaving Redeye as he ran back to the rest. "Run!" he shouted. "Run, they're coming!" All of his men did exactly how he wanted, jumping from the walls and landing harmlessly on the ground below outside the city. All of them were fearless but Boban. The Kalesian man had probably never jumped out of a tree, let alone off of ten strides of wall. He couldn't summon the courage to jump just as Redeye predicted. It was all so perfect. Redeye caught him before he could go over. "Not you," he said, pulling the man off the edge by his belt.

"Wha—?" Boban looked a mess of terrified and confused.

"They're your people; make them chase us!" Men of the city began pouring into the scaffolds to climb up onto the walls. "But first, push me off," Redeye said, lifting a knife over his head theatrically. "Be one of them."

It took Boban a moment before his eyes went wide as he gained understanding. The Kalesian grabbed Redeye's hand before he could pretend to stab him. "Good. Now, throw me over," Redeye whispered only a fragment of a breath before Boban, all too aggressively, shoved him from the wall. Redeye was in the air, really falling rather than pretending. The ground met his back with jarring pain that usually crushes a man. He lost everything for a brief moment before remembering where he was. Redeye made himself get dizzily to his feet and tumble away from the wall toward his men.

"Don't let them get away!" He heard men saying as great wooden gates creaked open enough for pursuers to begin pouring out.

The Hockleets were regrouped, waiting for Redeye.

"Hurry, draw them out of the city!" came his orders. So, the men retreated farther, letting time pass. Soon, sixteen Hockleets had what Redeye thought may be seventy men chasing them through the small city, not far from the gate of the city. He heard a noise to his left as all of Gorring's men charged out from alleys and houses into the Kalesian pursuers. Redeye led his own charge straight into the confusion.

Kalesians began to die immediately. It was too late for them. As soon as Gorring's men began to run for the open gates, the Kalesians shut the huge doors to keep out the much greater number of Galanoans and Kalesian turncoats. Redeye's men killed less than ten men as Gorring and his men ripped through the desperate soldiers of Krahl. Some of the men gathered to fight, like devils in Redeye's opinion, at the base of the wall. These cornered men were armored and well-trained Kalesian soldiers fighting without the chance of survival. Many of them huddled tight, killing their own number's worth of invaders. Galanoans and young Kalesians began to hesitate and get back from them as they aggressively retaliated. It was then that Gorring showed why Yellowtooth chose him as his warman.

The huge man charged and jumped, kicking hard into a shield with all of his momentum. His weight launched the man back onto the ground. Gorring swung what looked like a wood axe backwards to bury in the next man's head. He didn't slow, pushing and chopping against shields so that men charged in again, now filling the hole he made. Several men divided the city guards and picked them apart.

Soon, guards were above them on the wall and throwing rocks down, forcing them back away from the walls. They were stuck outside the walls and Yellowtooth's force could be seen coming to finish off the city. Redeye sighed that the walls were still not breached.

"We need to see to that thing, Redeye," said Igoss, tilting his head to Zifix, "Yellowtooth will be here soon."

"Oh, yeah . . . that." Redeye had forgotten to let Igoss kill his oldest ally.

Yellowtooth's men were still a long way off when Redeye called for Zifix to meet him in the village to plan. Redeye wasn't sure what was so hard about this. He'd killed more men than he cared to count over the years, so why was this different? Was he different? No, he may want to be like Tork and Cicero, always fighting for the good. But both men were killed by their own countrymen. Bloodway was in charge and Redeye needed to get used to this kind of thing. Redeye remembered when he lost his eye on the walls of Hocklee. How the pain made him wild and feared by men who attacked him. That made a little pride bubble up. That's why Yellowtooth chose him. Redeye was only good for one thing!

Zifix ducked his head under the cloth that hung over the threshold of the house. Igoss walked in close behind him, sealing the three of them inside.

"I'm sorry about the wall, boss. I didn't mean for the stack to fall—" Redeye cut him off with a raised hand. "That wasn't your fault Zifix." Redeye shot a glance at Igoss. "But listen. I want to thank you."

"Thank me when we get in the city, Chief!" said Zifix.

"No, I mean for the times. You've been worthy of trust." Redeye was finding it impossible to meet the man's eye.

"The times?" Zifix asked, somewhat confused. His eyes went

wide as Igoss put his knife into Zifix's side. Redeye expected his retaliation and caught Zifix's hand as he wheeled around to strike Igoss. He had a confused look as he dropped to his knees with Redeye keeping him from fighting back against his own murderer. It surprised Redeye to see that Zifix never went for Redeye. The man just dropped his head, looking like he couldn't work all of this out.

"I don't . . . get it," he rasped, wincing up at Redeye.

"Neither do I."

"But—" There was a sharp ring as the weight of Igoss's small hammer pinged off of Zifix's skull above his brow. Zifix was soon dead after that. Redeye's breath was drawn violently in from a horrible gasp.

"What was that?!" Redeye yelled, about to take his chances even with no weapon in his hand. Igoss had a knife ready, having ripped it from Zifix's side.

"You can't take the pain out of death, and you can't keep the ally you betray," Igoss said as he wiped the blood on his knife off across Zifix's shirt.

"You were never his ally!" Redeye spat.

"That would mean I didn't betray him. And since I'm the one who finished him off, you are off the hook." Igoss smirked and nodded. "Yellowtooth will be pleased." Igoss turned for the door. "I wouldn't stay long. Wouldn't want anyone knowing you're the one 'at did this. Well, anyone except Yellowtooth," he said over one shoulder. And with that, the bald man was out into the street, leaving Zifix and Redeye alone.

CHAPTER THIRTY-FOUR

WARD OF WAYMAR

PINELLA

Riva and Omera were instantly companions. After a few days of learning, she was already helping Riva in her work. Pinella had been right; numbers were her game. If her older brother was to become a Tribune one day, she would make a great ward after Pinella. Pinella made good use of the new position by delegating much of the work to the other chargers who she made accountable to Riva. The day-to-day responsibilities gave Pinella the time to make things more efficient and solve problems. Initially she thought it would be overwhelming to have so much more work, but with it came authority. Authority she used to organize and streamline the procedures into efficient chains of action and communication. Chains that all ran through Riva.

The voice of a herald carried into the her office from the Arcade. He shouted about how the rebels had hardly been slowed by the Alcott army and how the Fowler was only fifty miles from the city. Pinella wondered what she would do if the Fowler and his rebels seized the city. She hadn't actually stopped to wonder what would become of all her work for the Waymars. As she did, a knock came at the door. Pinella invited whoever knocked to enter, and in walked Greyah Aspin.

"Lady Bennault! It's good to see you. I'm sorry for coming unannounced."

Pinella stood in greeting. "No, no. It does me good to see you. How's your father?"

Greyah sighed and spoke regrettably, "He's better than we feared, but not as good as we've hoped."

"I'm glad you still have him."

Greyah agreed before setting a purse of singing coins on Pinella's desk. "I took it upon myself to deliver This month's Tribute."

"Greyah, your brother delivered the payment last week. He was two weeks ahead of schedule as you always are."

Grayah smiled patiently at Pinella's misunderstanding. "This is our Tribute to you, Lady Bennalt." She continued before Pinella could refuse. "I've learned of the Tribunal's suspicion of you. I want you to know how firmly the Aspin family disagrees with their unfair treatment of you, as well as the Waymar's failure to defend your honor."

Pinella sighed, moved by Greyah's words and gestures of high regard for her. "The Waymars have supported me through this. They are doing everything they can for me. They're under so much scrutiny as it is. The Tribunes wrongfully accuse them of collusion."

Greyah's expression darkened. "The Tribunes endeavor to protect the state. I uncovered this." The Aspin woman offered a rolled-up paper in her hand.

"What is this?"

"A letter we intercepted from one of Lady Kessa Waymar's close friends sent to Tertayin's allies." Pinella felt the calm leave her as Greyah continued to speak. "We dutifully fulfill our service to the Waymars, but to undermine your honor is no different to the Aspin family than undermining your father's honor. To him, we owe a great deal."

Pinella wanted with everything for this not to be happening. "Who knows about this?" she demanded.

"My brother, who discovered it, and myself. We won't use it. I give this to you."

Pinella thanked Greyah and dismissed her before sinking into her chair and crying.

❧

Before Pinella could return to the Upper City to attend what she hoped was her final questioning, she recieved a letter from Lady Waymar. The letter she expected to be a short recommendation or question regarding the Tribunes turned out to be a lengthy letter in which she required several stewards to sizably increase their Tribute payments. After taking time to consider Octavia's ill-advised order, she opened a drawer and left the note there with a few other unheeded requests.

There were many things Pinella had done slightly different from Octavia's exact directives, but never had she ignored one of her requests. The money could be found in other places, and it was not right to raise taxes. Pinella often used the personal Tribute she received from the Aspins to supplement the late or lacking payments of other vassals, many of whom were struggling to keep their own subjects paid. She knew that Octavia had not seen things correctly since her brother had died, and soon it would become more difficult to think clearly with the news of her own sister-in-law giving up information. Octavia had spoken of her own shortage of trustworthy subordinates when Pinella first came to their house. Now that most of the subordination was dead, Octavia was responsible for more. Things seemed to get continually worse for the Waymars.

That herald came back to her attention. Turning to look out the window, she listened to the proclamations. A man saying something about Storinian immigrants who were veterans being offered a higher wage than other mercenaries.

"They seem desperate." Pinella was caught off guard by Omera's voice. She hadn't even heard the young lady enter her study.

"Yes . . . or perhaps it's just a good time to be a soldier. Mercenaries from Storins are thought to be the greatest quality. Many of the wars in Alssae are won with the help of Storinian armies."

"I know that." An awkward moment lapsed. "But we must be in trouble if we're calling for Storinian locals to fight. My brother says that other mercenary armies won't fight for Trofaim because the rebels are too strong. He said the Storinians aren't willing to fight against the Fowler."

Pinella found it difficult to respond to Omera. Clearly she'd been listening to war politics, which were precisely the type of politics Pinella had worried herself with least. Lower City affairs were more than enough to occupy her focus. She hardly had time to keep up with the current events of the Tribunal, beside the fact that Octavia was making social enemies and losing allies by the day.

"We still have over two thousand Shrikes and some eight thousand professional soldiers. If we can field another Songbird Army, we will have the one of the greatest armies of our time."

Octavia's young niece sat in the chair on the opposite side of Pinella's desk and began pulling apart knotted ends of her beautifully black natural curls. Her eyes were distant, looking out Pinella's window. "I'm scared of the Fowler. I sometimes think of what may happen to us if we are defeated again and the rebels take over the city and there is no one left to protect us." Tears began to fill the young girl's eyes.

"Oh, don't be afraid, Omera. There are many things that would have to happen before we should worry. They are much further from attacking than the heralds suggest."

Omera began to speak with a whimpering tone, "They defeated my father's army . . . I know I am supposed mourn like everyone else, but ever since my father died, I'm scared of the men who killed him. I keep thinking of what will happen. What they'll do to us . . . to me. My mother and aunt Livra are just like you. Just like all the adults, they seem to not be afraid of what might happen to us if Trofaim is taken. Will we be killed? What if we are made to be concubines?"

Pinella thought about that. She had to think about that, unaware of why they weren't as afraid as they should have been. "I think we seem less afraid because us mature women of Trofaim have been through a similar situation. We lived in the time of the Mottravan invasion. We were scared then, dear."

"Yes, but your father was victorious . . . mine was killed." Omera let her first tear slip down her cheek. "And now, neither of them is here to fight for us. I wish we could just run away."

CHAPTER THIRTY-FIVE

OPENING THE GATES

REDEYE

Redeye watched as Yellowtooth's men, a full company of six hundred soldiers and thirty scouts, came swarming into the city. Hezro, the youngest, tried not to laugh at the Kalesians moving in the rows and files all moving to the beat of their marching songs. Redeye tried not to look at any of the evil Galanoans, each one looking around as if they wanted to fight the whole world. Zeux, on the other hand, didn't miss a single opportunity to glare right back at them, inviting whatever threats they made with their eyes to test him.

"These Galanoans from the land around Thrivdon are the worst kind of men. Why would Bloodway want any of them?" Zeux asked like a true man of Hocklee.

"He's a known man, and it speaks of his reputation if these men came from as far as even Kalaus to fight for him," said Rector, walking up from the other Hockleets. "There is no telling how he gets all these Kalesian stiff necks to follow Yellowtooth, though."

The aforementioned chief of nearly ten warscores of Southern soldiers came riding on a painted horse laughing at the talk of some Galanoan riders he was keeping company with. Yellowtooth was one of those who was always famous with new and obscure companies while the men who knew him longest could hardly bother with him. Redeye sighed at his leader. You wouldn't have thought he was reinforcing his company with how careless he looked. You'd think he was riding up to his own house after a night of celebration with old friends.

"Didn't Igoss say he was charging in with the last wave?" asked Rector.

"Could you imagine if we were inside the city waiting for him?" Zeux shook his head at his own rhetoric. "Our only hope would be that his jokes made the soldiers of Kathleen laugh to death."

"I'd better go talk to him; he'll be wondering why we aren't inside." Redeye sighed, starting over toward Yellow and his entourage.

"Redeye! Just the man I wanted to see," he said with that gaping dirty smile. "Why aren't any men marching through those gates? Why are you and yours resting out here rather than fighting?"

"Well—"

"He took the walls with no casualties and retreated before we could do any real fighting," said Igoss, cutting him short. Redeye felt his face flush with anger. How could Igoss . . .

"Why'd you leave the wall, Red?" Yellowtooth was starting to sound angry. "Why aren't you fighting?!" Redeye couldn't believe what he was watching. Igoss betrayed him after forcing him to kill Zifix. It was impossibly evil to Redeye. To make things worse, all of the strangers from Galanoa, who hadn't known Yellowtooth half as long as Redeye, all looked angry, as if Redeye had been given an easy task and not done it out of pure laziness.

"I . . . uh . . ." He felt his face burn bright red with embarrassment with every eye that accused him. Yellowtooth's eyes began to harden even when Redeye thought they couldn't get any more furious.

"OY! The gates!"

Redeye watched Yellowtooth's sick stare shift up to the walls and study. Redeye looked up at what it was everyone else looked at. At first, he didn't recognize the Kalesian man without his armor.

"Is that Boban?" some of Yellow's Kalesians asked, and Redeye knew that the fearful man had done it.

"There's my man!" Redeye said, laughing to the joyful agreement of all the men around. They all laughed. All of them except Igoss, who avoided Redeye's gaze.

"What did I tell you?!" shouted Yellowtooth triumphantly. "He's an evil devil, Redeye. You were raised for this business! Just like me! Just like Bloodway!" All as if he had always trusted Redeye, even before asking him to kill his own friend and take a town with a few men who all disagreed with one another. It hurt him to hear that, that he was made to kill. Redeye wondered if he'd really just been made to soil himself and somehow come out smelling like a champion.

Men cheered for him, Galanoans clapping his shoulder and Kalesian men nodding their salutations before charging into the open city. Yellowtooth and his Hockleets cheered for Redeye and his own warband. But Redeye felt alone in the moving sea of men, like a rock in a river. No doubt if Rector, Zeux, or the others knew what he'd allowed to be done to Zifix, they'd do it to him. No doubt he'd deserve it. The only man who knew him at that moment was Igoss, who no doubt wanted him dead for unknown reasons.

A month ago, all these men were searching for him to kill Cicero and those two children. Somehow he'd loved it. Cicero was not as evil as they said. Hoodless had made things like family. Even the old memories in Hocklee were different than this. It wasn't just Redeye, but all the Hockleets were different now. All of them suspicious of the Galanoan and Kalesian men that followed Bloodway, even though they used to be Galanoans and Kalesians before Cicero united with Tork and said they were no longer either, but one united men of Hocklee.

He watched them pour into the city, cramming through the gateway.

"Good work, Red! This is the work only a Hockleet could produce," said Yellowtooth with his wide, ugly smile that made you think you could smell it from afar.

"Yes, sir. You asked for the city, didn't you?" said Redeye, more curious about what Zifix must've done to get Yellowtooth to order him killed.

"Ha!" Yellow forced out that conceited bark of a laugh. "True enough, true enough! You set the bar high."

Redeye looked around to make sure no one would hear before whispering to Yellowtooth through shut teeth, "What'd he do?"

Yellowtooth caught up again, realizing what Redeye was asking. "Oh! Zifix? He had history with you and Rector. I almost had you do Rector or Zeux instead, but we all know Rector is a good hand in a fight, and Zeux is almost as unpredictable as the Hood himself! Zifix was hard to let go of, but still worth the price of knowing I can still trust you." Yellowtooth set his hand on his shoulder like always, like he hadn't betrayed Redeye. "Had to be sure that time you spent with old Cicero didn't make you soft. You're just as mean as ever though. Rest now, you've earned it." And the old mercenary was off toward the fortress of Krahl.

Yellow didn't care if Redeye needed rest. It just meant more plunder for him. Soon only a few men were outside the city, most of which were his Hockleets watching him from a distance. They probably wondered what he and Yellowtooth had kept secret from them. Were they now doubting him? What would happen if they found Zifix's corpse? When they find it, would they know? He killed a friend to earn a madman's feeble trust.

Now he knew he was alone among these men.

CHAPTER THIRTY-SIX

THE SOUTHERN LARK

FINNION

Finnion stumbled behind Reff, sneaking through the quiet village of Tolon at night. They weren't sneaking, not really. The rain fell heavy like the whole sky had become too dense to stay up. The village was small and close enough to the border of Storins that the mercenary law was largely undisputed here. Many of the people here had been under the arm of the mercenaries long enough to settle into a sort of normality. That was not to say it was any less tyrannical. Every town they'd seen over the last week since leaving Harmony-Ford had been nearly abandoned. The foreign mercenaries gathered more densely in cities where crime had escalated due to self-perpetuated poverty, which was the result of feeding thousands of foreign soldiers from Storins. Some soldiers even created small tax rules for the people who couldn't afford to give food or supplies to the mercenaries.

Finnion remembered sending envoys to Storins to secure the state of Trofaim while he led its rebellion to take the capital. It had been nearly two months since his generals betrayed him just after laying out the most intricate victory of his military career. Their mistake, though, was leaving him to die rather than cutting his heart out while they had the chance. Now Finnion was following a young noble of Trofaim, helping him to put down the rebels and stir up any patriots they could find.

Finnion, if given the chance, wouldn't make the same mistake. Each one of the men who killed Jonas Blakes and orchestrated Finnion's betrayal would have to die. The young Trofaimen nobleman, Reff, didn't know he kept company with the man who assembled the rebellion in the first place. If he found out, doubtless he'd get them both killed in some act of patriotic justice. *Better*, Finnion thought, *to use the young man for a second chance at freeing Trofaim from its corruption*. He would follow this time rather than lead. His leadership had taken Trofaim from a corrupt peace into a corrupt and bloody civil war. This young man may surprise everyone with his patriotic naivety. How may a story turn out with a pure-hearted patriot at the front of it? It was dangerous, he knew, to have an inexperienced leader of things, as he may act from heart over head. But Finnion would be shrewd while protecting him. The odds were long but maybe the young man would truly prove to be the son of a liberator and grandson of a protector.

"You're still limping?" asked Reff incredulously. Finnion's mind came back to the reality of the rainy village of Tolon. Wet dripped from the tip of Reff's nose and eyelashes.

"Does it matter?" asked Finnion again, losing patience for the impatient young man. "It's not like they're going to hear us in the middle of a complete rainstorm. And, in case you haven't noticed, this village isn't exactly crawling with Storinian mercenaries. We'll be fine."

"We'll be late," said Reff. "Your leg, I fear, is an excuse for your age. It slows you down."

Finnion hadn't any urge to argue. Enough arguing had been done on the road here over political differences. "Just lead the way!"

They stepped under the small house matching the description Benneck had given them. They enjoyed the moment without words under the covered porch. It was good to be out of the driving rain. It would be even better to be out of the cold soon. They looked at each other and at some unspoken cue, both men pushed into the house through an unlocked door. The warmth from a hearth fire broke like a wave over Finn's numb face. His leg made him want to scream in agony, but he had to sell the appearance of a capable fighter.

"Benneck is owed a debt!" he said with fiery menace, the way the old man had instructed. Finnion's eyes adjusted to the bright room. There was a man cooking over a hot cauldron.

"NOW!" said Reff, advancing a step toward the stranger.

"Relax, both of you," said the man. "Benneck said you'd be coming. We're alone." The man held up two soup bowls toward them with a lax smile. "It's Benneck's recipe. But I should warn you, I don't pull it off as well as him."

Reff didn't waste a second before dipping his hands into the closest bowl to taste the contents.

"It's delicious," he said with a smile.

With that, Finnion dropped the sword and hobbled forward like a crippled old woman to have his portion of the soup. Reff fell into a chair against the wall near the fire as Finnion took the other bowl, nodding his thanks to the stranger.

"Hard travels?" he asked. Some grunts from each of them was all the response they gave as they poured the hot chunky soup down their frozen throats. It tasted the way it was supposed to, the way old man Benneck said it would.

"So you're a lark then?" asked Finn, feeling the soup drip down his bearded chin.

The man nodded and, smiling, he said, "My name is Leighton. You two must be the remainder of the Wing!" Finnion noted how much they knew about each other without the other knowing. The Larks still felt somewhat like his enemy from when he was the leader of the rebellion. It made him careful. Every time one of the men of this guild of the Lark spoke, he questioned their truth. It was King Barrence I who said, "A spy, a true spy, is no man's but his own. This is what makes him powerful. It's what keeps him alive, his own self trust." So Finnion watched closely, building his understanding of them.

"Benneck said you'd have money for us?" asked Reff, as straightforward as ever. Leighton smiled and motioned to a drawer near Reff. With no other subtleties or formalities, he pulled the drawer open with the hand that wasn't still holding his soup. Finnion wanted to apologize for how abrupt Reff was being.

"We're thankful for your conTribution to the state," said Finnion as his young companion counted the jingling Brevaltine coins from a black sack.

"And I'm thankful in turn for yours," said Leighton. "Your efforts will yield a great profit for me if you're successful. I'm more of an investor than a patriot." That got Reff's attention. "But don't misunderstand me. I agree with the rebel motives but not the moves they've made."

"Agree with them?" Reff asked. Finnion was glad for once that Reff questioned someone so he didn't have to.

"It looks like you need more soup, friend," said Leighton, reaching for Reff's bowl. Finnion almost laughed at how Reff's attitude, again, so easily changed. This man was suspicious and sly, but Finnion liked how he controlled the hot tempered youth. "Let me explain, friend. Have either of you been this far south before now?"

Reff's eyebrows wrinkled in confusion. He looked at Finnion and, speaking for the both of them, he said, "No, but I have met the Tribune delegated from this region." Reff spoke as though that were the same as being a native of the far Southeast Borderlands.

"So you don't know anyone who actually lives here or struggles? The hardships?" asked Leighton to Reff's silence. "Their effort is to make places like this governed justly. The way the streets of Trofaim itself are safe, they plan to make it safe for all."

"The Songbird Army has kept everyone safe for generations," said Reff dismissively.

Leighton smiled and tilted his head. "There is a reason — a good reason — why men would leave their own reform in Trofaim. Mercenary law is a desperate option, but necessary for thousands." Leighton ladled a scoop of soup into Finn's bowl before he was even finished. This man knew how to keep men from interrupting. "Am I the only Lark this far south? In the city of Lavinth, there are six more. Each of us have been here all our lives. We have lived under the law of the Tribunes. We've been ruled by the Oligarchs of the Wing. I know things that Benneck does not about you Shrikes." He smiled a little wider at Reff's troubled look. "I may even know more about the Wing than you."

CHAPTER THIRTY-SEVEN

THE CONFESSION

PINELLA

Today was the day. Pinella had put off the inevitable long enough. When she initially learned of Kessa Waymar's betrayal, she tried not to believe it or to rationalize why it was best to bury the information in hopes that Kessa would remain uncovered. But the more she she thought about it, the more she understood that Octavia and the other Waymars had to know no matter how painful. Pinella dreaded the idea of exposing Kessa. She wasn't as close to her as Octavia, but Pinella always felt a deal of pity for Kessa. Livra was the love of Owen's youth and Karianna was his youthful love. Livra had his heart and Karianna had his attention. But Kessa was caught in the middle, always unable to compete with either of her sister wives. Kessa understood more about the city and its nobility than almost anyone else in the family, but she was still no match for Octavia's public prowess. She was like a clear crystal in a ruby mine. For all her beauty, she was avoided for what others deemed more valuable.

Pinella was reluctant but she knew that in order to clear her name, she had to come clean with what she knew about Kessa. No one would believe that she wasn't involved as long as there was an informant among the family. This was her way to step out from the shadows of her past and stand for the Waymars. Octavia would hurt when she found out, but the rot had to be cut away from the family before it could heal.

Pinella entered the Upper City, arrived at Waymar Manor, and made her way inside. Upon entering, she was greeted by one of her favorite of the servants. A young girl maybe fifteen who Omera spoke of often.

"Good morning, my Lady."

"Good morning, Nadi. Is Lady Octavia home?"

"Yes, ma'am. She is in her study. Would you like anything?"

"You can take my coat." Pinella smiled warmly as she handed her outer fur coat to the young maid, but kept her thinner leather jacket. "Thank you, Nadi."

"Of course. I will bring some tea up. Riva told me how you like it in the case that you ever came without her."

Pinella shined on the humble servant with an approving smile. "If you keep this up, I'll have to steal you from Hess as well."

Nadi fought an indulgent smile and left after bowing her head to Pinella. For all of Hess's fractious behavior the old servant really could train a hospitalian. The young woman had offered a moment of refreshing reprieve before the meeting Pinella dreaded.

As soon as she entered the study, she sensed an aura of oddity. Octavia had her back to Pinella, looking out the window toward the Lower City. Had she watched Pinella walk up to the house? Every time she'd seen Octavia in the past month, the noblewoman had been flocked by counselors and chargers demanding her input on a thousand affairs throughout the city and territory.

"Good morning, Octavia. It does me good to see you with a moment of calm. Thank you for meeting with me. I'll try to be brief."

Octavia stood up and, meeting Pinella's gaze with a weak smile, said, "It's done me a world of good to stop and take the time to look over our affairs. It has been enlightening."

Pinella nodded in agreement. She searched her mind for the right words. How to begin, she thought. "I hope you've found the goings on of the Lower City satisfactory. Riva is a genius at summarizing those reports. She was able to fit twenty strides of scroll into a journal page." A long moment unfolded in which Octavia couldn't meet Pinella's gaze. Pinella felt the weight of what she was about to revel about Kessa growing heavier.

"Pinella, the investigators have followed you closely. You knew they would."

"Yes." Pinella discerned that Octavia also struggled to speak about something. Then Octavia met her eye.

"They told me everything." Octavia's expression and tone took on the frailty of one betrayed. "My one hope is that you have come to tell me everything, no matter how it may hurt. That you keep nothing between us, Pinella."

Pinella swallowed, cleared her nervous throat, and spoke. "I did not mean to tarry in my coming to you. I knew in my heart you had to know, but I tried to think of a way to tell you without hurting you. I decided that you had to know so that you could deal with things your way. That's when I requested this meeting with you." Pinella took a moment, looking out the window to recollect. "Nearly a week ago, one of our stewardesses approached me. She explained how her desire was to restore and preserve my honor as ward of the Waymar family. I did not ask her to help me. And . . ."

"Pinella." Octavia's tone had sharpened considerably. "I know you have been disobeying my orders and implementing your own directives without my consent. I wanted desperately that you had come to tell me of your disloyalty and seek restitution."

At first, Pinella was confused. She reviewed what Octavia had just said. Disloyalty? "I don't understand." Her toes curled inside her shoes. Octavia didn't know about Kessa. She was talking about Pinella's work as ward. The investigators must have told her about Pinella doing differently than what Octavia had said. Disloyalty, though?

"Pinella, I entrusted more to you than anyone outside my family—"

"I have made everything you have given me prosper." Neither of the woman were accustomed to Octavia being interrupted. "I had to do things differently. Your initiatives to tax and question the stewards as if they're mutinying is cruel. These are the people who make your wealth produce for you."

"I must lead this family. It's not your decision how I deal with my vassals. Your job is to carry out my vision." Octavia's voice had elevated in volume. "The stewards are fortunate to be given the honor of their position. I would just as soon find a steward to replace one if I knew they could produce more." Octavia honed her words directly at Pinella. "I would crush the steward who disobeyed me."

"You elevate yourself too high, Octavia! Do you even remember how much your family lost to corruption and embezzlement before I began my oversight? Nearly a third!" Pinella matched Octavia's tone. "We found no sign of any fraud for the last month. And you direct me to raise their taxes? Why would I punish their loyalty?"

"Pinella, these are not your holdings. They're not even the steward's. This is all owned by the Waymar family. Our vision must be followed." Octavia increased her volume as she spoke. "I am sacrificing everything to reestablish our family as we face insurmountable turmoil. I trusted you to implement my insights without fail! If I am not obeyed, this house will crumble!

Pinella almost shouted her reply. "You haven't had the clarity of mind or the grit to manage any of the Upper City affairs. Our allies distance themselves. The senior families alienate us. We have never been weaker above the orchard. It's only by the loyalty and productive hard work of the stewardship that this family has kept its substantiality. You ought to be pleased that your leadership hasn't cost you the Lower City!" Pinella slowed her tone to an accusatory hiss. "Ask yourself how you have remained in supremacy. You can be sure, it is not because of—" Pinella was cut off by the door opening. Both women looked to see Nadi awkwardly standing in the doorway with a steaming cup in her hand.

Nadi read their expressions and her face ran pink with embarrassment. "I've brought your tea, Lady Bennalt."

Pinella only nodded as the girl hurriedly set the aromatic cup on the desk, the ceramic cup clinking gently against the saucer. Nadi couldn't keep the tears out of her voice as she dismissed herself. "Please forgive me."

The door shut and the woman were again alone, only now the fire of argument had settled into a civil disagreement. Before they spoke, both woman paused to breathe, waiting for the other to speak.

Octavia broke the silence with a humble extension of peace. "Pinella, I concede that you have managed the vassal families with exceptional acumen . . ." Octavia was graceful at last, having been corrected. Pinella would have never thought anyone could defy a woman like Octavia Waymar on politics. But here she was humbled, the look of guilty realization had crept into her expression. And Pinella had been the one to correct her. It was good to feel right. To feel vindicated.

Pinella decided not to wait any longer. "Do you know why I requested this meeting?" Octavia waited for Pinella's reason. "I came to tell you who has been disclosing secrets with the Fowler. I sent a courier to request the meeting as soon as I found out." She lied. The truth was that she sat sick to her stomach with the information before reaching out. "I could have approached the Adhemar family or Alcotts, but I only stand with the Waymars. I'm sure if I were the one to unmask the betrayal, it would clear my name. Truthfully . . . I haven't considered that until now. I brought it for you to deal with in your own way." Pinella took a pause, then looked to Octavia's eyes. "You called me . . . disloyal."

Octavia's face was laden with regret. "Pinella . . . I should have asked you about everything first. I wish I hadn't accused you. I didn't see clearly. I trust your judgement in the Lower City." Even though she attempted to make amends, Octavia did not apologize. Pinella nodded but remained hurt and distanced by her.

"It's Kessa. One of her friends is gleaning information from Kessa's gossip. She has illegally disclosed Tribunal secrets as well as privileged family secrets."

Octavia received the news without expression. "Which one of her friends?"

"They weren't so foolish as to sign the letter they sent to Elmo Deep's allies."

Octavia took the information slowly, thinking on the consequences.

"That's not her only trespass . . ."

Octavia's jaw clenched awaiting what else Pinella knew.

"Kessa is sleeping with Vestin Alcott since she found out about Owen's death. There is no telling what he knows." Octavia remained silent. Everyone knew Kessa Waymar was busybody and a gossip. It must have been painfully hard to discover that Octavia's only beloved brother had been so easily forgotten by his second wife. "No one knows except me and the steward who brought it to my attention. How do you want me to proceed?"

Octavia took a long moment to consider, visibly conflicted.

Pinella felt relieved and justified all at once. She took a slow, satisfied sip of her tea. It was good. Riva had taught the girl well.

When Octavia spoke, she said the most unexpected thing. "I will bring Kessa to heel and inform Livra and Karianna. We will deal with this before it becomes public and we become disgraced. Until then, keep this secret and make certain that the steward who told you remains quiet about this. The Tribunes still suspect you, which will give us time to sort this issue."

"Octavia, they called my honor into question. While I was exiled, I held my husband's name, but when I joined your family, I was restored as inheritor of my father's legacy. As long as they question my honor, they question my father's honor." Pinella was sincere. She hoped that Octavia wasn't so unconcerned with Pinella's reputation that she would use her to draw attention from her own family's guilt.

"I will be able to vindicate you, Pinella. But for now, give me time to straighten this all out. I need to speak with my sisters-in-law. This affects the entire family. I commend you on your progress with the vassal families." Octavia wore her typical smile that was only sincere because Pinella had defended herself to the woman who should have been defending her.

Octavia gave Pinella a reassuring squeeze of the hand that offered no reassurance before standing and leaving Pinella alone in the study with her tea. She probably thought all was good between them, but Pinella's heart was further from Octavia than ever.

Chapter Thirty-Eight

Waking Up

Cicero

He was tied up again. The jump must have knocked him out. He didn't know how, but they must have pulled him out and tied him up. Cicero was sure the water would've killed them both, but thankfully it only slept him and unthankfully didn't hurt the beast. The body trader sat cross legged in front of him, humming that horrid tune. He must have come to take the leg back. Well, at least Cicero wouldn't be needing it anymore.

"I didn't know!" Cicero's voice was strange and youthful.

"No. But you must be the one to pay," said Jaco, smiling sadly. The beast grabbed his leg painfully tight, and Cicero noticed the leg had lost its tattoos and the seam where the new leg met his was gone. The beast lifted a meat cleaver the size of a small axe to chop down onto his leg.

"Ahh! *Kaghhh*! *Kaghhh*!" Cicero coughed up brown water.

He sprawled and kicked at nothing, realizing he was alone. The river bubbled nearby. He had no idea of knowing how far the river had taken him or how long it'd been since he first went in. Pain and feverish mind fog radiated from the leg. Something about the water had damaged the bond on his leg. The tattoos were hardly the way they'd been and he could barely move the leg.

It was painful, but it held his weight as he stood. The woods were quiet all around him aside from the river's peaceful bubbling. He had to drag his leg at first but as he went, the seam between the legs was pressed together and he regained enough control over it to take slow, unbalanced steps. It wasn't like a normal limb with bone and interlocking muscles. It was soggy now, visibly affected by the water. It looked like a doll's leg sewed to his stump of a thigh. He limped, leaning against trees for balance as he went. At times, he would fall and rest where he lay before forcing himself up again. His eyesight was blurred and every joint ached.

Which way is south again? No, I'm going north, away from Hocklee. Is he still humming? How did I get on my back? Did I fall? I don't feel anything. Is the body trader coming? Is the big shroud he keeps with him nearby? Where is Swain? His thoughts swarmed his head, but he needed to lay there and try to rest. Swain was a good boy; he would be okay. He'd be back soon enough with some firewood.

Cicero was dry again, warm even, resting by a campfire. *Tied up again?* At least his leg stopped hurting, but how did he get dry? Cicero noticed it was nighttime.

Abruptly, he snapped back. Pain in the leg — no. *agony.* He was wet from the river. Cicero forced his way onto his feet. His leg was a problem. It didn't work, except the part that felt pain. The limb was worse than dead. Ever since he'd come out of the river, it affected the rest of him. The leg pulled out strength from the rest of his body, leaving feverish aches throughout. It was death.

Cicero heard some whistling somewhere out in the woods. Jaco Tro-Horm's tune, or Kerrick's. He recognized it instantly from the dreams the leg had given him. He also remembered them from when he changed the leg out. The whistling got closer. As it did, the other sounds in the forest became quieter. Cicero searched his possessions for a weapon. Foolish, he didn't have a weapon.

He didn't have any possessions. So he stood there, quietly hiding behind a thick tree trunk. As the whistling came closer, the pain became distant. His mind felt clear, filling with music. It was like being back in Trofaim again. He almost came out from behind the tree but remembered he was hiding from the sweet music. He thought he should run, but how far would he get before pain mounted in him again?

"Hello?" The whistle stopped and Cicero almost fell over for the sudden lack of balance. "I've been looking for you. Cicero of Hocklee, is it?" said the stranger. It wasn't Jaco, but a woman's voice that called out. Cicero poked his head out from behind the tree. He had no more fight or give. But he would do anything to get this woman to start whistling again. What were things coming to? Oh well, he just could not take the torture any longer.

He stepped out and looked at the woman, red of hair.

"Still alive?" she asked. Her body contorted in his slurred vision.

"I . . . I'm a little . . ." was all Cicero could manage.

She stepped closer toward him.

Cicero in turn stepped out toward her but toppled forward onto the ground.

"Your way has been difficult, I assume?" she said, sounding concerned. Cicero's mouth moved to say yes but nothing came out.

"Come help me, Bluehands," she said.

He felt himself giving over to sleep. He had nothing left in him.

Chapter Thirty-Nine

The Man with the Hood

Redeye

Vanno stepped between the bodies of soldiers who no one deemed worthy for a burial or so much as a shallow pit with enough dirt to cover their heads. Vanno wondered if any of them would consider him worthy of a few minutes of work for a burial. That made him start at burying some random dead soldier. He'd never met the man, but strangers would be his only hope if he went into a battle. All of his friends he'd only trusted until they could use him for their own gain, always at his loss. Battles, raids, and the rest were the best ways to trust a man in these wars.

"That man's one of Woodenhead's." It was Trego. He didn't spare any disgust for the dead man. He led like Cicero and was another noble, admirable, and feared man, all for good reason. You would have almost thought Trego couldn't lose a battle, the way the last few had turned out — particularly yesterday's.

"My mistake!" said Vanno, letting go of the dead man as though realizing he'd grabbed a snake. "Thought I recognized him for a moment!" He chuckled nervously, brushing the dirt off his hands. "So, are we making camp here chief?" Vanno was nervous to be speaking to the new High Chief.

"No, of course not. The dead make poor company." Trego had that way of speaking that made you always feel foolish. Vanno considered the living to be the most vicious company. At least you knew a dead man wouldn't kill you in your sleep for what you had in your pockets. He'd seen more than a few living ones do it, though.

"We will move east to gather more men and support before this new man everyone's talkin' about comes and presses us," said Trego.

"Shouldn't they fight alongside us? We're Galanoans too, aren't we?" Vanno knew it wasn't that simple, no matter how hard he wanted it to be. "How come Kalesia fights under one flag while we have as many flags as we do towns, each one going its own way?"

"Because Woodenhead was more evil than the Kalesians are. His nephew Bermand is the worst of all. As long as he's chief in Galanoa, we can't rest." Trego was always too intense. He never smiled and always had a reason to scowl. "This new man, Gallo, won't fight with us because of some old feud he's got with the chief of the Hockleets, Cicero. That's the only reason we haven't defeated Bermand in this territory."

"Aren't you the High Chief? Can't you tell Cicero to talk it over with Gallo? You could save us from all that trouble." Vanno, again, found himself doubting his own simple solution. Trego shook his head, looking up to where Cicero and his men made their camp.

"Not this time; it's not like it was with Yellowtooth. The blood between him and that man, Gallo, is even deeper than the blood between me and Endo Woodenhead, and I thought Woodenhead and I would burn Galanoa to the ground before our fight was done."

"You killed him at Begatto two winters before I came to fight with you. His presence is not missed from what I can tell," said Vanno.

"It's not quite forgotten. I understand a third of Gallo's men are sent to fight for Bermand, Endo Woodenhead's nephew. They're calling him Bermand Broadback. He's consolidating his uncle's chiefdom while his warman Gallo comes to fight us." Trego's face had grown dim. "Woodenhead's men ruled Eastern Galanoa before I even started fighting. I don't look forward to fighting 'em again. Sometimes I wonder if my alliance with Hocklee is worth more war with my own countrymen. With every day that passes, I see how different the men of Hocklee are from other Galanoans." Trego commented as Cicero started to come over with his closest, Lain and a young man from Hocklee, intending to speak with Trego.

"Zifix and Zeux say you can't be defeated," Vanno replied.

"Those cousins from Movatto? They're kin to me. They started that rumor because I haven't lost. Not because I won't."

Vanno wanted to believe Zeux and Zifix, but he was learning life wasn't as simple as he wanted it to be. Nothing was.

"Trego!" called Lain, still a ways off. "I've got a good youngster here for you to meet. This is Rector," Lain introduced the tall young man. "He comes from Brevalti, where my sister was married." Vanno figured Rector must be a few years younger than him. Vanno also noticed that the boy couldn't grow a beard. Vanno couldn't fault him though; Lain never could either.

"Always good to have another hand with us," said Trego, shaking the boy's hand. "You can learn from Vanno here!" Trego patted Vanno on the back. "Don't let Zeux mess with him too much." Vanno was surprised to be put in charge of anyone. It seemed odd. "Cicero, you'll take the whole flock of these Hockleet boys. I trust you'll make men of 'em."

Cicero nodded in response to Trego, nothing to say except, "Chief." That must have been why people called him the quiet man.

"We're heading north, eh, Chief?" asked Lain.

"Right," Trego nodded. "After the Kalesians. We'll finish them off before their reinforcements come."

And that was it. Vanno had a boy following him who knew nothing about war. He didn't know how to lead. He'd only been taught how to use people. He watched how Lain admired Cicero as he spoke to him. It'd be a fine thing, Vanno thought, to be admired like that. He decided to do what the quiet man did. Maybe in time, Rector would admire him. Zifix and Zeux would too. Well, not Zeux. That man admired nobody and seemed to mildly hate everyone and everything he saw. Truth was, Zifix, Zeux's older cousin, had been the closest person Vanno had to an ally. He wondered what it might take to turn him into a friend.

ॐ

Redeye blinked the rain out of his one eye as Rector pushed the last of the dirt over Zifix's corpse. The man he would've readily called his friend was now under the grass and Redeye was the one who put him there. Zeux stood still, finally, after not ceasing to move for the past hour of burial for his cousin. Some of the Hockleets had gathered at the mound to honor Zifix, but not as many as Redeye thought his friend deserved. They stood there in the cold wet wind, their hair and beards dripping rain, all of them silent. The shouts of people looting and being looted inside the city of Krahl nearby. Redeye knew he'd smell fires burning once the rain let up.

It was a man named Cilio that spoke first: "Zifix is gone. I met him when the Hood did his work at Brierly Hill. He was a rare man. Maybe the rarest ever. He was one of few men you could trust in and out of battle, the way you could trust Tork or even Trego." Cilio's voice began to falter. "May we all get a slice of the trustworthiness he had." Cilio stepped back into the crowd with the other Hockleets, the men around him nodding and voicing agreement.

Next to speak was Rector. "We didn't have much peace in Hocklee between the wars and now." Rector shifted his feet, looking down thoughtfully at the mound. That's the only emotion Redeye ever remembered Rector showing — thoughtfulness. "But what little peace we did have wasn't enough for Zifix. Zifix first saw things the Hood's way when he decided to give up war with Tork. He even helped convince Lain. I reckon he'll have peace now, but we should keep up the fight. Now that Tork's gone and Zifix is with him. We will keep the fight going." Rector stepped back into his place in the crowd.

Moments began to give way to more time past, and after a while, they became silent as the battle-hardened host had far too many emotions to fit through their mouths for their fallen ally.

"Zifix is my cousin. You all know that." Zeux was the one who spoke, his voice brimful with tears but refusing to overflow. "And, you know . . . I think I'll tell folk he was my brother."

Chapter Forty

Cazipran and The Fowler

Finnion

Reff was clearly annoyed but also subtly curious about the Lark of Tolon. Leighton had to be older than Reff but younger than Finnion. He was smart, and with how he'd conducted himself over the past day with them, Finn could tell there was a great deal he kept secret from the other Larks. Finnion didn't fault him for that though. The Battle of Brierly had confused them into distrust of one another.

"You said you know more about the Shrikes than me!" Reff's voice spilled from him like steam from a hot kettle. He was eager to hear out this Lark. Finnion could tell that was the desired effect. Whereas he admired Leighton's charismatic prowess, Finnion was careful to make sure he wasn't deceived by Leighton's words. Finnion was still Reff's ally. No amount of rash words spoken would keep Finnion from protecting the young man.

"Well," said the Lark, "I don't know what you know; we've only just met." Finnion could tell he was figuring out Reff much quicker than Reff was learning anything. "But, I've lived here all my life. I worked in intelligence south of Lavinth before the first rebellion."

"No way!" said Finnion. "You would've been no more than ten years old back then!"

Reff's gaze darted to Finnion then back to Leighton.

"I was eight," he said unexpectedly. "I carried information between spies for my father. That was before they called it the guild of the Lark. In those days, they began calling my father the Lark. That's where the groundwork for the Highwater Rebellion came from." That was surprising for Finnion.

"The Lark is a loyalist guild. It makes no sense that they would work against the Wing for the rebellion," said Finnion, half asking how it could be possible.

"The Songbird Army has always been a formidable army, but it was a force unparallelled in those days." Finnion remembered when the Songbird Army was comprised of five thousand and seven hundred men.

"They were a horror of a thing," Leighton continued, "but it's how they wage war, not simply how they fight their battles that is truly horrific." He put the ladle back in the soup cauldron and set the entire cauldron off the fire to cool.

"The city-state of Trofaim doesn't just wage war with its sword. That's not even foremost among all of its weapons." Reff appeared to be beyond patriotic woundedness. He was so surprised by all the new things challenging his limited understanding that he just sat listening.

"So what is their foremost weapon?" asked Finn, already knowing, but testing to see the Lark's understanding of politics in Trofaim.

Leighton smiled. "It's not the Chamber of Tribunes! I'll tell you that with confidence!" he laughed. "It's their total control of law and order."

Finnion knew he was right.

"If there is no law, the state falls into anarchy. This is what happened when the Highwater Rebellion arose. The men of the Songbird Army have never delegated the duty of policing anyone outside their own families. They do this so that if there is any protest to corruption from the people, the Shrikes leave the area lawless."

"Commoners aren't capable of policing themselves," Reff said, shaking his head.

"Of course they are," said Leighton. "But the men capable of judging and enforcing laws are removed in their rebellion against the Company. This lawless, vulnerable state is why we're currently under mercenary rule. Cazprien understood that in the creation of this new uprising. He couldn't trust the mercenaries to fight the Wing because he knew Trofaim would pay the Storinian Army a substantial amount to turn on the rebels. He made the hardest decision by leaving his country to the tyranny of mercenaries in order to rid it of corruption."

"Why did Cazprien abandon the Highwater Rebellion?" asked Finnion.

"He didn't abandon it. He gave his life for it, but he must've understood that it was time to start over."

"Who is Cazprien?" asked Reff.

Leighton smiled, considering something.

Finnion waited for what the Lark thought he knew. Whatever it was, almost nobody knew who Cazprien was.

"Your last name is Bennault, right?" The Lark asked Reff. Finnion felt his brow furrow. Reff nodded.

"Akten only had a single daughter, though, so what was your father's last name?"

Finnion's eyes opened wide. He wanted to stop the madman. Reff might become wild if he found out the truth. But he couldn't give himself up to the Lark.

"Talister, isn't it?"

Reff lost some of the color in his face. The boy slowly nodded again.

"Ronald Talister is your father, yes?"

How could this obscure man know the truth about Ronald Talister? Finnion now wondered if it'd been this man who betrayed Reff's father. Maybe Finnion would kill him if he found that to be true.

"You probably thought your father died years ago."

"He did die. But my father wasn't a . . . he wasn't . . ."

"A rebel?" asked Leighton. "He was *the* rebel. He was Cazprien himself. How do you feel about being Cazprien's son and the last threat to the Wing?"

Finnion was amazed. This man was more than a spy.

"That must be a lie. My mother is a Wingman's daughter," said Reff, retaking composure. "My father was family, son-in-law no less, to the Hero of Paveneli!"

"Why do you think he began his rebellion shortly after your grandfather's death?" asked Leighton. Reff's eyes scanned the floor for answers, evidently finding none. Leighton spoke after a long moment. "Akten Bennault was betrayed by the Wing. That's what sparked the whole thing."

Finnion couldn't believe he knew. He would've never thought he'd see anyone who knew Cazprien's true identity beside himself.

"I'm considering you to be a slanderer of my father," growled Reff. "You must be a rebel, trying to turn me against my people!" Leighton seemed calm. Finnion was not calm. Reff had spoken endlessly about his family's honor and constantly looked for a reason to draw his sword.

"How had I slandered your family? Both your father and grandfather were heroes." Leighton had his hands lifted in surrender.

"Why don't you follow the rebels now then, if you consider Cazprien to be a hero?" asked Finnion, slicing through the tension with the right question.

"Cazprien is either lost or he's been betrayed. The rebellion changed after their latest victory at Brierly. He's alive, though. I think that's how his son here was the only survivor."

That hit Reff hard. He stood up and left the house, saying nothing. No doubt it crushed him to hear so much so abruptly. Finnion was also surprised that the Lark knew so much, but he was also wrong about some speculations. It was good to see that this man, as informed as he was, didn't know that Reff's father was dead and that Finnion was the real Cazprien that took his place.

"He will need time to consider all that you've told him. It may take a long time," said Finn.

"I'm surprised it took him so long to discover any of this," Leighton sighed. "I'd almost say he's naive."

"And I'd say there's worse a man could be," said Finnion.

Leighton studied him. "You should be careful with him. Leaving him alive was the greatest mistake the rebels or the corrupt nobility could've made."

"I'll take my chances. His family needs someone they can trust." Finnion's tone was subtly accusatory.

"What's that supposed to mean, exactly?" demanded Leighton.

"It means some Lark must've betrayed Trofaim for the rebels to deliver such a crippling defeat to the Wing." Finnion had to get him to think defensively to defend himself from this man's genius. Finnion had thought of the old man Benneck as honest and patriotic, but this man of the guild of Larks struck him as dangerous. He showed a clear willingness to only protect his own interests but held the trust of enough of the remaining Larks to speak for his better intentions. "You're telling me you didn't betray the Wing, but you consider Cazprien a hero and the rebel cause to be noble. If I were looking for a rebel sympathizer among the Larks, I'd say I found one."

"The rebel cause is as noble a cause as a man could ever find." Finnion agreed with the Lark's statement but didn't show it. "But all their actions are not justly warranted. Cazprien's generals are more corrupt than the ones they aim to replace." Again, Finnion agreed and again, said nothing of his agreement. "If he obtains power, they'll assassinate him immediately after they take Trofaim." Leighton stood up, brushing crumbs off the table. "Take the money. No traitor of yours pays you."

Finnion stayed seated, considering everything. He was right in that they tried to kill him to take control. He watched the Lark clean the cauldron and wondered if this man was an ally or an enemy. Whatever he was, Finnion would use him as a resource.

"What should be done to the rebellion, then?" asked Finnion.

"It must be rebuilt," said the Lark.

Finn agreed.

CHAPTER FORTY-ONE

JUSTICE FOR TRAITORS

PINELLA

Pinella recieved a certain joy watching young Omera Waymar learn from Riva. Pinella watched in amazement as a woman who had been a slave her whole life taught a girl who grew up with everything how to find joy. Omera had been so gloomy and reclusive after her father's death. Now her face radiated light like a lamp post, amazed by the many different words Riva could write with the few letters Omera had allowed. In so many of her mannerisms, she resembled her aunt Octavia far more than her mother. Seeing Omera's growing bond with Riva made Pinella's heart ache for how her own relationship with Octavia had become so strained.

Pinella had returned from the Upper City at the request from the ladies Waymar. It was the first she heard from them since her explosive confrontation with Octavia two weeks earlier. She was left to wonder if Octavia would do the right thing and expose Kessa's treachery, or if she would do what was best for the Waymars and let Pinella be suspected as the rebel conspirator.

A while later, Hess retrieved Pinella, escorting her into the conference room guarded by an armed Waymar soldier who Pinella hadn't met before. The table was surrounded by Octavia,

285

Livra, Karianna, and Kessa Waymar. Kessa, she noticed, had the puffy red eyes of someone who had been crying. When Pinella sat down, they all rejected Hess's offer for food and drink. Octavia thanked the servant woman and dismissed her, every word formal and painfully tense. The door closed and the women were alone for a silent moment before Livra spoke.

"Good afternoon, Pinella. Thank you for coming all this way to meet us and discuss our next course of action as a family. We have a lot to tell you, so please allow us to explain everything."

Pinella fought the urge to roll her eyes. Livra always spoke like she was the most senior member of her family. She was just the oldest. "Of course," said Pinella with a smile and nod.

Octavia spoke next. "We have brought you in as witness to our decision of justice as a family." Again Pinella nodded. "Our sister has been proven guilty of giving away secrets of our family amidst acts of debauchery, a dishonorable offense against her own family and late husband. She has also befriended and disclosed secret information to certain individuals who have aligned themselves with murderous enemies of Trofaim."

Kessa began to cry again as Octavia cited her crimes.

Karianna smiled knowingly in a way that interested Pinella. The woman didn't have the same look of justified anger that her eldest sister wife had.

Octavia continued. "As a family, our decision is that Kessa Waymar be completely ostracized from House Waymar." Kessa wimpered. Octavia and Livra both endured the formality, while Karianna kept looking carelessly around the windowless room.

Pinella could sense the pain in each of Octavia's words as she spoke them. It made Pinella regret despising Octavia for not judging Kessa immediately. They had been sisters for nearly two decades.

Pitiably, Kessa said nothing in self-defense. She just sat and cried, looking down at her lap, ashamed. Octavia addressed Kessa now, "Kessa, now that you are stripped of your familial standing, we are going to give you over to the Tribunal to be judged for your crimes against the state. You will not receive legal support or defense from the Waymar family. We have arranged for you to be detained here in your room until you are escorted to the prison. Do you have anything to say?"

Kessa just slowly shook her head in humiliation. It was a shame, but it was just.

When Octavia finished speaking, the room became quiet enough for them to hear the noise of a crowd of people and footsteps coming from all over the house. Pinella and Octavia looked at each other, looking for answers and finding none.

Livra spoke first. "Sounds like the children have become rowdy." She stood up and left the room. It was clear to both Pinella and Octavia that the sound was more than just the children playing. Kessa was unmoved, swallowed in tears. Then Pinella noticed the ghost of a grin on Karianna's face, like she was trying to hold back a laugh. When the door opened again, it was not Livra who entered but the strange face of bald man. A Shrike in his ceremonial armor. The Waymar guard drew his sword to protect the Waymars.

The Shrike looked at the guard who was in the room, with his sword now drawn. He paud him littlen regard, similar to how one might view a child who pretends he's a dangerous warrior just because he's found a sharp object.

Without any hostile demeanor, he spoke to the table of women. "My name is Rien Alcott, Ward of the Alcott family, and I have come with my men on behalf of the Tribunes of Trofaim to place . . ." He took a moment to identify the faces in the room. "Most of you into custody for withholding affairs of treason from the Tribunal." Rien looked off into space in an effort to remember something. "I think that's all of it. On your feet. Let's get going. I'll be waiting outside."

Before he made his exitm, Rien looked once more at the guard, still ferociously intense with his sword still drawn. "Unless you'd like to take a try . . ." When the guard did not attack, Rien smiled and winked at him before leaving the room.

Octavia directed her attention from the door to Pinella. "What is this?"

"I don't know. I haven't told the Alcotts. I haven't told anyone."

Octavia's expression accused Pinella, but before she could say anything, Karianna spoke for the first time since Pinella had come: "I did."

Everyone paused at what they just heard. All three women turned to the youngest widow of Owen Waymar. Even the guard stared at her as she stood.

"What do you mean, Karianna? Sit back down! You did what?"

She did not sit back down. Like a satisfied cat slinking off to a nap, she left the room. After a moment of baffled looks to one another, they stood up to follow her.

Pinella followed Octavia out of the room where they were herded by more soldiers out of the house. Scribes and counselors were all forced out like criminals and put into a large group with the Waymar women and children. Scribes and counselors were brought out as well, but Pinella never saw Riva with them. Karianna stood apart next to Otrin Waymar, both of them unguarded. The man named Rien Alcott spoke to them with a friendly manner.

Octavia called to him. "Otrin! What is this?!"

The young man swept his eyes across his own family being

treated like criminals. "This is you being imprisoned for treason." Otrin looked over one shoulder at Rien. "You told them, didn't you?" Alcott nodded. "He says he already told you . . ."

"Otrin, tell them that we haven't withheld anything. We were about to present your mother before the Tribunal within the hour."

"No, no, Aunt Octavia. Karianna stands witness to your commands to conceal acts of family treasons."

At that moment, Kessa cried out. "My son, what are you doing?! We are your family!"

Otrin made a show of his next statement. "They are my family, but they have committed treason against Trofaim. I will not endorse or sanction such crimes." Turning to Rien Alcott, he said, "This is everyone. The children were not involved."

The soldiers commanded servants to take the young children so that the woman could be led away. Pinella was so confused. Octavia only looked heavily inconvenienced. Kessa clearly had no idea what motivated her son to accuse his family of her crimes.

Octavia hardened her voice as she addressed her nephew. "Otrin, this is very serious. Confess to your little conspiracy immediately, or your mother won't be able to protect you from me."

Otrin just looked from Octavia to Rien, and after nodding to the soldier, he turned to Karianna, who Pinella noticed to be wearing a hungry smile at her nephew.

Then a guard shoved her toward the Upper City prison.

CHAPTER FORTY-TWO

THE WALL

REDEYE

Vanno woke up suddenly to the alarming sound of a dog barking. Before his mind had enough time to separate dreams from reality, his sword was in hand and he was on his feet. Vanno peered over the battlements of Hocklee, looking for Bloodway's men. Seeing nothing in the pale morning light except the naked stone between expanses of enemies, Vanno looked inside the walls of Hocklee instead, seeing only typical early morning stillness. Aside from Cicero's dog barking and circling his tent at the base of the wall, the soft chimney smoke was the only movement behind the walls. The new scout that had Vanno's old job was named Lairo; he stood watchfully looking over the wall. Vanno became aware of his heart beating fast and tried to slow his breathing. He wiped the sleep out of his eyes, but when he touched the left one, the pain reminded him his eye had been gouged out. The eye did not hurt half as bad as it had a week before but was not fully healed either.

He pushed the awful memory of it down and tried to find a distraction from the things he'd lost in the last months. Just over an arrow's shot away, the Galanoans sat at the bottom of the Green Hill where the Mudway washes out endless amounts of soil every year. It had been nearly seventy days since Gallo and his entire maniple, composed of ten warscores of men, had set siege to Hocklee.

In over three months, Cicero and less than two warscores had pushed back four of Gallo's attempts to take the city. Thanks to Cicero's leadership and the rains making the Mudway soft, the city of Hocklee was still free. A few survivors from Movatto were among the Hockleets, along with some farmers-turned-soldiers. The Galanoans waited for Cicero to defend the city from the Kalesian Army at the Highpines. While the Hockleets were away, they sacked the city and made the Mudway into a river of blood with all the Kalesian people who lived in Hocklee. Cicero and his small band of outlaws came to relieve Hocklee, only to find hundreds of dead and the city largely abandoned. Vanno had found his mother dying in her home for no other reason except that she was born a Kalesian who chose to raise her boy in the town of Hocklee. They found little aside from dead and wounded in Hocklee that night.

When the sun rose the next morning, Gallo had the city surrounded with Cicero's small band under siege in the pillaged hilltop fortress. As a child, Redeye remembered the city elders throwing down ropes and helping invading armies into the city in order to avoid a sack or being starved in a siege. Cicero offered no surrender even after Gallo had killed so many and raided the town. For as long as the siege lasted, the Hockleets lived on what little resources hadn't been taken. To make it worse, Gallo left many innocent wounded and maimed so that Cicero would have to spend what little resources they did have to take care of them.

Vanno realized the dog had stopped barking and looked back into the city as Hockleet soldiers began to stir. Cicero stood outside his tent, speaking to Lain, who stood as Vanno's chief. Rector and the cousins stood nearby, all in their armor with weapons at their sides.

"Ready for Blood, Redeye?" came the voice of a fellow wallman named Elmo. Vanno wasn't completely used to people calling him Redeye yet.

"Why would there be blood today? The enemy hasn't even left their camp yet," he said, not understanding what Elmo meant.

"Ask Cicero," Elmo told him with a nudge. "I'll watch the wall for you." With that, Elmo made his way up the ladder and Vanno made his way toward the men congregating around Cicero's tent.

"Chief?" said Vanno, attempting to get Lain's attention. The cousins, Zifix and Zeux, both clapped him on the shoulder in greetings. Vanno and Rector each nodded to one another as always. He didn't trust anyone as much as Rector.

"Good morning, Van," said Lain with a nod, "Are your weapons ready?" Vanno nodded. He had spent the night prepared to defend the wall. At that, Lain nodded to Cicero. "My men are all here," he said.

Cicero, the recent chief of Hocklee, looked at all the men eagerly looking to him for orders.

"We have been here for thirty-four days without sufficient food or supplies. In our current standing, we can go for maybe another month before we starve to death. The only resource we have in excess is water from the spring. The rains have stopped for the season, and soon, the Mudway will dry. When it does, Gallo will come up the hill and fight us while we're starving and, by that time, even more outnumbered." Many of the men shuffled and shifted uncomfortably at the bleak reality.

"Even worse than that, they may test our strength and, when we're weak enough, they will leave a small enough force to keep us trapped here while they take the rest of our land." Their high chief was speaking more than he had at any one time since they'd been locked up in Hocklee together.

Cicero pointed to an adolescent boy, too young to be of any experience in war, but he had a devil's expression that made him look meaner than Zeux. "This is Hezro of Movatto," Cicero said, introducing the youth. Cicero nodded and Hezro cleared his throat.

"Movatto has fallen!" Hezro's voice cracked with the proclamation. Men began to murmur at the news of the only other town allied with Hocklee's revolution having been taken.

"Hezro climbed the cliff last night to bring the news that Trego's family was killed in the sack of Movatto," announced Lain. Vanmo's heart sank. Men were stirring all around. Cicero motioned for silence before speaking again.

"Men of Hocklee. You and I are the last who still believe in the dream of freedom from Kalesian kings and Galanoan feuds." He drew his sword swiftly from its scabbard. "We will not wait for them to take us down. We will not starve either."

Lain pulled out his own sword as support for Cicero. Yellowtooth drew his as well. The sound of weapons clattering soon filled the air.

"Eat well, men of Hocklee. If they want to make monsters of us, they will have monsters of the worst kind imaginable. Tonight is our last night under siege!"

⁊⦁

Redeye sat among the Hockleets watching the Southern Army pour into the fortress of Krahl from atop its mighty stone walls.

"Do you think he will make another Bloodway for his namesake?" said Zeux with a disgusted look on his face. Many of the others expressed their own grumblings, but never as blunt as Zeux.

"I would help him if he did!" said Callox. "When Gallo made the Mudway red, it was those Kalesian trespassers that he used to do it."

To Redeye's surprise, some of the men on the wall agreed with him as well. Zeux must've had his fill of death because he remained uncharacteristically silent. But Hezro, one of Zeux and Rector's closest, who they called The Youngest, stood up to reply.

"Some of those Kalesian trespassers had lived in Hocklee for generations. I lost a half-sister because her father was from Dalrock!" Hezro's voice got deeper and louder with emotion. "You all who hate Kalesians should ask Gallo why he joined Tork. It's 'cause Hoodless pushed him off the Hocklee wall and down the green hill four times. Cicero's victory decided that there were no more Kalesians or Galanoans." Callox squared up with Hezro, who was much smaller than himself.

Callox was a big man, and known for it. He had that big frame that men of Western Galanoa had. To Redeye, Hezro looked just like Zifix for a second. The short Hockleet looked stout but not as tall or as broad as the big Westerner. Redeye thought he might have seen Hezro twitch, and he felt shivers go up and down his spine. *Who was going to interfere? Someone should stop this,* he thought. Then he remembered it was his task.

"Hold it!" Redeye shouted. His voice, even to him, sounded cold and harsh. "Whereas I don't care for you Western Galanoans, Youngest is right." Redeye stepped forward and paced between the two men. Callox gave no ground, but Hezro backed up to give space for him to stand between them. "I agree with how he says there ain't Galanoans or Kalesians anymore." Callox and his men snarled their disagreements while the outnumbered Hockleets behind him were silent. Redeye knew it wasn't fearful silence though. He recognized it to be the silence Cicero and Bloodway had. It was the type of silence the men of Hocklee used to think together. No doubt they watched him intently for a hidden cue at which they would snap like a dry twig in the wind.

"I think it's wishful thinkin'!" said the big Galanoan.

"Tell that to Broadback," Redeye snapped back. Callox's brow wrinkled, unable to understand Redeye's meaning. "See those Kalesian dead down there?" he said, pointing to the stacks of dead being piled up outside the gates. "They agreed with you. Bermand Broadback agrees with you as well. But we fight for Gallo Bloodway. It was him who said we're uniting the South. This city ain't Kalesian or Galanoan. Fact is, it's not even Hockleet. It's Southern." Redeye was speaking cooler now. It took time adjusting to the role, but adjusting he was.

"Look," Redeye said, eyes narrowing and voice quieting as he sank back into the familiar role of killer. "I understand if you find it hard to follow a man you haven't heard of — but look around, Callox," he said, pointing to all the scattered dead as they were being gathered and carted outside the gates of Krahl. "See how many men I have killed today? Not *nearly* enough. I'm afraid that some may call Redeye merciful." His voice was low enough that everyone else was silent to hear him. "I let Yellowtooth in, and I don't think he'd mind me spending a proud Galanoan to buy the fear of his men."

Callox loomed in front of him with exactly the same fearless expression. The big man didn't show it, but by the way he shifted his weight from one foot to the other, Redeye could feel that he put fear in him.

"You want a name?" came a deep voice behind Callox. "Our old chief is coming to Krahl."

The Hockleets said as little as the Galanoans. Redeye was not expecting that. He thought if he gave some hard words like Yellowtooth, then they would follow him like men followed Trego or Tork.

"We will play along until then," said Callox.

Why had Redeye thought they would start trouble with him while the advantage was his? Of course they'd give him the hollow victory for now and come back for it later.

Callox backed away, eyeing the other Hockleets.

"He'll put himself with Big Crooked," said Rector.

Hezro put his hand on Redeye's shoulder. "Don't worry, boss," he growled. "We beat Galanoa once. Cicero said, 'Whatever it is, we can do it if we trust each other.'"

Redeye looked at Zeux, who stood at the edge of the wall, looking at the spot where they had buried his cousin below. If any of them found out that he had allowed Igoss to kill Zifix, Redeye would be alone in his fight with the Galanoans.

The fight went cold, and Rector sent the Galanoan troublemakers into the city. They slept that night on and around the wall. The wall was the closest thing the Hockleets had to home.

CHAPTER FORTY-THREE

MONSTER MAKER

REDEYE

In war, you prepare. You prepare your weapons when they're not sharp. You clean your armor if it can be cleaned. You feed your horse if you have one. You prepare for a thing as close to hell as you'll get in life. War is the time spent preparing for battle.

In battle, everything breaks. Your horse leaves you if it isn't killed. Your armor gets wet with blood and heavy on your body. Your sword breaks from the use. In battle, you fight until there is no preparation good enough, no sufficient arrangement. If you live long enough in battle, you see men break one another with broken hands and breaking hearts.

Redeye knew it all well enough. He knew war and battle like a farmer knows the ground. And still, he found himself in war again. Like a drunk asking for another drink at a new tavern, he tried telling himself it wouldn't be as bad as the last. He knew, though, that he would lose himself again, the way Vanno had been lost to Redeye. *Is that why Cicero protected those two little kids? Was he only saving them, or could he have been looking for something he'd lost? Does one find themselves in doing differently? Could he overcome evil with good?*

As Gallo Bloodway rode his horse next to Gristax, he tipped his head to Redeye, somehow picking him out of the men on the high wall. Redeye's stomach dropped. Only a week since he'd seen Bloodway and now the man dominated half of Kalesia. What measure of good, Redeye wondered, could overcome the evil in this man? At that moment, he heard Yellowtooth's splitting whistle come from behind him down in the city of Krahl. Yellowtooth, standing amongst Gorring and many more killers, motioned for Redeye to come down. He felt all the eyes of his men on him.

"Rector, stay with the men." The fact that he would be in charge didn't need saying. "Hezro, with me." Redeye didn't want to leave Hezro for fear he'd cause more trouble. Without any acknowledgement from his men, Redeye turned to the stairs. He could feel Zeux looking at him but didn't want to look.

Yellowtooth was one of the most cutthroat men to ever walk the hills of Hocklee. He stood with Cicero until Cicero made peace, then his old ally became an outlaw. Redeye wanted to believe in peace, but when Cicero bought land far out in Begatto, saying he wanted to restore the land he'd burned, Redeye found that peace was as complicated as war was simple. Soon enough, he was back with Yellowtooth.

Igoss was there as well, not meeting Redeye's gaze. Yellowtooth smiled hideously when he saw Hezro and Redeye approaching.

"Where's Rector?" he asked, looking around just a little nervous.

"I left him with Zeux." Redeye answered.

Yellowtooth nodded and looked at Hezro. "Your daddy still alive, boy?"

When Redeye turned to Hezro, he noticed a calm look on his face.

"He died a little after you all passed through," Hezro said as he spat on the smooth stone street.

Redeye wasn't sure what they were talking about. Yellowtooth just nodded.

"Shame! I'm glad you're with us at least," Yellowtooth said, turning back up the street toward where Bloodway had gone. His long curly hair blowing in the wind as he went. He didn't ask or even tell Redeye to follow, he just went assuming they would. Gorring, The Bridgeman, and Greyblood going behind him. Those men were the darkest Redeye could think of among the living. He couldn't get his head to understand how these were nearly his equals now.

"Pretty hard to find a darker set of men from Hocklee," said Hezro grimly.

Redeye just looked forward and gestured his agreement. They made their way after Yellowtooth into the captured fortress city of Krahl.

⋅♠⋅

Redeye watched Gristax duck under the low door frame just before him as they entered the Governor of Krahl's court at Bloodway's summons. Boban stood guard at a sort of throne with a man in expensive clothing tied to the ornate metal chair. The captive in the chair had a hood covering his face, the sack cloth stained dark brown with blood spots.

"Hello, Chief!" said Boban enthusiastically. It took an expectant moment before Redeye realized Boban was addressing him. Redeye responded with a nod. *Chief?* He wondered if that would ever feel normal. Redeye looked around the room, seeing the rest of Gallo's men of war. Crooked and his men stood to themselves in a group. Some spoke quietly while Big Crooked eyed Yellowtooth.

Redeye noticed the same man who locked eyes with him after the death of Tork. Redeye didn't let the fearful shiver that ran up his spine show.

"Who's this man that challenges you with his eyes?" asked Hezro with a whisper.

"I just think he wants to be my friend," Redeye replied. Hezro snorted, trying to keep in a laugh. Soon, Redeye heard a familiar sound that washed the whole room in uneasy tension, which by comparison, made the national rivalry seem a light affair.

Jaco Tro-Horm's tune echoed down the hallway, getting closer as he came. The only person who didn't seem uneasy was Yellowtooth. The old mercenary-turned-man-of-war picked something from under his fingernails as if speaking with the most feared man in the South was a mundane activity.

Gallo Bloodway was not a man easily identified. He didn't wear distinct clothing like Yellowtooth and the Galanoan men of war. He didn't mind if his enemies knew what his face looked like, somehow making him more feared than the rest. He didn't care if men demonstrated their respect for him or gave any kind of salute or bow. It caused an unease, not knowing how to behave around him. Bloodway entered the room casually, studying the stones of the courtroom floor. He didn't nod, or glare, or smile. He was different, different like Cicero except much more greatly feared.

Redeye cringed at the sight of the switch Jaco Tro-Horm.

Jaco smiled so widely at the sight of Redeye, his face must have hurt.

"Good Redeye!" said the switch. "How have you fared since we last met north of Hocklee-Town?"

Redeye hesitated, disgusted. Suddenly he missed the man's humming. "I've fared," Redeye said, leaning back and looking away.

"What a relief!" he responded with a huge white smile before moving on with Bloodway to inspect the man in restraints. Red-eye watched as the two huge-bodied shrouds followed after them. These characters were covered in dark cloaks, following Jaco like dogs after their master. They wore canvas hoods over their heads with no slits to see through, yet they didn't stumble.

"Yellowtooth, I'm pleased with your taking of this city," Bloodway said, appraising the room they stood in.

"I'm just as pleased to give it to you, as I was to not lift a finger in the taking."

Bloodway looked at Yellowtooth with a ghost of curiosity; that was the most concern Gallo had given thus far.

"Red here had most of the work worked out before I could so much as ride up." Yellowtooth winked at Redeye, showing another row of plagued brown teeth.

Gallo Bloodway nodded thoughtfully in consideration before apparently considering Redeye. "Have you ever visited this fortress, Redeye?"

"No . . . Chief. I haven't. I sent men from Kalesia, and some of them are from Krahl. They knew how to sneak in. I leaned heavily on this man." Redeye pointed to Boban, at whom Bloodway spared a quick unimpressed glance.

"Thank you, Redeye." said Gallo as warm as one who speaks to a brother.

Redeye had always wanted to be praised in front of other jealous men. How many times had he imagined a thing like this? But it was empty, worthless compared to the friendship he'd lost with Zifix.

The man in the chair gasped as Gallo removed the sweaty hood that veiled the restrained man's head. Through long glossy curls, the man's swollen eyes strained to see around him. Muffled grunts came out of his gagged mouth.

"Hello!" Bloodway smiled warmly. "I am Gallo Bloodway, Commander of the Southern Army of Alssae. I'm honored, as you must be Governor Balt." Redeye couldn't find a trace of sarcasm or mockery in the way Bloodway spoke. "I heard of your victory in the white woods against Cicero. As I understand, you were closest to Tork in those days. That would've been before Tork betrayed you to join Cicero and drove you from Hocklee." Bloodway rested a palm on the governor's shoulder and spoke fondly, like he was catching up with an old friend. "I sent word to you offering an alliance before we attacked," Gallo said, as if the message had been lost in the rain rather than sending the messenger's scalp with one ear still attached. Redeye cringed at what the man's near future must have entailed.

"Perhaps I am to blame. I should've offered my help back when Tork betrayed you and after Cicero betrayed me. In those dark days, the circumstances would've made allies of us." He looked out the window over the fortress to the city of Krahl. Bloodway's expression revealed a desire to return to the past with a second chance. "How sad it is that circumstances are now so unfavorable for us." A sad look spread across his face as he looked back at the governor. It seemed like Gallo was sincere. "The young man I sent came with men from this city to ask for help. They offered my friendship to you."

As the governor moaned through the rag that stuffed his mouth, Gallo studied him. A tear left a streak down the man's grimy cheek.

"I sent a young man who would've died for me." Gallo looked up at Boban. "Did you know any of the Kalesian men that I sent?"

Boban stared straight forward in rigid attention. "My nephew was among them," said Boban.

Gallo set his other hand on Boban's shoulder. With a sad face, he said, "I did not know that, Boban. Do you have blood with this governor now?"

"You could say something like that," the Kalesian said grimly.

"Please relax. You don't owe me all of this honor." Boban's shoulders slackened and his eyes came unstuck from that place on the wall to look at Bloodway. "Would you like to be the one who deals with this man?"

At that, Governor Balt struggled against his ties and failed to speak with his throat stuffed with cloth.

"M . . . Me, sir?" asked Boban in amazement.

"This is your town, isn't it? He was your chief who wronged you, wasn't he? Why not you?"

"Sir." Boban shook his head in protest. "I am not a commander in this army. I should have little say."

Bloodway looked around the room, his face puzzled. "You took the city, didn't you? Why wouldn't you have a say in this matter?"

"Redeye is my chief. Let him have the decision," said Boban reverently.

"Redeye has no blood with this man. Neither does Yellowtooth. You and I, though, we have a great deal of blood."

Boban looked around the room. When his glance reached Redeye, it stopped there a moment, waiting for approval. Redeye nodded his endorsement, and only then did Boban look back to Gallo.

"I would not be here, on the right or wrong side, unless I was your man, sir."

Redeye worried for Boban, as he was a good man and honorable fighter. It seemed the noble Kalesian was starting to believe the legend of Gallo Bloodway. A man of so much honor . . . Would Bloodway ask him to kill one of his own to keep trust he thought he already earned?

"Boban," said Redeye, "I do have blood with this man, but I will give my right to settle up with him to you." Boban's eyes widened.

"After all, none of us would be here," Gallo gestured around at the courtroom's opulence before poking a finger into Boban's chest, "if you weren't with us."

The men in the room stood silent. Redeye could tell Boban wasn't accustomed to the Galanoan spoil traditions. The Kalesian man stood nervously, a foreigner in this room of Galanoans. No doubt he was worried after Gallo's consolidation of the Southern Army following Tork's death.

Gallo smiled. "I have an idea!" he said, turning to the Kalesian men flanking Boban. "Go get the rest of the notable men of this city. Bring liars and gossipers. Men you don't mind sparing." As the men left the room discussing their options, Gallo smiled at Boban. "How would you like to earn a name for yourself among your enemies?"

CHAPTER FORTY-FOUR

THE PHYSICIAN

FINNION

Several days were spent in Tolon under the protection of Leighton, The Lark of the South. The whole southern region of Trofaim had been under mercenary law for over six years while Finnion conducted the rebellion. The conditions of mercenary law were rarely smooth, but the conditions in Southeastern Trofaim had gotten so bad that famine had begun to set in as farmed goods or livestock was hoarded by the farmers and ranchers who raised them. People were forced to hold onto any resources from supporting the mercenaries. The Storinian Mercenary Army, that numbered in the thousands, weighed down on the locals.

Finnion spoke to many of the Lark's loyalist workers, discovering that the mercenaries, lazy and used to ruling the struggling people of Trofaim, had implemented gangs of young locals to collect taxes and supplies for the mercenaries. These gangs, composed of criminals and war refugees, were the exact type of individuals that the mercenaries were there to ward off. They were used to sapping life from those they were there to protect.

Finnion sat on the Lark's porch as the rain persisted for the fifth day in a row. His leg had begun to heal but he could tell it wasn't healing the way it should. The pain decreased but his mobility grew worse in the knee. He had that feeling of worry constantly nagging at him, telling him to let a physician see it, but he had so much to do, so many of the Lark's men to meet with. Trust had to be built with these men. Procrastination was also, in part, due to his fear of hearing the leg would have to be amputated or that it was past the point of proper healing.

In the past, Finnion only trusted his personal physician, Greenan. The man had been a local doctor before joining the rebels, and he had always taken care of the leadership of the army. Finnion had trusted him, and Greenan used that trust to steal the army and spend these poor people for their own conquest.

While he sat on the porch, waiting for the next man in the body of Larks to approach the porch, he thought about the past. So many moments of comradery and generosity were shared between him and his friend, Jonas Blakes. How many nights had they spent staring at a dying fire, dreaming about the days when Trofaim would be free. Before the fighting began, they went from home to home, asking old farmers to pick up their plows again so that their young able-bodied sons could free Trofaim. Their number grew and they began to free farms and villages until they defeated mercenary armies that were hired by the Shrikes. It wasn't long until governors and city elders joined their cause and its legitimacy grew. It all grew until it defeated the Songbird Army, the mightiest body of soldiers to ever march Alssae.

All those memories of war and victory, shared with his best friend.

Jonas Blakes was killed by the same men he called brothers. They cut him down because he had been too close to Finnion. Simply because of this, they deemed him worthy of death. Finnion gritted his teeth at the familiar anger. They may have killed his friend, he thought, but little did they know, they had come too close to Finnion to think it could be over. It wasn't over. Finnion would rebuild this rebellion, and when he did, he would—

"Hello!"

Finnion's train of thought was severed by a young woman with a basket hanging in one hand.

"Hello," he said, wary of the woman. "Can I help you?" Finnion motioned to stand up.

"Oh, don't get up! Please, I know your leg is hurt." She set down the basket. "That's actually why I've come."

Finnion stayed seated. He was not going to argue for a reason to stand on the useless leg anyway. "Who told you to come here? My leg is fine," he lied obviously.

"Leighton sent me. He will be here soon."

"Who is Leighton?" he asked, this time not trusting the woman.

She rolled her eyes. "The man whose house you sit at," she said before taking a look over each shoulder, leaning in close to whisper, "'m a Lark."

"I have no idea what you want or what it is you're talking about! I don't know you. You don't know me. Just go on looking for whoever you're looking for." Finnion spoke straightforward, tone flat, hands gesturing for her to go.

The woman sighed as she opened the basket she'd brought. Finnion sat forward, his hand finding a dagger's handle in the belt around his waist. He settled though, as she opened a pot with steam rolling out. The smell of Benneck's soup greeted his nose.

"You should be careful!" he cautioned, looking around to make sure none had heard her. "Anyone could hear you and tell the rebels." He gestured for the woman to come inside.

She laughed and followed without protest.

The room darkened as Finnion shut the door behind him. He settled into a chair by the table, eager to relieve the agonizing leg, now inflamed from use. The woman set her pot over the low coals of the fire.

"Leighton sent me, you know?" she said over one shoulder.

Finnion rubbed at the pain in his knee fruitlessly. "He sent you to expose us in the middle of town?" Finnion wondered how stupid a person could be. "If the rebels get word . . ." Finnion's imagination started to wander and he couldn't even find the words to describe how bad it could be. "The rebels are killers. A Lark . . . If they found out about our plans—"

"You're too worried about the rebellion," she said, shaking her head.

Finnion couldn't believe what he was hearing. The rebellion was taking over the entire state. He just sat there, waiting for her explanation as to why he shouldn't be concerned with the rebellion.

"Cazprien and his army are encircling the Fork Region." The woman closed the furnace door with a squeak. "You and I are in an unimportant town named Tolon near Lavinth, but not near enough to be important." Finnion let his lack of understanding show on his face. "The rebels are about to have the greatest raid in the nation of Alssae. The Fork Region surrounding Trofaim is wealthier than any whole Southern State except Brevalti, and it's smaller than most townships. They aren't concerned about us, and we have another problem currently at hand." She slid her coat off and hung it near the fire to dry.

Finnion, even though still offended in disagreement, couldn't help but notice the woman's figure. It wasn't a bad figure. She turned around to catch a look of guilt betraying his thoughts. The woman eyed him, looking self-satisfied as though she had just put a spell on him without even trying.

"And what problem is that?" he demanded, unamused.

"Well, assuming I am not a problem for you," she said, laughingly, her eyes smiling, "our problem is the mercenary law that oppresses Southeastern Trofaim." Finnion was growing increasingly frustrated. He could've been looking for hidden weapons on the woman, couldn't he?

"How are you a Lark? And I'll have your name! Trust doesn't just fall with the rain these days, and I am a wanted man." Finnion didn't like any of this. So far he'd dealt with only men and he had always been a step ahead. Always knew a stretch more than the next. Then here comes this woman and she's already telling him his plans and disregarding his opinions. Not to mention, she was trying to make him feel guilty as a disobedient child. He was be on-guard now. After All, this woman was a self-proclaimed spy.

"My name is Venna. As I told you before, Leighton sent me. I am a physician by trade." She sat down at the table across from him. "I will tell you more once I learn about you."

"Me?" he asked, his voice filled with suspicion. "You're the one who claims to know who I am. Don't you know enough?"

"Leighton has told me about you plenty, but that's because *he* trusts me. That does not mean I trust you with free knowledge about me. You don't live long as a Lark by openly giving out information. First, you must trade for it."

Finnion somehow felt like this was a youthful flirt rather than a dangerous conversation with someone trying to find and assassinate him and Reff. Was it a flirt? Finnion worried about the dangerous men from his army. But, the longer he considered their intellects and the facts surrounding this woman, he thought less of the risk. She had brought the ridiculous soup, hadn't she?

"What do you want to know about me?" he asked after a moment of reluctance.

Venna smiled. "Were you a rebel?" she asked.

Finnion's eyes squinted. "Was I a . . .No!" he exclaimed. "I was a farmer until this young would-be hero conscripted me." He knew immediately she didn't believe him.

"Then how did you break your leg?" she asked with the certainty of a person who remained unconvinced. After a brief hesitation from him, she spoke, "If you're trying to gain my trust, you are not succeeding." He sighed.

"Let me try the soup."

Finnion and Venna spoke slowly, suspiciously, in turns at first, then more fluidly until they were deep in conversation. She told him of their need to first rid the region of the Storinian mercenaries before any able bodies would have the confidence to leave their homes to come north to save Trofaim from rebellion.

"Many of the women who can't pay for their tax to the Sorinians while their husbands are gone have been raped. Other 'payments' have been taken from these people."

Finnion was inwardly ashamed. He had been the one to employ the help of Storinian mercenaries. Was this why Cazprien did not make use of mercenary law in the Highwater Rebellion? Even if Finnion had been triumphant, could he have ever been truly victorious, having paid such painful prices with the lives of so many free innocents. He was lost in his own head for a moment.

"What is it?" she asked, noticing his concern.

Pulled back into the conversation, he regained his focus. "I understand. The Storinians have to be pushed out." This time, he agreed with the woman's plan.

Finnion heard a rustle at the door and saw fear on Venna's face for the first time. Then saw relief as Reff and Leighton walked through the door. "It's okay, Venna. This young man here is Reff."

Reff made a suspicious look at Venna, then at Leighton, then at Finnion.

"Finnion, who is this strange woman?" Reff turned to Leighton again. "Why is she in your home?" he asked Leighton.

Finnion gestured wildly to Leighton and replied. "I have no idea! He sent her!"

"This," Leighton said, gesturing to the silent woman, "is Venna. She's a physician by trade and belongs to our organization. She can be trusted."

Reff's eyes accused Leighton wildly. Then suddenly softened in curiosity with a look to Finnion.

"Did she bring soup?" Reff asked, trying very poorly not to let his hunger show. Venna said nothing, just pointed to the pot resting over the fire. Reff took a slow stride toward the fire that the pot rested on. Then, as if possessed by something otherworldly, lunged toward the pot and opened the lid. He took a deep inhale of the contents and sighed as his posture relaxed. Reff turned to Finnion. "Smells like trust to me," he said, reaching for a bowl and a ladle to give himself a serving of Benneck's recipe.

Finnion felt guilty for judging Reff having just finished his third bowl.

After a moment of silence, Venna left to get the medical opinion and counsel for how to address Finnion's leg. Reff and Leighton, tired from morning business, ate and went to bed early that evening. That put Finnion alone once more with his thoughts.

When he considered the Lark woman, Venna, he couldn't help a deep stab of guilt. Throughout their whole conversation, he had not thought of his long-lost wife. It felt like betraying her, to let himself notice another. Even after all those years, he was still hers. He was still a man in love. When he laid on the bedroll next to Reff's, he went to sleep, fearing the fact that he could've been so easily distracted. When sleep eventually came, it took him slowly.

CHAPTER FORTY-FIVE

DELIVERANCE

PINELLA

Pinella would have guessed it to have been late evening or early in the morning. She was somewhere between sleep and death when the door of her windowless room opened abruptly. Her sore back lanced with pain as she jerked from the surprise. She wasn't sure if the guard who led her out was pushing her to some quiet place where they'd cut her head off, torture her, or give her some fake trial, but she was somehow a little relieved. She wasn't scared. She hadn't been for over a week. She was through with a hole of room she been left in and trying to guess at what time it was based on when her meal plate was shoved under her door.

Now, it must have been midday by how the sun stabbed her eyes through clinched eyelids.

Then, someone's voice — *Riva's* voice spoke to her.

"My Lady, I'm sorry it took so long. We need to get to the Aspins in the Lower City. Otrin Waymar may know I'm here. If he does . . ."

"Where is Octavia?"

Either Riva didn't know or she couldn't say, but Pinella had so many questions. "When is our trial?"

"I . . . don't think there will be a trial."

Clearly Riva had an entirely different perspective, so Pinella forced herself not to ask as many questions as came to mind. "Go ahead, Riva. Tell me what's happened."

Riva pulled Pinella's arm, forcing her to leave the guard and walk away from the prison. "Karianna told Otrin what his mother did, how she committed treason. I'm not sure who is still alive, but The Tribunes made Otrin head of the Waymars. He's Sire and he condemned his mother and threw her from the cliffs. He has gone absolutely mad. He smothered his little brother and gave Omera away in marriage to one of the regional Tribunes. Her new name is Omera Lemrott. The Lemrott family paid the most for her. He's hired many soldiers now, and he's killed so many families and vassals already. Everyone thinks he will kill his aunts next. I was so terrified for you. I thought . . . that maybe . . ."

"How did you get me out?"

"Greyah did. She told me she would have you out soon, so I waited here."

"Greyah?" Pinella nearly twisted her ankle against a crack in the stone. "Ah!"

Riva's face was full of pity. By her expression, Pinella must have looked disheveled. "A little farther. I have a cartman waiting."

"I'll walk. I'm fine. It's not even a quarter league."

Riva stopped and looked straight at Pinella. "We cannot go to the Waymars. Otrin does not know I am helping you. I need to take you to the Lower City; the Aspins will have a plan and means. I am taking you to the Lower City."

"Riva, how did you keep favor with the Waymars?!"

Riva sighed. "I think it was because Otrin saw how his sister loved me. He promoted me to your position as ward. He needs someone to manage the stewards until he replaces me. He thought it wasteful to give up the position as ward back to one of the old corrupt family affiliates. Karianna must be teaching him all this."

"She must be. She's using him to rise above the family . . . I can't believe he killed his own mother. What could she have offered him to betray his closest family members?"

Riva looked at the passing buildings as they made their way down an alley street. "He . . . Otrin took Karianna as his consort . . . They're married." Both women were quiet for a moment. "She has always been his tutor, but they must have began sleeping together before his family coup. Probably after his father's death."

Pinella remembered the look on Otrin's face as his aunt breastfed his own niece in front of him. "What of his nieces? Did he kill them too?"

"No. Karianna tells them to call him father. He's already promised Owella's hand in marriage to another distinguished regional family, but I don't know who."

The alley emptied into a street where Riva found and waved to one of the cartmen. The man pulled his small two-passenger wagon up to them, clearly recognizing Riva.

"This is my associate, Arkin. He will take you to the Lower City where you can hide and gain flight out of the city." Pinella looked at Riva, not understanding. "They may kill you here. You're still subject to the Waymars. Otrin could have you killed. I'm sorry, but you have to leave. I will make sure Greyah has everything she needs."

"No." She held on to Riva. "I want to stay with you . . ." Pinella felt her lip begin to shake. She had only just reunited with the woman. "Don't leave yet."

"I have to go back to report to Otrin now. He needs to remember that I was with him the day you were set free." Riva was right, and Pinella knew it. As Sire of a distinguished family, Otrin could execute anyone pledged to him. That included Pinella and Riva. She decided to trust her friend.

"Thank you, Riva." Parting from Riva with a hug, Pinella turned and stepped up into the wagon.

⊱

Pinella was dirty. She smelled her own putrid odor after the better part of a month in jail. Despite her dejected state, the Aspin family service greeted Pinella with more care and respect than she had ever received from a Waymar servant. The Aspin home was as modest in appearance inside as its exterior. While it was large with many rooms, many of the rooms were small and absent the pomp that was typical of most prominent homes. Pinella was shown to what she knew must have been Greyah's own bed chamber. A hot bath of spiced water was drawn for her, along with many parcels of clothing.

"Lady Aspin will meet with you when she arrives back home." The servant poured Pinella a cup of pine needle tea. Riva somehow thought of everything. The young cartman named Arkin, who had carted her over four miles, sat two stories below Pinella's window in his own cart, breathing heavily. His breath smoked in the cold weather.

She was safe for the time. She had no idea how long she would have been jailed. She'd been considering her own death in solitude when she was delivered from the prison two hours earlier. She was anxious beyond reason. Would Waymar soldiers arrive and have her head severed in the next two hours?

Pinella took a long sip of the tea she'd often dreamed of while swallowing the dirty gray water that kept her alive for the past five weeks or so. It was hot and smooth. She enjoyed the smell of the sweet steam as she drank the warm drink. Every muscle reluctantly relaxed. She breathed slow, holding the tea close to her face to inhale the smell of it.

Then she opened her eyes and set the tea pot on the small table next to the bathtub. Though she'd done little more than stand up and lay down in her cell, Pinella was exhausted and sore. She pulled her dress off her shoulders where the fabric left pale grooves in her skin. It was ripped and shortened from the many times she used it out of necessity during her menstrual period. The hair of her body was grown out everywhere. Pinella had been a farmer and even a whore, but never so dirty as she was now. She nearly flinched seeing her own decrepit form in the mirror. Her red hair always shined with its light undertone leftover from her adolescence. Now it was a dark bird's nest full of debris. Her ribs and sinew were visible through her abnormally pale skin. She had been left for dead in a hole.

She looked away from her horrible reflection and stepped into the hot bath. Something about the good pain of the hot water and the smell of her tea made her want to cry, but she resisted. She sat still, cleared her mind, and trying to remember what her son's face looked like. When she could not, she succumbed to tears.

CHAPTER FORTY-SIX

THE HAPPY SWITCH

CICERO

Cicero woke up to the switch woman working on his leg. The pain is what woke him.

"Good morning, Cicero," she said with that morning cheer.

He had gotten to know little about her now. Her name was Alora, and he wondered how she always seemed so happy. Cicero had been on the trail for so long, he was finding it hard to be happy at all. Really, the trail wasn't so bad to him, but he'd been wounded for so long with the odds so heavily against him that now all he could think about was laying somewhere dry and warm with something to eat. They'd always said Cicero was lucky enough to never get wounded in all that war. Seemed to him now that he'd just been storing up a debt that he was forced to pay off all at once. His leg burned, of course, but was often soothed by the switch's workings. He had cut wounds from his fights on the run. Brutal sprains from a hundred stumbles during his flights and fights among the Northwoods of Hocklee. Across his entire body were miles of dark, faded bruising from his fall into the chopping river. It was like he held a lifetime of wounds all at once. It was a wonder that he had been able to go for as long as he did.

"Where are we?" he asked through the phlegm in his throat.

Alora smiled back at him. "We're still in the state of Brevalti.

That is the city of Stromega. We will arrive there by noonday." Cicero could just see the tops of buildings off to the distant east.

Cicero had never been to Stromega or anywhere else in Brevalti's heartland. He'd met Brevaltines though. All of them were from Trofaimen heritage. That meant that they didn't know they could lose a war to anyone but each other. Any man that thought he couldn't lose a fight was always eager to fight over something else. The culture of the men Cicero had met was to never let anyone touch your belongings — a stark contrast to the men of Kalesia who shared everything and knew no strangers. Galanoans were considered strange to both for their constant bending towards trusting no one at all.

"Why are we going into the city?" he asked.

She sighed, looking at his leg. "I have an old colleague in Stromega, under whom I did a length of my studies. He is the one who pioneered the practice of undoing a shroud's mental deterioration."

Cicero didn't even know a shroud could be put right. "You can heal a shroud?" He didn't even try to hide the cynicism from his voice.

"What do you think I've been doing with my two shrouds?" she asked rhetorically. "There would be no use trying to teach him to speak any more than trying to teach a rock, unless their mind could be healed from its deteriorating."

"He can't speak though. So why try to teach a rock if it's never really spoken?" he asked, feeling triumphant.

"Shouldn't your leg have killed you by now?" she asked, raising one eyebrow. "How have you not died from its poison yet?"

Cicero didn't know exactly how to respond to that because he wasn't a switch. "I've been unconscious for days at a time. If you're saying I am getting better, you mistake my condition."

"Well then, who is Rhett?" Cicero's flesh prickled with goose-bumps at that question.

"I don't know him. Why would I?"

"What is your name?"

"Rhe . . ." Cicero caught himself in the process of telling them his name is Rhett.

"Who gave that leg to you?"

"A man who worked for the body trader Jaco Tro-Horm. Ker-rick, he said his name was."

"And you've seen him in dreams, yes?" she asked as if she knew all the answers, which was slightly annoying to Cicero because she was right so far.

"Well, yes. A few times. How did you know that?"

"Because when you dream about him, sometimes bits and pieces of his consciousness will spill out. It's like you're sleep-walking, but instead of Cicero, it's Rhett who is talking." Cicero felt extremely uneasy at that. Had his mind been poisoned by some other man's leg? "You see, Cicero, all research states that your leg would have to be removed if you are to live. Now that you've been entirely submerged in water, most switches would say that you'll die for certain." She smiled a little wider. "But my theory is that you can make the leg your own. My goal is that you do not have to cut off the leg higher than where it was cut before." She stood and picked her bag up as Bluehands picked Cicero up just as easily. "You see, if your mind can overpower the infection and adopt the limb, it proves that Bluehands too can be himself again. If a shroud can be healed, the entire practice may be used for healing rather than war."

Cicero had fought several shrouds. Many of them were danger-ous because they fought as reckless and fearless as feral animals. "What makes a man to be a shroud?" he asked.

"Well, when a limb is attached with tattoos, it rots away faster than a normal body part. The limb also rots the flesh it's attached to. This flesh doesn't rot as fast, but it does if the limb is not removed."

"When will mine rot?"

"It has already begun to decompose," she said plainly.

"Why haven't you cut it off then? If it's rotting the rest of me with it."

"Because I want to prove the effects can be reversed. That's what I just said. Weren't you listening?" Alora had a look of anger at that.

"I'm not a shroud. I'd like to not become one either," Cicero said. "How is it already harming me after such short a time?" That would have to be the question he settled with for now. He had so many.

"The effects of a limb all depend on the elements and methods used in the process of attaching it. Your leg in particular was poisoned so that it would plague your mind. Most shrouds have several old limbs. That's what causes them to lose their minds. They eventually go wild or are controlled by the switch. You were almost made into a shroud with only one limb. You would have been a powerful shroud with all your original arms and remaining leg."

It made something burn in him that Jaco Horm had planned to enslave him. But deep down, he'd always had his suspicions. Cicero had seen dozens of men ask for new arms and legs, eventually losing more and more of their sanity, becoming more and more reliant on a switch for peace of mind and even sleep. Cicero wouldn't have thought he'd ever be in danger of becoming a shroud himself.

"So you think I can keep this leg?"

She looked at it, studying it with squinted eyes. "Well, for the most part, you're able to stay awake and think clearly because of the elixirs and mixtures I've given you. But I have seen some small signs of deterioration reversing. The process, if successful, will not be brief, but if you do keep the leg, I will have a better idea of how to reverse the damage in Bluehands and Shadows as well."

Cicero wasn't sure how he felt about being a switch's experiment. The more he considered it though, her experiment saved his life. Saved him from being a shroud maybe. He thought about all the strange things they'd talked about and all the shrouds and switches he'd interacted with over the years.

꣠

Stromega sat high on the edge of a river valley. It was surrounded with squatty wooden barricades that looked like they hadn't been used in years. Cicero thought no Brevaltine had used them to defend the town. Probably they were used last when the Kalesian king fought the Rumeneddan king for the land that eventually became Brevalti.

The buildings were old but hadn't aged, each one beautiful in its antiquity. Some old buildings in Galanoa were of a similar style but poorly maintained over the course of their long existence. Each one was made like Trofaim's River District. Each with white exterior walls and red tile rooftops.

He observed smoke gently lifting out of chimneys high into the bright blue sky. Cicero hoped they found a warm dry place with a hot fire to stay near. The weather had grown cold as the season had dragged on. He'd been on the road for so long, Cicero was beginning to forget the feeling of settling down in a peaceful place. Hopefully no Brevaltines had followed them or even knew they were trespassing here. That made him greatly hope none of the Hockleets were hunting him either.

"Have you ever been here?" Alora asked.

"No, only to the river towns on my travels. What about you?"

"I haven't been here either. My old colleague was said to be here because of the nearby wars in Storins."

"And war is good for your studies?" he asked. She looked at him from the side of her eyes.

"By nature, yes," she said. Cicero thought she probably didn't want to think she had her part to play in war. He knew, though, that everyone had their parts. Even if they couldn't accept it.

They chose a place where the shrouds were allowed to stay, but only because Alora begged and offered to pay more than double the cost of a normal room for them. Cicero couldn't blame the woman. He'd always thought of them as monsters. Some shrouds killed at random outbursts of anger. Typically shrouds and switches were isolated, considered strange by regular folks. Now that he was with them, Cicero was too. Nobody had told the townspeople he was a switch's experiment, but they all looked at him as though they knew. Each one eyed him as though he planned to take their body parts for his switch. If they only knew that he could hardly piss on his own, let alone hurt anyone . . . He just ignored them.

The inn was small with small rooms but it was dry, and that alone was a world of improvement from the trail. The rickety bed Bluehands laid him in seemed to embrace him with more love than he'd ever felt before. It was not a good bed, he knew, but to his pained body it was life. Cicero heard Alora talking to the innkeeper woman about their stay but he couldn't stay awake. He felt his muscles melt as he gave in to his exhaustion and let sleep take him.

Cicero woke to a cow lowing just outside the window near him. The smell of livestock filled his nose and the rest of the cheap room. He saw Alora standing at the edge of the bed. She was brushing her long red hair using a foggy mirror where her eyes met his in the reflection. She smiled.

"Good morning Cicero!" she said as happily as ever. She was beautiful, he noticed. He also noticed she had shared the bed next to him. That somehow made him feel uneasy, like he'd done something wrong or trespassed, but he knew he was too broken and wounded to be a threat in any way. She smiled warmly, the way he would've wanted her to, to say she didn't mind his company.

"I could've slept on the floor," he said with a rasp.

"But the bed was good! No need to sleep on the hard ground without cause," she said, ignoring his shy attitude.

"Couldn't you have slept in your own room?" he asked.

"The price was already a lot for Bluehands and Shadows to stay here. Another room would've been far too much," she said, pulling her overcoat over her shoulders. Cicero was nervous as he realized he'd never spent the night with a woman before, certainly not a beautiful one. She had the look of a Southerner but he wasn't certain where in the South. But Cicero knew for a fact she wasn't Aravacan.

"Where are you from? Really." His voice was still raspy with sickness. He coughed at the tickle in his throat.

"I was born in the Broken Isles on the island of Euodia. My clan was first from Silisia before that." She smiled, turning to look at him. "Are you strong enough to stand?"

Cicero thought it should be obvious since he had barely moved.

"I can't feel anything unless I move. When I move, it's very painful."

She looked a touch surprised by that. "Your leg, you mean?"

"Both legs," he said. "My arms, and ribs when I breathe deeply, are worsening as well." Cicero marveled at how he'd gone far. Knowing that the children, Swain and Noon, would be killed if he stopped had been strong motivation. Now though, he'd gotten used to being carried and resting. Every movement was painful and therefore required a deal of motivation.

"Hmm . . ." Alora pursed her lips in thought. She had a mild look of concern that concerned Cicero in turn.

"What?" he asked.

"Well numbness isn't good. It's been a source of relief for you, I am sure, but it means that the leg is taking your body over rather than your body taking the leg. Pain in unrelated areas of your body shows that your body fights the death spreading out from the leg."

Cicero tried to make sense of that. "Am I becoming a shroud?" he asked.

"No. Worse."

"Worse?! I'd rather die than become a shroud. That's why I jumped into the river!"

"What that switch poisoned the leg with is mixed with some of his own body. He did that to control your corpse as an extension of his body."

"That sounds like a shroud to me," Cicero said, still trying to simplify it so that he could understand what was happening.

"Yes, but shrouds are autonomous, while you would be utterly subject to the switch." She shook her head and her eyes became distant. "It's an old forbidden practice called necromancy. This is the first time I have heard of it outside of old texts and older legends."

"So how do I keep from becoming a puppet corpse? Can't you

just cut off the leg?" He knew that would be far too easy.

"If we cut off the leg now, you won't have a chance anytime soon to walk normally. You've already built a bond. If you can make a foreign leg your own, you'll prove a shroud can be redeemed. You'll give hope to Bluehands and Shadows and many more. What's more, the leg has already spread poison into your body . . . so prove my theories correct and make that leg your own!"

Cicero wasn't sure that he cared for a shroud's hope, but he owed this switch woman a favor for saving him in the woods. So he nodded, sighed, and said, "Tell me again. What do I need to do to make the leg mine?"

She smiled at that. "Just move everything that hurts. Replace the numbness with pain. Remember, the numbness is not yours, but the pain is. Soon the pain should subside, and the leg will be yours."

"How soon?" He asked skeptically. She smiled and put her hand on his.

"As soon as you can bear."

❧

Cicero winced at the pain, fighting back the urge to cough. His ribs were like a caged fire. Everything inside them burned with each deep breath. The switch, Alora, had said he should move as much as he could and cause as much pain as he could in order to make his transplanted leg the same as his own leg. He stumbled around the street block in the early morning, holding his breath and tears caused by the pain in his body. The sun was still below the horizon. Each step produced the kind of pain that made him wonder more and more why he had to be the one to live this out.

What had he done to warrant all this?

Cicero kept going, pushing through the agony. While his body was so close to the grave, his heart was ascending. He thought back on a life of hurt and he remembered why he was so close to death now, the way he had been so many times before. He remembered starving and shivering at the bitter cold in Hocklee as a young boy. He remembered seeing room in every house, no matter how full they were, room that he could have put to good use, warm and dry. He wasn't mad that nobody took responsibility for him, just wished that someone would.

As a boy covered in mud, he promised that he would do the unusual. Cicero would be the type of man that took responsibility for others who couldn't take care of themselves. Thinking back to the cold, burned out people of Hocklee and how the wars had divided them. More Hockleets went hungry than ever so that a man from Kalesia could say it was his, or because clans from Galanoa thought the tyranny of kinds would threaten their way of life. Cicero remembered the little city on a hill and how it always made him think of himself, alone and hungry.

Years went on and he made a name for himself and saw a young man in need without the means to help himself. Swain didn't know that he reminded Cicero of his own self, but he did. Swain also reminded him that he'd chosen to take responsibility for others. It wasn't a roof over his head that he needed as a boy. He needed the love that gives food and shelter. Cicero had needed the love that helps. Swain needed help and Cicero had made the promise to help. That's why so much had happened to him.

Cicero smiled and thought of a young man planting the apple seeds they'd picked. Swain would have the means to help someone in need because someone else had once helped him. Would he have done anything differently to prevent this pain he found himself in? Cicero felt the answer deeply, loudly, and overwhelmingly within him. No, he didn't regret what he had done for the two children from Hocklee. So he welcomed the pain, loosened his jaw, and walked.

The quiet cobblestone street between peaceful homes was the stage on which Cicero's life's drama unfolded. One of many scenes in his painful, unusual life was here. This is where he learned to choose his decision all over again. That would be his trick to taking another pain-filled step.

❧

"Breathe in as deeply as you can, Cicero."

He was bent over a cauldron of boiling oils mixed with mint and tea to open his burning lungs. She had put other herbs into the liquid, but Cicero had forgotten what they were called as soon as he heard their names. It was hot. The steam rolled up from the boiling pot and beaded up on his face like sweat. The mint filled his aching chest with a contrast like ice on a burn. At first it was overwhelming but became soothing as he allowed the stuff to bless him. He coughed up blood and dark chunks of tissue just as Alora said he would.

Cicero heard the door squeak on its hinges. He was too consumed by the hot steam to look out from under the towel draped over his head. "Good morning, Bluehands!" Alora said. "Have a seat on the bed there." The giant's footsteps became familiar to Cicero as the huge shroud crossed the creaking floorboards. The wooded framework of the bed groaned under the weight of Bluehands' huge borrowed body. "Just keep breathing, Cicero." She squeezed his shoulder before turning her attention to Bluehands.

"Alright, my blue-handed friend. You lead today, and I'll keep time." The shroud gave small growls and moans the way shrouds do. Alora began clapping her hands together slowly with rhythm. A moment passed and Bluehands just made an attempt to speak.

"Remember . . . Haven't remember." His voice sounded desperate.

"You have to remember, Bluehands," she said, stopping her clapping, "I know your mind feels strange, but your mind it is. So remember! Once you start the song, I'll finish." And she began clapping again. Slowly, with time, the shroud began to produce a noise somewhere between a humming and a singing sound. At first the song was tasteless, as Bluehands was painfully out of tune. In time though, Alora's voice subtly joined his and the song became sweeter to Cicero's ears. As she sang the foreign words, his pain was drowned in melody. His body was soothed by the steam of the pot and the song of the switch. Cicero was at peace for the first time that morning. It was like bathing in warmth.

Cicero woke up in the bed again as usual. It was unusual, though, to feel this alert. Cicero was well rested. The sharp pains were reduced to dull distant aches.

"Good morning again! You've had two mornings today," Alora said, laughing at herself.

"I think your song helped me," he said before clearing the sleep from his voice.

"It helped you rest," she said. "Aside from that, it only numbed the pain. It came from me, the way the leg numbs you." She was cleaning the pot Cicero had been breathing over. He couldn't remember how he got into bed.

"How did I get into bed?" he asked.

"Bluehands put you there," she said, not even looking up. "He is out feeding the stable animals brought in by travelers."

"He works here?" Cicero wondered how they let a shroud work

in the stable, so he asked, "How does a shroud work in a town labor?"

"Well, 'Brevaltines have to make our money somehow,' as they say. It's actually becoming more commonly practiced in Central and Eastern Alssae, to make use of shrouds in this way. That's why they send more and more local men out to war as mercenaries." Cicero had always wondered how so many Storinians could afford to leave their homes to fight someone else's war. It made sense to him now. "Storins and Carnae become more powerful every year this way."

"How do you know so much about this country? Aren't you a foreigner?"

She smiled. "To most foreigners, the affairs of your country have an effect on their trades. When kings united Alssae and pacified the threat of a violent South, trade flourished from the far east to the distant west. You see, Cicero, peace in Alssae once meant prosperity for many nations." He doubted that she meant Hocklee and the Southern States.

"Do you mean Trofaim? They're the ones with power."

"Trofaim certainly leads the affairs of Alssae, but the Southern States make up most of the narrow stretch of land that bridge the seas together." She smiled knowingly. "If the Southern States are divided, the only practical trade route is river passage."

Cicero's eyes widened slightly as he was educated about his own country's politics. "Do you mean to say that Trofaim wants to divide the South?"

She smiled as he understood. "I would've been killed without my shrouds just for the small purse in my bag." Cicero knew she was right. Thieves were common. Just look at Redeye and Yellow-tooth, always making war on peace. "This is how Trofaim controls the nation's wealth. The nobles there regulate trade throughout the country. Why do you think Brevalti charges a travel tax?" She barked out a short, sarcastic laugh. "By ensuring that they are the only place safe enough to travel through."

"In the old wars, a large Brevaltine family named Gladney sold weapons and armor between armies." Cicero added.

Alora's eyes lit up in response. "You see?! I didn't know that, but it proves the point I am trying to make. Controlling trade may have its place, but inciting war between states is criminal. They cripple the states around them for their own wealth and power." She sighed and examined Cicero's health. "But that's enough of that. Has the pain come back to your leg?"

He noticed it hadn't returned.

"No," he said, knowing her response.

"You should force it to return. Remember the pain is good."

He sighed. Cicero didn't want to reenter the agony. "Why doesn't Bluehands need to suffer?" he said with a deal less patience.

"Bluehands' condition is different from yours," she said with painful understanding. "He was not poisoned. He must be trained to live with his malady before he can control it. That's why I'm teaching him the song to soothe himself. When the switch or switches changed out his body parts for larger, stronger ones, he slowly went mad with the phantom dreams that they gave him. I am trying to reverse his madness by giving him control over it. You, on the other hand, have the one leg. Like other switched limbs, use of them causes decay to the point at which they're attached. My theory is that the opposite should be able to occur, and the living host can take over the limb. If you can make that leg your own, you will prove that Bluehands can be redeemed. I will have incentive to continue with other shrouds."

Cicero was barely following everything she was trying to lead him to understand, but he still forced his weak body up from the bed. "Fine. I'll walk around the inn again," he said in defeat.

"Three times before you come back this time," she said.

Instead of protesting, he just struggled up and out the door. Cicero did his best.

&

"How'd the morning circles go?" Alora was referring to the circles that Cicero made around the inn each morning.

"Painful as usual, "said Cicero through clenched teeth as he stepped into the room. He was exhausted. Nearly two weeks and the leg had barely healed enough to allow an extra trip around the building.

"But you went faster today than last week. That's your improvement!" She said that as though all of her theories were proven right. He almost mentioned how he'd gotten up sooner and that if anything, his leg seemed worse, but that wouldn't put her in a good mood so he thought better of it and chose to stay silent. It was hard to do that. The pain wasn't so bad anymore, but the repetition wore on his patience severely. He wanted nothing more than to have it off.

"Could you just cut it off now that you know I am improving?"

"I don't know that yet, though. Until you can use it as well as your right leg, I won't be confident." That wasn't what he wanted to hear. Cicero wondered if he'd ever heal. What if she was wrong and this test was doing irreparable damage? Cicero tried to put that out of his mind.

"How's the big monster of yours?" Cicero asked.

"Bluehands, you mean?" It seemed to Cicero that her patience wasn't quite wearing down as much as his. "He's content with his work at the stables. The people in town sometimes speak poorly to him, but the stable hands love him." She smiled at that. "I told them he'd do all three of their labor for half their pay. They're getting half the money without working. That pays our stay at the inn."

"And what about the spider-looking fellow?" he asked, falling into a hard chair, perfectly comfortable to his exhausted body.

"You're talking about Shadows. He survives on his own outside the town. Unlike Bluehands, he cannot be confused with a person. So the people treat him like a monster." Alora sighed.

"That's a shame." he said, trying to mask his insincerity.

"It's not so bad for him. He was made to live like an animal by an Aravacan. He is capable of hunting and surviving on his own like an animal. He prefers it that way. When his phantom dreams get too severe, he comes back for a song to soothe the pain, then after he gets a piece back, he returns to the wild. He also watches for strange bounty hunters. Anyone that might be looking for us."

Cicero was impressed. "He can do that?" He'd never heard of such abilities possessed by a shroud.

"He can do much more. He was soon to become the property of the king, sold by the duke of the Tirona Province in Northern Aravaca. He was made to be a scouting tool for the Aravacan Army."

"Against Alssae?" asked Cicero. Alora was silent at that.

"For what the king purchased him exactly, I do not know, but I protested the sale for him as a weapon by the duke," she said distantly. "So I freed Bluehands, captured Shadows, and fled northward."

Cicero said nothing to that. He wondered if these affairs had anything to do with his hamlet being raided and Swain's family being killed. He thought longingly about Swain and Noon, hoping they made it safely northward.

ॐ

Cicero woke from his daily rest a little after noon. All was quiet in the humble room. Alora quietly read a book while making notes in a kind of journal. He could hear the pages turn and her charcoal pencil scratch against them. As she studied, he studied her. Her brow furrowed, deep in thought as her lips silently pronounced the words that she read. Then she noticed him watching her.

"Good morning, Cicero!" She said it just as she always did, her voice flowing with well-wishing cheer. Cicero smiled back at her.

"Is it good that when I sleep, I am awoken by pain now?" His body was covered in a stagnant ache, all except his leg. It was replete with needle-like pain.

"Yes, it is!" she smiled brighter. "That means your body is taking responsibility for your leg! Is the leg in more pain or a different kind of pain than the rest of your body?" Cicero was surprised by her knowledge of his body.

"Both," be said without masking the pain.

"I'm both sorry and glad to hear that. Pain means progress now." Somehow Cicero knew that she would say something like that. He felt that she was more glad than sorry though. "The pain will most likely get worse, I should warn you. During that process, I won't be able to soothe the pains at all, as they're becoming more necessary."

"How, then, will I find any relief?" he asked, his mind filling with dread, "The pain is almost too much already."

The remnant of her smile withered. "You wait." There was a slight pause as Alora calculated the next few steps of the process.

"When your fever breaks, the pain will begin to subside."

An exhausted sigh flooded out of Cicero's chest after hearing that. "Another fever?"

&

Cicero laid in bed, staring out the window through squinted eyes. His teeth were clamped so tight, his head throbbed with pain at every heartbeat. Everything hurt. Cicero's body felt like it'd been dipped in pain and pulled out, all except his leg, still immersed to the hip in agony. It was bad, but nothing was worse than the seam between the stranger's leg and what remained of his own. That small part of him was the source of a unique pain more severe than the rest. At times, it made him puke. Tears chapped the skin of his face where they had trailed down his cheeks. His teeth were so tightly shut, he thought they might crack. But if he opened his mouth, he knew he would scream.

He remembered the episode in the forest with the children, when he lost the leg in the first place. It was nostalgic by comparison to what he went through now. Part of him wished he could've just been killed by the river instead of this. Back then, he thought of ways to survive. Now he thought only of how he wished he could die.

Although Alora occasionally visited the room to check on him, Cicero was usually alone. She said he couldn't be soothed by the medicine songs she sang to Shadows and Bluehands. He wished she could still be there, even if for no other reason than to cure his loneliness. He missed her joyous attitude. She had told him good morning every time he woke up, without regard for what time of the day it was. He had enjoyed watching her as well. The longer he was alone, the more beautiful she seemed to him. He missed her. As he thought about it, though, he also missed the two shrouds and everything he had before this pain had come over him.

The door swung open. The shroud's face peered without emotion through the gap between the door and doorframe.

"She's . . ." Shadows was still struggling to form words into a coherent sentence.

Cicero held back an almighty urge to cough. "She's down the hall." His voice was hoarse and breathy. Shadows looked at him a moment before closing the door. Cicero thought it might have been pity that he saw on the shroud's face. It was welcome, he thought, to have someone else. But shrouds don't have pity so Cicero chalked it up to wishful thinking.

Empty blocks of time spent in agony crawled by at a snail's pace. Cicero watched the shadows of trees outside, but the sun didn't move them. Each minute was magnified by the pain. Time swelled like dead wood in the rain, each moment heavier than the last. He should've been thankful that his only task was to wait, but waiting felt impossible now that pain was his chief companion.

"Good morning, Cicero!"

Cicero awoke from a half sleep into the pain again. The pain was consistent, but it always dimmed when he slept. He never appreciated it until he was awake and the pain sharpened.

"Good morning," he whispered.

Alora smiled, pulling the bed blanket that served as the room's curtain. "It isn't morning anymore, but it sure is good." The light splashed over her and poured warmth into the room. Cicero hoped she would stay longer. The last several times she had left him because he begged her to sing so the pain would ease and he could rest, but she always left when he did, so he forced himself not to ask.

"Can I eat?" he asked weakly. Her eyebrows rose up.

"Do you think you can keep it down if I give you food?" Cicero felt weak and thin after a week of fighting to keep down any food at all and mostly losing that fight.

"I need it, so I will try." He half coughed the words. Cicero saw some pity in her expression before she turned her face away to look back out the window. He hated that she felt some of his pain, but it made it more bearable in a way, having someone to share some of it with.

"How're the shrouds?" Cicero tried to stifle the pain in his voice. "Bluehands still singing your song? Heh!" He masked an unstoppable cough with a laugh. "First time I've ever seen a shroud sing to his switch!" He hacked out another laughing cough at his own poor humor. He noticed her shoulders shake slightly, and through the noise she made, Cicero thought he may have heard a giggle. "Maybe you could have him come sing to me!" This time she turned around, her face filled with laughter.

"I think you're making a good amount of progress!" She took a moment to study him, his leg in particular. "Does this hurt?" She poked the bottom of the new leg with a pin from her hair. He felt the sharp pain and nodded that he felt it. Alora pulled back the lock of hair that had fallen and secured it with the pin. As he watched her, Cicero felt a feeling for her deep within him.

"You should feel better soon." Her eyes smiled brightly with the good report. "It may be sooner than we thought that your fever breaks. Training the leg completely will take time, and then there are the tattoos to address, but the pain should subside soon." After what felt like so long in agony, he could hardly believe it would end.

"Bluehands is going to sing to me though, right?" He smiled and Alora smiled back.

"He's busy working to keep us under this roof. And you can't hear a binding melody until the leg is yours. It may undo some of your hard-fought progress."

Cicero woke up with a start for the second time that day. Instead of the light of day waking him up, it was the light being snuffed out by the curtain that brought his consciousness back. Alora peered through a small opening, a streak of sunlight lighting a portion of her face. He didn't have to ask to know something was wrong. You don't cover up the windows unless you're hiding from someone.

"Who is it?" he asked. Alora closed the gap and looked down at the floor.

"Some of the men I am running from have caught up to us." Her eyes met his. "They're dangerous."

"Why are they looking for you?" Cicero was made of questions. How was he again being sought out by dangerous men?

"Because I'm trying to heal shrouds. They are men of the South. They work for the duke of Tirana like I used to." She crossed the room and locked the door. "They have a Brevaltine sheriff escorting them." Cicero pushed himself slightly, sitting upward in the creaking bed.

"I don't understand. Why do they care if—"

"The duke wants Shadows back. I've made him look foolish to the Aravacan king."

"How many men are there?" Cicero asked, breathily.

"Only two very dangerous men. The duke's men."

Cicero thought it could be worse, but he hadn't the ability to fight or anything to fight with.

"Can we just hide in here?" he asked. "How will they find us?"

She closed her eyes tightly. "The sheriff will ask the innkeeper eventually. We have no reason to think he won't tell the sheriff we're here."

"I should stand if we're going to hide somewhere else." Cicero feared the prospect of walking. He could imagine the pain, but . . . *If you're gonna have to go, it's better to go willingly*, he thought.

"It shouldn't be long, Cicero. I'll find a place and Bluehands will carry you." She made for the door. "I'll go get Bluehands."

"Don't get caught," he said as she left. Cicero laid back flat on the bed, the room now dark. The pain had been bad, sure, but more death seemed even worse. He soaked up the comfort of the bed while he still could and tried not to think about the agony of being carried like a child again.

CHAPTER FORTY-SEVEN

NOBODY'S WHORE

PINELLA

"I'm not leaving, Greyah. Octavia could still be alive eating dirt in that dungeon. I won't leave her while ensuring my own safety."

The head of the family to whom Pinella spoke so defiantly brushed a shock of her silver hair to the back of her head. "She is a convicted criminal. If you make an effort and you get noticed, they may reconsider you as a conspirator against the city. You must let me take you to our land outside the city. You can build support there."

"I don't need support. I need to free Octavia. I owe it to her. And once she's free, she will know what to do. She will have allies. She deserves a trial." The two women struggled together, unwilling to cede their own side of the argument. "If your connection could get me out, he must be able to do the same for Octavia."

Greyah blinked her eyes rapidly to conceal her frustration. "Let me explain it this way: Octavia and Livra Waymar are some of the most commonly spoken of names in the Upper City right now. The only reason you aren't discovered yet is because is because their reputations dwarf your own. You are safe because there are many Waymars imprisoned. They may even think you are still in that prison."

Pinella got a mental image of her food plate piled high with rancid slop and no one there to eat it. "Greyah, I will not leave her. You can either help me free her or hang a bell for me, because I'm going." A moment passed.

Greyah considered before acquiescing. It hurt to think she was helping a Pinella out of a sense of duty to her. But Pinella was indebted to Octavia, and she had to save her.

"Well, if you're are bent on saving her, you won't be able to do it as a criminal. You will have to vindicate yourself. Once your name is clear, you may be able to make some sort of—"

"Appeal!" Pinella finished for Greyah.

Greyah laughed to herself. "It would take a silver tongued noble with as much influence and leverage as Owen Waymar did to make an appeal like that. You cannot simply appeal them. Once you're of clear repute, you would need powerful distinguished allies to make the appeal for you." Pinella tried not to look as discouraged as she felt. Greyah Aspin seemed to know all the inner workings of the distinguishment, even though she herself belonged to the lower, prominent class.

"That's not such a bad idea . . . I met many distinguished men and women in Octavia's galas. We could send messages out to them . . . Couldn't we?" Pinella was finding her own ideas harder to believe.

"Many of the nobles who aligned themselves with the Waymars will be reluctant to align themselves with you against Otrin. They have either taken the opportunity to cut ties with him or they support him as the new Sire of the Waymar family, applauding his patriotism. He uncovered a great information leak. Now that he lent his soldier's to the Alcott war effort which has won it's first victory, there will be few nobles willing to support you against him. Don't take this the wrong way . . . but without any ownings or allies in Trofaim, you have little to offer right now."

Pinella spoke before Greyah could continue. "How much ownership would I need?"

Greyah sighed and gave Pinella's farfetched scenario a chance. "You would need enough that your voice was representative of more than your own opinion. A wealthy noble who owns a great deal of city or regional assets with many under their subordination will speak in representation of those under them. With the influence that wealth would bring you, it's easier to find allies — allies that you would need in order to ratify your bail and obtain a trial."

Pinella sighed and rubbed her face with both hands. They smelled good. The body oil Greyah had given her to use was scented like cinnamon and rosemary. A genius mixture.

Pinella sighed at the futility of entertaining that idea. Valuable assets had to be inherited or bought. "Oh, Greyah. What does an impoverished woman without any station do for a friend who has given her everything . . . Greyah, she even made me Ward of her own house, and I'm not even a relative."

Greyah coughed a sober laugh. "Heh. If you were still Ward, you could just sell some Otrin's estate to yourself." Pinella looked up at Greyah to see her eyes spark with the same realization. "Wait, Pinellla! *Assuming* they wouldn't catch Riva and kill her, you would still need allies. You're still accused of crime with no support. They will just take your assets and redisTribute them." Greyah tried to reason Pinella out of it, but it was too late. It was a good enough idea to try.

"Greyah, send for Riva. I need to speak with her soon."

CHAPTER FORTY-EIGHT

THE BLAKES

FINNION

Finnion and Reff walked up to a small farmhouse about two miles away from Talon. Finnion fell after his hurt knee buckled, sending him to hands and knees. His knee was becoming more and more stubborn, ironically, each time he rested it. He picked himself up off the ground for the second time that morning.

"What did Venna say about your leg?" Reff asked with a concerned tone.

"You can't just trust any physician who says they are one. Do you think I would let her do anything to me simply because she calls herself a physician?" Finnion didn't want to think about another woman taking care of him. It hurt his heart to think of trusting another woman.

"Not sure what she's done for us not to trust her," said Reff from his deep lack of experience. His ignorance showed itself as arrogance.

"I don't trust her, nor will I," said Finnion with resolve. It took Finnion a second to understand what Reff said next. It sounded like "Keep falling then," and Finn fought the urge to spur on the argument. Instead, he looked at the farmhouse, remembering the task at hand.

Leighton had said a woman lived here with her three sons who asked to pay her family's tax to the war effort in advance. That was people's way of saying they wanted to conTribute to the Lark and claim their loyalty to Trofaim over the rebellion. "Nobody pays their taxes early," Leighton had said.

Finnion marveled at all of this, at everything Benneck had created. It was genius. Finnion had always felt that he was so close to catching the Lark when he led the rebellion. He was never close at all. He thought the Lark was a single person and that one of their informants would betray the truth, but he was wrong. The Lark was composed of many moving parts, each with its own discretion and autonomy. The fact that he outsmarted them before his battles with the Wing was nothing short of a miracle, Finn was convinced. These agents were powerfully connected and distant enough to remain safe. Finnion might have won a few battles against them, but had he taken Trofaim, they would've proved to be nearly impossible to discover and put down.

Reff knocked on the wood door. They looked at each other nervously, each of them gripping handles of hidden weapons. You couldn't be too sure if something was meant to be a trap. You couldn't be sure if something may go wrong due to some accident or misunderstanding. A voice came from a window to their left, and both of them jumped at the surprise.

"What's your business?" said the person inside. It was a woman's voice.

"Storinian law requires that you pay early," said Reff, just as Leighton had instructed him to. That was what the hidden message had instructed them to say when they arrived, a kind of password to prove they weren't gangsters or Storinian authorities. After a moment out in the cold morning wind, the door opened to them. A woman that couldn't have been more than forty years old welcomed them. She offered them a seat and poured them hot soup. Soon, three young men sat down at her instruction. Each one wore clothing that looked like sewed-together blankets or rags. They looked strong in their youth but skinny from great hunger. The boys didn't eat but eyed the food eagerly. Reff and Finn shared a look when they realized it was mostly just bone broth.

"I've heard there is a Shrike still alive," said the woman. "There are whispers that he is gaining loyalists to fight for him."

Finnion cleared his throat. "We're not sure. They haven't told us much. We ourselves are scarcely trusted, as we both are deserters of the rebellion." Reff gave a look of agreement to Finnion, communicating his endorsement of Finnion's story. So Finnion continued, realizing how often the two of them were speaking without words. They'd grown close in their efforts together, close enough to have read each other's minds a handful of times. "We were sent with instructions to thank you for your help in carrying the burden as well. The food and supplies will serve Trofaim greatly." The woman said nothing at first, looking into the weak fire. Even it appeared small for the preservation of resources.

"You were in the rebel army?" she asked distantly.

"Yes, ma'am, before it became the corruption it is now."

She just stared blankly, deeply into the fire. "Did you ever know a man named Jonas?" she asked.

Finnion's eyes widened, but he quickly corrected his expression. "I . . . no, I haven't. But I've heard of him. Heard great things," he said, his voice concealing his surprise. "A great man that many followed."

"I am his mother. Merna Blakes is my name, and these are his sons."

Finnion felt his heart thump and his breath catch. Suddenly he could see the resemblance. Each youngster looked the same, the only difference in appearance was each one was younger than the last. They looked just like him, just like Finn's best friend.

"Where is their mother?" Finn asked.

Merna shook her head. "Jonas was conscripted by the governor of Bilton at the time. He told me he'd met Felix himself, saying hundreds were joining and that it was his responsibility, too. I know he isn't coming back. Neither are his brothers . . ." Mrs. Blakes looked up from the fire. She pushed backed some deep emotion before she spoke again. "There is talk of corruption having overcome the rebels after their victory over the Songbird Army. Before the battle, we received enough money to pay our tax and keep ourselves fed. He sends no letters now . . . and my boy wouldn't abandon us." She looked at Finnion now. "My husband. My three boys. A daughter in law. I've given all I can afford to rid us of these mercenaries in our lands."

"We thank you for that," said Reff, his voice full of respect and remorse. The woman's eyes drifted to her grandsons.

"Now I am giving all that I have left."

Finnion looked at the boys, wondering what she meant. They looked close in age, the youngest no older than seventeen and the oldest no younger than twenty.

"Jonas said not to tell anyone their age or they'd be conscripted. They've worked hard, tending to the land and livestock so we could live peacefully. But the tax burden was so high we couldn't store enough for winter." Finnion could see where this conversation was headed, and he almost couldn't believe it. "I suppose if you're honest about this new uprising, this effort to free us from Storins and defeat the rebellion my son fought for, then my grandsons can go with you."

Each young man bristled with youthful intensity. Finnion could tell they wanted to go. He was starting to see how much they were like their father. Each one certain. Each one respectful of their grandmother, letting her speak. Finnion had to clear his tightening throat. *I'm sorry Jonas.* His friend had lost so much for Finnion's cause, and his family paid the price for his loyalty with their own.

"I won't survive much longer on bone broth boiled in melted snow, but if these boys can at least eat, if they can make it through, I will have done what I could for my boy and his sons."

Finnion knew Reff would insist that they were too skinny or inexperienced to come, so Finnion readily agreed. "It would be an untold honor to have each of you!" he declared, standing. "This betrayal of their own people that the rebels have committed — it wouldn't be happening if your father were alive."

Finnion stuck an already shaky hand out between him and the young men, and he introduced himself. "My name is Finnion."

The oldest took his hand. "My name is Bracken," he said.

Finnion shook his hand. Nice, firm grip.

"I'm Logan," said the next. Weaker, yet still firm.

"Griffin is my name, sir," said the youngest. The weakest, but more mettle than the others.

Each of the boys gave Finnion a nod that reminded him of their father who would return that same exact nod before all of their battles.

"It's an honor to serve you," said Logan.

Finnion stood there at a loss for a moment. He remained stoic, trying to conceal the emotion that had been washing over him. "If you'd known what your father did for this country, you would see that the honor is mine." Finnion wiped a wet eye before it could let loose another tear. He was grateful that Reff was focused on the men instead of him.

"There are other young men," Merna said. "The boys will bring them to you when you call for them. It was a pleasure to have you in my home. If I live long enough, I will hang bells for you." And with that, she stood up and left the small house, and Reff then introduced himself to the Blakes brothers.

Finnion wasn't sure how, but he was going to take care of these young men however he could, no matter what it took.

&⋅

Finnion poured water in the residual of Benneck's soup. It wasn't going to be nearly as good this way, but food was scarce and Finnion had bragged to the Blakes brothers about how good the soup was. He put the nearly empty pot over the furnace and waited for the mixture to simmer. Reff and Leighton were out giving money and food to support known loyalists of Trofaim. Finnion's leg needed time to heal, so he stayed back, doing Leighton's work.

Venna, the newest Lark, had gone with them, saying she needed supplies and took the Blakes brothers with her. Leighton had suggested they keep the young men busy so that they wouldn't discover too much about their secret dealings conducted from the house. While everyone was away, his task here in Tolon was to stay at Leighton's home and coordinate with other workers who sent messengers to the Lark. Many of them brought word from other Larks as well. Every day, men and women brought their food or extra clothes and blankets with hidden messages or money inside.

Reff had laughed at the irony, remarking about how the Storinian mercenaries stationed soldiers to protect Leighton. He was, after all, a man collecting valuable goods and resources, and he should not be left vulnerable. "They're guarding the people who plan to kill them!" he'd said. The Storinian authorities hardly ever checked the goods, and why would they? These people had asked them to come since they could not protect themselves in wartime. The rebel army was away and, without mercenary law, Southern Trofaim would be prone to invasion. So the foreign soldiers had become lax in their patrol, never suspecting a rebellion of their own. The negligence led to the use of gangs and borderland brigands like Cuften Bander to do the hard work of intimidation and enforcement of tax penalties for people who couldn't afford to pay.

It's a shame, Finnion thought, *to leave so many people to starve like this in one of the most severe winters. The new generals of the rebellion would take at least five more years to swallow the city of Trofaim. Maybe three if they were brutal on the patriots in the Fork Region. How many more people would die of starvation, or even cold, after years of being taxed out of their own food and blankets in the wintertime? It's shameful. Felix and Magellan should've sent a detachment to send the Storinians home.* That's what Finnion would've done. Instead, the selfish commanders raided all around the city, devouring its wealth and abandoning their people in the South — he same people that supported their meager beginnings.

"I think I can smell soup!" he heard Reff saying from outside the house.

"No way," said Venna's voice. Finnion's eyes rolled almost involuntarily. The woman was always trying to outwit them. "I ate the rest of it."

"Oooh, don't tell Finnion. He always saves the last bit so he can really enjoy it," said Leighton.

Finnion was suddenly furious. She'd eaten his portion!

"Seriously?" she asked, "It's just sou—" The woman was surprised to see Finnion glaring murder at her when she walked in.

"You took the last of the soup!" he accused.

"I see a whole pot right there," Venna said, pointing to a soup-flavored pot of water. He almost let himself shout profanity, but Reff interjected, trying to change the topic.

"How's your leg?"

"My leg is fine. You'd better be able to make more of that soup, or—"

"Of course I can," she said. Finnion squinted, all suspicion. Reff's head jerked to look at her along with Leighton's.

"You can?" asked Leighton.

She smiled, looking from one disbelieving face to another. "That's why I asked for these ingredients."

Finnion was skeptical to say the absolute least. Benneck was an old spy for a notorious group of informants that survived by never trusting or speaking more than they had to. The notion that he'd just given her the recipe was ludicrous.

"We were talking to a physician a few miles from town," Reff said out of nowhere.

"Did they say they would support us?" asked Finnion.

"That's not why we went," said Reff, like he was scared of Finnion's reaction. "Venna consulted him about your leg." Reff was failing to meet his eye. Leighton and Venna were soon too preoccupied to look at him either.

"So? What'd he have to say?" Finnion wasn't sure what their strange mood could be about. "It's bad. I already knew that."

"When Venna described it to him, he asked how long it had been since you damaged it. So I told him. He, uhh . . . He said your leg is trying to heal itself, but because of overwork, it may be permanently . . ." The young man struggled to find the words. ". . . permanently . . . the way it is now . . ."

"The soup is ready!" said Venna.

Reff and Leighton cheered their excitement, eager to think about something else.

Finnion could only think of the horrible reality he had just heard.

CHAPTER FORTY-NINE

THE SIEGE

REDEYE

The sun sank on their seventh day in Krahl. Redeye sat in his usual spot on the high wall with Zeux and Rector, just above the spot where they climbed the wall when they took the city. It was just above the spot they'd picked to bury Zifix. The cold winter breeze kept blowing Redeye's hair into his face. It was a soft wind that spoke gently of a winter that followed it. All the troubles he'd had in peacetime were gone. He was alive the way he only ever felt in war.

Rector played that small thumb harp that he and his uncle, Lain, always played at times like these. A hollow wooden box the size of a man's hand. The instrument had several wooden tongues that, when plucked, produced lullabic music. The birds sang with it at times from where they roosted in the surrounding treetops. It was then, when Redeye heard a different birdsong, that he knew he was truly far from home.

Zeux's furious presence was made smooth after the loss of Zifix, like the two vastly different spirits of two men had joined within Zeux. Maybe that was his mourning process. Or maybe it was Zeux's inability to let go of his cousin. Redeye noticed that distant look of a man and the depth of his many memories. Just beyond him sat two Hockleets, both looking over their weapons and cleaning yesterday's battle off of them. You might think their blades were crafted by a talented jeweler from the way the crimson sunset shone off of their blades. Redeye could tell this is all they've been up to since Zifix's burial ceremony.

Rector's music played softly, uniting the Hockleets on the wall with shared memories and emotions that words could not capture. The tall man leaned against the high tower the same way Lain would have. All the men, though strangers in a foreign place, somehow felt at home in the familiar company surrounded with the music.

Cicero and Tork always said war should only be fought for peace. But the only peace Redeye had ever truly felt were in the quiet moments spent with the only family he'd ever had. Was there only peace in war for Redeye? Why couldn't he understand the peace that Tork and Cicero had spoken of?

Redeye could see a rider in the fading hours, pushing hard towards Krahl. A moment after he noticed the man on horseback, a voice called out, "It's Boban's man! He's back!"

When Redeye noticed, he instructed a voiceman to retrieve the news. The rest stayed until they received orders from the higher-ups. Rector's music stopped along with the men's care of their weapons. Redeye came back into reality, leaving Zeux entranced in the rich peace of the moment before. Redeye gave a simple nod, showing his approval of Hezro's orders. The chief's endorsement was necessary for the men to act. At his cue, the two men hurried down the spiraling steps of the tower to the city street.

Redeye entered the court that had once been the governor's court. This time, Bloodway, Boban, and the Bridgeman sat listening to the Kalesian scout's insights from the Army of Kalesia. Redeye's entrance interrupted the conversation.

"Good to see you, Redeye," said Bloodway, gesturing to a chair at the table for him. Redeye did as any sensible man would when in the presence of a madman and sat.

"Likewise, Chief," he said with a nod. Redeye had heard from his voicemen that the greater part of the Kalesian Army had come to retake the city of Krahl. From Cilio's report, it sounded like they were greatly outnumbered by the more well-armed body of soldiers that came to retake Krahl.

"Go ahead, Saul," said Boban before looking at Redeye for his opinion. The exhausted man cleared his throat and began to speak.

"The Kalesians have come in numbers!" He sounded terrified. "I spoke to a man in a distant township here in Krahl. He said there were at least eight thousand and many more light footmen. I'm not sure how many horsemen they have but they were close behind me when I neared the fortress. I have my spirits to thank that my horse didn't give in."

"You have Yellowtooth to thank," said Boban. "Those Galanoan horses are swift and smooth as the breeze." Redeye was liking Boban more and more. He knew that Bloodway had special use for him or else there would be more of Gallo's warchiefs here.

"My orders, Chief?" asked Redeye.

"How are your men?"

Redeye was confident in all of them. "They're anxious to do the will of their high chief," Redeye said in respect.

"Because you took the city, they receive honor throughout our Southern Army. Galanoans and Kalesians agree on the one thing that divided them, the men of Hocklee." He smiled, sitting forward. "Redeye's Hockleets have done the fighting and given their portion to the men who didn't fight to take it."

Redeye felt nervous at the tone of admiration in Bloodway's voice. "The fighting is Hocklee's portion. Let the other men bravely take the victory." The Bridgeman grunted his approval of Redeye's words. Bloodway's smile stretched.

"You've brought us honor, Redeye. I'm starting to think this Kalesian of yours is from our town as well," he said. Boban stiffened in honor. If Cicero were here, he'd be proud to see Kalesian soldiers honored at being compared to a Hockleet. Galanoans called them traitors and dogs. The men of Kalesia had always viewed them as lesser. The king of Kalesia, conquered Hocklee for slaves and taxes. Now Redeye, a Hockleet born to a Kalesian mother, sat at a table, being honored by a Kalesian man who proudly called Redeye his chief.

"Maybe he fights like one of us," Hezro said, pointing at Boban with a chuckle, "but if you saw him trying to scale a wall, you'd be cured of the notion."

After a moment spent laughing at Boban's expense, Bloodway began to speak again, "Saul here is the only scout to return of the twenty-one I sent out. If he's correct, they will encircle the fortress by evening tomorrow. The other scouts, if alive and still loyal to us, will return with more information. According to Yellowtooth and Boban's plan, I will send you and your best men of war, no more than two dozen, to go out into the countryside around the Kalesians to be a thorn in their side. Yellowtooth is willing to give up his best man of war, Gristax of Mandt, to go with you." Redeye felt a sense of fear at Yellow's deadliest man going with him. Redeye wished that snake, Igoss, would go with them. It would've been the ripest way to kill the man. Bloodway held out his hand to Boban who set a rolled-up piece of paper in his palm. "This is the most reliable map he has found in the court. It's a powerful tool of mine, Redeye. I will send it with you to help in your efforts." Redeye felt the anticipation beginning to spread through him.

"Only Hockleets, sir?" He didn't want to question the bloodiest man in the South, but it would've been comforting to take a man who knew the land, one of Boban's men maybe.

"I know it probably sounds good to have a few local men with you, but if I send Kalesians, they may defect and give you up to the Kalesian Army. I can't trust many Kalesians except Boban and a few of his closest. It will be a siege. I know it. I can feel it. I need every trusted one of them in the city to help defend it and operate the city. I will rely on them to keep the other Kalesians loyal." Redeye agreed, knowing all too well the importance of having trusted men in a siege.

"How long can you last, Chief?" asked Redeye. At that, the Bridgeman opened the door. Boban excused Saul.

"We're keeping this secret from the army as we don't know who to trust. Boban and his men found grain stores and dried food to last us. It was stocked up so that governor Balt could withstand a siege long enough for the bulk of the army to smash us against their walls, but you took the city in a single day." Redeye considered what that meant.

"Attrition?" Redeye asked. Bloodway didn't disagree.

"They plan to starve us out. We can last long for a siege, but we are over a hundred miles into Kalesian lands. Even in the cold of winter, they will be richly supplied with endless caravans. They will not leave, as our whole army is here. If they take the city, they will retake Hocklee. It will be worth whatever the price to kill us." Redeye felt his nerves weaken at the thought of so much at stake here. Somehow, Gallo didn't see this as a certain defeat.

"Shouldn't I wait for more information about the enemy from returning scouts first?" asked Redeye, trying to build a plan.

"Each of the scouts were told false information about our numbers and resources. In the case that they are captured or rejoin the enemy, they will pass on confusion." It sent chills through Redeye to see the genius of Gallo Bloodway in his element. He was feared by his enemies. Redeye knew, as well as any, what it was like to be against him. All horrible memories. "It is your task," said Bloodway, "to disturb their supply chains and cause shortages of every kind among them. Weaken them and make them break off the siege."

Redeye and Hezro walked up the long stairway to the Hockleets. Gristax waited for them by the gate to the stairs at the base of the wall. They had spoken little to each other. Not that Hezro didn't want to. The man continually spoke of his eagerness to wreck the Kalesian Army. The men's faces were grim in their expectation. They knew orders were coming. They were suited up, each one of them with armor salvaged from Krahl and many other defeated enemies to form the perfect equipment for each man.

"We have new orders," said Redeye, surprising none. "The Kalesian Army will soon be all around the city in numbers. We're going out to fight 'em." Redeye grabbed his pack he left at his place on the wall.

"Why not just fight them here? We've got the walls," Drux asked in surprise. It was clear none of them saw the sense in going outside the walls after having just taken them.

"The rest of the army is going to fight here. But we . . ." Redeye looked around at his men, ". . . are going out to cause trouble for them."

Rector stepped in in the midst of the other men's hesitation. Zeux a moment later.

"Better we get down into the countryside before Tork's cousins show up," said Zeux.

With that, eighteen men collected their things and left the city to make war with an entire army.

Chapter Fifty

The New Rebellion

Finnion

Reff and Leighton stared at Finnion as he tried to put his boot on. The right leg took him a minute for all the pain it took to bend his knee to get the shoe on. He tried not to wince and grunt but found that to be impossible not to.

"If you can't get your boot on, do you think you'll be able to walk to the council ruins?" asked Reff, a touch of amusement in his voice, but mostly pity.

Finnion saw that Reff still kept with his childish competition.

"You should stay here another day," suggested Leighton, "I can go with Reff."

Finnion didn't even properly respond at first, just grunted in opposition. "I'm going."

The oldest and youngest Blakes brothers watched as Finnion stood up, putting the brunt of his weight on his good leg and using the bad leg only to support his balance.

"Okay, now can you walk?" asked Leighton skeptically. It was as if this were only a waste of time for him. Venna had relocated his leg horribly two days earlier, leaving Finn painfully bedridden until today. It was the day she had told him to try some light motion and practice, but she had not said to walk a few miles. Finnion felt that Reff needed him. These Larks may have been helping him, but these were people who protected themselves by breaking off contact with desperate allies. Finnion would help Reff and, if the Blakes brothers were anything like their father, they could be trusted even more than himself. Reff needed strong, trustworthy allies that he could call on in a desperate situation.

"Mister Bennault!" came a voice with a knock on the door.

"Logan," said Griffin as the oldest, Bracken, opened the door with Leighton's permissive nod. The door opened, revealing the second of the three brothers. Logan was smiling wide.

"I was out with Venna collecting support from some of the elderly in Tolon, people who can't make their way here to pay taxes," he said, excited, one hand behind his back.

"You should still be with Venna," said Leighton. "Why aren't you?"

"Because," he said, revealing the hand's hidden contents.

Reff gave Finnion that same look he'd repeated a hundred times in their months together. The unspoken, *you're old*, reflected from his smiling eyes.

>

They were late because of Finnion's periodic rests, but they made it to the council ruins thanks to the cane Logan Blakes had found for him among the elders of Tolon. The council ruins were thousand-year-old ruins of an old performance theatre. Before civilization pulled people into towns, the long-abandoned stone arena was the place where locals brought stories to share with one another. Now, for the first time in centuries, the seats were filled with people, all strangers to one another.

"Funny how you can partner with so many people and know none of them," Reff said, still a little ways off from the ruins.

Creeper vines and lichen clung to the snowy walls of the cracked arena. The entire thing couldn't have held half of the people who lived in Tolon or a third of those who lived in Harmony-Ford. Finnion wondered how sparsely populated the region must have once been.

They entered the half-moon-shaped seating and sat at the bottom of the cascading bench rows. Here in this strange and remote place were gathered nearly every member of the Lark. Most of them wore partial face coverings like scarves or blindfolds with eye holes cut out to mask their appearance from one another. People muttered shallow remarks to one another in hushed tones. Clearly the Larks were tense, unaccustomed to being in the presence of more than one other Lark. Finnion felt a smile rip across his mouth at the sight of a familiar face.

Benneck sat, smiling back at Finnion, smoke from his pipe exaggerated into a larger cloud because of the cold winter air. The old man waved back at Reff, who smiled widely at the familiar man who'd reached out and made this all possible.

"It's good to see both of you survived long enough to put a rebellion together," said Benneck.

"All thanks to your trust in us and your soup," Reff said, laughing. "It's amazing how a skeptical spy will trust a man with hot chili soup!"

Benneck's smile showed that was why he'd done it that way. "Trust is built most securely on friendship," he said, patting each of them on the shoulder. After taking several puffs from his pipe, he stood in the middle of the arena, looking back at all the faces in the seats. The small crowd of nearly three dozen slowly quieted in expectation of what he'd say.

"It's good to see you all, friends," Benneck said with a unique comfort that spread a contagious sense of hope rather than the very common tone of fear that loomed over the entire country. "Many of you hide your face to protect your identities from the Storinians and authorities of the rebel army. I chose not to mask my appearance because many of you already know me and my chili soup!" A small laugh united the crowd slightly. "The last leader of the rebellions has done this to protect himself from assassination." *And not well*, Finnion thought. "But now we have a brave new leader! A leader who does not hide himself from us, but trusts us instead. He is a son of the orchard but uncorrupted by its power! He has come to wage a new war on corruption; he's one of the last Shrikes and avenger of Trofaim. You all have placed your trust in me. Now place it, as I've placed mine, into Reff Tro-Bennault," Benneck said, motioning for Reff to speak.

Finnion nodded in an attempt to reinforce the young man. *Just speak the words I've told you*, Finnion thought.

"I've come here from the far east territory near Darmstadt to begin building a resistance. I came here because my own father was born south of the Fork Region. I'm not only a commoner like him, though. The father of my mother was the great Akten Tro-Bennault, hero of Paveneli. It is with the name my humble father gave me that I claim the legacy my distinguished grandfather passed down for me!" Reff was warming to the position now, feeling more confident with every word he spoke. "Once, there were many evil people who moved to take Trofaim for their own greed. My grandfather broke their tyrannical spirit and turned them back."

Tyrannical spirit? Finnion held back a smirk. He hadn't taught Reff to say that. It was good.

"Now his grandson, with your help, will crush the same spirit within this new evil collection of men!" That got a cheer out of a few of the Larks somehow. Finnion just thought Reff had read a few too many storybooks, but whatever worked was good for him. "For over a month, you have been collecting supplies and money with the purpose of saving Trofaim. You have asked us when we would begin." Reff nodded to Logan Blakes.

The young man sprang up at his cue, hoisting the full bag he'd carried from Leighton's house. Logan set it on the ground in front of Reff and loosened the drawstring. Reff theatrically plunged his hand inside and pulled out a handful of bronze and silver brevalts, holding them in a handful thrust high into the air above his head. Finnion's eyes rolled.

Benneck sat eagerly at the edge of his section of bench, inspired.

"This will buy us time and purchase us men who can take up arms." Reff gestured to Griffin, who brought another huge bag. "These will bless the starved, freezing people who support our efforts." And Reff let spill the contents of Griffin's bag. Potatoes, carrots, and corn poured out. Last, Reff nodded to the oldest Blakes Brother. Bracken hoisted his cargo with an effort and set it next to that of his brother's.

"These will be given to those trusted men who you send for us." And Reff drew out a shined simple short sword from Bracken's bag. By this time, people cheered after each bag was opened, most of them standing in their excitement. "When will we begin, you ask." Reff took his time to make eye contact with several Larks. "Get your people. Send your men who've known war. The time is now!"

CHAPTER FIFTY-ONE

PROPOSAL

PINELLA

Pinella made her way to the king's forum in the Upper City. It was late in the evening, three days until the Tribunal would reconvene. It would be her first time to attend with land holdings and a presence that was fully her own. The sun had only recently dropped below the horizon. She hadn't slept since she received the threat letter two days before. Rather than telling the Aspin family what had happened, Pinella decided that the only way to deal with her enemies, who now had too much power over her, was to gain an even more powerful ally.

It had been dark for some time, leaving Pinella alone to tread the waters of her endless guilts when she heard a voice behind her.

"Good evening . . . Lady Bennalt. I'm sorry to have kept you waiting. I didn't think you would come."

Pinella turned slowly. She hadn't seen Fabrien alone since she left him for Reff's father. The man was always crowded by political advisors and prominent supporters.

"I haven't been waiting long," she said, looking around to make sure none overheard their conversation. The widely paved streets surrounding the forum were vacant of the citizens who filled them every day. The two of them were alone here in the old city center. They just looked at each other for a long moment. The two of them had been greatly opposed to one another until now. Now that their independent standings had both been so greatly shaken.

Fabrien had been the most well-known and powerful Tribune of the last decade, with seven years as charger in her father's house before that. She remembered a time when they both thought they'd marry one another. His entire career as a Tribune was now being threatened. Fabrien had begun fighting a losing battle to keep his own influence intact with the families who appointed him their Tribune. Pinella had heard that Fabrien had personally gone into the Fork Region to raise morale among the stewards there. His goal was to encourage their production of food and not to abandon their post due to a false report of rebels everywhere. She'd heard rumors of assassins sent to kill him out there.

She wasn't sure what was true or not, but it seemed Fabrien faced a personal war of his own. Pinella didn't know nearly as much about Upper City politics as she did about the Lower City. She new almost nothing about regional affairs. Her attention was upon her greatest threat.

With the support of most of the Songbird Army and a success in the battle, Alcott had the fickle support of a huge majority in the Tribunal. The self-preserving Tribunes agreed with little of Alcott's policies, but now that she controlled an army, the nobility swarmed to join the safety of her party like ants to a cake. They did her bidding so that Greyah Aspin could make no progress.

Pinella believed that if Fabrien resumed his place in the Tribunal, he could split the majority. Fabrien had so many enemies that would become her enemies if she allied with him. Pinella would sustain his dying popularity among the masses, though, among whom she had immense and favorable popularity. It would be worth it for all support she would receive from the other nobles who owed their power to Fabrien's counsel.

Fabrien broke the silence after a long moment, "I'm surprised to gain an audience with you, considering my current standing. I half-expected to be jumped and beaten in the street." Fabrien cracked a tight smile. "I'm not sure that isn't still a possibility." Pinella stood confused. He continued, "But before you order Otrin's thugs to attack me, let me ask: How can I, a man with so many powerful enemies, help a woman of such growing popularity?"

"You have many enemies, but your allies are highly distinguished and loyal to you . . . They're the kind of people who can ratify my position as Dame of a distinguished family. I will take on your enemies with you if you help me achieve nobility."

Fabrien's brow pinched together at her statement, and he looked off toward the distant Tribunal chamber. "A political alliance . . . And what if I give you this? What if I help you rise, and you have no greater reason to help me in return? Will you betray me?" Pinella noticed Fabrien's mouth almost form the word *again*.

"I can't betray you if our alliance is made public," she said, knowing what she must offer. It was what he really wanted.

"An alliance between us would be illegal. Making a political alliance now in time of war wouldn't be permitted. Our enemies would argue that to ally with one another publicly would be outright dishonor to the dead Shrikes. It's ambitious, but it won't work." Fabrien was almost humored. He had a disappointed look that seemed to wonder why he'd come.

"That's why our alliance can't be political."

His smile faded, considering her words carefully. "What kind of alliance are you suggesting?"

Pinella considered everything for a long moment. She had

thought about this for days, and now she was faced with the choice. If she went forward with her plan, there would be no turning back. Her eyes met his again in darkness, and she met skepticism with steel.

"A marriage."

MARK MILLER

Mark Miller, residing in Fort Worth, Texas, has always been drawn to the wonder of imagination and creativity. He believes there is something truly special about the hidden beauty life has to offer—whether found in quiet moments of reflection or the bustle of everyday life. For those who search, beauty often reveals itself, hidden in plain sight. This endless curiosity has fueled his journey as a writer.

Mark's goal is to craft stories that captivate, pulling readers in with their intensity, and inviting them to see themselves within the narratives as he does. He hopes to offer his readers a measure of healing joy. To Mark, writing is an adventure—a way to explore the depths of creativity and see where the heart can wander when given permission. Every story is a new discovery, a fresh way to embrace the passion that has been with him all his life.

He is always excited about the possibilities ahead and can't wait to see where his imagination will lead him next. Mark invites readers to join him on this journey, hoping they will love it as much as he does.

ABOUT THE PUBLISHER

Di Angelo Publications was founded in 2008 by Sequoia Schmidt—at the age of seventeen. The modernized publishing firm's creative headquarters is in Los Angeles, California. In 2020, Di Angelo Publications made a conscious decision to move all printing and production for domestic distribution of its books to the United States. The firm is comprised of eleven imprints, and the featured imprint, Reverie, was inspired by the long-lasting legacy of fiction and adult literature.

www.ingramcontent.com/pod-product-compliance
Lightning Source LLC
Jackson TN
JSHW020918020125
76325JS00013B/47